THE FIENDS
IN THE FURROWS III

Final Harvest

THE
FIENDS
IN THE
FURROWS III

Final Harvest

Edited by David T. Neal
& Christine M. Scott

N*P

NOSETOUCH PRESS

CHICAGO | PITTSBURGH

For the Hive

CONTENTS

INTRODUCTION

Every harvest sees the cycle of the seasons, the transformation of planted seed to growth and tending, and we've seen Folk Horror continue to expand from a literary afterthought to something more substantive, enjoying its own pop cultural moment (particularly onscreen), as well as something more enduring.

When Christine and I set out to publish *The Fiends in the Furrows* in 2018, it was at a time when most people didn't ever think about literary Folk Horror, and we were happy to curate our vision of what Folk Horror was and could be, and we're happy to see *Fiends I* still drawing enthusiastic readers years later.

When we came out with *The Fiends in the Furrows II* in 2020, it was right when the COVID-19 pandemic was surging and fundamentally changing people's lives. We saw in the pandemic elements of its own kind of Folk Horror as people reacted both sensibly and irrationally, depending on their view of the world and their place within it. *Fiends II* continues to draw interest and attention from readers yearning for a Folk Horror experience to perhaps make sense of the pandemic madness we all experienced.

We saw Folk Horror gain still wider interest and acceptance, and it's been an interesting journey for us, seeing it evolve, and how people both understand and misunderstand Folk Horror in all sorts of ways. This reflects the chimerical landscape of Folk Horror, which is rooted in particular ideas and themes, but those same themes permit the exploration of borders and breaking them down into new folk rituals.

Now, in 2023, we return to the fields with *The Fiends in the Furrows: Final Harvest*, with the wistful understanding that we set out to do what we intended to with the anthology series, and are at peace with the idea that while this may be the third and final *Fiends* volume, the trails it has blazed has made it a worthwhile effort we were proud to take.

From our perspective, there are always new places to go with Folk Horror, and we intend to go there, wherever it precisely takes us, even as we do honor to *Fiends* with this third, final, and largest collection of stories, yet.

This anthology opens with the legendary Steve Rasnic Tem's "F is for the Farm"—a disturbing, chthonic exploration of the tenacity of cult relationships in the face of abject horror. Next is "The Motley" by Charlie Hughes, which puts a twisted community to the test in its allegiance to an arcane ritual involving fealty to a monstrous prophet.

Thersa Matsuura provides a Japanese folk horrific exploration of family obligation in "Child of the Gods", while Richard Thomas explores the spiritual rigors of a supernatural sentinel in "The Keeper of the Light". "The Last Honeyboy", by Ryan Cassavaugh, serves up a platter of folksy horror in the personage of a doomed harbinger tasked with a dreadful duty.

Fox Claret Hill's "Mrs. Badger's Bones" conjures up an old menace in the form of Bloodybones, and the fateful decisions involving that awareness. "Cooper's Hill" by Matt Elphick offers absurd folk rituals that have far deadlier manifestations under the cover of darkness. "As the Thing is Needed" by Damien Raphael, provides folk magic as both a solution to and a source of trouble.

"Come Sing for the Harrowing" by Dan Coxon leads an unwary soul to a horrifying fate in the service to dire rituals. Lyssa Szydlek's "Back Yonder" races along back roads that transport unwary travelers to unfamiliar places. And "Mulberry Silk" by Rae Knowles mixes colorful concoctions in the service of supernatural considerations. Coy Hall's "Herald of the Red Hen" travels back in time with an occult detective and his canine companion sleuthing out sinister goings-on.

"The Gods That Drift with Us" by Zachary Rosenberg pits the emissaries of ancient religions against one another. "Radegast" by J.M. Faulkner crawls deep in the Czech wilderness in the service to old gods. "Paper Coins" by Die Booth uncovers abusive secrets in a forsaken setting. Catherine McCarthy's "The Sickle and the Tithe" delves into a folk community's unique approach to ageing and death.

"Sarsen Wood" by Timothy Granville journeys with young souls spiritually polluted by dark forces, and "Malleability" by Alex Wolfgang takes folk art to dark places in a community held fast to wicked traditions. Finally, Tracy Fahey's "Witchwalking" wraps up the trilogy with the ardent invocations of a community of witches out to protect their own and punish their enemies.

The cinematic Folk Horror offerings continue to excel, with *Gretel & Hansel* (2020), *Lamb* (2021), *Antlers* (2021), *In the Earth* (2021), *Men* (2022), *Enys Men* (2023), and many others providing outstanding Folk Horror forays on the big screen. There was also the fantastic documentary, *Woodlands Dark and Days Bewitched: A History of Folk Horror* (2021), that we expect will serve as a primer for cinematic Folk Horror for many future fans of the subgenre.

The television screen delivered some excellent Folk Horror shows, such as the fascinating treatise on mourning that was *The Third Day* (2020), while *Yellowjackets* (2021) takes a drink or two from the Folk Horror well to deliver chills to fans who may still be unfamiliar with the folk horrific landscape. *The Pale Horse* (2020) even saw an old Agatha Christie mystery get dusted with some Folk Horror flourishes that offered an impressive new life to her work.

Also, we wanted to vigorously praise *Hellebore* and *Hwæt!*, both of whom have been exemplars of Folk Horror aesthetics over the years. We hope that they continue to do so in the future! Further, we have to mention the folks at *Weird Walk*, who offer their own spirited approach to the genre's link to the land.

We're sure that Folk Horror will continue to evolve and grow as more become transfixed by the possibilities it presents. Nosetouch Press sincerely thanks everyone we've worked with throughout the trilogy, and all of the readers who keep the *Fiends* anthologies close to their hearts. Oh, the places we'll go....

David T. Neal
Christine M. Scott

STEVE RASNIC TEM

F IS
FOR THE
FARM

ANDREW hadn't seen Beth in months, so when he received her note inviting him to the farm, he rushed from the apartment without telling anyone where he was going. He'd stopped being cautious with love. In his experience you seldom got a second chance.

He'd expected wide open spaces, chickens, and cows, but the address was for a house in an older urban neighborhood with vintage bungalows, nearby schools and grocery stores, and a grand library at one end of the street. It was hot, so he parked under a large shade tree.

He checked the note again; this was the address Beth gave him, # *F Alphabet Row*. Above the house's dusty mailbox, a tarnished brass letter F was screwed into the brick.

The property appeared ill-kept. He stood on the stoop, a few fractured concrete steps rising from the failing yellow grass. Vines poked from yawning cracks in the foundation.

He knocked. He waited a minute and knocked again. An ancient woman in a stained beige dress opened the door. Her pale face was corrugated and mud-stained. "We don't welcome salespeople."

"*Mother*, he's here for me." Beth appeared and turned the woman around and nudged her inside. She embraced him fiercely. "I'm *so glad* you came."

He squeezed her gently. It scared him how much he liked this woman. "That was your mother?"

"We call all the older women here 'Mother.' Did you have any trouble finding us?"

"I thought you lived on a farm."

"You'll see." She grinned and pulled him inside.

The crowded mess in the front room initially made him think they were hoarders. Then he realized the trash was dead leaves and decaying flowers. The floor vanished beneath them. A muscular young man sat in the corner, reading under LED grow lights. He absent-mindedly, and blissfully, chewed on a plant. Torn blossoms spilled from his lips.

"That's Joseph," Beth said. The young man glanced up briefly and returned to his book without speaking.

Thick, woody vines covered the walls with broad leaves and those voluptuous blossoms. Vines grew into the bare brick. Multiple brick rows, around the windows, above the door, were distorted, pushed askew by the aggressive growth. Andrew doubted this structure was safe.

Beth caught him staring. "Aren't they great? They're all descended from the original plant Father discovered growing here when he bought the property." She squeezed his hand and led him further into the house.

The house was small, but packed with people, the furniture minimal and the interior doors removed. In every room a team tended not only the vine but several potted plants, pruning, watering, dropping bits into jars and bags.

The residents varied in age, although he didn't see any children, and many were quite old: seventies and eighties, nineties. They were all dressed in work clothes, nothing nice, and nothing clean. They paid Beth and Andrew no attention.

Beth kept moving, saying *Hi!* to various people, and *This is Andrew! Say hello to Andrew!* as she dragged him along. Despite her enthusiasm, no one said hello.

The kitchen was large, with two stoves and plentiful counter space. Industrial-sized pots kept the room steamy. An elderly woman wearing a headscarf stood at each pot, watching, stirring. Andrew couldn't have described the flavor. Just green—the air inside the kitchen tasted and smelled exceptionally green.

Beyond the back door a ramp led them down to ground level and a vista of plant rows receding into the distance, corn and peppers and tomatoes and a few crops Andrew didn't recognize. The omnipresent vines lay across the ground like fire hoses. People stepped over them carefully as they walked the rows with baskets, harvesting the swollen crops from the plants or off the ground. A high fence around the property shielded them from prying eyes.

An enormous antique plow hung from a pole nearby, the kind a horse or a mule pulled, with handles the farmer could hold onto. It was painted enamel black and had a giant shiny silver blade.

"That's so we don't forget how hard farming used to be. Isn't it *fabulous*? Father used it to create the first furrows, but we have a rototiller now. He bought the lot behind us so we could plant more rows."

A tall, black-haired man in filthy bib overalls stood beside the plow, glaring at them. "That's Karl. He's one of the originals. Don't mind him—he's a sourpuss. He doesn't like anybody, and nobody likes him."

A large man sat in a faded lawn chair with a glass of green juice. He was bare-chested and bronzed, had squarish white teeth, long white hair, and a wiry silver beard streaming with greenish stains. He looked up and smiled at Beth, glanced at Andrew, and nodded, returned his attention to his clipboard.

"Sorry," Beth whispered. "Father doesn't like surprises. I should have let him know you were coming. I'll introduce you later."

The farm had no proper bathroom. Beth showed him to the latrines at the far back corner, hidden behind plank walls and a rough-made roof. He was fairly sure this was illegal within the city limits.

"We've got three farms in one," Beth explained. "There's the house farm, and there's the field. Then we have a place underground. The Below Farm. I hear that's something to see, but you must earn an invitation. Even I haven't been there."

Andrew hadn't planned to stay long enough to earn anything. "Where does everybody sleep? I didn't see any beds."

She laughed. "You sleep wherever you can find a spot. Everybody gets tired eventually. They just lie down wherever they are. Most sleep somewhere out here between the rows."

"And if it rains?"

"If it's a light summer rain, and you're well-covered, it can be refreshing. When it pours, or when it's cold, everybody crowds inside, like a giant slumber party."

"Doesn't seem to be much privacy."

"But we're all family here, even the ones who weren't always."

He looked around. He didn't want her to see the doubt in his face. "You take showers?"

"Outdoors, when necessary. Father says modern folks wash too much. They scrub off their natural protective oils. I know you'll love it here. You can stay at least a few weeks, right? Tell me you have nothing better to do."

"Beth, you know I like being with you. But I'm not sure I can live like this."

She put her arms around him and kissed his neck, his ear. "I think you'll feel differently after you've stayed a while. We're the folk of the farm, of the plant and the vine. Soon enough you'll understand."

She had the same wide-eyed expression she wore when he first saw her at lunch that day, sitting on the ground just outside campus, feeding little green bits to the birds. When the birds became too many and too eager, he'd stepped in to rescue her.

She gave him some clothes to change into, battered old jeans and a faded T-shirt. "And your cell phone? I'll need that. I'll keep it safe. I promise."

"What the hell, Beth."

"Didn't I tell you before? I'm sorry. You can't have a cell phone here. We don't have wireless or cell phones. Don't you know those things give you cancer?"

Dinner was a vegetable, or plant stew, eaten from clay bowls. It had a bitter aftertaste, but it felt substantial. He became satiated, and sleepy. Andrew would come to hate the feeling.

He met more family members. Brothers and sisters, and more old Mothers than he could count. A few old men, who were reluctant to talk. No one said much more than a first name. The presence of the older people began to make more sense. Perhaps they had no family or income. They were taken well care of here.

Father walked among them as they ate, whispering, laying his hands on heads or shoulders. He whispered into Beth's ear, patted her on the head. He ignored Andrew.

After dark people wandered off singly or in pairs. She dragged him into the soft dirt near some tall corn and began pulling off his clothes.

"You love me, right?" she said breathlessly. "Tell me you love me."

"I am—I'm falling in love with you."

They made love and rolled out of the corn onto freshly-plowed ground. There they slept curled together between the furrows.

Andrew never made the decision to stay, but after a few weeks he was still there. Every morning they ate a light breakfast—dry, chewable plant material—while Father, still ignoring Andrew, delivered a message or rambling reminiscence about living naturally, supporting the plant, and what the plant gave back. It sounded like poorly organized New Age mush, but Beth listened with rapt attention.

Each day, they tended plants. At first it was tidying up, trimming a few dead leaves away, smoothing out the ground around the crops where someone had been sleeping. Beth talked to the plants, and urged Andrew to touch them with tenderness, because it facilitated growth, and was the right thing to do.

When they worked in the house farm, it felt a lot like house cleaning, because the vines were always dropping bits and pieces. In between they sneaked kisses and grabbed opportunities for quick sex. Andrew could barely keep his hands off her, even though he often felt faint. This new plant-based diet, with the occasional offal added, was a challenge. He made frequent, exhausting trips to the latrine. He was sleepy but learning how to work through the drowsiness.

The entrance to the Below Farm was a low, crudely built masonry structure with a rusted hatch in the middle of the field. Two young men were always stationed nearby. Since Father still ignored Andrew, his going below seemed unlikely. That unpleasant fellow Karl supervised the Below Farm, so maybe it was just as well. Most workers with access were elderly, especially the Mothers, including the old woman who first greeted him at the door.

Those workers slept and took their meals below. Given the crowded conditions in other parts of the farm, it made sense. Andrew rarely saw them after they went down.

Andrew frequently tripped over some bit of the vine, and he had to be incredibly careful not to nick or damage it in any way. Eerily quiet most of the time, these people became loud and irate when such mistakes occurred.

At the end of Andrew's fourth week, Father came and sat with them both and addressed Andrew directly:

"Once this land was forest, then farmland. Then the farms were abandoned, and nature took them back. Human beings in their ignorance plowed it all under again, building industries instead. When these industries failed, as all human activity eventually must, they scraped them off the land, and they built these houses.

"But something persisted, hidden within layers of time. A generous plant, unlike all others, a plant willing to give back to those who gave it care. If you are to stay here, you must honor this plant and our ways."

With Beth watching, Andrew felt he had to agree. But he was hardly a convert. He distrusted most religions, including societies, parties, clubs, whatever they called themselves. They were always trying to recruit you. He was content if he could spend more time with Beth. Life here wasn't exactly unpleasant. It reminded him of long camping trips when he was a kid, but with sex involved.

"Do you believe everything your dad says? I moved out of my parents' house years ago."

Beth looked unhappy.

"First off, he's not my dad. We call him 'Father' to honor him. I did move out of my parents' house. I was sixteen and I haven't seen them since.

"I used to fantasize having an apartment downtown, coming and going as I pleased, but I outgrew it. This land is more important than we are. The vine is more important than we are. We are temporary. But the land and the vine are not."

Andrew stopped asking questions. He would have to watch for an opening, then somehow talk her into leaving with him.

After several months, Andrew realized it had become a voluntary incarceration. Beth was perfectly happy here. If he said anything negative, she became cold, and he became isolated and alone.

He'd been assigned the nastiest chores: maintaining the latrines and filling the giant organic compost vats, which often included the dead animal remains. He himself tossed in a dead fox he'd found by the fence.

This was their way of testing him. There had been other newcomers since Andrew arrived, and as far as he knew, all remained. One or two were given the right to represent the farm at various farmer's markets around the city, where they sold their potent green juice. This was a major source of the farm's income. Several had even made it to the Below Farm. This offended him. Hadn't he done everything they asked?

The other major income source was the "endowments." Some of those old people hadn't been destitute. They'd had resources, money, property, which they signed over to the farm.

"They believe in what we're doing. We're they're family now. They either don't have kids, or their kids don't appreciate them. You would do the same, wouldn't you?" Beth was enthusiastic on the subject.

"Sure. But I'm broke. I've left school. At this point my roommates probably think I'm not coming back. I don't even have a place to live anymore."

She smiled. "Then you'll just have to stay here with me."

Andrew closed his eyes. He was so tired. And maybe Beth wasn't who he wanted after all.

During Andrew's first month, one man accidently cut deep into his palm with a harvesting knife. Such accidents weren't uncommon. The knives were sharp, and they were encouraged to be more productive. Sometimes they rushed. Andrew was nearby and grabbed some rags to bind the wound.

The fellow pulled his hand away angrily and ran to the nearest vine and allowed the blood to flow generously over it. Then, staggering, and pale, he came back to Andrew and presented his hand for bandaging.

Andrew witnessed this ritual several times. Giving the blood to the vine was always the first step, before any medical aid was administered, usually by the Mothers. As far as he knew, no one was ever taken to the hospital, although sometimes it appeared necessary.

The Mothers intentionally bled themselves. Numerous times he saw them gather near the crops, and one would enter and hide herself and come out bleeding, or the other Mothers had to go in after her because she'd done too much with the knife and passed out. They'd carry her away, with bloody bandages wrapping both arms.

He pointed this out to Beth.

"We have to show respect," she said. "The Mothers will do anything for the plant and the farm."

At the end of every month, they held a festival, a party, meant to blow off steam. Father would deliver a speech, enumerating their accomplishments that month, items harvested, and bottled juice sold, and then the drinking and dancing began.

The drink was an alcoholic version of the farm's green juice. He didn't know where they got the alcohol. Maybe they brewed it in the Below Farm. After two drinks, even the quietest were singing, dancing around half-dressed, couples dragging each other off into the darkness.

But what was unique was the chanting, the rhythmic recitation of sounds and words in a language he did not recognize, including lots of odd, painful throat sounds. It sounded like the Appalachian Holy Roller speaking in tongues.

Several times he interrupted Beth's dancing and asked her if she was okay. She certainly didn't look okay. He stopped when she became angry and turned her back.

He didn't feel the same euphoria. Maybe the alcoholic juice hadn't been in his system long enough. He felt a slight fuzziness, a pressure in his head which went to the edge of a headache without crossing over, and everything appeared darker and further away. He sat for a while, watching Beth dancing, listening to the non-words she spoke. Finally, he risked asking her, "Did Father teach you this language?"

She turned around, laughing. "Oh, we don't *learn* it. Over the years it comes into us, and we let it out in speech. We know if we don't let it out periodically it will build up in our flesh and make us ill. You'll discover it, too, when you've been here long enough."

The celebration went on all night. Andrew didn't remember falling asleep, but he was swallowed up and smothered within a cloud of sound. For a time before sleep, he forgot his own name, her name, and where he was.

One morning, a few days later, Karl rousted them awake. "Come with me. Congratulations. We've assigned you both to the Below Farm."

The two guards beside the hatch were sleeping and Karl wordlessly kicked them awake. He guided Andrew and Beth below.

From its first details the Below Farm filled Andrew with dread. Overly bright halogen bulbs hung from the ceiling casting a harsh white light and generating much heat. Compacted vines lined the walls. The vine had coiled around itself repeatedly to create a support system for both the slanting entrance tunnel and the multiple chambers which followed. The staircase had vines trailing beside and underneath it. An old man with an acetylene torch was stationed near the stairs. Periodically he burned a flame near any vines threatening to grow where they were not wanted, such as over the steps or other apparatus. Vats and drums, some connected to hoses and pumps and other equipment, were arranged throughout the space.

A forest of roots and vines hung from the ceiling. Mothers and elderly men were scattered throughout, tending to these roots and vines, cutting some and dropping them into the carefully watched vats, preserving, and protecting other sections, tying them back to get them out of the way.

None of these older folks looked at all healthy. Andrew wondered when they'd last experienced daylight.

A few workers were Beth and Andrew's age. They were used for the more labor-intensive jobs. Karl put them to work rolling fresh vats into place, stationing full ones to be hauled up the stairs. Other workers were in the far reaches of the Below Farm, digging and rearranging vines, extending the farm's reach, but Andrew never saw them.

Andrew had a fear of enclosed spaces. His impulse was to run back up the stairs and leave the farm. He controlled his claustrophobia for Beth's sake, but his hands were shaking, his throat dry as bark.

A yellow liquid skim lined the floor of the Below Farm. Drainage from the irrigation system, juices dripping off the vine and from the various dangling roots. They stood in this liquid all day, every day. After a few weeks, the bottoms of their feet were furry with fibrous growths. They shaved them off using disposable razors, but they came back.

He felt for the oldest Mothers, none of whom seemed fit for this environment. He tried to talk to them and see how they were feeling, and unlike in the farm above, down here they didn't seem to mind talking.

Beth, on the other hand, went quiet. She seemed depressed, and they rarely had lengthy conversations anymore. She was still affectionate, and at night hugged him even more tightly than before. But he felt a desperation in it. She seemed defeated.

Andrew had assumed the Mothers weren't to be trusted. They were watching everyone else, and he frequently saw them in conversation with Father. But here they were more relaxed, even eager to chat, although sometimes the relaxation seemed more like fatigue, and the chattiness more like delirium.

Hatches had been placed here and there on the floor of the Below Farm, and once he'd seen some Mothers open a hatch and descend. So, there was another, lower level, and who knew, there might be levels even further down.

Usually, a Mother was stationed at each hatch, but not always. Rules below were more relaxed than rules above. Or they thought no one wanted to go deeper into a place which was already wet, unpleasant, and barely tolerable.

Over time, the population of Mothers in the Below Farm dwindled until there were only a few. Andrew assumed they'd been reassigned upstairs. The ones who remained were a listless bunch. Beth said they needed more older women to join the family, and they had members out in the city recruiting. He'd never heard her use *recruiting* before.

"Is that why I'm here? You recruited me?"

She looked embarrassed and couldn't look him in the eye. "Of course not. I *liked* you. I *wanted you* here with me. You've been good for me."

"You could have been sent out recruiting, and still liked me. Those two things are not contradictory. Now maybe you're a little less interested now I've been here a while? Is that what's going on?"

"Andrew! No!" She became weepy. "It's just this *place*. Everybody has talked about the Below Farm as if it were something special. I thought being assigned here was an honor. But it's *awful* down here! I'm *miserable*."

"You can talk to Father. Get him to reassign us. He likes you. It's obvious."

"I can't disrespect him like that, asking for special favors."

He put his arms around her. "Maybe if we do a little more exploring into how everything works here, we can figure something out. Maybe starting with this hatch." He pointed to the one he'd recently seen Mothers access.

She wrinkled her face. "Are you kidding? It's terrible enough at this level."

"If it's too bad we can leave, but maybe we'll find out something useful."

They lifted the hatch and slipped in, trying not to make any noise. There was plenty of light. But also, an overabundance of vine. Stepping off the stairs they were confronted by thick vines leaving a narrow passage through. A loud thrumming noise pulsed ahead of them.

They found the first body ten yards in. Andrew had no idea what it was at first, a swollen vine, like some sort of plant tumor, with a mass of filaments on one end of the bulge. His eyes wouldn't quite focus with the gloom below, the scattered bright bulbs above. Then he saw the facial pattern in the bark of the tumor. A woman's wrinkled, disintegrating face. And those greyish, fragile-looking filaments was her hair. He touched it. It fragmented and dissolved like cobwebs in his hand.

He walked a little further. He couldn't quite figure out where the corpse stopped and the plant began. There were many more in diverse sizes, more than a dozen. Many more. Besides the vine, the bodies were connected by a fatty-looking fungus, and it was the fungus making the thrumming noise. The fungus was overwhelming, yards long and wide.

He froze, unable to move further. The corpse plant writhed with bugs, many flowing over the dead faces. He reached down and scraped them off a face. It was the Mother who'd answered the door when Andrew first arrived.

"You have to understand." He realized Beth had been speaking behind him. "Some of these people were already dead, and the rest were going to die soon. They gave their bodies willingly. That's why we need the older ones in the family. There are never enough. The vine—"

"You *knew* about this?"

"I've been told. I've been told how beautiful...I've never actually *seen* it."

"What *else* haven't you told me?"

The alarm went off above them, sounding like overlapping screeches of pain. They hurried back to the ladder and climbed.

Workers were running toward the exit. Andrew wondered if there was a fire, or flooding, but he didn't see anything obvious.

"The plow," a Mother said nearby. "The plow." Several others repeated it.

Behind him, Beth said, "Our presence is required, but Andrew, you're not going to want to see this. Just do what they say, but keep your eyes shut. That's what I always do."

People had gathered between the house and the rows of plants. Several young men were taking the plow down from the pole.

"We live on fertile ground. When our income falls there must be other reasons!" Father was walking back and forth before a naked figure staked to the ground. "This man has been with us since the beginning, but all this time he has betrayed us. He has stolen from us, and he has stolen from the vine. He has behaved not as family, but as one of the strangers who lie, cheat, and steal beyond these walls." Andrew and Beth pushed closer. The man on the ground was Karl.

He'd been severely beaten. His mouth moved sloppily, but no sound came out. Father spat. "Bring up the plow."

The crowd separated, a few stronger men grabbing the plow handles and positioning the blade between Karl's squirming legs. The rest formed a line on the harness end, which had a long rope attached. Family members latched on to the rope. A couple of the Mothers pushed Beth and Andrew toward the end of the line.

Beth waited until the Mothers found their own place, then dragged Andrew away toward the house. "You don't want to be a part of this. You don't belong here. Joseph's one of the plowmen so there won't be anyone guarding the front room."

They made their way along the fence behind some tall plants, then to the back door. Everyone was focused on Karl and the plow. Father shouted "Now!" and Andrew turned his head.

As they entered the house, he could hear the huffing and the laborious grunts behind them, as if from a giant beast. "I guess Karl will soon be below feeding your precious vine."

Beth jerked his arm urgently. "Forget him. His bits go into the compost."

"You've seen this before?" She didn't answer.

They reached the front room. She opened the door and pushed him onto the threshold. "Go! Before someone notices!"

"Come with me!"

She dropped his hand. "I can't."

He stared at her. "So, I was just a recruit, right? That day in the park you were waiting for someone like me."

"It was my assignment. I waited until the right guy came along. We need new young guys, just like we need old women, Mothers. They fit the plan. But I liked you. I *really* did. Better than anyone—"

"Anyone you'd recruited? There were more like me? This Joseph, was he one of yours? Is that why he seemed so standoffish when I first showed up?"

She looked up at him. "You must *leave*, Andrew. They're my *family*."

He turned and went over the threshold, almost falling as he stumbled down the concrete steps. He heard the door slam behind him. The house's exterior looked the same as it had the day he arrived. He crossed the quiet street. His car had been towed, probably some time ago, but he'd expected that. There were kids on bicycles, teenagers with books headed toward the library at the end of the street. Everything possessed this strange, bright normalcy. He was embarrassed by his slovenly, dirty appearance.

He passed three black parked cars. Two men in ties and jackets sat in the front seats of each. One had a cell phone, talking as he stared at #F.

Andrew wanted to tell them what was happening inside that house, but guessed they already knew.

CHARLIE HUGHES

THE MOTLEY

Who told The Motley,
You kissed that girl?
Who told The Motley,
You stole that pearl?
It wasn't Tammy Jenkins,
It wasn't Mistress Drew,
So, nobody knows how The Motley knew.

SHE remembered her father as a huge man, towering above his friends, bulky and muscular. Now, the weight had dropped away and he stooped, even as he sat in his wheelchair. His hands, holding the knife and fork, shook like leaves in a gentle wind.

Eloise raised herself and wiped away stray flecks of cod caught in his moustache.

"Tell me, Eloise," he said, "What did The Motley show?" His eyes were bright and wide.

He had moments like this when he asked questions and talked politely. Once, she'd taken these interludes as a sign of hope, even recovery. But over the years, it became clear they were nothing of the sort, just cruel reminders of a father she'd already lost.

"I haven't been to the meeting yet, Dad. My first one is tonight."

"Oh."

Eloise rubbed the bridge of her nose, then took his hand in hers. "Dad, can I ask you something?"

"Of course." He smiled with fatherly indulgence.

"At the meeting, will it tell us what happened to Rachael?

"Will who tell you?"

"The Motley," she replied.

He spoke in stages, constructing the sentence out of each individual thought. "You want The Motley, to tell you what happened, to the little girl, your friend?"

"Rachael. Her name was Rachael. You remember."

"She went missing. Poor little girl."

A lump rose in Eloise's throat.

His eyes shifted from side to side, then he smirked, as if Eloise had said something amusing.

"Wonder if you'll get some fun at the meeting. I always liked the funny ones."

"Fun?"

"The sex ones are good," he said.

Eloise grimaced and prayed he would stop. He'd forgotten who he was talking to.

"Someone screwing someone they shouldn't or stealing or fraud. They think The Motley won't know. They stick their fingers in the till or cook the books. I remember Ronny Jenkins getting caught…" He trailed off, losing the thread of his thoughts.

His eyes went wide, then fell, the look he always gave just before she lost him. In these moments, she was convinced the horror of it all settled on him: his impotence, his dependence, the bonfire of dignity.

He looked dully at the blank TV screen in the corner of the room.

Eloise stood and wheeled him around in front, then switched it on. A programme about wildlife in South America. "Is that okay, Dad?"

He stared, silent.

She kissed him on the forehead then whispered in his ear, "I love you, Dad."

He looked up at her. She wanted him to say it back, just like he always had.

"Cunt." he said. There was no anger in his voice. He could have been commenting on the weather. "Dumb cunt."

———————————————

Eloise pushed through the door of the town hall and found herself reciting an old nursery rhyme under her breath, one the children still chanted in the playground.

Who told The Motley,
You kissed a girl?

She removed her coat and hung it on a peg in the reception room.

Across the room, Roland Peebles sat on a chair outside the assembly room. He wore a blue tunic which strained to cover his bulk, the crest of the town council sewn to the pocket. Roland got paid for a few hours each month as assistant to the Town Clerk, checking off the councillors as they arrived among other menial tasks. Eloise suspected this was his only income. She approached and stopped beside him.

He whispered, not looking at her, almost without moving his lips, "Don't say anything," he said. "Just nod."

She shuffled on the spot, wondering if she should move on.

"You're still going to try?" he said.

She nodded.

"Do it quickly, as soon as you have the chance."

"Okay," she said.

"Be quick, they'll drag you away as soon as they twig."

Eloise walked into the council chamber.

Inside, fifteen or twenty councillors were taking their seats or talking in small groups. The chairs were set out in a broad U-shape, five lines deep, all facing toward a grand bench raised on a stage.

"Three from the left, two rows from the front." Her father had reminded her many times. Eloise found the appointed place and sat.

She offered a tiny smile to Oliver Hemsworthy, seated next to her.

"Aha! The new girl," he said.

"New, yes," she replied. "Girl, no."

"Quite right, quite right." He grinned. "Looking forward to it?"

"Oh yes, good to get going."

"That's the spirit!"

She noticed his shirt cuff had ridden up, exposing his forearm. Two- and three-inch scars striped his skin, the same as her father. Hemsworthy saw her looking and shifted his shirt down to the proper place.

Eloise looked up to the public gallery where several groups were settled, including wide-eyed children staring down on them.

On the stroke of the hour, a loud knocking from behind the stage and the room fell silent.

A snaking line of suited men emerged from behind the stage, winding up the steps and into their seats. In the grandest chair, chains of office draped around his neck and chest, the Town Clerk peered down at them.

His name was Oliver Maynard, a rotund, po-faced man who owned a land drainage firm on the town's industrial estate. Maynard had once been close to her father but hadn't visited once since his illness became evident.

"Be seated," he said, "We have plenty to cover this evening and I will begin by noting apologies…" And so, he proceeded with the public meeting: A tree preservation order, a licensing application, and a new contract for mowing the grass verges.

The mundanity of it allowed Eloise to relax. How could she be nervous when grown men spoke gravely of dog fouling on the rugby fields?

Some of the councillors engaged with these items, raising points and asking questions, but Eloise got the impression the majority viewed these interventions as poor form. Oliver Hemsworthy huffed and puffed each time someone raised their hand to speak, as did several others.

When the Town Clerk moved onto the final item, the room came to life. The councillors shifted in their chairs, shuffled papers and stretched limbs.

"That concludes our formal business. Thank you one and all for attending." The Town Clerk nodded to the officers sitting beside him. They stood and walked out of the hall. Maynard remained in place. He motioned to the public gallery.

Slowly, reluctantly, they began filing out. One boy, no more than eight or nine years old, stayed rooted to his seat.

His mother turned back and raised her voice to him. "Come along then!"

When he continued to gawp down on the assembly, motionless, she went back, grabbed him by the collar and dragged him after her.

"But I want to see," he screeched. "I want to see it, Mum."

"You're not allowed," she replied. "Only the Councillors are allowed."

———————

They were not sisters. Her mother would remind Eloise of this whenever Rachael could not sleep over or stay for tea.

"It's nice that you have a friend, Eloise, but Rachel has her own family."

Inseparable since nursery school, they spent every possible moment together, playing, taking long bike rides, building dens in the woods behind Eloise's home.

Rachael's parents were not wealthy like her own, they lived in a tiny cottage on the other side of town. Her father fixed cookers and washing machines for a living. Her mother cleaned other people's homes. Neither would ever sit on the Town Council, like Eloise's father.

If Eloise ever noticed these differences, it was only as obstacles to her time playing and adventuring with her friend.

The day Rachael disappeared, they were supposed to go fishing in the Stour. It was a pastime her parents hated, her mother describing the sport as "common" every time it was mentioned.

Rachael Peebles had learned to fish from her own father and proved a patient teacher to Eloise, even gifting her an old rod and a box for tackle.

That day, Eloise had rushed home from Sunday school to collect her equipment from the shed, pausing only briefly to tell her father where she was going.

Eloise waited on the riverside in their favourite spot, soaking in the sun, watching the heavy brown water of the Stour flow past, reluctant to cast her line until her friend arrived. When she thought back to those moments, the reflection of the sun on the river and the sound of the water sloshing past

always came back in vivid detail. Her world was changing ir-
revocably and she knew nothing of it. She waited and waited.
Minutes passed, then hours and the sun began to fade. Eventually, downhearted, Eloise trudged toward home.

On her way over the fields, a figure appeared bobbing up
and down in the distance. For a few paces, she was sure Rachael had finally come, complete with smiles and excuses for
her tardiness. Then she noticed the short hair and heavy gait
of the figure coming towards her and realised it was not Rachael, but her brother, Roland.

He was a year older, but the kids at school teased him because he was an inch or two shorter than his sister. He was
strange, insular. Always telling stories about The Motley
which nobody wanted to hear.

When their paths met, he said, "Mum sent me to get her."

"Get who, from where?" Eloise already knew the answer,
of course, but the narrowing of Roland's eyes was enough to
catch a breath in her throat.

"She's still fishing? Mum wants her home for tea."

Eloise felt a sudden sinking sensation in her chest. "She
didn't come."

"Where is she?" Roland said. "Where's my sister?"

———————————

Only the councillors were left in the room now.

The Town Clerk looked up from his desk and gestured to
two councillors seated in front. "Gentlemen."

They stood and went behind the stage. The room fell silent.

A minute later, the despatched councillors reappeared,
moving slowly, clumsily. The structure they carried resembled
a miniature sedan or litter. Instead of an emperor or ark riding between them, they carried an object encircled by drapes.
Its outline reminded Eloise of a bird cage.

She'd heard rumours of the cage, the stories told by children in the playground, tales the adults of the town soon
learned to avoid.

From the back of the hall, Roland Peebles appeared, carrying a silver tray. A huge slab of meat, grey-green in texture rested on top. Even from metres away, she smelled rancid flesh. He placed it on a table and walked out of the hall. Only the closest of observers would have noticed the look he gave to Eloise as he went by.

The Town Clerk came down from his platform, stood beside the tray, then picked an object from beside the meat. He twisted it at eye level, the steel glinting in the light.

A dagger.

Maynard turned and looked towards the councillors. "The Letting." he said, his low, stern voice filled the chamber. "Approach."

From the nearest line of seats, they rose and filed towards him, a congregation rising for communion.

The first to reach the Town Clerk was Frederick Costard, a tall thin-faced man, who looked as if he were sucking a boiled sweet. He stood proudly before Maynard, pulled up his sleeve and presented a milky forearm.

Maynard presented the blade and slid the tip across Costard's wrist in a short, sharp motion. A crescent of blood bloomed against his white skin. Quickly, Costard held his arm over the meat and let his blood run onto it.

From beneath its covering, the cage rattled. It was a small sound, a minor shift of mass from within, but all eyes turned toward it.

Eloise stood and followed the flow of councillors into the aisle, joining the queue.

The Town Clerk cut, and they bled onto the meat. Cut and bleed, cut and bleed. After each new supply, the cage shuddered.

She reached the front. Maynard gave a sly wink before beckoning for her arm. She hesitated, then complied. Eloise gasped at the jolt of pain, but kept her expression neutral, her stance steady.

She leaned towards the meat.

The smell here was thick and rich with decay. She covered her nose and mouth with her free hand. Red, red, red dripped onto the mouldering flesh.

The cage rattled again, more violently this time. And there was a sound, a voice. Throaty, sickening. "Yes."

She was supposed to scurry back to her seat now, but she had a promise to keep.

"Where is Rachael? Who took her?" she whispered.

A cry of "No!" came out from behind, but Eloise ignored it. She had reduced her universe to the curtain and the cage and whatever lay on the other side. Nothing else existed.

"Rachael Peebles," she said.

There was another shifting movement from inside. It was about to say something, she was sure of it. "I tell...."

But before she could hear more, two sets of arms were pulling her away, dragging her back to her seat.

───────────────

By the time the last of the councillors had passed by, the meat was immersed in a soupy claret mixture.

The Town Clerk turned to address them and began with a deep sigh. "Before The Sharing, I must remind all Town Councillors of their solemn and sacred responsibility to follow custom and protocol in this chamber at all times." These last three words were given such emphasis that The Town Clerk's voice descended to a primeval growl. "We must never use the access granted to us to pursue personal obsessions or vendettas..." and so it went on, his eyes and those of her fellow councillors boring into Eloise whilst she sat among them, isolated and shamefaced.

Maynard shook his head as if to rid himself of a terrible memory. "Now for The Sharing". He turned and addressed the cage, "Motley, Are you ready?"

A voice from inside came, "Yes," then a pause. "I'm awake. I'm ready, sir."

To Eloise's ear, the voice sounded adult and childish, simultaneously mocking and desperate.

"Please give, sir," It said.

Maynard picked up the platter and placed it on the table in front of the cage. Carefully, deliberately, he reached up to the curtain and pulled a cord. The drapes moved back and the thing inside was revealed.

Eloise leaned forward. She had known, deep down, that one day she would see it. And she had known that it must be something fantastical to hold a town in its hand for so many years. But all that knowledge, all those stories, every hint and rumour, every nursery rhyme and poem could not have prepared her for this.

It moved.

It writhed and moved and breathed. She could see its little chest rising and falling. And yet, it should not have moved or breathed, most definitely should not have made sounds or spoken. Every instinct told her it should be inanimate, unliving.

And yet, there it was, a hideous amalgam come to life. She prayed it would stop moving, but it kept on.

"I am hungry," It said.

The central column of this abomination—the part that they called its "body"—was covered in a leathery layer of skins, stitched together with thick black twine. Some said the skin had been human once, taken from the bodies of children back when the passing of an infant was a common occurrence. Inside, they also said, it was stuffed with grass or straw. Small stems poked out of its exterior, here and there.

On its oversized head, where eyes might have been, were two simple cross stitches. The Motley was blind, in the conventional sense of the word.

Its arms and legs were made of sticks. Small, but thick and robust, broken tree limbs which bent in places where a human arm might also join.

The Motley sat with its legs out in front, the same way a baby might sit when it learns to hold its head upright. "Can I have the food, sir?"

"You can have the food if you share your secret," The Town Clerk replied.

"I have a good one," It said.

"Then you will feast." Maynard leaned forward and un-hooked the latch on the cage.

Eloise wished with all her heart that it would stop being alive.

It shifted its weight to one side, then hopped up onto its stick legs, and walked out of the cage, onto the table, scuttling like a spider.

"Sir ready for secret?"

The Town Clerk nodded.

The Motley reached out both hands and Maynard took them in his. His entire body jolted, as if subjected to a shock of electricity. He continued to judder and flail, somehow staying on his feet and keeping his hands clasped to the doll's. This went on for almost a minute, the other councillors watching, enthralled.

It ended suddenly, Maynard suddenly rigid, still, then re-leasing its hands. He turned to the councillors, "I have the secret," he said.

There was a murmur of approval from his audience.

"Can I eat, man?" The Motley asked.

With a wave of his hand, Maynard gave his permission.

It descended onto the meat, its face plunging into the blood and flesh. The head bobbed up and down, side to side, and tiny pieces of meat sprayed around its head.

Eloise cast her eyes down. She could not look, did not want to think about its sharp little teeth or why it wanted the rotten meat drenched in the blood of the town councillors.

Hemsworthy spoke to her out of the corner of his mouth. "Eloise, you must watch. It is your duty to bear witness."

She looked back to the thing and saw it had taken the meat down to the bone, was near finished, had devoured its meal with incredible speed. The Motley pulled back from the plat-ter, blood smeared around the hole that was its mouth.

The words danced from her lips again, whispered before she could stop herself.

...It wasn't Tammy Jenkins, It wasn't Mistress Drew,
So, nobody knows how The Motley knew.

When it was finished feasting, The Motley shuffled back into its cage. The same councillors carried it back to its room behind the stage. Meanwhile, Maynard prepared his speaking notes, readying himself to share The Motley's secret.

Eloise entered the market square an hour before the Giving of the Truth. She pretended to look at shop windows and chat with acquaintances. Her eyes kept drifting to the corner of the square, where a curious wooden structure squatted, hunched over like an ogre.

The occasional outsider who saw the stocks would assume they were a whimsical hangover from a bygone age, or perhaps a prop for some harmless tradition. Unsuspecting tourists posed for photos, pretending to be locked in, pulling pained faces for likes and shares on social media.

Shipstonians did not like to see this, and local shopkeepers and others would shoo them along if they stayed too long.

"Not for playing on," Bobby Mayo, the butcher, would say, "They're not toys."

The sharp-eyed newcomer might, as they reluctantly shuffled away, notice the rouge tint to the stocks and the paving around it.

On days like this one, the third Tuesday of the month, the square was sealed off from prying eyes and a ritual was observed.

The Giving of the Truth.

Right on time, June Chandos was marched around the corner, held by three men, two holding her arms and another, the Town Clerk, gripping the scruff of her coat. She looked grey-skinned, petrified.

Eloise knew her well. She'd served on the parent-teacher committee of the primary school with her mother. June

Chandos was near sixty years old, but that morning Eloise would have guessed nearer eighty.

There was no mob, no fire and brimstone, not yet. They took her to the stocks in silence and the Town Clerk's minders locked her in. When her head and hands were held firmly in place, the Town Clerk stood next to her and rolled out a piece of paper. He read aloud.

"Our people know the soil and know our ways. We are better for it. Here, we look out for our own, and punish the misdemeanours of our brethren. It is the only way."

As Maynard spoke, more and more of the people in the square moved across to the area around the stocks. A group of larger, younger, more physically imposing men edged themselves to the front. There were some in the town who enjoyed participating in the Giving of the Truth, more than they would admit.

The Town Clerk continued, "We do right by each other and allow no thievery, nor fornication nor cruelty to our fellow man. We listen to The Motley. It shows us the error of our ways and allows us to correct them."

He went on: "Ms. Chandos and her neighbour Ms. Dillis Cooper have for many years quarrelled over petty things. They grew to hate one another. On the sixteenth of September this year, June Chandos decided to take vengeance on Dillis Cooper. She tempted her neighbour's dog over to her back garden and fed it poison…."

"I did not! I did no such thing."

"Quiet!" Maynard snapped.

"Shut up," came the shout from one man at the front. There was a murmur of assent from the others, who had grown in number, perhaps thirty or forty now.

"The poor dog died a horrible death. Ms. Dillis Cooper is most aggrieved. June Chandos, this is a good town because The Motley knows our secrets, the truth of our actions."

"No" the old woman whimpered.

From behind the crowd, a wheelbarrow emerged, pushed by one of the Town Clerk's assistants. He struggled to keep it steady, such was the weight of its contents. The barrow was full to brim with rocks and stones.

June Chandos saw and wailed again, frantic this time, the sound of utter desperation.

Eloise had seen the Giving of the Truth before, many times, but this was different. This time, she had raised her hand, along with all the other Councillors, and agreed to the proposal for her punishment. Her father had always reassured her that the system was just, that The Motley kept the town pure, disciplined.

She tried to turn and walk away, when large hands gripped her by the shoulder, long fingers digging into her collar bone. Oliver Hemsworthy's face was smiling down at her. "Going somewhere, Eloise?" he asked, his voice was low, conspiratorial. He leaned in toward her, "You're on the Town Council now. You must bear witness."

June Chandos called out again, "Please, no!"

Her entreaties were joined by the sound of rocks and heavy stones clicking against each other as hands took them from the barrow.

Eloise closed her eyes.

─────────────

Her father's head lolled to one side; his mouth half-open as he snored. Eloise turned off the TV and tried to summon the energy to get him onto the stairlift, then into bed.

Ever since the meeting and June Chandos, this was how it had been. She went through the motions—shopping, cleaning, cooking and caring for her father—but it was harder now. Eloise was tired, weighed down by her participation in the town's unforgiving traditions.

Before she could dwell any longer, the doorbell rang.

Eloise opened to find Roland Peebles standing in the rain, his thin hair stuck to his head in clumps, leaving ugly islands of white baldness. She was about to chastise him for being out without a coat or umbrella when she caught the look on his face. Eloise had seen sadness before, many times—the town was a breeding place for it—but this was something else, something much worse. Desolation? Something had broken Roland Peebles.

His skin was pale, almost blue.

"Please…" he managed, a raw edge in his voice.

"Will you come in, Roland?" she said, gently.

But he was too far gone. The words tumbled out, "Her name was Rachael. A little girl called Rachael…."

"Roland?"

He was shaking uncontrollably.

"Please help me, Eloise. You're the only one. I see her in my dreams every night, I see her in the street even when I know it's not her. I can never reach her, never tell her I'm sorry."

Instinctively, she held out a hand, touched his cold arm. It was like flicking a switch. He fell to his knees, and folded into the foetal position, sobbing right there on her doorstep.

She hovered over him, unsure what to do. Slowly, the shaking calmed and the sobbing subsided. She coaxed him into the house. After a time, she had him sat in front of the fire, wrapped in blankets, a hot cup of tea beside him.

Eloise checked that her father was still sleeping in his chair, then sat opposite Roland. Eventually, without prompting, he told her, in a distant voice, as if speaking from the other side of a thick dark cloud, what had happened.

Roland had been feeling unwell, depressed for a long time, and it got much worse after the Town Hall meeting, he said. That night, to take his mind off things, he'd gone to the rugby club to watch an evening game. Over the sound of shouting spectators, he heard the chatter of kids playing on the playground. A parent walked over to them and shouted for their child to come.

Roland held his hands in front of himself and spoke to them, as if the secret of his disintegration could be found in his palms.

"He called the name of the child, over and over. 'Rachael! Rachael, Come here darling.' The girl rushed to her father. It was her, Eloise. Just like *our* Rachael. Bright and so alive."

"You've had a breakdown, Roland. There's no other way to put it."

"Have I?" He seemed bemused by the thought.

"Yes, I think so," she said.

"Oh."

"You need to rest, and then you need to see a doctor."

"Why"

"To help you get better."

"So, I can do it all over again next year? Or the year after?"

"This isn't the first time, is it?"

"No." he looked at his hands again.

"You must take better care of yourself."

"I need to know, Eloise. I need to know what happened to her." His voice was soft, but resolute.

"But I tried," she said. "It didn't work."

"We could try something else."

"Careful, Roland. Remember…" she spun her finger in the air, as if The Motley were hiding, waiting for them to make a mistake so it could pounce.

"It's my sister I remember, and you should, too. Or is that seat on the Town Council a little too comfortable already?"

It cut deep. Eloise rocked back in her seat. They had spoken about Rachael many times over the years, but he had never blamed her, never lashed out like this.

Her voice cracked as she spoke. "That's unfair, Roland."

"We should try something else…"

She brought her finger to her lips. "Don't say another word."

"We could take The Motley," he said. "Kidnap it. Make it tell us."

"Shut up, Roland!"

"We could find out what happened to Rachael, once and for all."

She stared at him, unable to believe he'd been so reckless as to say it aloud. Silence filled the room, closing in on them.

She said, "They keep it in the Town Hall. They guard it." The words were out before she could think to stop them.

"Then we need to find a way of getting past them."

"Like how?"

Roland cast his eyes to the floor.

"How?" She kept on. "You're going to beat them up?"

"I haven't thought it through. I don't know."

"You want to be a hero now?"

He held his head in his hands, and Eloise regretted speaking so harshly.

"You could get in by the attic." The voice was hoarse and sleepy. Eloise's father turned in his wheelchair and grinned at them. "That's what we used to do."

Eloise gawped, open-mouthed.

He went on. "That's what we used to do in my younger days. Me and Ronny Maynard would get up into the rafters from the stage ladder. Then up into the attic. Every room in the Town Hall is linked by the attic. There are no walls up there, you just have to get up and find the right hatch, and you're in."

Roland looked at Eloise, amazed, then back to the old man. "Mr. Phillips, you used to sneak in to see The Motley?"

"Oh yes, all the time. We liked to talk to it. Find out some extra secrets."

"And you got in from an attic?"

Eloise's father didn't respond.

She saw it, that look again, when he understood what he'd become.

"Find the girl," he said. "Find her." And then they lost him again to the clouds in his mind.

She could've crawled across the dusty, cobwebbed boards in a minute or so, but she had to wait for Roland. He wheezed, heaving his body over the top of the ladder and into the loft.

THE MOTLEY ☙ 53

She shuffled along on her hands and knees until she reached the hatch for the room behind the stage. When Roland arrived, Eloise twisted and pulled the handle. A haze of dust flew up around them. Below, through the opening, there was only darkness. She wondered if they'd made a mistake, but then picked up a gentle metallic rattling sound coming from below.

Roland tied his end of the rope around his waist. Eloise lowered the rest down into the room below. She clambered through the hatch, Roland took up her weight and she began the descent.

Eloise suddenly thought of its hutch as a delicate, breachable thing, and remembered the council meeting and how The Motley returned to it after feeding, peaceably and without coercion. It stayed in the cage because it chose to, not because it couldn't escape.

The descent took an age, the ridges of the thick rope rubbed her hands sore. As her feet touched the floor she whispered to Roland. "I'm down."

She released the rope and stepped back. In the dark, something pulled on the back pocket of her jeans. She lost her balance and stumbled, banging her hip into something hard. There was a loud crash, so shocking that Eloise dropped flat on the floor, as if cowering from an explosion.

"Jesus, Eloise! You okay?" Roland's voice was shrill, panicked.

"Yes. Shut up."

Slowly, her eyes adjusted. Outlines emerged against the lighter colours of the walls. There was a table next to her and, now fallen to the floor, the cage. Toppled on its side, the cage rolled back and forth, creating a metallic, jangling sound. The little door on the side flapped from side to side, wide open. Eloise scanned the room for The Motley but saw nothing. She took out her phone and switched on the torch.

Scratchy steps.

She swung around, the crystalline beam from the phone flaring against grubby cream walls.

"Hello?"

More steps and she turned again, back towards the cage.

"Mr. Motley, hello." She cringed. Did it even know its own name?

Without warning, without sound, it was on her.

There was the physical sensation of its weight arriving on her back, like someone hitting her with an old lumpy pillow. Next, and much worse, its bizarre twig arms wrapped around her neck. The suddenness of the invasion stunned her to silent, rigid stillness.

It spoke into her ear. "Lady have treats!"

Every instinct she possessed told her to reach back, rip it off and fling the freakish doll across the room. Somehow, she held the impulse at bay and answered.

"Yes, I have treats for you. If you let go, I can get the treat."

"You don't like close, do you, lady?" Its mouth was beside her ear, but no breath escaped, just the faint whiff of something carrion. The Motley shuddered against her when it spoke, like a clockwork toy wound up too tight. "Lady doesn't like Motley close."

"Oh, that's not true," she said. "I just want to get the treat."

"Sure?" Its tone was babyish, mocking.

"Oh yes. Real sure."

She felt its scratchy arms loosen their hold and its body slid down her back. Eloise turned to find it settled on the floor, sitting, its awkward large head swaying like a waning metronome.

"They won't like. Visits not allowed," The Motley said.

The voice retained its strange mixture of innocence and sarcasm, but in the lightless confines of the room, there was menace too—hatred, even. Eloise felt a momentary sense of gratitude for the darkness. She could see the outline and position of its black cross-stitch eyes, but not the detail of its hideous movement.

Slowly, never taking her eyes from The Motley, she took the meat from the bag.

"I want you to tell me a secret," she said. "And I'll give you this."

"Does it have blood? Right kind?"

"It does. My own."

The Motley paused, like a patron considering which wine to order. "Yes. You on council. You asked about girl."

It remembered her. She hadn't expected that. "Yes, I did."

"You want know 'bout little Rachael."

She bit her lower lip. "Yes, yes. Will you tell me?" Eloise held up the meat again.

"You promise to give me?" Its stick hand pointed to the meat.

Eloise pulled the package back into the crook of her arm, "If you tell. Only if you tell."

"Bad question, lady." The Motley's twig arm tapped its cheek. "Hurt my head."

"Why?"

"Why! Why, she says." It laughed, and the sound was awful, like sandpaper rubbing on coarse stone. "'Cause I told. Secrets, secrets, secrets, they want. Never listen. Motley Secrets should be used, not forgotten."

"What do you mean, 'you told'?"

It yawned and then grinned at her. "I got sharp teeth," It said, ignoring her question. "Motley take meat. Tell no more secrets."

She had hated the idea of being near The Motley but hadn't considered being in actual physical danger. Did it do that? Would it bite her? All it wanted was the blood from the town's people, the councillors' blood.

Panic rose through her chest and throat. Her breathing quickened, but unevenly, without rhythm. "Why would you want to hurt me? I don't know what happened to Rachael. Nobody does. That's why I'm here."

It smiled and even in the dark, she could see the points of its teeth jutting out at bizarre angles. Eloise glanced up towards the hatch and wondered if she could climb the rope quickly enough to get away.

"Big boy up there." It said, chuckling now, "He's a greedy boy."

She whimpered. Her body was shaking now, riven with fear.

The Motley's head tilted to one side. "You ask. At meeting. And I show him, the man. Just like I did before."

"You didn't tell."

The doll shook its head.

"You told us about a dog. A fucking dog. A woman died, horribly, because of a dog." All the years of anger and frustration and pain welled up inside her and poured out. "Children go missing, but The Motley tells about dogs."

"Lies, lies, lies," it screeched.

The Motley leapt up onto the tabletop and then dived, full length, at Eloise. For a fraction of a second, she saw only teeth coming toward her. In that moment, she knew everything was over, that her life was would now end in terrible suffering, without ever knowing what happened to her friend.

The teeth stopped in mid-air, The Motley's gnashing incisors reaching for her face, but somehow suspended before her. Eloise stepped aside and saw Roland in the dusky light, still holding the rope, reaching down and gripping the monster on its back. He wheeled away and slammed it down on the table, pinning it in place.

"Tell us! Tell us what happened to my sister."

The thing gagged and spat and a substance flashed past Roland's head.

"I'll tear you apart, rip you to shreds. Tell us," Roland said.

Roland dug his fingers into its soft body and began to pull apart. The Motley squealed in agony.

"Stooop! Stooop!"

Roland relaxed his hold, just a little.

"I see Rachael," it said, wheezing, in a weaker voice than before. "I always tell. Every time. I tell for the meat."

"Who? Who do you tell?" Roland had bent down, his face pressed down towards The Motley.

"At the big meeting. The man with the chain. Many years now, I tell. I show."

Eloise experienced the dizzying sensation of sudden and unexpected understanding. Tiny interlocking fragments of truth began to click together in her mind. The way Maynard always returned The Motley to its room before The Sharing, the look he gave her when The Motley released his hand.

"He knows?" she asked.

"He knows. Motley Secrets should be used, not forgotten," it said.

Roland wept as he spoke, still pushing down on The Motley. "They didn't tell us. We didn't know."

"You're her brother?" The Motley said.

"Yes."

"Let go. Give me my feed. I show you."

"He's lying. Keep him there," Eloise said, but there was the unmistakeable lilt of doubt in her voice.

"I need to know." Roland was trembling.

"Don't, Roland."

He released The Motley.

Slowly, it raised itself up and stood on the table, its face directly in front of Roland's.

It proffered a mangled limb of twigs and sticks. "Take hand, boy. I show you sister."

Three from the left, two from the front, Eloise sat in her chair, doing everything in her power not to draw attention. She nodded and smiled and frowned in all the appropriate places. The casual observer would not have noticed the insistent twitch flickering beneath her left eye, nor the way she pressed her hands together on her lap, as if holding herself in place.

At the end of the public meeting, the gallery was cleared of everyone, except for her father. There were raised eyebrows from those who'd spotted him but, as a former councillor and Alderman of the Town, he was permitted to stay. Roland had wheeled him up to the gallery several hours before. There'd been no outbursts or reasons to attend to him. The familiar rhythms and rituals of the gathering seemed to sooth his temper. Despite everything, he was still a man in his element.

Eloise forced a smile and waved. He returned the gesture, looking for all the world the proud and loving father.

They carried The Motley out from his room and placed his cage on the table next to the Town Clerk, just as always. Maynard said his piece and the councillors were brought forward to give their blood to the meat. Eloise followed obediently, never taking her eyes from Maynard as he cut her arm.

For its part, The Motley gave nothing away. It rattled and snarled and pretended this meeting was the same as all the thousands which had gone before.

Eloise and the rest of the councillors returned to their seats. Maynard and The Motley spoke the words of ritual.

"May I have food, sir?"

"You will have the food if you share your secret," The Town Clerk replied.

"I have a good one," It said.

"Then you will feast." Maynard leaned forward and unhooked the latch on the cage.

Eloise glanced up to the gallery and saw Roland had taken a seat next to her father. He was not supposed to be there, but if anyone had spotted him, they gave no indication. Roland caught her look and raised a finger to his lips. She nodded back.

At the front, The Motley held out its hand for Maynard to take. They touched, but the Town Clerk did not jolt or spasm as he had last time. A look of confusion spread across his face.

"You come closer, mister man." The Motley said.

And he did. Maynard leaned his head down towards the doll, as if it were about to whisper its secret to him.

The Motley raised itself up, so that its head was above the Town Clerk's. Maynard had no way of seeing its teeth emerge from behind those strange, mangled lips. A fraction of a second before it struck, some of the councillors understood. Shouts went up, but it was too late for Maynard. The Motley's fangs came down on the side of his face, and a red haze sprayed up onto its patchwork skin.

There was pandemonium in the room. Some screamed, some leapt to their feet toppling chairs around them. Next to Eloise, Oliver Hemsworthy backed away, wide-eyed, transfixed by the butchery ahead of him, but knowing he needed to move away, fast.

Eloise had expected councillors to rush to Maynard's aid. Several approached, and The Motley raised its head and hissed viciously at them, spitting Maynard's blood in their direction. Timidly, they retreated. None were prepared, it seemed, to risk personal harm to protect their leader.

Maynard lay on his side and The Motley berserked his way from the face to the neck and the chest. The spray and splash of Maynard's insides followed its mouth like little red fountains, each snap of its jaw producing another burst of blood.

There was a crush at the exit to the assembly room as councillors fled.

Eloise sat in place, watching The Motley eat, occasionally glancing up to the gallery to see her father's reaction. The old man was almost impassive, only furrowing his brow at the scene below, as if sensing a misplaced note in a symphony.

The sounds of human flight and fright dissipated, almost as quickly as they arose. With the councillors gone, only Eloise and The Motley were left in the expansive hall. The doll slowed its feasting, as if sensing urgency was no longer required. What remained of the cadaver rocked to the rhythm of its inquisitive teeth. The front of Maynard's body now resembled a soft fruit, peeled and opened.

Eloise felt nothing for him. The Motley had shown Maynard Rachael's fate many times over, but the old man had chosen to conceal the truth. They couldn't have members of the town council, his own friend no less, being thrown into the stocks, could they? Instead, he used the situation to his advantage and sought to settle old scores.

There was a clatter from behind, and Eloise turned to see Roland manoeuvering her father's wheelchair through the broken doors.

She got up and met them in the aisle. Roland stopped and Eloise bent to be at eye level with her father. She took his hand in hers and patted it. "Rachael arrived early, didn't she Dad?"

"Silly, silly girl." It wasn't clear if he was referring to Rachael or his own daughter.

"She arrived early, so she came to the house to see if I was there." Eloise continued, "and you told her to come in and wait. She didn't want to. She'd sensed something wrong in you long before. Rachael was smart like that. I was blind to your demons, but she could see them, even if she wasn't able to put them into words."

"I'm thirsty. Get me a drink, girl."

She ignored him. "Rachael came into the house and you did terrible things. Unspeakable things. She never came out again, did she, Father?" She spat out the final word at him, as if to expel their relationship, to deny it had ever been part of her.

"I said, get me a drink!" He was shouting now, fury coursing through his every word.

"We know, Dad. The Motley showed Roland. And Roland told me."

"You're a disgrace, girl. Get me…."

"I found her. Buried in the garden. You put the fishing rod in her hand, didn't you? That was your little joke, wasn't it? Did that make you laugh, Dad?"

He began to pant, short shallow gulps of air taken through clenched teeth, "Take me home."

"No more laughing. Rachael deserves that, at the very least."

She stood, took one wheelchair handle, and Roland took the other.

The Motley had stopped eating Maynard and now stared down the aisle through cross-stitched eyes.

"Bad man." It said. "I can smell."

A few metres away from the doll, both Roland and Eloise gave the chair a firm push, and it rolled to The Motley.

"Bad man," It said again, grinning, hissing, baring its bloodstained teeth.

THERSA MATSUURA

CHILD OF
THE GODS

TEMARI

"KAKA, he ruined it." Aoi held the shredded *temari* in both hands. Her little brother had ripped out the delicate embroidery with his teeth, then used his dirty fingers to pull apart all the colorful pieces of silk and stuffing. Her precious handmade ball was destroyed. Aoi wanted to lunge across the room at Jiro with pinches and slaps and kicks. Only her heart was too broken at the moment. She couldn't move. She hated him.

"He's just a baby," her mother said, squatting on the clay floor, fanning the wood fire in the *kamado*. The newest child, secured with long lengths of soft cloth to her back, made mewling, hungry noises. He was always hungry. Aoi's sister, Kaya, bounced the two-year-old she was carrying and feigned concentration as she chopped sweet potatoes with a heavy knife, secretly enjoying the confrontation.

Jiro was not a baby. He was old enough to walk and talk and stare at her for long periods of time with his unblinking, fish-like eyes. He was right now across the room, single-mindedly poking a hole in the bottom of the shoji door, pretending he didn't know what he had done. But Aoi knew it was him. She'd been told, even where to find her lost toy. She knew he was listening.

"Kaka," the girl begged once more for her mother to do something.

Just then, Aoi had a thought and dropped to her knees to re-examine her most prized possession. The painful lump in her throat grew and threatened to choke her. Tears ran quiet and hot down her cheeks as she remembered last winter, sitting on Baaba's lap every night for weeks. The old woman's fingers curled into dead spider-like claws from a lifetime of sewing, carefully pieced together all the most beautiful kimono scraps she'd collected from her richest customers. Aoi sat perfectly still, the crone's arms around her, maneuvering the needle like a *yamamba* mountain witch. When she pricked herself, she didn't bleed.

Before Baaba sealed the ball by covering the outside in a complicated design of colorful thread, she took the *fude* made from Aoi's own baby hair and dipped it into a ceramic bowl of glassy black ink. On a tiny slip of paper, she brushed a wish for her granddaughter's seventh birthday. After it dried, she folded it and tucked it inside. It was a secret wish. Its power, her grandmother told her, was in its secrecy.

Aoi rifled through all the shreds of cloth in front of her. The wish was gone.

She turned to Jiro, who now sat looking at her with his stupid drooling face and always running nose. He shoved a handful of torn *washi* paper into his grotesque mouth and chewed. He smiled.

"Kaka, he ate Baaba's wish."

Why did she have to endure this monster? All of them. It wasn't fair.

"A-chan, he's a boy. It can't be helped." Mother watched the toddler swallow and reach for another fistful of paper. Her face went slack. She looked so tired these days. Aoi remembered when she had been filled with fire and laughed. But that was before Baaba died. Before the two-year-old and the baby. She was busier now.

"He's willful," Mother finally said and looked away.

Aoi stood up and stomped out of the house, leaving the mess on the floor. She ran into the forest.

THE KITSUNE JINJA

Mother picked her way through the fallen limbs and overgrown path. She knew where to find her daughter. In the woods, curled up under one of the moss-covered *kitsune* statues that stood in front of the abandoned *inari jinja*.

No one came this way anymore, not since Old Man Tamari who used to tend the shrine was found gored by a boar, body parts strewn everywhere, even in the trees. Rumors quickly spread that it wasn't a boar that had rended the old man. If the gods couldn't protect a tottering grandfather who swept away leaves from the path, spiderwebs from the rafters, and left fresh water in the bowls he'd placed at the fox's feet, then maybe they weren't gods after all. No one continued his devotion after he died, and the place was forgotten.

Mother scolded Aoi on so many occasions, telling her to stay away from the dilapidated shrine. It was dangerous. But her daughter was unafraid. Maybe that was one of the reasons she was so unlike the other children. Maybe that's why Mother felt such an overwhelming need to protect her. A burden she worried would never end.

Passing the headless *jizo*—only the weathered stone and the filthy, tattered remnants of a bib remaining—Mother knew she was almost there. She remembered back to the day her daughter revealed to the family that foxes visited her at night and when she was all alone. She said they sang to her and told her things. After that her brothers and soon the neighbor kids teased her relentlessly. Aoi wasn't one to cry easily. But she finally broke down. That was the first day she took refuge at the shrine.

It still puzzled Mother how the young girl found it though. Hidden in a chilly copse of trees, the falling apart building with its two fox guardians being devoured by the forest were almost invisible. Old Man Tamari had died years before Aoi was born, and no one from the village spoke of the place, much less dared visit. She had almost forgotten it existed herself.

Except the other question that unsettled her. While the whole family spent that day searching everywhere for the missing girl. It was Baaba who finally told them where to look. How had she known? By that time, the old woman could hardly walk, so there was no way she could have led her granddaughter into these dark woods. Giving directions to such a young girl and such a strange and haunted forest would have been impossible, too.

Intuition, maybe. There was the girl's matter of fact announcement over the evening meal that she communicated with kitsune along with other signs. How sometimes she'd show up with hawk feathers woven into her hair and smelling of honeysuckle and pine. Like how once she returned home, muddied and smiling with her sleeves full of flat brown wax tree seeds. When questioned, she declared it was *kitsune no koban*, fox money. And explained how for every hundred she collected, she'd be granted a wish.

That day Baaba had hinted where to look and Mother found her daughter at the shrine, sitting on a broken stone step with a wild look in her eyes, she carried her home. Everyone was relieved that she was safe and for a while, life continued as it usually did. But children were cruel when they decided one of them was different and the teasing started again. Several days later, in the middle of the night, the entire village was shaken awake by horrific cries echoing from the forest. Almost human-like chirps and howls and screams that made one's hair stand on end. Foxes.

Aoi ran to the window and squealed in delight. She said she'd gotten her wish. The children turned cold after that, refusing to play with her. Mother tried to keep her close, but there were fields to work and children to raise. Aoi didn't seem to mind the shunning though. She preferred to stick close to her grandmother, except when she'd vanish for half a day as she did from time to time.

Once Jiro was born, Mother thought it would be good for Aoi to take care of him. It would teach her responsibility and help more quickly tether her to this mundane world she so hated being a part of. Her sister Kaya—only one year older—had always been obedient and hard-working. For the most part, the others, too. But Aoi disliked Jiro from the start, saying he had the face of a carp and thought evil thoughts. She was such a difficult child.

Mother approached the unmoving girl. She was covered in leaves at the foot of one of the statues. It looked like she'd been there for days. Mother sat down beside her, shivered, and looked around. She disliked this place. It wasn't holy anymore. The wooden *torii* gate was splintered and peeling and covered in spiderwebs. The stone kitsune's stern expressions, sharp noses and tapered ears, not at all softened by the rich green that blanketed them. Every time she came, she couldn't help feeling someone was standing in the distance, just out of sight, watching her.

"I know, A-chan. I know. He's a very obstinate boy," she said.

Her daughter didn't move. It wasn't a good idea to talk about Jiro.

"I was thinking," she continued. Her hand hovered over the skinny girl. She pulled it back. She needed to judge her mood first before touching her. "Remember last fall when we visited Tenjin-sama's shrine to celebrate your seventh birthday?"

Something in the forest stepped and snapped a branch behind her. Mother turned quickly to look. Nothing. Something wanted her to know it was listening. The urge to hurry grew.

"It was me, you, and Baaba. We walked all the way there. We sang songs and then ate sweet *dango* on the shrine grounds. At the jinja we bought a *kifuda* just for you, for your seventh year. You asked what was so special about that year and Baaba told you all children up until seven are children of the gods, *kami no ko*. The *ofuda* was a talisman asking them to continue protecting you and keeping you safe and healthy."

Aoi stirred but didn't speak.

"Those gods must really favor you, look how big you've grown and how healthy you are." Mother rested a hand on her daughter's leg. "You can run all the way here and you're not even out of breath."

A breeze swept dry leaves across the ground. The sound made her think of the dried bones on Ubasute Yama.

"It's been a year and I think it's time we return the *fuda* and properly thank them, don't you?"

The girl sat up, leaves cascading from her hair and shoulders.

"Go back to Tenjin-sama?" Her mood bright again, the only sign of tears were the dried dirt-streaked lines down her face. Aoi smiled.

Mother laughed in relief. But the feeling of being observed still itched at her. There were more eyes now. This was her daughter's part of the forest, not hers. She needed to leave.

"I've been talking to your father about it for a while now. Ever since Baaba passed away," she said, getting to her feet. "I think we should."

HITOBASHIRA

They woke before dawn and quietly got ready. Kaka, carrying the ever-present baby, secured a large bundle of everything they'd need for the trip on Aoi's back. The girl didn't care if it was heavy; it still wasn't as bad as Jiro. She hated carrying him. The heat of him, the smell. And he was always pulling at her hair with his slobbery hands. The thought of being rid of him and the noisy, nagging others for the day, of venturing all the way to the mysterious Tenjin-sama Shrine made her stomach feel like she was being swooped away by a mountain *tengu*. Only instead of soaring above the landscape, disconnected and dreamy, they were going to travel through it. This was always more thrilling and dangerous. Also, that it would be only her and Kaka made it that much more special. Nothing could ruin her day today. She would try hard to be a good girl.

Mother and daughter knelt in front of the family altar. Kaka mumbled a *sutra*, the same one Baaba used to pray. Then she asked the dead grandmother and all the other ancestors for fair weather and a safe passage. After that, she removed the kifuda they'd purchased last year, wrapped it in cloth, and slid it into Aoi's bag. Aoi had grown fond of the talisman. Mother had to smack her hands to keep from playing with it. It was a long rectangle of wood with fancy calligraphy written down its front. Baaba was teaching her how to read, but these seaweed-scribbled characters were indecipherable to her. They must be magic.

Mother let Aoi carry the lantern as they left home in the dark and made their way through the still sleeping village. Once dawn broke, the *chochin* was cooled, folded, and tucked away. Villagers were waking and the smell of grilling river fish on wood fires made Aoi hungry. On the outskirts of town, the girl buoyantly called out greetings to the bent-over farmers, swinging curved blades through shafts of golden-tasseled rice. Nearby children helped their mothers lash together bamboo racks to dry the bundles before threshing. Aoi felt special not to be one of them today.

The morning continued slowly with the girl chattering nonstop, stories she never dared share with the others. Kaka listened and respectfully didn't ask any needling questions. Or maybe she was distracted with other thoughts. When the girl got too far ahead, she turned and trotted back with another unbelievable tale she had just remembered.

It was sometime after midday when they reached the big river. On the other side rose the hills, then more distant mountains jutted beyond that. They wouldn't have to go that far, but it made the hair on the back of the girl's neck stand up to think about what lived in those darker forests. Aoi noticed it was taking them longer than last year, even without her grandmother and her bad hip. Kaka moved as if pulling her feet through muddied fields. Was she feeling okay?

At least they were almost there. They could have carried on except the baby was getting fussy, Kaka's feet were sore, and they were all hungry. They stopped on the raised bank next to a gorgeous field of bright red spider lilies. Mother spread out a *furoshiki* cloth and took care of the baby before readying for lunch. The girl, still full of energy, skipped through the flowers. When she returned, she was wearing a crown of red spindly blooms and had a long chain of them around her neck.

Kaka was cradling the feeding baby and looked up.

"A-chan, no!" she scolded. "It's bad luck. Get rid of them. All!"

"They're not bad luck." Aoi was hurt. Her mother didn't usually yell at her these days.

She tore off the flower chains and threw them back into the field.

"Pretty things can't be bad," she mumbled under her breath and sat down.

Mother patted the ground beside her and spoke carefully.

"Those flowers have many names and none of them are good."

"Names?"

"Ghost flower, funeral flower, corpse flower," Kaka said. "Their roots are poisonous, too. There's a reason they're planted around rice fields and graveyards."

Aoi plopped down with her back to her mother, facing the river. Her mood was perfectly spoiled.

"I don't understand why we have to give the fuda back anyway," she mumbled.

Mother handed her a salted rice ball and waited. A few minutes later her daughter pointed to the other side of the river. There was a large group of men preparing to build something big.

"What's that?" she asked, unable to stay upset.

"They're building a new bridge. The old one is not very strong and keeps getting washed out when the storms come."

"But they're digging something." Aoi new the four bamboo poles strung with rope and white papers meant some kind of ceremony.

"It's a prayer to the gods. It'll keep the shore and the bridge strong. It's called a *hitobashira.*"

Aoi didn't have time to ask what that was before Mother had laid down the baby and was digging through the bag her daughter had been carrying.

"I have a present for you." She said as she pulled out a small package wrapped in paper. "Hold out your hands."

Aoi turned quickly and knelt politely in front of her Mother, holding out both hands.

"A present!"

"I was never as talented as Baaba," Kaka said and handed over the bundle.

Aoi pulled away the paper to see the temari restored.

"Kaka!"

The intricate threading was different, a much rougher design, but the pieces of silk she recognized. They were the same ones Baaba had used. She loved it.

"Thank you." She clutched to her chest and then her cheek. She tossed it into the air and caught it again. Today was the best day. Nothing would ruin today.

STICKY RICE DUMPLINGS

Aoi was tossing the temari high in the air and seeing how many times she could clap before catching it, when the trail that led through the trees turned and widened. She dropped the ball at the sight and had to scramble to pick it up again before reaching over and grabbing a handful of her mother's rough kimono to steady herself.

The torii gate was even more magnificent than she remembered. Two vermillion columns, taller than three men standing on each other's shoulders, rose on either side. A black lacquered piece across the top and underneath that hung a braided rope as thick around as Aoi herself. Delicate rectangles of white paper fluttered in the breeze.

"We're here," Kaka said, placing a hand on her daughter's shoulder. "Come on."

The two passed through the gate along with other fancy-dressed visitors. Every one of them holding their own secret prayers and wants to be delivered in-person to the gods. But Aoi wasn't paying attention to them or the grand red building with its thickly thatched roof and intricately carved lintels at the end of the long path. She was examining the ground at her feet. There should be some sort of line, something that separated the regular world they were leaving from the sacred one they were entering. At least that's what Baaba had told her before she passed away. That's what the torii gate meant, she'd said. But Aoi didn't see anything. She didn't exactly feel any different either, although she half expected to.

"Let's sit over there under the *kinmokusei* and rest for a moment," Kaka said and pointed to the large tree covered in tangerine-colored blossoms.

It was early enough in the season that the fragrance of ripe orange mixed with apricot perfumed the crisp autumn air. A week from now, the tree would carpet the ground with the tiny starlike flowers and the heady scent would vanish. Exactly like the spider lily field, they'd come at the perfect time.

Kaka spread the furoshiki cloth on the ground again and asked Aoi to tend the baby. She'd be right back. Earlier her mother had seemed plodding and distracted, now she was buzzing with wasp-winged nerves. She hurried away toward the row of simple food stalls leading up to the main shrine. Next to the girl, the baby kicked and waved his arms, delighted to be able to stretch. He was a good baby. Aoi could tell he was going to turn out okay. She patted his belly and sang to him for a while. She told him he was going to grow up strong and smart and kind. When he got older, she'd introduce him to her kitsune friends. Although recently they'd turned a little skittish. Her stomach growled and she searched for her mother among the people purchasing sweets and savory snacks from the vendors but couldn't find her.

She'd be back soon. Aoi's legs ached. Her whole body shimmered from fatigue, and she was so hungry her stomach bit relentlessly at her insides. She laid down beside her little brother and gazed up through the canopy of leaves and flowers. The dappled light painted them with sparkles and made her sleepy. She closed her eyes.

"*Hai, mitarashi dango, douzo,*" Kaka sang out.

Aoi jolted awake, confused for a second about where she was. Kaka was kneeling on the cloth holding out a skewer of five *mochi* balls. She took it and immediately pulled off one of the still-warm sweets with her teeth and chewed. *Mirin*-sweetened soy sauce filled her mouth. She rolled her eyes and thought these were even better than the ones Baaba used to make. Sorry, Baaba. These dango had been roasted over a fire so they had a slight crunch to them. The insides, though, were so soft they melted in her mouth. She licked the syrup that ran down her fingers, then pulled off the next dango.

"Slow down. There are more." Kaka patted the ground where four more skewers lay half wrapped in a bamboo leaf. Aoi ate and watched as Mother held the hungry baby to her breast.

"Will we be able to name him soon?"

"Yes, I think so," Mother said. She rocked back and forth. "I just spoke with the head priest." She nodded toward the shrine. "After we return your kifuda, I'll get a smaller talisman for him to put on the altar back home."

They sat like that, not speaking, for a long time. Aoi devoured the sweets, picking the skewers clean of all sticky treat as she gazed off into the distance. She was imagining what kind of creatures haunted this forest and if they were friendly. Did the torii gate keep them out? This jinja didn't have foxes out front and why was that? Aoi was about to ask her mom when she noticed in the late afternoon light, it looked almost like she was crying. Was she sick?

"Kaka?"

Mother started out of her trance and looked around quickly.

"A-chan, we have to hurry." She returned the baby to her back, grabbed the temari and slipped it into her daughter's sleeve. "Hold on to that."

Aoi swung the lucky ball and giggled.

Kaka then retrieved the kifuda from the bag and unwrapped it.

"Here. You can give it to the priest. He's waiting for us."

Aoi took the long piece of wood, heavy with spells, in both hands. She was surprised. She was so rarely allowed to touch it. She wished she could keep it.

"Remember to return it like this." Mother demonstrated. "With the calligraphy facing him. It's the polite way."

They stood and Mother shook the cloth, folded it, and returned it to the bag her daughter had been carrying which she
shouldered.

"I'll take this," she said, kneeling to look the girl in the
eyes. She brushed her hair back behind her ears and plucked
away some leaves from her clothes. "You're in charge of the
ofuda. Remember to bow low."

Together they walked to the main shrine and the jumble
of people lined up to shake the braided rope and jangle the
metal bell. Everyone clapped their hands, lowered their head,
and spent a few minutes silently asking or begging for some
bit of fortune.

Suddenly, Aoi had a bad feeling, a sickening clench in her
stomach and the urge to flee. She checked the trees to see if
her kitsune friends were there, but there was nothing. She
didn't think they'd trek this far, anyway. She distracted herself by imagining the stories she could tell them about the trip
when she got back.

Instead of lining up to ring the bell with the other wor-
shipers, Mother steered the girl alongside the shrine toward a
different, but just as ornate building set farther into the surrounding forest.

Aoi fought her uneasiness as she marched solemnly toward
the priest and his two female attendants who were waiting
out front. He was dressed in layered brocade robes of cream
and rich purple and wore a silly tall black hat, tied under his
chin. The women were dressed just as prettily but had long
shiny black hair.

"Please," Mother said. *"Yoroshiku onegaishimau."*

Aoi held out the kifuda and bowed. The priest took it from
her and stepped back. When Aoi stood back up she found it
strange that the two attendants were now on either side of
her, one hand each gently cupping her elbows.

"Would you like to see inside?" one of them asked.

"A-chan." She heard her mother's voice crack and had to
turn around to see she had moved some distance from where
she had been seconds earlier. "You were always the strongest."

Judging from how upset her mother was, Aoi understood something was terribly wrong. She didn't know what.

"Kaka!" the girl cried. "Kaka, I'm sorry."

MAY THE FOXES SING HER TO SLEEP

She bowed low, closed her eyes, and concentrated on things that would keep away the outside world. First, prayers and then when prayers no longer worked, her children. The baby heavy with sleep, hot against her back. The kids at home probably right now bickering as they readied for the evening's meal. And the one in her stomach, still a twist of recurring nausea and constant exhaustion. And hope.

"Kaka!" she called.

Something sharp like flintstone sank into the older woman's chest. She choked back a sob. It was the right thing to do.

Aoi was born too early and too small. The midwife warned she wouldn't survive and offered to take care of it. Mother refused and the girl surprised everyone. Except, she was different. The thread that tethered her to this world shimmered more tenuously than the others. Every morning Mother woke with Aoi on her mind. Was she okay? Was she still in her futon? Had the gods stolen this *kami no ko* back? She had a thought. Maybe it wasn't that the gods didn't want her. Maybe the girl just refused to go.

Her daughter was tenacious and for reasons the older woman didn't understand, not so easily taken. In her short life, she survived coughs, fevers, and the pox that claimed the stronger ones in the village. But why? Mother thought back. Maybe something happened that first time she disappeared as a toddler. Gone. Snatched right from under the eaves of the house when no one was looking. Later the girl was discovered scratched up and bruised but otherwise okay. It was mother, while bathing her, who found she had tufts of cinnamon-colored fur in her mouth. Perhaps she could take care of herself.

All mothers who cared for more than one child understood them profoundly. One more difficult than the others, one smarter, kinder, more sensitive, or more cruel. But all were equally loved. Mothers didn't have favorite children or children they disliked more than the others.

Aoi would not tear into the temari. No matter what happened, she wouldn't open the ball. She'd hold it close as a handful of *miko* swept into the sweet-smelling tatami mat room to calm her in polite sing-songy words and prepare her. Her daughter would marvel at the way their billowing layers of embroidered silks made shushing noises when they moved. Their glossy black hair combed through with *camellia* oil, intoxicating. Their white-painted faces and red lips, otherworldly. Her daughter might imagine what it would be like being them, movements precise and elegant, in control. They, too, looked as if they could fly up to heaven at any moment. And wouldn't it be nice to live here and have no little brothers to argue and fight with anymore?

After it grew quiet, Mother opened her eyes again and stood back up. The autumn sun was slanting harsh orange light through the neatly trimmed maple trees lining the courtyard. The crowd had thinned out, too. It was a long way home. She was so tired. Right now, she just wanted to lie down somewhere and close her eyes. But she needed to leave. Already she had stayed too long.

She imagined walking along the narrow pass in the dark without Aoi to hold the paper lantern and chatter excitedly about made-up adventures and danger. Something like a winter ghost passed through her and she shuddered. It was a silly thought, but even though she'd given this greatest gift to the gods, she felt less protected now.

Mother bowed once more to the shrine and turned to make her way back down the long, pebbled path toward the looming torii gate. There were blisters on her ankles where the straw sandals rubbed through her skin and her lower back ached from the weight of the child. It was a long way home.

Her thoughts went back to Aoi. There'd be prayers, elaborate meals, and obscure explanations that a seven-year-old couldn't quite understand. But she'd be told how special she was, and learn she was chosen. That night the young girl would sleep in a large room lit by oil lamps that flickered feathery shadows behind pure white rice paper and didn't reek of fish oil. Her futon would be thick and soft, the pillow fragrant with this season's rice husks. No sibling's feet would kick her. No sleepy fists would dig into her ribs, keeping her at a distance. No *dani* would bite at her freshly-bathed skin. All that everyday suffering reverberated in Mother, too.

Once her daughter realized what the next day held, though, it would be impossible to sleep. She'd be so scared. Mother collapsed to the ground and wept freely at the thought. She pulled a rough sleeve across her face. Would Aoi gather up her small toy then and press it to her face. Were memories still trapped there? Letting the cloth soak up her always-silent tears, she'd want to run away. But she wouldn't. Because by then they would have told her she was going back to the gods, she was going to see her Baaba again soon.

She'd stay.

Mother got back to her feet with the help of a passing stranger. It was almost dusk, and the bell crickets chirred in the shadows. She wondered if Aoi could hear the same song. Then later tonight, when everyone else was asleep, would the foxes gather at her window to tell her things. She hoped they'd whisper stories about brave girls who did brave deeds. She hoped they'd sing her to sleep.

When the day came there would be chanting that hypnotized all those gathered, a constant rhythmic jangling of bells and scream of flutes, but her daughter would remain fully aware. When the cool dirt was up to her waist and splattering her face, if she decided to use her teeth and fingers and rip open the poorly-mended toy, she'd find a folded slip of paper. On the paper in her mother's fine hand with the same brush Baaba used were written the words: *You were always my favorite. You were truly a child of the gods.*

Mother sobbed knowing Aoi would never open it, knowing that keeping the wish secret made it stronger.

RICHARD THOMAS

THE KEEPER OF THE LIGHT

IF you drive north, away from the city and bright lights, up toward the cornfields, and then on beyond into the darkness of the forests that thicken as it grows colder, you will find some semblance of a man living in a dilapidated house at the end of a long, gravel road.

The frame is not so much built as it is trembling in its feeble existence, clinging to something that must be anger or magic or fear. To look directly at this faded shack is to stare into the shadows of the dark, damp corners of your basement—swirling images that ebb and flow, the sharp, rancid smell of feral urine, and the ongoing creaks of diseased wood trying to collapse after years of service.

When the wind blows, it sways back and forth, the shutters often slamming into the rotten wood, a few of them hanging crookedly, missing a nail or two here and there. If it once had a paint color, it has long since faded into something closer to dust or bone or sickness. Now and then, a thin wisp of smoke drifts up out of a brick fireplace that coughs bits of mortar onto the torn, weathered shingles, smelling of tobacco and meat and a sickly sweetness. It usually sits in darkness, the trees in a ring around it, not quite touching it, not quite hovering over it, bushes thick with a dark green foliage that is spiked with ruby red thorns. In the distance there is the sound of a bubbling brook, running deep and cold, with mottled fish haunting the waters, a slick moss creeping all around the rocks that line the crooked creek.

On the thick oak door is a singular knocker, that of a lion's head—expansive mane, sharp incisors, mouth in a growl—as it somehow holds onto a large brass ring, its eyes two black, smoky gems. It is rarely used, but when heard, the clatter and clang of it resonates throughout the woods—birds stunned into flight, the odd fox or squirrel fleeing without a glance back, the bushes dropping their withered berries onto the dead earth that covers the front yard.

Sometimes he answers.

Sometimes he does not.

There are so many urban legends about him that if you asked five different people, you'd get five different answers. One story is that he used to be a professor of ancient history at one of the state schools downtown, respected and embraced, until a series of relationships over the years came to light—mostly young women, but sometimes men, extra credit, failing grades, and a basement where the pain and pleasure were dispensed in equal amounts. Another is that he was a genetic scientist at a well-known laboratory to the east, and that one of his experiments went horribly wrong, killing several of his associates, and disabling him for life. One speaks of his past as a man of the cloth, at an odd little church out west, where they used to perform rituals with snakes, baptisms that sometimes went wrong, darker celebrations depending on the season, or moon, or alignment of the stars. A fourth tale speaks of something native, a shapeshifter of sorts, this part of the state originally the tribal headquarters, and burial grounds, of the Dakota Sioux, desecrated and paved over, but still hungry for vengeance. But the most compelling might be the alien nature of his ongoing life—there and not there, older than time and yet sometimes quite young, never eating, strange lights in the forests, a meteorite once found in his back yard, taken away by officials, never to return.

Very little of this is true.

———————————————

The first time I saw him in the flesh, it was on a dare, with several of my friends, as we drove around the cornfields, drinking beer, and tossing the empty cans out the window. We had nothing better to do. The girls we knew were never interested, we were perpetually broke, and this gave us the chance to try out our bravado, in a setting that probably wouldn't hurt us.

Probably.

The story of this man, his house, and the bad things that happened out that way held just enough intrigue to encourage us to gas up the random minivan we had that night, and head north toward his encampment. The other three jokers in the car with me aren't important—call them Jeff, Matt, and Steve if you want—they were three interchangeable assholes, with bad teeth, pimples, greasy hair, and fading futures. I know, because I was the same. We were all destined for mediocrity, and that was just fine with us.

But I also had a secret.

There was something wrong with me, something the doctors hadn't been able to figure out. My parents quickly went from worried, to annoyed, to entirely ignorant. They no longer asked why my urine had blood in it, or why I woke up screaming as I swung my fists at shadows that loomed over my bed, or why there were sloughs of skin and iridescent scales in the shower tub every time I finished. I'd brush my teeth, only to find a stray hair caught in my throat, pulling and pulling as it grew longer and longer, trying not to cry, or scream, as my eyes watered, and the clump of matted fur finally dislodged from my endeavors, landing in the sink with a dull, wet thud. The first time, I gagged, washed my mouth out, and then flushed it away. The second time, I cried for an hour. The third time I poked at it, opening it up, to reveal something reminiscent of a bezoar—the indigestible material of a deer, hawk, goat, or even eagle. I was horrified, but curious, and inside that ball were tiny teeth, bits of shiny glass, claws, and a bit of flesh and bone that must have been an embryo or baby bird. It was then that I threw up into the toilet, lowering myself to the cool tile, passing out gently into my expanding fear.

So, when we approached the house, I had something in mind. I wanted answers, or I wanted vengeance, or I wanted to die at the hands of some macabre witch. I was ready to end it all, and none of my friends knew this.

The house sat quietly, the cold winter air running through the skeletal trees, the music in the van off now, just a dull echo of bass reverberating in our rapidly beating hearts. I took a swig of my cheap beer, crushed the can, and left. They snickered, leaned out the open windows to spit tobacco, and mutter insults, lighting cigarettes as my skin grew cold and clammy. I was empty inside, dead and gone, seeking any sort of response from this monster, just to be able to feel something again.

He did not disappoint me.

───────────────

When an hour went by, they came to the door and knocked.

No response.

At two hours, they got worried.

At three, annoyed.

They'd been drinking all night. We all had.

So, cops?

Unlikely.

That sounded like trouble.

So, they went home in silence, hoping that the morning would provide some answers.

And it did.

───────────────

When he first opened the door, the only light in the entire house was a candle far down a long, extended hallway, on a kitchen table, where a glass of mead sat waiting. I couldn't see him, not his hands, his face, and certainly not his body. It was as if there were a net or cloud or dark sheet wrapped around him. As the door opened wider and the shadow that was his shape retreated, I understood what he had said, or offered, so I followed him into the house.

He didn't ask for my name, and I didn't give it, his presence both comforting and unholy. When he pushed through the kitchen, out the back door, and into a yard that overflowed with a garden unlike anything I had ever seen, I followed.

There was a stone path down the middle of the grasses, bushes, and overhanging tress. Flowers bloomed, but in the darkness, they stayed monochromatic—shades of black layered one on top of each other. Even though the moon was bright overhead, it was hard to see anything in great detail— rose bushes that had long, dripping thorns, that must have been red in the daylight; tall grasses and weeds with spores and fluff floating around them, motes of some kind swarming in and out of their long, sticky blades; the ground covered in moss, and clover, and other creeping varieties, so soft underfoot that I felt myself desiring a long, endless rest.

When I opened my mouth to speak, he held up a hand.

"No. Do not share more with me than I need to know. If you ever want to leave, that is. I know why you are here. The same as all of the others. And when your friends leave, we can begin."

I closed my mouth, opened it again, and then swallowed, shutting it for good.

"Keep your name. Keep your affliction. I can see that you are tainted, touched, that a presence has found you, and is trying to call you home. That's all I need to know."

In the foliage and bent trees around us there was a gentle sigh, that had started to match my breathing, the nightbirds crying out in despair, the rustle of hungry critters on the edge of our muted Eden.

"It's important that you see me before we begin. It's important to understand your fate, to come into this with your eyes wide open. Not everyone can survive what happens here, and very few are chosen for service. As well as what lies beyond. I can remove what courses through your veins, what resides in your bones, but it will come at a price, dearie. I just want you to know that, first, before we begin."

When he stepped into the moonlight and dropped the veil, I screamed.

When I got home the next day, my parents were furious. They yelled at me until they saw me, *really* saw me, and then their voices went quiet, and they began to cry.

There were cuts all over my body, from head to toe, and I was bleeding from all of them, just one mark shy of a thousand. It stung. It wept. It exorcised the last of my demons, in tiny amounts, no worse than a common cold, or stubbed toe, or crick in the neck. My eyes were so bloodshot that there seemed to be no white left, as if they too, were filled and overflowing with my blood. My hands were swollen, my fingers bent, not quite broken, but stretched, and bruised, like the claws of some beast.

They managed to ask if I was okay, and I nodded.

"Shower," I said. "I have to get clean."

When they came closer, I stilled them with a glare.

"No, don't touch me. Not yet. It's too soon."

I started to undress in front of them, told them to burn my clothes, to use tongs or gloves, but to not touch anything with their hands.

I wanted them to see me, to see how I had suffered, and to know that I had survived it. Because I wouldn't be with them forever. My time was now spilling grains of sand, the ticking of the hands of a clock, the eroding shores of a distant land slowly falling. It could happen at any time.

They would think poison ivy, I later heard them say, over the rash and boils that ran across my skin. But as the memory of this night faded, they found so many ways to push this all away, to deny it ever happened, to find rational answers to irrational manifestations. The yellow seeping wounds, they were ringed with purple, weaving in and around and over the cuts, the only other places on my skin that were left, covered in raised welts, that throbbed as if alive. Everything hurt. I pulsed with pain and a creeping uncertainty.

What hair I had left on my body had grown dry and brittle. When I pulled off my shirt, patches and clumps fell to the ground, some of it already turned white. The rest went down the drain, when I'd finally managed to pour myself into the steaming shower, stifling my sobbing, weeping voice with the knuckles of my right hand.

I stayed in the shower until it ran cold, and then I stayed there a bit longer. When my parents knocked on the door, asking if they could do anything, if I was okay, I shivered and nodded, reaching for a towel. They turned the knob and opened the door slightly, like two children peeking into a gingerbread house full of treats and terrors.

"I need time and space to heal," I said.

And they gave it to me.

They knew something had been wrong.

They knew this wasn't right.

But perhaps it would get better.

And it did.

In a way.

For many years, I went about my life. Always looking over my shoulder, always staring out windows, waiting for his call, his appearance, but it didn't come. I went to school, fell in love, and then screwed that up, as I would quite a few relationships over the years. I graduated, traveled the country, found my calling, and started to head toward the light. I got a job, fell in love again, had kids, grew old, and thought that maybe I'd gotten away with it. Maybe this wasn't going to happen. Perhaps I'd dodged a bullet. Maybe it had all been imagined, and none of it was real. I thought about a great many things when I lay in bed at night, but most of the time, I just prepared myself for the inevitable.

I was heading to an estate sale up north, away from the city, up past the cornfields, and into the woods, that grew darker as I drove farther into them, when I started to feel a wash of sickness creep across my flesh. The GPS told me where I was going, but I had a sinking feeling in my gut that it wasn't working.

One thing the lore doesn't tell you is that not everyone can find him, only those that are broken. My friends, when they left, they *did* come back. They felt guilty, but couldn't find the house. And the next day, when they sobered up enough to tell their parents, they *did* go to the police, and the officers drove up and down the county lanes, unable to find the shack, eventually getting angry, taking haphazard notes about some stupid kid that got drunk and disappeared. I wasn't technically—legally—missing until 24 hours had passed, and I came stumbling home of my own weak volition before that actually happened.

The house.

The man.

The old shanty appeared in front of me as the gas tank needle settled on empty, sputtering to a halt, but I'd already been crying, already had my ribcage filled with fluttering birds, already resigned myself to the fact that I'd never see my family again.

And I was okay with that.

When he opened the door, his shadow larger, much bigger than before, I followed him to the back yard, which was in full bloom now, the sunshine splitting the dense greenery with a brightness and purity that coated me with grace. The lavender was thriving, the purple flowers dotting green, leafy plants. And around them were all manner of lily—orange and Easter and tiger—in a smattering of orange and white. The roses were indeed red, and I inhaled deeply as I prepared myself for his presence.

When I finally took him in, saw him in all of his hideous glory, I blinked, and stumbled backwards, unable to look away, and yet, trying so very hard to do so. His pale, pasty skin was swollen, wherever it could be seen, his face covered in a ratty beard, long hair hanging down in greasy tendrils. His two main human arms were long, disturbingly long, with rough hair, and meaty biceps that held scabs, pustules, and weeping sores. As he raised his eyes to me—in shame, relief, and horror—they glowed a sickly yellow, as a white pus leaked out of them, running down his cheeks. His human legs were hairy as a beast and bent at an angle that looked excruciatingly painful. They seemed to end in some sort of deformity—the toes fused together, or perhaps cloven hooves. And that was where the humanity stopped. Out the back of his head spiraled two long, curling horns, like that of an antelope or gazelle. Tufts of fur sat at the base, as a sickly grey skin seemed to peel off of them in large flakes. On his back were a pair of diseased wings, hanging down in a mangy, crooked decline, the dull feathers falling off in dusty flutters every time he moved. A multitude of eyes gathered under his chin, chittering beaks opening their mouths where his nipples should have been, four purple tentacles erupting out of his stomach and back, greasy white suckers helping to move him across the lawn. He was encircled by motes and flies and bees and moths. When he opened his mouth to speak, spiders trickled down his chin and over his neck, a mist of musk and urine spraying from orifices I couldn't quite see.

He coughed once, and then reached up to his mouth, to pull out a long hair, that kept coming and coming, the end of it holding some ball of fur and teeth and claws.

What I had been once, he had taken.

His body was a shrine to every sick, broken, and cursed lost soul that had found their way to his doorstep.

In a shrug, it all fell away, and his body glowed in the absence of the weight, shimmering for a moment, sparks of light refracting in the quiet of the glen.

And then I stepped into his place and took the yoke from his neck.

"It's so much longer than you think," he said.

And I nodded as he evaporated into the quiet of such awful wonder.

RYAN CASSAVAUGH

THE LAST HONEYBOY

BROODS HOLLOW, NORTH CAROLINA
LATE SUMMERTIME, 1923

"BEES! Sammy Jay said he saw bees! Down by the river!" Honeyboy is running ahead of me as usual. He skates down the dirt embankment, breaking out in a run where the ground levels out towards the border to the Old Wood. "Big black an' yeller ones, fat as yer thumb."

He's an old man now, the Honeyboy. Seventy. Eighty, maybe. But damn, can he run, when the spirit takes him. Like most of us only do when we're kids, carefree and explosive. He's not even out of breath, and his skin glistens the color of late season honey.

For a quick moment, I catch a reflection of the Honeyboy my Gran'pap knew, the golden god of some long-ago summer; I close my eyes and the moment passes, leaving only the broken-down old man-child who ruined everything for everyone in this damn town.

My Gran'pap was a true believer in Honeyboy right up to the end. Thought for sure Honeyboy's Flower Maiden would come back. "They'll all look foolish then, Koritsi," he'd said. He always called me *Koritsi*, since I was little, it means "girl" in Greek. I really miss that old man.

"When She comes back, we'll all drown in honey, and I'll die happy!" he'd say with a laugh. But She never returned, the town went to shit, and my Gran'pap died crying, blind, and pissing blood in the bed.

Worst thing is I know Sammy Jay's lying. Honeyboy screwed us all over, he chose beauty and truth, and now we are all spiritually and organically fucked in a pig's ass. Cursed. What else is there to do with your day except get drunk and humiliate the Honeyboy? I hate this god'amned Holler.

Honeyboy was at Janet's on Wednesday for his donut and coffee, which he still gets free each morning because he's the Honeyboy, even though there's been no honey in fifty years and it's his fault the town is in ruin. Still, he eats for free at the donut shop, which means a lot to him. Sammy Jay came in with one of the Card brothers; they knew Honeyboy would be there. He was always there first thing in the morning when the shop opened, so he could be gone before anyone else arrived. Except that day, that day Sammy came looking for him.

"Looked like they'd been out fishing," Honeyboy says, halfway across the dust field, nearing the edge of the Old Wood. "Owen Card was in waders, and Sammy was wet as baptized chicken, looked like he'd fallen in the river."

"He probably did," I say, "He's been known to do that when he's drunk, and Sammy Jay is almost always drunk."

I'm in a foul mood. My knees are killing me, it's hot, and there's still so much field before the dark shade of the trees.

"Weren't drunk that day," Honeyboy says. "He did fall in the river. Not because he'd been drinking, but because of the bees." He is happily unbothered by my lack of interest in hearing the story for the dozenth time since Wednesday morning. Here it was only Friday afternoon and a god'amned hot one, too. I don't like this place. It's eerie. The ground is dead, and the noise of the river sounds like angry, whispering voices.

"Not wasps, or nothin'. Not that anyone'd confuse a honey-bee with a yeller-jacket," Honeyboy says, vanishing into the trees ahead. I slow, hoping Honeyboy gets far enough I'll no longer have to hear him. He's not talking to me anyhow. He's talking to himself, or the wind, but especially to Her.

There's no way she wasn't all he's thinking about since Sammy lied about the damn bees. So, I promised him I'd go check with him today 'cause I'm off work. Making him wait two days just about god'amned killed him, but I don't mind that so much. Irritating old bastard.

Broods Holler had been alright with Honeyboy at first. Religion is like that. You can't just go changing religion, or it's not religion. It's just some story you tell yourself to make life a little less miserable. The town knew Honeyboy had no choice in what he did, but that didn't mean they forgave him. A man had to eat, and it was hard to eat when the honey went dry. That was always there, just under the skin: A man has to eat, Honeyboy.

Now the town hated Honeyboy, and they didn't even remember why. Just that it was his fault everyone was poor and miserable. Everything else was just a fairytale, a warning about believing in something with all your heart. Which is a pathetic takeaway from any fairytale, but that's what happens in real life: shitty moral lessons.

Demetri never minded being called the Honeyboy. Even after Broods Holler turned the name from a title of honor to a joke and finally a cold epithet. He always wore it with pride. Being the Honeyboy means free donuts and coffee every morning at Janet's; it means not having to work apart from checking the hives now and then. Of course, being the Honeyboy also means he's a god.

"Small god." Gran'pap would say, "The useful kind."

It's impossible to see this hunchback old drunk and think: Honeyboy, the God of the Summer Fields! He nearly gave us everything, and fuck him for it.

He had not been the youngest Honeyboy ever chosen. That honor had gone to his father Andrzej, who was also seventeen but an entire two months younger when called. But Demetri would be the longest, the proudest, the best, the worst, the most honorable, and undoubtedly the very last Honeyboy. And he was by far the most natural choice the Holler ever made.

It had been the job of the Flower Mothers, women who played the role of Flower Maiden in years past, to choose the new Honeyboy on the first evening of Summer. The Mothers would meet in the center of town, by the stone Honey-cellar, and walk in a solemn, silent processional, through the Holler and into the Old Wood carrying nothing but their sewing kits. They would emerge hours, sometimes days, later. Their dresses torn, stained with blood and sweat and beeswax. They would have made their choice, and they would be carrying his body.

———————————

Gran'pap was there the night Demetri was made the Honeyboy. Sammy Jay was too, though he was just a babe at his mama's tit. "Best night of my life." Gran'pap told me, towards the end. "The hives never sang so sweet, the night never smelled so clear, and I never had so much hope for the world, for the Holler. I wish that night had never ended, Koritsi."

But that night did end; and Gran'pap's hope never came t' nothin' but ruin and death. Makes it hard to see Honeyboy as anything other than a ruined, miserable old man, and I'm the only person in this town who…well, I certainly don't believe in him, but he thinks I do, which means everything to him. It's hard to believe it now, but for one summer, everyone believed in Honeyboy.

"No Honeyboy was ever chosen quicker, not even an hour." Demetri will say when drunk enough that he wants to talk about it, which was most nights now that Sammy Jay started in with the bees. Most years, there would be a crop of young men wanting to be Honeyboy. Every farm boy in town hoped to see the Flower Mothers return carrying their effigy, a near-perfect rendering in beeswax, straw, and flowers. That year no one could have stood beside Demetri Andropolis. Nearly six-and-a-half feet tall, broad and wide and strong. Golden like summer, like honey, like the sun itself.

No man was not envious of Demetri that summer night or for many nights to come. Those nights would come soon enough, and they would be beyond count. But he was the Lord of the Summer then, "the great sun that warms the seeds

in the earth that sprouts the flowers for the bees to make the
honey that feeds us all" made man, and the world was his. I
know by the look in his eye, something far away and out of
focus but more real than anything else in his mind. Like a
rock polished smooth by the river, he returns there any moment he can spare. In his mind, he is still the Golden God of
Summer, and she is his Queen. Before autumn dawned and
everything was torn apart.

———

"What happens when no one believes anymore?" I asked.
Maybe last night, maybe Wednesday. I've been drinking my
share, too, lately. "You know, what if you die and she hasn't
come back?"

"I can't die."

"If there's one thing I can tell just by looking at you, Honeyboy, it is that you are very much able to die. And probably
very soon." I poked his side, and he winced.

"You'd like that." He sounded like a scolded child, "Then
you wouldn't have to spend your nights looking after me."

"I don't have to do that now, you old horse's ass; I do it
because…."

"Because you believe in me," he said, finishing my sentence
and then his beer. "I can't die until she returns, maybe soon if
the bees are back. Are you sure we can't go tonight? I'm not
tired."

I shook my head.

"I can wait," he said. "I've waited this long. I know she'll
be back because I believe, and I'll make it because you believe."

And we'll drown in honey and all die happy.

———

Only two people can check on the hives: the Honeyboy,
and his squire. It's a stupid term and makes no sense, but I
guess I am his squire since no one else is, and someone's got
to go with him to check for bees. He'll likely just die of disap-
pointment anyway, and then I'll be shut off this whole damn
thing. This town can find something else to blame their miser-

able lives on other than who or what some old man fucked in a hole in the ground in front of the whole village fifty years ago.

That summer, his squire was a girl whose name he refuses to tell me, "for modesty's sake," though he swears he does remember it.

"She had breasts like plump beehives, so it seemed fitting." He told me. "And she believed the way I did. Really believed in the furrow and the field, the flower, and bee." He sighed, "If things had gone differently, I might have married her."

"It's never too late," I joked.

"It is for her. She died of the fever when the honey dried up." He paused, staring at his feet. "And who's damned fault was that?"

It's forbidden for the Honeyboy or the squire to report on the state of the hives. Though it was often gauged by the wheat, corn, and tobacco crops; that year had been the best the Holler ever recorded. The actual harvest, the honey yield, was not revealed until the final night of summer when the ground was prepared for hibernation. When the Flower Maiden was chosen and The Dance of the Furrows took place.

"I'd seen 'em, of course," he'd said the night we were drunk. (Last night, I think, In the shack we share outside town.) "Thirty-seven hives, a dozen more than my father who had held the record. Not only that, the hives never gave so much honey, girl."

He only calls me "girl" when he is particularly drunk. I only allowed it when similarly inflicted, as I was that night.

"I know," I said, "sixty...."

"Sixty pounds per hive...that's right, have I told you this? It was the night of the Harvest festival...my last night as Honeyboy...." He whispers that last part like it will be a surprise later when it turns out not to be his last night as Honeyboy.

"Tell me about the food," I said. "You used to, and now you skip that part and get right to the part you want to talk about, and I don't." I picked two warm beer bottles from the floor, opened them, and placed one on the table in beside him. "I know you have to talk about that eventually because we're going back tomorrow to…."

(Tomorrow. It *was* last night. No wonder my head hurts. No wonder everything hurts.)

"To see the bees," he said, incorrectly finishing my sentence for the second time in an hour.

"To see *if* there are bees."

"Sammy Jay said…."

"I know what Sammy Jay said. And he was sober?"

"Do you want to hear about the food?"

"If I have to hear the rest of it, I want to hear the food. The rest is sad."

"Not for me."

"Especially for you. Maybe not to you, but definitely for you."

He didn't like that.

"You'll see," he said smugly.

"No, I won't. Gran'pap thought he'd see, and he never did. You're the only one who can see it now, so tell me about the food so you can get to the part you have to get to."

"All right. If you're getting angry drunk, drink your way to the other side, and I'll tell you about the food."

The table for the Harvest festival was the massive oak door of the Honey cellar, carried through the town by six strong men and laid across the four tree stumps at the edge of the Old Wood.

The honey-cellar, which stands smack-dab in the center of the town, had started out as the First (and only) Broods Hollow Baptist Church. Some great-great-grand uncle of Owen Card's named Albussa come over from all the way in Shelby to try and establish their religion here in the Holler. It didn't catch on, and the preacher contracted a strange fever and died soon after, with a lot of screaming and calling on his God. He passed a day before construction was finished on the church, he never even got to give his first sermon.

Following the untimely and apparently unsightly passing of Reverend Card, the dark stone church with its large hall and small, cool chambers had been found perfect for storing honey barrels. As if it had been constructed for just such a purpose. Its only other use was the yearly surrendering of the door.

Once the table was installed, the Flower Mothers would bless the table with a song. Gran'pap said you couldn't hear the words no matter how hard you listened, but the melody was beautiful and sad and made him dream of endless stars. All the while, the Flower Mothers whirled in a complicated dance, their fire-red end of summer dresses floating and dropping like leaves in the wind. Each movement a complicated action, both elegant and practical. With one great swing, they would dress the table in white linen snapped high in the air, gathering wind until it looked like a ship's sail, then spread it out and across the table with yet another rolling movement. Some moves carried plates and dishes pulled from high wicker hampers. Other softer actions sprinkled the table in clover, wildflowers, and royal jelly mixed with the ashes of a queen. They twirled and bobbed, spun, and floated. Never a wrong step, never a flawed action. And when they were done....

———————————————————————

"Food like you've never seen, girl!" he cried, a Cheshire grin across his face. He was right, I had been angry drunk, but I'd come through it with another beer. "Meats of all kinds. Roast beef the size of cotton bales, goose, duck, chicken and fowl of every kind, and usually a whole pig. That year there were two, a roasted black boar and a red wattle sow stuffed with onion and sage and carrots. You could smell it from a mile away; so sweet and warm. And the vegetables!" He clapped his hands and stamped his feet, childlike.

"Corn, carrots, potatoes. I miss the potatoes, baked, fried, or mashed with sweet cream and rosemary. You sure this isn't boring you?"

"No," I said sharply. "I've never seen a 'tater that didn't come chopped up in a tin of soup. You're bored because you want to get to her, and then you'll get all shitty, and the night will be done. If that's what you want, we can just call it an early night; I've got a big day tomorrow taking some old jack-ass out to see that there are no fucking bees!"

"There are!" His beer bottle barely missed my head, clattering unbroken to the floor behind me. His eyes were wide. His hands had already covered his mouth, which sagged open in panic. "I…I'm sorry."

"You really fucking are." We both sat there for a long time, in silence.

"Do you want me to go on?" he finally asked sheepishly.

"You're getting worked up. It's not good for you."

"Nothing's good for me."

"Then just skip to the dance, huh?"

━━━━━━━━━━━

Once the feast was over, and the best meats and vegetables had been eaten, finished with a keg of last season's honey-beer, and the sweetest baklava you have ever tasted, the men and ladies would sit and smoke their pipes and wait for night to fall. Nothing began until the first star was spotted in the sky. The younger children climbed to the tops of trees for a better look, hoping to be the one to spot the harvest star. Only then could the furrow be cut. A horse plow was yoked with a long leather strap. At the end of the strap were tied ribbons. One ribbon for every young woman of the town who wished to be considered for Flower Maiden, which was all of them that year. The women pulled the plow gently across the field for a length of eight feet, the plow would then be carried back, and the furrow was cut a second time, deeper into the soil, a third time, and a fourth. For the four seasons, I suppose. I piece things together from what Gran'pap told me, what Honeyboy tells me, and what he doesn't. And everyone else doesn't either.

━━━━━━━━━━━

"Where were you? Were you just waiting?" I asked. We were out of beer, at least that's what I'd told him. He didn't seem to mind.

"I was off in a grove nearby with the Honey Lords. My father was there, and all the men who had been the Honeyboy were there. I was being...prepared."

"Prepared how?"

"I can't tell you, girl." He tried to laugh but coughed until he spat red-black phlegm into his shirt sleeve.

"There are no Honey Lords left, are there?" I asked.

He tried to sit up and argue, but my hand on his head rocked him back into his seat like an upside-down turtle. "Listen, Honeyboy, what if the bees are back? (Why would I ever say that? Don't get his hopes up.) There's no more Honey Lords, you said so...Do you think...that if the bees are back... if she's back..." (I remember all this now, god, I was drunk.) You really think you'll live through to come out t'other side?"

(Oh, and apparently, I was a brutal asshole.)

"So tell me what you were doing, in case I need to...take over or something."

"Yeah, alright."

(Damn! It worked.)

―――――――――――

The Flower Mothers had the real magick, but the Honey Lords had something equally important. A special kind of local magic all their own. A red and yellow domed mushroom that grows along the rocks by the river. The Honey Lords brewed a special mead with the stem.

―――――――――――

"An hour after I drank the mead, it started. The night was dark and clear...countless stars. I stood naked as the Lords brushed a tincture of beeswax, oil, and sandalwood on me until I shone and smelled of summer night air and the beginning of autumn.

Then the singing started, a prayer for the town washing over the trees. Voices singing, rising, hands clapping, feet stomping until the whole grove felt as if it might shake apart, and above it, all the bees hummed. Back then, the sound of the hives could be heard throughout the town. Day and night, the ground vibrated with the drone of the Hives.

Alone, I followed the singing through the trees until I came to the field…and there it was. The furrow. A bed turned of soft and fertile soil; both sides lined with young women, each willing…wanting…to be the Flower Maiden and do The Dance of the Furrows in the fresh-cut ground. Each was as beautiful and deserving as the next, and I had to choose.

I thought I had, I'd had all summer to decide, but the actual choice had to be made at the moment. Some girls of the town had caught my eye, but that was all gone. I didn't recognize any of 'em. All I could see was…a light. From inside 'em, glowing softly. It burned with their love for the old ways, for our ways. That was what I saw most of all.

Thirty-seven lights drawing me like a moth to a candle…." He stopped then, his eyes years away in a different life, a better life. "Then the entire world went white with a blinding radiant light, and I was with Her somewhere beyond the stars.

Most of the townsfolk say they saw a woman, a stranger, walk out of the woods and take her place at the end of the line, but I knew exactly who she was. You know who she was, don't you?"

"I want you to tell me." Everything was a game with Honeyboy.

His smile widened, his voice just above a whisper.

"It was her. The Wood, the Land, the Honey, the River. She who is the everything made flesh, and she chose me. Because I was more…more Honeyboy than anyone. She chose me."

He stopped, momentarily unable to speak. When he does, his voice shakes.

"How could they not see her? Any of them? The Honey Lords, the Flower Mothers, no one saw her for who she was?"

He wasn't telling it all, of course. I knew what the townsfolk saw come out of the woods that night wasn't just some woman. No one could agree on what they saw. Gran'pap said he saw a girl, "'real pretty girl, naked as the day she came in.'" But not everyone saw that. My father, who never told me much, told me his mother said it was a woman, but not young or pretty. A thing old and withered. Decayed, that was the word my father used. "'A decayed thing.'"

Others saw nothing, only a black emptiness and man-god entwined in some mockery of The Dance. One of the Elaides', old Anthis Elaides, said he saw a worm. A grub. A pale, eyeless thing, writhing with Honeyboy in a black gash in the soil. But the Elaides' had been tainted by the word of God, the big one that lived in the cities. Brought it back with them when they visited Salem to put their uncle in the ground.

The sun is relentless today, but I've somehow managed to make the forest's edge, the cool shade and roaring of the river surround me and I feel lightheaded. I find a rock and sit down, my knees giving me no other choice. And still, Honeyboy can't stop moving. Floating, bobbing, weaving, the waggling dance of the Honeyboy.

Also, I'm a coward—I know it. That's why I've been hanging back, waiting.

I can't be there with him when he finds the hives empty. Dead. As they have been ever since that night.

I don't want to start moving again, but if I don't, I will lose him. I need to be near enough that he doesn't do something stupid, but not so close as I have to see his heart break. Not again. It's my own little dance.

The last time this happened somebody told him honey was flowing from a rock east of town. He couldn't wait for my day off and went out by himself while I was at work. Three kids from town were waiting for him. Beat him somethin' awful and broke his arm, which had never set quite right, and he gets headaches now when it rains. But the worst was afterward. He sat in our little hut for two months, sober as a judge, and sobbed. Had to break out a stash of the old stuff, the real honey-cider. Wasn't much left, and it took all of it to get him back last time. I can't do it again.

My knees scream at me, and I scream at the sky, unsettling a tree load of bright blue birds. Honeyboy doesn't even turn around, so I stand and press on, trying to dislodge more of the dust from last night.

He'd started to nod off when the fire died down. He always did that, get lost in a thought or a memory he didn't care to share, and chase it right off into a pleasant sleep by the fire.

"Go on." I kicked his foot softly. He stirred and grumbled.

"You know what happened next. Everyone knows. The town went to shit."

"I know what you tell me, but I know what others tell me too. If you want to go tomorrow, I want you to tell me."

"You're bluffing," he said, spitting at the floor.

He's right. I am bluffing. I never go back on my word. It's my biggest problem; it's how I ended up here. I loved my Gran'pap more than anyone, so I made a promise. A foolish, un-thought-out promise.

"Just tell me."

"You know where there's more beer." It was not a question, "One more bottle."

"Each?"

"I'm not sharing," he said coldly. I fetched three bottles from the larder, opening two and handing one to Honeyboy.

"A third one to split, if you tell me everything."

"Almost anything," he's said, reaching for the bottle in my hand. I snatched it back and sat down, holding the bottle just out of reach.

"No, you have to tell me…."

"NO!" Before I knew what was happening, Honeyboy stood over me, his eyes slits of pure anger. His balled fists shook, but his voice did not.

"I don't care about your bottle or anything in this world. Someday you'll see. You'll all understand why I did what I had to do." His face was streaked in tears, but his eyes were narrow and predatory.

"Alright, alright. Tell me almost everything." I hand him the third beer to have. All to himself. As soon as I do, he deflates back into his chair.

Fine. I let Honeyboy keep his secret.

"Next thing was the hives," he says after a long pull from his bottle. "There'd been some commotion because of...Her. Eventually, some of the Summer Lords remembered their jobs. They put the five biggest hives on the edge of the furrow, cutting deep into the flesh with long curved sword, swords that belonged to the Greek sailors who first discovered the hives. Then the town waited for the honey to pour over us, feeding the land for another year. Only no honey came from the hive. Just black ichor and clouds of biting flies.

And then the hives collapsed. Not just the ones by the offering site but all of them. Gone."

"And then the silence?" I don't want to push, but he had never gone this far before.

"Our bodies were there, but we were somewhere else. She told me something then, whispered into my ear before everything crumbled, and I woke up alone in a hole in the ground with the whole world hating me."

"What did She say?" I ask. He smiles sadly, and I know this is the thing he won't say.

"The second She whispered to me is the moment the bees stopped humming and silence fell over Broods Holler." I expect him to stop now, but he's resolved. "You never felt it. It moved the ground. And suddenly, the world is silent and still. It hurt...that emptiness. It still hurts."

He leans forward, his hands between his knees. "That's when everything changed. Faith can only last so long. Generations change, and they haven't seen it. You have to see the miracle, or it's not a miracle. It's just a story."

He stares past me, "Maybe I'll tell you tomorrow. Why I'm still the Honeyboy, and why I was right."

"Is that so?"

"And what She said to me. I'll tell you if the bees are back and She's back. Tomorrow."

And I'll bleed honey, and we all die screaming.

———

The river roars from somewhere nearby, but I can not tell the direction. Where the river runs through towns doesn't have trees, it doesn't have anything green or living. Only tumble-down shacks and the mill. Since the honey stopped flowing, everyone's been sick, and the mill has less and less to do. Only my grandfather's old grain truck keeps food in the pantry and beer in the larder.

I know I need to find him, but I'm so tired. The warm breeze, soft grass, and the relentless sound of river lull me. I feel light, happy. I'd no idea there was anywhere green left in the Holler. I look up at the sun, flashing through the leaves, dappling my skin in patches of warmth and shade. Shit! The sun is nearly on the horizon. How'd did it get so damn late?

I heave myself to my feet, and after a few stumbling steps, my knees agree to start walking. The hives lay along the river bank to the west. That's where Honeyboy will be. I just need to follow the setting sun. We'd set out before midday, but soon we'd be walking back in darkness.

"Honeyboy!" I yell, but it is swallowed up by the thick foliage and the drone of rushing water. The sun is so low that I can hardly find it through the trees. I try and follow the sound of the river, but it is overwhelming, coming from all directions at once. I close my eyes, shut out the forest and the sun, and just listen.

And then I hear it. What I should have been hearing the whole time. A soft sound. Like the wind, like breathing, like water flowing over rock. It's the river, straight ahead, but....

Oh god! Oh shit! I'm an idiot, a fucking fool! And he's known this whole damn time. That sound. The fucking unceasing roar we've been following for miles…it was never the river.

That sly old bastard. No wonder he never slowed down. He wanted me to chase him. Honeyboy and his games.

I come up over a small ridge and see him at the top of the hill. Waiting, smiling like an ass. Of course, I can't see his face; he's too far ahead, and the sun at his back only renders him a black shadow in the center of a golden halo. But I know he's smiling, radiant with self-satisfaction, and good for him.

I'm crying like an old woman, but I don't care. I see him now. Really see him. Not the godchild of Summer, but something more. The Amber God of Autumn, a glass of late-season mead ablaze in the last light of summer. And the forest hums, and the ground moves, and the world buzzes.

Honeyboy drops down into a small glade below, leaving me staring into the sunset. I close my eyes and let them adjust, the last burned image of Honeyboy on the ridge fading from my eyelids.

When I open my eyes, Honeyboy is nowhere to be seen.

The wood is deeper here, older. Heavy pine branches reach down from the monstrous, primordial tree at the center of the Old Wood. And the Hives. I didn't know. Gran'pap told me, but I…I didn't know. I'm sorry.

I can't see Honeyboy, but I know he's close. Through the hum of the hives, something else rises above. High and steady, like singing, coming from above me.

I don't want to look. I don't think I have the right, and I'm afraid of what I'll see. It's Her. She Who Sings Above All. And I want to see the right thing, the good thing. My grandfather said it was a beautiful girl, but Gran'pap was a believer. I'm not, or I hadn't been. I am now, but that doesn't count; that's not how faith is rewarded.

I think of Anthis Eliades and his worm, his grub. White and blind and wriggling with Honeyboy in a hole in the ground. But I'm no Cross-lover, for what it's worth. They find evil everywhere except when it looks and acts just like them. That's their flaw. Here we see our own lousy shit every day for what it is.

The noise is getting louder, insistent. She wants me to look at Her, to see Her. I never had faith. I knew people who did too well to say that, not in Her anyway, and not in Honeyboy the god. But I always believed in Gran'pap, and Honeyboy; not the god, but the frail old man who believed so much in himself. He grew on you. Look around Broods Holler; there are certainly worse ways I could have wasted my life than looking after him. Maybe that counted something towards faith.

I close my eyes and lean back against the largest tree, the heart of the Old Wood, sinking to the ground, a bed of soft pine holding me. I don't know how to look at a god. I've looked at Honeyboy every day, and he's a god. But the only time I saw him as a god, I almost blinded myself. I know that's because I was looking into the sun. I'm not foolish enough to let a fluttering of belief rob me of all my damn senses.

I'm still crying, fat tears welling out of my eyes. It's hard to keep them shut. I turn my face up towards the sky until Her form blocks the sun's red glow from my eyelids; an hourglass eclipses the world. The Hives hums, thrums, buzzes, and She with them. Deeper, kinder, but insistent, the sound swells around me until it is part of me. I understand Her now.

I open my eyes.

———

I never thought I'd be meeting Sammy Jay, of all people this time of the morning. But I was up. I couldn't sleep again last night; it's been almost a year, and I still can't quite get used to the hum, not that I'd ever tell anyone that. Shit, how would that look? Fuck, I promised Honeyboy I'd stop swearing so much. I promised years ago, and he's dead now, but it feels like something I should work on. A promise is a promise, and I always keep my promises. Like I promised Sammy

Jay that if I were up this early, right when Janet opens…and damnit-all, I am.

Don't get me wrong, Sammy's a good guy. After the bees returned and the honey started flowing again, many people claimed they never stopped believing. Sammy's one of the few I believe.

Only I know what he wants to talk about, and I'm still not ready.

I honestly can't say what I saw. That's what Sammy wants to know. Did I see Elaides' grub for what it was? Something larval, unformed then, now returned fulfilled? Honeyboy impaled on her barbed sting, her Queenly abdomen pulsating. His eyes wide, mouth hanging open in a smile of pleasure as slick golden honey poured from every part of him until it took him, ate him into itself. How the hell would that sound? Or should I tell him that I saw Honeyboy, reborn as the Amber God of the Autumn? He and his Winter Bride locked in an embrace somewhere beyond this world, dancing on the edge of endless stars in a forest deep all their own.

Both are just as much true and just as much bullshit, is it any wonder I can't sleep?

As I open the door, I smell the coffee, the hot lard in the kettle, and the dough rising and see why Demetri liked it so much.

"Honeyboy!" Sammy Jay yells from the counter and waves. There's no one else here. Did he think I was going to miss him? I take the stool next to him and Janet puts two cups of coffee on the counter. Sammy's old, the oldest man in town now that Demetri's gone. Small, but strong. Straight-backed, with dark black hair and eyes as old as the hills.

"Buy you a jelly donut?" Sammy asks, smiling.

"You joke, but the Honeyboy only gets one free donut a day, and hiking out to those hives is hungry work. I will let you buy me a donut."

I expect Sammy to complain, but he doesn't. He smiles and nods at Janet, who stops sweeping and pulls three jelly-filled from the tray, setting them before us on brown paper napkins. They're fat, round, and dusted with rock sugar. The donuts had always been good, but now they were so much better, the coffee, too. Everything was better sweetened with a touch of Holler honey.

I don't know how long it will last. Broods Holler's time is growing short. I can sense these things now. They seem like things I have always known but had forgotten even though they haven't happened yet. Being a god is strange. I don't know as I like it. What other choice was there, though? I'm the only one who knows the role.

Sammy stirs his black coffee, the spoon clinking inside the mug.

"You been out to the hives?" He finally asks.

"Not today. It's early. Went out two days ago." I say, "You know I can't tell you about the hives."

"Oh, I know. I didn't want you to tell me." He pauses and closes his eyes, sighing deeply. "Can I see them?"

I was not the question I had been expecting.

"You know I can't do that, Sammy." He was one of the old faithful. He knows the rule. "That's only for the Honeyboy."

"And his squire," Sammy says, a bit too loud for the empty shop.

"You want to be my squire?"

"Why not?" He asks, meeting my eye. "I'm not too old. Not with the honey flowing again." He does look healthy. The sickness that had held the town in its grip slowly faded once the mill opened up.

"Alright," I say and smile at him. "We'll go out after this, Squire Sammy." He beams and looks like he's going to cry, so I shove an entire jelly donut into my mouth and make a face at him, which makes him laugh instead.

Life's good as long as Broods Holler stays off the map, but how long can we keep that up? There will be more Eliades, more non-believers, and they will win in the end.

There will never be another Honeyboy like my Honeyboy. They made me Honeyboy, so what does that tell you? A woman as Honeyboy? I will have to perform the dance of the furrows soon, with my pick of the young men in town, and then…then I'll become a Honey Lord and never have to do a thing for the rest of my life. Maybe, but things are changing, and I was never one for sitting around.

I thought Demetri would be the last Honeyboy, but he wasn't, and I won't be either. But its end is not far off. The hives will grow smaller yearly, and the honey will grow less sweet as the blue skies fade to a cloudless grey. Progress, they call it. The outside won't understand, so they will mock us and our ways until no one will dare to believe. That's how gods die, isn't it? In pieces. Let 'em have the future. Right now, the world hums with the song of the hives, and there are many good harvests left.

———————————————————

Demetri never got to tell me what She whispered to him that night, right before the great silence settled on the Holler. But She did.

It was a promise to return, not just to end the silence, but of something bigger to come. I saw a world on fire, glowing in dark amber and yellow flames that engulfed the earth. Only it wasn't fire, it was a world where She reigns above and below and the universe moves with the sounds of the hive, a world drowned in honey where we will all die happy. There are certainly worse ways to go.

FOX CLARET HILL

MRS.
BADGER'S
BONES

MORE hugs. More condolences. More black. Breathing in charcoal, swallowing tar, Freddie stoops to receive kisses from two different mothers. One is here for him; the other is here to grieve. His mother, Deborah, leaves an oval smear of vanilla Chapstick on his bristly cheek, and Gabriel's mother, Sharon, leaves teardrops on his shirt collar.

They walk him to the taxi, two squat ducks flanking a heron. One clenches the cheap fabric of his suit jacket, and the other carries his suitcase. Deborah tells the driver where to go, opens the door, puts the case in the boot, and guides her son into the back seat. It's too small, the driver's seat too far back, and Freddie's knees press into the imitation leather. Together they share a smile, not quite a laugh, and she gently places a palm to his throat. A miniature hug that permits her to feel the reassurance a pulse provides.

It takes too long to shut the door, and Freddie apologises profusely to the taxi driver, a thick-necked man with cauliflower ears and rolls at the base of his polished dome. The driver brushes him off with a grunt, clearly uncomfortable with the rising pool of grief leaking into his backseat..

"Battersby Station, is it?" the driver asks, twisting in his seat, his thick Yorkshire accent jovial.

Freddie splutters, thinking of the past two months spent in his far-away flat. The half-empty bed, the rotting food, the takeaway boxes, the unwashed clothes, the drawn curtains, and nocturnal nights filled with mindless reality television. He shakes his head and retrieves a crumpled, neon sticky note from his pocket. The address for their new start. Freddie hands it to the driver and keeps an open palm, impatient for its return.

The driver's demeanour changes; he tenses and opens his mouth as if to say something before thinking better of it. He dutifully types the address into his GPS and returns the note to Freddie, who admires the cursive loops of his husband's handwriting, before tucking it safely back into his wallet.

As the cab begins to pull away, Freddie and Sharon wave at each other, a tumultuous relationship severed by death, and he watches her collapse onto the gum-scarred ground. Grateful to still be standing, Deborah wraps Sharon up in ample arms and leads her away, back towards the closed casket and noxious lilies. Freddie looks at his hands. Silence settles, and numbness takes hold.

After a few minutes, the stillness is shattered with condolences, and after Freddie offers well-rehearsed gratitude, the driver asks, "Are you local?"

"No. My husband was, once."

"Have you been before?"

"Never. Never had reason to. Guess he's given me on by being buried here."

The driver pauses. "At least it's pretty, eh?"

Freddie smiles as they leave civilisation and hurtle past golden fields set against steely, storm-brewing skies. He wants to say what good is a beautiful view when all you can see is the inside of a coffin, but he doesn't. Instead, he says, "It is."

The cab rolls to a stop at the end of a muddy incline, a thick wall of fog concealing what lies ahead, and Freddie looks up, confused by the sudden halt.

"Are we here?"

"This is as far as I can take you. It's been pissing down. Don't want to get stuck in the muck."

"It looks fine to me," Freddie replies sharply. It's the tone he slices his lazier students with when they fall asleep in lectures. He hates how it sounds, and so does the driver, who raises meaty shoulders like a dog raises its hackles.

He turns in his seat, bushy brows hanging heavy over beady eyes. "Give us a break, lad. Nobody and I mean nobody, goes to this house. You're lucky I took you this far."

"Why?"

His broom-like moustache quavers in irritation. "That there, that's Mrs. Badger's house." He gestures to the charming chimney and thatch roof that protrude past the earthbound clouds.

"Mrs. Badger? You mean Irene?"

"You want my advice?"

"Not really."

"Don't go in. If you've bought it, sell it. Someone will take it off your hands and flatten it. It's not a house to be living in."

Freddie shakes his head, strands of paprika and pepper falling across his face, his mouth upturned with disbelieving laughter. "Oh, please tell me it's haunted. I'd love some proof of the afterlife."

They make eye contact in the rear-view mirror, and Freddie's wolfish grin melts as he looks at the sombre expression on the other man's face. He looks like the one who's just been to a funeral.

"I'm late," he tells Freddie.

"Pardon?"

"For my next client. I'm late."

"Oh, of course. Sorry." Freddie fiddles with his wallet before handing over his fee and generous, guilty tip.

"Ta," the driver says, wrapping the cash up in a rubber-bound wad.

Freddie nods and opens the door. Unfurling like a poison-sprayed spider, his long limbs slip in separate directions as he scrabbles towards the popped boot. The moment he grabs the handle of his leather case, one foot finds a patch of black ice, and the other finds a puddle of blacker mud, sending his legs into an impromptu split. Offering an apologetic wave as the horn beeps impatiently, he finally finds his footing and totters through the sole-sucking mud to the side of the road.

The wheels churn against the muddy lacquer on the make-shift road, and though they fleck his clothes with mud, Freddie doesn't move for fear of falling over in front of a fellow middle-aged man. The car gains traction, and as the driver passes, he offers Freddie a look that one would imagine a British bulldog wearing if faced with broccoli instead of beef.

So much for befriending the locals, Freddie thinks as the scrutinising gaze passes and the car vanishes from sight. He turns, pulls his dress shoes from the earth with a wet slurp, and pierces through the film of the fog like a needle.

A padlock holds the gate firmly shut, and he half-jumps, half-steps over the rusty bars. It takes too long to hit the ground. The extra ten-inch drop stops his heart, and by the time it starts back up, he finds himself in a countryside booby trap. The cattle grid. He spews a series of half-sobbed curse words, and the woodland that borders the clearing bounces them back in needling echoes.

Skinny ankles at risk of snapping, he struggles to escape, and his suitcase slips from his fingers and hits the ground with a bang. The flimsy clasps come undone, and overstuffed clothes fly into the air with force and rain down upon his head, shoulders, and the boggy surroundings. He sniffles as he pathetically crawls on hands and knees and gathers the sodden garments, shoving them back into the case.

The painful, lapping cold keeps him moving, and frozen feet wade through the overgrown fields of decaying grass until he finds what he's looking for. A plastic rock nestled in a bed of dead roses, mentioned in his final correspondence with Irene. The one where she informed them that she would not be well enough to provide a tour of the property. Fleeing woodlice fall like lemmings, and a trapdoor reveals a set of jingling house keys.

Bronze swallowed by rusty hole, he wishes Gabriel was here, to do this together, unlocking their first house. However, when the door creaks open, he's unexpectedly glad that

Gabriel is not here. The front hallway is so full of knick-knacks, boxes, and unopened mail that there might as well be a brick wall on the other side of the door. It turns out "Mrs. Badger" was a hoarder. Feeling like the dead have gotten the last laugh, he mimics the idiocy of his past self as he slams the door shut. "Oh no, Mrs. Badger. We couldn't *possibly* take the house for so little!"

Angry stalking carries him to a smaller door, a back entrance accompanied by filthy sun-bleached wellington boots, and he tries his luck here instead. It opens, and he's happy to see nothing but darkness in front of him.

Ducking as he enters, a too-tall man in a too-small house, Gabriel's laughter rings clear. "Have we spent all our savings on a house you can't even fit in?" the ghost asks, doubled over.

"Yes," he replies to the empty room, looking down at his feet in embarrassment. "It doesn't matter because *you* can fit," he says. *It doesn't matter because I bought it for you*, he thinks.

When he receives no response, he remembers that he's alone and worries about the effect of the negative temperatures on his brain function. He shuts the door behind him, hoping to defrost in the stillness of the house, but it doesn't help much. The single-pane windows rattle and do little to keep the cold out. He shivers violently, gooseflesh emerging on purple, cold-burnt skin.

He wipes his ruined shoes on the doormat, tar-coloured streaks painting the rotting fibres. Slush drips from saturated trouser legs which renders the action pointless. Too filthy to proceed, he resorts to removing the two items, leaving his bottom half covered by nothing aside from baggy tartan boxers and white cotton socks. He steps further into the room, searching for a light switch, wet socks slapping the linoleum.

He finds one, plastic stained from oily fingers, and the ancient filament of the hanging bulb hums as it wakes. Yellow light turns the baby blue kitchen a sickly green, and Freddie stares around at the doily-laden dollhouse surroundings. Stacks of books, newspapers, letters, catalogues, and magazines obscure the dated floral wallpaper from the floor to his hips, and patches of discoloured damp consume the upper half. It smells like mildew, and he fears the insects and rot that lurk behind the piles.

Scrape. A scratching of overgrown nails on a rough surface, and he presses a batwing ear to the closest wall, checking for rodents. Whatever was there moments ago falls into silence, but the smell of rat urine and a spattering of defecation confirms his fears. He sighs wearily as he adds hiring an exterminator to his growing list of things to do. *At least you'll be busy,* he thinks in a voice that sounds more like his mother's than his own.

Wanting to get the horrors and surprises over with, he dips through another doorway designed for a much shorter generation and pads across the dirty carpet of the hallway. The softness underfoot provides the illusion of warmth, and the hordes of rubbish that coat the walls insulate that feeling. He stops shivering and cautiously makes his way through the maze of debris. Halfway between the kitchen and living room, something stops him dead in his tracks. He backs up and does a double take. There's a small door under the stairs. The problem is not the door; the boards that cover it are. His mind reels, trying to decipher the purpose of the barricade made of bent nails and wonky planks. He grinds his teeth as he thinks, and when the sound of bone scraping against bone ceases, it's replaced with a tapping, a rattling, on the other side.

Curiosity piqued, he looks for tools to help him access the mystery cupboard. The only good thing about hoarders is that they usually have everything you need and then some, and he soon finds a wobbly hammer. Using the back end, he pries the poorly applied nails from the boards, and they plop to the ground. A rattle comes again, like bowling pins mowed down by a strike, and he tries to place the sound as he turns the tiny iron handle.

As it opens, the sound stops, and by the time his eyes adjust enough to see inside, whatever was there is gone. Unlike the rest of the house, the room is empty, barring a skeletal rat, and the only other thing of note is a hole in the wall at the back. Convinced that there's a host of animals dwelling in the spacious foundations, he squats to further assess the damage and runs his fingers through the pile of plaster chips.

Something smooth and hard stops him from leaving. He didn't see it at first, it being the same colour as the cream debris. He places the ivory object item in his palm before flinging it away in disgust. A human tooth skitters away, root intact, too small to belong to an adult. Something lurches inside of him, and he recoils into the hall, kicking the door shut, his back pressed against the wobbling wall of books.

She was a babysitter, he tells himself, *for rough working-class boys*. A tooth is just a tooth without context, so he makes up his own. Under the stairs was a time-out for naughty boys with quick fists. A knocked-out incisor belonging to a now-grown man is nothing to worry about.

Once his stomach is settled, he pulls himself away and rounds the living room, and, using the lighter in his pocket— left over from his time as a smoker and his dad's funeral five years ago—he manages to get a modest fire going. Opening his suitcase and clambering on top of a wobbly stool, he hangs each soggy item with twine and watches the amber-lit ghosts dance in the cold draft. He wraps a knitted blanket around himself, the wool crunchy from age, and appreciates their show in silence.

As he paces, he ferrets through the amalgamation of Mrs. Badger's life and discovers an exceptionally well-preserved box amongst the detritus. Inside are a series of illustrated children's books by Irene Green, the covers depicting folklore monsters and offering some credence to her local reputation. Flipping to the first page, her nickname, too, makes sense. Her black hair, styled into a bouffant bun, is marked by two white stripes. Her expression is thin-lipped and cold, her writing a warning of what happens to picky eaters and thumb suckers, and Freddie shudders to think of her babysitting style.

One story catches his eyes in particular. The cover illustration depicts a skeletal red monster waiting for a little boy, up past his bedtime, to descend the stairs. Bloodybones. The name rings a bell. A dinner party, scary stories, Gabriel. A supposedly true tale from Yorkshire, from his childhood. He reads it, hearing a dead man's voice instead of his own.

"Rawhead and Bloody Bones
steals naughty children from their homes,
Takes them to his dirty den,
And they are never seen again."

It tells of a young man named Tommy Rawhead, strange-looking and skittish, who lived in Yorkshire in the 16th century. One day, while he looked at his reflection in a pond, a group of men crept up behind him, accusing him of hurting a child. He'd never done such a thing but couldn't speak well enough to plead his innocence and ended up at the bottom of the stagnant pool.

They left him, hidden and forgotten, and the fish flayed his flesh until nothing was left to eat. By the time he crawled from his watery grave, he was a poorly held together puppet, controlled by hatred and made up of blood-soaked bones. After that, he snuck into local homes, hiding under sinks and beds, making dens in dark cupboards, waiting for a child to utter so much as a cruel word.

Thinking of his discovery under the stairs, Freddie slams the book shut with a dusty puff and places it back amongst the other moralistic tales. As he sets the box back down, he freezes, blood running cold. Next to his own silhouette on the wall is another head. He pictures Tommy Rawhead's fleshy face and empty eye sockets staring at the back of his skull.

Upon turning, he finds himself face to face with a paperweight nesting in a fox fur stole. He disassembles the precarious illusion before checking his clothes. Finding them dry, he brushes the dirt from the surface, covers himself in tweed and decides to take a break from Mrs. Badger and Bloodybones. Pulling on wellies that had belonged to someone much smaller, he ventures towards the local pub with curled-up toes.

According to the spotty Internet on his outdated phone, The Sleeping Pig is the only public structure within walking distance, and while the reviews are dubious, his eagerness for a pint makes him willing to gamble.

It's eerily quiet as he climbs the slippery steps, the rustic black-and-white building looming over him during the ascent. There's no music, no conversation, no clinking of glasses. Nothing except the high-pitched creaking of the sign—depicting a dead drunk pig surrounded by hops and apples—swaying in the breeze. Gold seeps from the sunken windows, and the door sits slightly ajar, reassuring him that the pub is open, and he makes his way inside. Hopeful that he'll be in a similar state to the painted pig soon enough.

Upon entering, he raises the pub's population to a measly five, and despite the low ceilings, dark wood furnishings, and generally cramped space, it still feels hollow. The first of the four strangers is a stoutly-built bartender with a face like a toad, her barrel chest decorated in shades of brown and beige knitwear. The following two are a pair of middle-aged women with shiraz-lacquered lips who whisper drunkenly and tout unlit cigarettes between solid fingers. The last is a man, silhouetted by the fire, wearing an olive green waistcoat, his face obscured by his newspaper and his hair hidden by a flat cap.

"A pint of lager, please," Freddie says, stepping closer to the bar, whispering just because everyone else is. Despite his hushed tone, the three patrons all turn to look. The women titter, and he's taken back to his school days. Too tall, too thin, too ginger. The old break in his nose throbs, and he tries to make himself as small as possible as the pint is poured and paid for.

He lowers himself onto a much too tiny stool that wobbles loudly as its shortest leg smacks the flagstone. He looks up at the paintings of pigs hanging on the walls, pretending to be interested in anything but the other occupants as he sips his room-temperature beer.

The newspaper in the stranger's hands rustles as it folds, and once it thuds to the table, a warm, Northern voice asks, "Fancy joining me?"

Freddie looks at the man whose lips are stretched thin to encompass his welcoming smile. He removes his boots from the padded chair beside him, shifts his lackadaisical reading position into something more upright, and pats the open seat. Freddie's body, cold and rigid, answers for him, and he's lured across the room on possessed legs.

He sits in the chair, which moulds against his sharp buttocks, and startles as a thick-knuckled and scarred hand is thrust towards him. He accepts the firm handshake politely and stares into the man's glacial eyes for as long as is socially acceptable.

"Freddie Walsh."

"Magnus Fernsby."

Freddie cocks his head. "Are you Scandinavian?"

Magnus laughs heartily. "Do I sound Scandinavian?"

The answer is no, and Freddie laughs to hide his embarrassment. "You don't meet many Magnus's around here."

Still beaming, Magnus removes his hat. The heat of the fire has left his temple sweaty, and he runs a hand through the jaw-length silver strands. As the stranger tucks as many waves as he can behind his ear, Freddie notices a puncture in the lobe. A piercing that has long healed over.

"Aye, you're right. I'm only joking. My mam was Swedish."

"Have you ever been?"

He shakes his head. "No, I've never gone further yonder than London. Even then, I only lasted a year or so in my twenties before God's own country called me back."

"You should go. To Sweden, I mean. Stockholm is great. Good beers." Freddie lifts his pint awkwardly as if Magnus might not know what a beer is and quickly takes a deep swig to disguise the gesture.

Crow's feet crinkle, and he looks into the fire wistfully. "You sound like my wife. She was always trying to get me to go to my motherland, as she called it. Our lad has taken over the nagging now. Calls me from all over. Paris, Amsterdam, Brussels. Says I'm missing out on the world. Maybe he's right, but I don't see the point in seeing much without her."

Freddie pauses, taken aback by the vulnerability of the admission. He waits for Magnus to change the subject, but he doesn't. He stares expectantly at Freddie over the top of his pint. He waits for him to speak as if he knows what he's going to say before he does.

"I went to my husband's funeral today," Freddie says, far more surprised by the sentence than Magnus.

"Ah, so that's what you're doing here. I did wonder because this pub doesn't see too many strangers." He doesn't offer condolences, just warmth, and Freddie's premature thank you gets caught in his throat.

He coughs. "Well, you might be seeing more of me if I stay. We bought a house here before he died. Not sure if I'm staying or selling."

"Too rural for you?"

"Too quiet. Too lonely. Too much work to be done."

Magnus goes quiet and stares into his beer, his brows knitted together in thought. He takes a deep glug before asking, "You haven't bought Mrs. Badger's house, have you?"

"I have. How did you know?"

"This village is small. Not a bairn cries without me hearing it."

For the first time, Magnus's smile slips clean off his face. He goes from rosy-cheeked to green-gilled as he holds up two fingers to the bartender. She sighs, delivering a bottle of whiskey with plenty of blustery breathing, and slams the glasses down on the table for good measure. Doubles are poured, and doubles are drunk.

"You should sell it," he eventually states.

"That's what the cabbie said."

"He was right. How'd you even come to possess such a house? You're clearly not a local."

Freddie scoffs. "My husband knew her, looked after him when he was a kid. He contacted her when his mum told him that she'd gone into hospice. She wanted money for her son's inheritance, and we got a great deal."

"First of all, Mrs. Badger never had a son." Magnus swigs his drink. "Secondly, if your husband was one of her lads, you should know all about the missing kids."

Freddie does not know about the missing kids, and it's written all over his pallid, freckled face. Magnus pours them some more drinks and tells him everything.

In 1986 a boy named Oliver Barnes went missing under Mrs. Badger's care. Neither she nor the other boys saw him disappear, and the police never found a trace of him anywhere on the property, aside from his fingerprints on a half-drunk glass of milk. Despite her possible negligence, most parents believed Mrs. Badger to be blameless, and even though Oliver was never found, most allowed their children to remain under her very affordable care. The boy was, after all, a wanderer who preferred to explore nature alone rather than play with the others.

Not long after that, Mrs. Badger began to claim that she saw Bloodybones in the house, a terrible monster that featured in her worst-selling book, and she warned the children to behave if they didn't want to be taken. Explained away by the guilt of losing Oliver and the desire to run a tighter ship, her paranoia was perceived as a convincing act. Even as her delusions worsened, Alzheimer's explained the rest of the ghoulish sightings. Then the children began to see Bloodybones, too.

The parents rolled their eyes until these children, too, began to vanish into thin air. Eight children, excluding Oliver, went missing between 1986 and 1994. It didn't matter if they were at Mrs. Badger's house or home in their own beds. They vanished quietly and without a trace, never to be seen again.

One boy is an accident, but eight is a pattern, so Mrs. Badger was blamed, and while she never saw the inside of a cell, she was ostracised in the community. She went from church piano player, respected author, and the saviour of working-class parents and single mothers to a murderer. Mrs. Badger became equivalent to the Bogeyman in the local lexicon, overshadowing her own creations. Only the surviving boys maintained her innocence and blamed the actual monster that had haunted their childhoods. Bloodybones.

"What do you think?" Freddie asks, head spinning, stomach churning. Grief, booze, and horror bearing down on him, forcing his shoulders forwards and his eyes shut. He swallows, keeping the bile down.

"I think you should burn that house to the ground."

Freddie shakes his head and staggers to his feet. "I don't believe in ghosts."

"I think you should stay with me," Magnus says, putting a sturdy hand on Freddie's swaying body, holding him upright with ease.

Freddie feebly breaks the contact between them, the warmth radiating into his hip. There's want hiding in that palm, and it's too soon for that. He squeezes Magnus's shoulder as he continues to right himself, opens his eyes, and stares down into icy blue. "No, I need to go home. Thank you for the story."

Somehow, despite the falls, the ankle-twisting, and the prolific puking, Freddie makes it back to the house in one piece. The light in the kitchen guides him like a moth to a flame through the mire and muck. Once he's only metres away, he sees the crimson streaking the brown. It oozes and beads from his battered knees and scuffed palms. It starts to throb, and his stomach, now emptied of the day's contents, rumbles.

The kitchen offers refuge from the cold, and the freezer offers a variety of ancient microwave meals inside its frosty guts. A tuna pasta bake seems safe, and he nukes it until molten, washing his hands with hot water while he waits. Unable to wait for it to cool, he peels the plastic lid and eats it gladly as he wanders toward the living room to revive the fire. The top of his mouth burns and bubbles, and he knows he'll regret this, but nothing can stop him. Except for the door under the stairs.

Lowering the fork, protected by his drunken haze, he opens the door again and finds that the tooth has disappeared. In its place is what looks to be a human finger bone. The logical part of his brain thinks about his pet cat, Frankie, long dead now, who used to bring him bird beaks and rat guts. It would be nice to have a friendly tomcat around, culling the pests.

His brain's illogical, fearful side, altered by ghost stories, thinks about Bloodybones. Yet, whether from a cat or a ghoul, it feels rude to not give something back. So, he lowers the rest of the unseasoned fishy gloop and takes the bone for himself.

Chuckling as he fiddles with the bone and places it in his pocket, he doesn't think about the link between a bone and a body. Or the bodies of multiple missing children. All of that settles like sediment in the back of his head, subdued by liquor. Right now, a bone is just a bone without context. There's no such thing as ghosts, and Mrs. Badger, killer or not, is deep in the ground, being devoured by worms, so there's nothing to worry about. The bone and the bake are quickly shirked as his mind relegates his functions to getting cleaned up and minding his step as he heads up the stairs.

The dated, dimly lit bathroom is behind door number one, and he opts for the tub, with its peeling finish and mildew-black grout, instead of the shower. The pipes gurgle and clank, but the pressure is good, and soon the bath is filled with steaming hot water. Sliding in, his skin turns red like a lobster, the grime lifts from his filthy body, and the amalgamation of his day floats to the top. Feeling like a pig rolling in its own faeces, he doubts the efficacy of the wash, but he's too tired to care. Muscles slacken, warmth permeates his many human layers, and the tile in front of him blurs and eventually blackens.

In dreamland, Tommy Rawhead stares into murky water and tries to make sense of his reflection. A strange face by any means, but one that indicates inheritance and survival. So many long, bent noses had to find so many sunken cheeks in order to make him as he is. So much history in a face, but he doesn't know this. The rippling surface turns a whetted countenance into a soft mass of clay, and he pulls at the lumpy features, trying to remould them into something better.

A group of young men, dressed in tunics and coifs, take his hushed moans as a threat and approach from behind. Their prey curls up like a frightened animal before the first kick comes. Though his attempts at friendship have long been abandoned, his attempts to bond have made him familiar with the sound of danger. As solid hands and dirty nails hold him under, danger sounds a lot like death, and all he can think is at least he can't see himself. Water fills his ears, nose and mouth, and black blooms beneath screwed-up eyelids and spreads until it's everything.

Bang. Bang. Bang. Gunshots. Fireworks. A panicked inhale. Lungs full of liquid. For a moment, Freddie thinks he is Tommy Rawhead being drowned in the pond. He's always been Tommy Rawhead. He opens his eyes underwater, looks up at the lemon-yellow ceiling, and realises he's in the bath and he, Freddie, is drowning.

Scrabbling, he manages to sit up and presses his sloshing abdomen to the porcelain edge, forcefully pumping the water from his body. The déjà vu consumes relief, a self-induced Heimlich required to save his husband from having to tell people he died via boiled sweet inhalation. They laughed about it after the fact, over the phone. Laughter doesn't come so easily now.

Bloodshot eyes stare down at the sick-saturated bathmat, and he takes a deep breath. He's fine, he feels fine. He's cold, exhausted, and his extremities are pruned beyond recognition, but he's fine. As he stands, coarse wet hair and bony body exposed to the freezing temperatures of the room, he remembers something. The bangs. The panicked sounds that woke him up, that saved his life.

There's no such thing as ghosts, he reminds himself, *but if there was, this one saved my life.* Wrapping a damp-smelling towel around his waist and brushing his teeth with a finger, he ponders the sound and tries to place it. Upon noticing the door to the bathroom is ajar, he writes it off as having been moved to banging by the constant draft and ignores the fact that it doesn't move now. Not an inch.

Thump. A new sound. Muffled, coming from somewhere else in the house. *Thump, thump, thump, thump, thump.* The stairs, something heavy colliding with the thick carpet and the infestation of moth-larvae contained within the fibres. Much like the wriggling worms, this sound indicates life but on a much bigger scale. There's something out there, but the question is, are they descending or climbing?

The bathroom door has no lock, so if it's the latter, there's no point in hiding. The light is on, and his fight for survival has been far from quiet. So, he opts for a running start and creeps onto the landing, nudity hidden only by a towel, and stands tall above the intruder on the landing. Facing the dark stairwell, partly illuminated by the bathroom light, he realises he's serving himself up on a silver platter.

He stares at the inky nothingness for a long time, waiting for a face to emerge from the darkness and slow thumps to speed up and grow louder. Nothing happens, nothing comes, nothing makes a sound. So, he steps forwards to investigate, and crouching down by the top rail, he observes the lower floor.

Movement. Something shifting behind the labyrinth of rubbish. Hope tells him it's a cat, and for a moment, he believes it. The evidence is all around: the bones, the dead rats, the smell of urine, the rummaging in the crawl spaces, the scratching in locked rooms.

The cupboard under the stairs opens with a creak, and when it slams shut, the force blows out the optimistic flame in Freddie's head. He has known some intelligent cats in his life, but not one of them capable of doing that. Acrid smoke in his nose, he half slides down the steps like an overgrown toddler, trying not to creak or lose his towel. At the bottom, he grabs the discarded hammer and approaches the door. Inhale. Exhale. Open.

Empty. Aside from a licked-clean plastic tub that once contained his dinner and another bone amongst the plaster. This one is obvious; it doesn't require touch to find. It's an intact jawbone, small but unmistakably human. He picks it up despite the fear and disgust brewing in his body, and with sobriety on his side, the penny drops with a resounding clunk. There are bodies here. Underground. Somewhere.

The locals are right about Mrs. Badger.

Or they were right about Bloodybones, he thinks, standing with a child's jaw in his hands. It feels like a gift, exchanged for food scraps. Freddie's gut tells him to keep the cycle going, that something, a ghost or a cat, saved his life in the bathtub. Concerned for his sanity, not his safety, he decides to wait until the morning and pockets the bone with faux gratitude. It'll be a much-needed piece of evidence when blue and red lights arrive and disrupt the washed-out colours of this rural hideaway.

The day hits him all at once, and even the bone, fleshless and delicate, weighs him down. Dragging his body to the kitchen, he takes his uneaten wrap from the soggy trouser pocket and leaves it unwrapped in the cupboard for his new friend to eat. The door is shut gently, thoughtful for the quiet of the house, and he lugs his aching carcass upstairs on heavy feet.

After collapsing onto the pillowy softness of the first bed he comes across, he hears noises from down below. Scuttling, rattling, bones clacking, and a hungry mouth chewing fill the suffocating silence. *Enjoy,* Freddie thinks, too tired and numb to feel anything else about the wet gnashing. He lets the sound turn into white noise, his new cityscape, and fond illusions take hold.

This dream is vivid and consuming, much like before, but these memories belong to him. In bed with Gabriel, limbs entangled, bodies pressed so close their sweaty flesh merges into one organ beneath thick duvets. Staying in bed all weekend, not even eating, just whispering and sleeping in a constant cycle that's too sweet to break. He rolls over to look at Gabriel, his brown skin and hazel eyes, but Magnus is there, silver and handsome. He's cold and coarse, but his wiry strength makes Freddie's blood pump. Freddie rolls onto his front and lets fingers stroke his spine, but they're sharper than he expects, like dry twigs. They scrape his skin, but at least the scratching feels like something, so he lets Magnus do what he wants to his flesh.

He wakes in the early hours, birds singing and cows mooing, feeling warm, refreshed, and a little hung over. Still, it's the best sleep he's had in ages, and he's thankful to have dreamt of love rather than monsters or murdered children. He looks at the jawbone on the side table of the double bed and knows he's in for another long day, but hopefully one that will bring comfort to many elderly residents who lost their children long ago. And once the bodies are gone, the house can become a home.

Thinking at first that the sensation is the remnants of his dream, he thinks little of the weight in the bed beside him. It's only when wet beads of blood run down his back and whatever is beside him moves that he freezes. Every muscle retracts, and he forgets how to breathe. The thing beside him notices and begins to tremble, with fear or pleasure, he doesn't know.

Not wanting to find out, he stands without looking and loses his towel as he walks out of the room. He maintains a confident pace but doesn't run, and he makes his way across the landing, down the stairs and into the kitchen. There he pulls on his muddy suit trousers and the wellies he'd worn the night before and exits the house as calmly as he can.

The dew in the field lashes his exposed skin, and only when he sees Magnus on the edge of the clearing does he break into the fastest run he can muster. The collision is only prevented by the return of the other man's strong, steady hands.

"I knew I shouldn't have let you come back here alone," he says, eyes wide as he looks at the sticky layer of blood that coats Freddie's torso. Nudity is covered by a smart hunting jacket, and hands rub at cold arms. Magnus pulls away, doing his best to muster a kind smile in the face of wild-eyed panic, but his expression fails as he looks over a shuddering shoulder towards the house and the open back door.

"What the fuck is that?" he asks, and it becomes Freddie's turn to stare.

"It's Bloodybones," Freddie croaks, paranoia and myth unfolding into nightmarish reality before his eyes.

They stare as the six-foot skeleton ambles towards them, a sense of desperation and longing in its outstretched arms and uneven gait. Unlike the illustration, the creature is not just made up of jam-covered bones, sinew, and tattered muscles. His organs slop around, poorly contained, and his heart still pounds in his exposed chest.

"No, it's not," Magnus replies gravely. "It's Oliver Barnes."

"He's still alive," Freddie squeaks. "Holy shit, he's still alive."

"That's impossible. I saw him die."

So, Magnus tells another story. A bullied boy, a pushing, a fall down the stairs. Mrs. Badger cradling a dead boy in her arms, trying to hold his smashed skull together, ten boys with poor outlooks staring at her pleadingly. He was put in the cupboard under the stairs until she could figure out what to do with him, but when next she opened it, he was gone. That's when they all began to see Bloodybones.

"He wasn't dead," Freddie says. "She put him in there, and he wasn't dead."

Oliver has nearly reached them when they both see the gnawing marks, where the rats ate his unconscious flesh, and then he ate them in return to stay alive. A feral boy living in the crawlspaces and haunting a house who grew up to be a monster.

Magnus raises a hunting rifle and points it in Oliver's direction, but Freddie makes him lower the barrel. "He killed eight of my friends," he pleads but keeps his weapon pointed at the ground.

Freddie pauses. "Why didn't he kill you?"

"I was outside. I came in when I heard the screams."

"You said there was ten. What happened to the ninth?" Freddie already knows the answer. Gabriel never told him what caused him to move away to Manchester to live with his dad, why he'd never been back to Yorkshire.

"He left."

"What about Mrs. Badger?"

Oliver is halfway across the field.

"I used to see her leaving food for him. Bloodybones liked offerings," Magnus is panting, confessing his childhood as if he's the one being held at gunpoint.

"She was his friend," Freddie whispers so quietly that only he hears it.

Puzzle pieces fall into place, and they all fit in their slots. It's why Gabriel bought the house when she went into hospice. He knew it wasn't a good deal. He knew Bloodybones wasn't real. Nothing comes after death. What is real is the suffocating guilt and responsibility for something horrible you did as a child. What is real is providing comfort to something so tortured and abused. Feeding it, making sure it doesn't have to be alone. Oliver Barnes, Tommy Rawhead, all they ever wanted was friends.

Freddie frees himself from Magnus's white-knuckle grasp and walks through the field, meeting the limping, desperate creature halfway. He's not human anymore, not really, but he is alive.

Freddie wraps his arms around Oliver Barnes and gives him his first hug in decades. When nothing happens except stillness, Magnus lowers his gun and leaves to call the police.

When the cars arrive, Freddie and Oliver are already gone. Hidden in the trees, waiting patiently to return home and for every death to be blamed on the woman who fed a boy to the rats. As Bloodybones watches the bright lights, wrapped in Magnus's jacket, he breathes, and the cadaver dogs leave him alone.

MATT ELPHICK

COOPER'S HILL

MARK looked out over the patchwork sea of tweed, rugby shirts, and hooded tops. People stood in small huddles, stamping their feet against the cold, clouds of breath hanging just above their heads like waiting spectres. The grass was slick with dew and at the bottom of the steep hill Mark could see the members of St. John's Ambulance drinking out of thermoses, patiently waiting. Even from here, Mark could tell that there would be hidden dips and strong tussocks of grass scattered all over the long, concave face of the hill that would clutch at feet, the dew ensuring that there was no purchase to be found. He was sure that within the hour there would be several twisted ankles, if not broken legs.

All for a wheel of cheese, the fucking bumpkins. I moved to get away from this shit, and now I'm back in the thick of it. Mark reached to his jacket pocket, to the pack of cigarettes that wasn't there. He tightened his jaw in frustration and then stuck another mint between his teeth.

A ripple spread among the groups and Mark followed the gazes of the turned heads to see the master of ceremonies, a portly man whose thinning hair was lifted from his scalp by the light spring breeze, scattering handfuls of broken biscuits. Mark jotted down *biscuits—why?* In his notebook and tried not to think about the murders or break-ins he'd be covering if he still lived in London. Real news. The wind changed and a breath of cigarette smoke streaked past his face. His mouth watered.

The fat man finished feeding the birds and the crowd seemed to swell as the first racers took up their positions on the crest of the hill. The cheese, a great wheel of double

Gloucester tied with ribbons, was brought forward, and held aloft for everyone to see. After a moment's pause, a bowler's flick of the wrist sent it bouncing and weaving down the hill, picking up speed as it went.

A heartbeat later, and the first racers fell over the edge after it, their legs barely able to keep them upright, arms pinwheeling for balance. It reminded Mark of a desperate and primitive people chasing the sun.

"It symbolises the moon, you know," a thick Gloucestershire accent said to his right.

"Sorry. What?" For a second Mark wondered if he'd spoken aloud.

"The cheese. It represents the moon." The man said again. "Most people don't remember. In fact, the scattering of biscuits and buns is about the only thing they does get right with the ceremony."

The man was dressed in a wax jacket that smelled of dog, a pair of worn-out jeans, and wellies. An antler-handled walking stick hung over the crook of his arm as he teased fine shreds of tobacco into a rolling paper.

"Why the moon?" Mark asked.

"Fertility thing, ain't it," the man said. He sealed the cigarette with a swipe of his tongue and clamped it between his lips. "Ensures a good harvest and all that."

"I always thought it was just a weird country tradition. I never thought there was any real meaning behind it."

"Well, there ain't now, not really, not the way they does it." The man drew on his cigarette and looked sidelong at Mark.

"Not from 'round here, are you?"

Mark smiled. "That's where you're wrong, I was born a couple of towns over."

"Don't sound like it. You sound like one of them yuppies from the city." He grabbed one of Mark's hands and stroked the lines of his palm with a calloused and scarred thumb. For a brief moment, Mark had a memory of holding his grandfather's hand when he was a young boy, his slim fingers swallowed in the grip of a great paw hardened through physical work. He shook the memory, and the man's grip, away in the same motion. The man smirked.

"That's what I thought."

"I moved away for work."

"And now you're back. And none too happy about it either, judging from your expression."

"It's just…there's not a lot going on. In London there was always something happening, something exciting to report on."

"You work for the rag?"

"The *Gazette?* Yes. Started a week ago."

The man nodded and leant on his stick, his cigarette jutting from the corner of his mouth. Another race was about to begin, and the runners had made their way to the cusp of the hill.

"You're wrong, you know. About nothing going on. There's plenty if you know wheres to look." He lit his cigarette and then held Mark's gaze through the smoke. "A few of us still remember the traditions, how they were meant to be. Wouldn't that be something? Being able to tell the true story of the rolling, what it means and where it comes from. It might not be big city exciting, but it'll get you readers enough."

Mark had looked through the archives before coming to the event, to see what he was in for. Although he'd grown up in the area, he'd never attended the cheese rolling, and didn't know what to expect. He scanned through ten years' worth of articles covering the event and they were all the same, the only variation coming in weather conditions and the number of injuries. For the last four years, even the winners had been the same.

Mark stuck out his hand and ignored the memories of his grandfather as the man shook it.

"Mark," he said.

"Bill," the man said, flicking his cigarette into the bushes. "Follow the Landy and we'll pop for a cuppa."

Twenty minutes later and Mark was driving along the valley of a narrow country road flanked by high and lichen-covered hedgerows. Bill drove his Land Rover with seemingly little regard for it or anyone travelling in the opposite direction and Mark had lost sight of it several times around blind corners and sharp bends. Its dark green paint was chipped and spattered with mud, the windscreen caked in filth apart from a pair of overlapping semi-circles where the wipes could reach. The exhaust had come free from its moorings and bobbed and weaved wildly under the rear of the vehicle like it was an excitable dog. Mark felt every jolt in the road and his Corsa bottomed out more than once on deep potholes.

They turned another corner, and the roads became worse, nothing more than loose gravel and mud. The hedgerows too became sparse with large gaps, and through these Mark could the dark lines of furrows. The crops, whatever they were, looked more yellow than green and were smaller than Mark had expected. In fact, nothing looked healthy. The hedges had hardly any leaves, and in the closest field, the biggest oak Mark had ever seen was naked when all of the trees at the hill had been in full leaf.

At the edge of that field, Bill stopped his Land Rover in front of a padlocked wooden gate and jumped out to open it. The track that followed was nothing more than two divots either side of a small grass hump that tickled the underside of Mark's car. It wound its way through a number of small paddocks before crossing a line of stone wall and entering the yard. Mark couldn't help but think that the walls, with their caps of upright stone, looked like rows of teeth separating the lips of the fields from the tongue of the farmhouse.

The yard itself was nothing more than a concrete square, hemmed in on either side by large barns, some of which housed machinery and others' animals. Everything stank of shit, and the floor was coated with a dark liquid that looked too much like black coffee to be mud. Mark followed Bill's Land Rover around the side of the furthest barn and pulled up outside the front of the farmhouse. The building seemed to glare at him as it squatted, toadlike, as though it purposefully hid behind the barns, not for protection but so that it wouldn't be disturbed.

Inside, Mark sat at the kitchen table on a chair that felt spongey with woodworm, while Bill filled a kettle with water and set it on the range to boil. A taxidermied squirrel holding an acorn sat on one of the chocolate-dark beams. Insects had chewed a large hole in its side from which stuffing showed and what little fur remained was grey with dust.

Through the single-glazed window that stood over the chipped Belfast sink, the ground slowly faded away into the fields, and from this vantage Mark could make out the ink-blot of the oak.

"It's a big tree, that," he said, nodding towards the window. Bill placed a faded and stained mug in front of him.

"Aye, it's a bigun. Should be, too, the age of it. Hundreds of years old, at least. Older than the farm, that's for sure, and that's been here two hundred." Bill slurped his tea with his back to Mark, looking out the window. "It's always been in the family, this farm. Dad said it were built by one of us. My ancestors bought this land because of that tree. They said you could always tell how good the harvest was going to be by the state of the tree. If the tree were no good, the harvest would come to nowt. Meant they could prepare, see. At least, that's what me Dad would tell me."

"Is it true?"

"Well, there's different sorts of truths, ain't there? Is the tree some sort of mystical barometer? No, lad, I don't think so. Is it planted in the same earth as the crops, does it drink the same water? Seems to me that it'd make sense for the crops to do badly if the tree is."

Mark thought of the yellow shoots struggling up in the fields. "The tree doesn't look that well at the moment."

"Aye, the harvest hasn't been doing so well the last few years."

"I'm sorry to hear that."

"S'alright. These things have a way of sorting themselves out." Bill drained his mug and turned. "But you didn't come here to hear an old man talk about crops. You wanted history." He strode across to a wooden dresser dark with age and began rifling through the detritus of a drawer. "Ah, here we go." He turned and threw something towards Mark who caught it in his cupped hands.

Mark held it up to the light between thumb and forefinger. It was a crude carving of a figure, almost like a chess piece, made out of a dark rock turned grey by dust and dirt. Mark licked his thumb and rubbed it over the surface, and it shone like dark glass. The figure had holes for eyes and two parallel lines marked the presence of a nose. Below this, a single curved line represented a frowning mouth. In contrast with these crude marks, the bunch of wheat that the figure held in its clasped hands was highly detailed and Mark could make out individual grains in the ears.

"Found that in the field a few years back. Some sort of idol or offering or something." Bill shrugged. "I think it's meant to be an old god. Seems pretty ordinary if it is. I thought they all had antlers or wings."

Mark took out his phone and took pictures of the carving from various angles, using a coin for scale. He opened the phone's browser to see if he could find anything similar but had no signal.

"You won't get any reception out here," Bill said over his shoulder. "Besides, you won't find anything about it on the Net. I had a young lad working with me the year we found it and he had a good look."

"But you know?"

"I've got an inkling, aye."

"More stories from your dad?"

"Something like that."

Mark was aware that Bill had suddenly become quite coy with details which made no sense as he had invited him to find out the history of the event. The *real* history.

"Look, lad, I could tell you the story," Bill began, "but wouldn't you rather see it in the flesh?"

"I'm not sure what you mean."

"I told you there were a few of us that still remembered what it was all about. Well, we don't just remember, we *do*. While every Tom, Dick, and Harry plays at chasing a cheese during the day, a few of us still act out the old ceremony at night."

"Why?" Mark asked.

"Why do people do anything that doesn't rightly make a lot of sense to them or anyone else? Tradition, isn't it? Someone's got to keep these things alive, or they'll be forgotten about and die."

"So you'll show me? You don't mind this being written up for the *Gazette?*"

"None of us are spring chickens anymore and the traditions can't keep going if no one knows about them. That starts with you getting involved and being a part of it."

"Do I need to bring anything? Do you have robes?"

"Only if you want them others to take the piss. Wear decent boots. That hill looks a hell of a lot steeper in the dark."

That night the sky was a dark blue canvas and the moon sat in it, fat and heavy and full. As instructed, Mark had left his car in the layby of a nearby lane and was making his way around the edge of a field of rapeseed that rippled and roared like the sea. Not many of the small yellow flowers had yet bloomed, those that had seemed to mimic the stars to where it looked as though the field was a great lake reflecting the image of the heavens back at it. Despite himself, Mark felt a small prickle of fear creep up his spine, being in the field so late at night, and the small puddle of light cast from his phone did little to calm his nerves. He was sure that he kept seeing the shine of eyes from the hedgerow.

He navigated one more crop field and crossed a style and then was on a gentle incline up a grassy bank to the top of

Cooper's Hill. Approaching the hill from the rear the slope was much more gradual and so he was only partly out of breath when he reached the top.

He could see the figures before he got there, silhouetted in the moonlight, and the haze of cigarette smoke that hung above them. He counted seven of them. Occasionally faces were briefly illuminated in the red glow of a cigarette cherry, although there were none that he recognised. He found Bill who clapped him on the shoulder.

"Ah, here he is. Our fresh blood. You ready to be a part of this?"

Mark nodded, and then, realising that they probably couldn't see him properly in the dark said "Yes. When do we start?" He took a Dictaphone from the pocket of his jacket and pressed record.

"Right then, follow me this way," Bill said, leading him to the edge of hill. "When we was chatting earlier, I said that the cheese represented the moon, right? Well, that's true, but it's also a sacrifice for it. We give a gift to her and then she, in return gives a gift to us in the form of a good harvest. We dedicate the gift by rolling it down the hill in her light, and then, wherever we bury it, good things follow. This year it's my turn to lead the ceremony and do the burying."

"Ok, I guess that makes sense," Mark says. He looked around. "But, if we're not using cheese, what are we using?" Mark could sense the others crowding round behind him.

"Ah, lad, there's something else that rolls and makes an even better gift." Mark felt hands, strengthened by years of hard work, grip his arms. Another snaked its fingers into his hair and pulled his head back.

"I am sorry," Bill continued, "but it's you or the farm and I'm not about to see it fail." The blade caught the light of the moon as Bill slid it from his waistband.

It flashed silver.

A second mouth smiled across Mark's neck and a curtain of blood flowed down the front of his shirt. The second slash of the knife opened his throat to his backbone, and he was lowered to the floor. Bill stood over him and, grasping Mark's hair with one hand, used the knife to saw through the cartilage between vertebrae and out the other side. He held Mark's head aloft for the others to see. Someone had already gone to fetch a pickup truck and it slowly backed up, lights off and hatch down, until someone banged on it to stop. Three people picked up Mark's headless corpse and tossed it onto the pile of waiting wood chips before covering it with plastic sheeting.

Bill took a small figurine from his pocket, the same one that Mark had been looking at earlier that day and placed it in Mark's mouth.

"A gift," he said before he kissed the head on its crown and dropped it down the face of Cooper's Hill.

The head bounced and flipped end over end as it rolled, much as the cheese had done, picking up speed as it went. Bill stepped over the edge and made his way down sideways, at a steady pace. He knew the head would be waiting for him when he got to the bottom.

It was. Mark's head lay face-up against the wire of the fence, blood-streaked and spotted with blades of grass. Bill watched it and waited. He rolled a cigarette, lit it, and then exhaled a great plume of smoke into the still night air.

With slow purpose, the left eyelid raised to reveal the staring eye beneath. The eye itself began to move from side to side as if searching for its body, and then a bulge appeared in the white. The bulge grew until the surface split, leaking fluid down the cheek, and a vibrant green shoot burst forth, the tip slowly waving back and forth, searching. The lips parted to reveal further shoots that reached up and entwined with the first. Soon, there were sprouts reaching from all of the head's orifices, twisting together to make a single thick vine that stood erect, almost like an ancient moss-covered horn, a foot above the head that was now almost completely obscured beneath young leaves and stems.

Bill picked up the head carefully in cupped hands and slowly made his way to the Land Rover.

It was still dark when he got to the field, although a pink finger of light was probing at the horizon. He carried Mark's head under his arm, taking care not to damage the shoots, and in his other he carried a shovel and a lamp. He picked his way between the rows of stunted crops until he arrived at the oak tree, and then he started to dig.

The soil was thick with clay and before long he was slick with sweat despite the coolness of the night air. Ten minutes passed until his shovel hit something hard and hollow. He used the edge of the blade to scrape the dirt away to reveal a grinning skull. Although it was too dark to see, he knew that there would be a small figurine behind those teeth. After all, he'd put it there.

He gently lowered Mark's head into the hole and scraped the earth back in around it until only the very end of the knot of vines was visible. He pulled a pocketknife, the blade barely a whisper after decades of sharpening, and drew it across his palm and let the blood water the ground.

With a jolt, the vine began to grow again, its tip tracing a large circle as it searched for purchase. When it met the trunk of the oak, instead of climbing upwards, it burrowed inside.

Bill walked back to the house, poured himself a drink and bandaged his hand. He watched from the kitchen window as the sun grew over the horizon and cast its light over his farm and his fields. His fields which were now hip-high with healthy green plants and the great and ancient oak that watched over them, in full leaf.

DAMIEN B. RAPHAEL

AS THE THING IS NEEDED

BABCIA had a way with words. She loved them. Foraged for them. Newspaper clippings. Scribbles in address books. Pages that were carefully scissored and stashed away in bottles underneath her sink next to jars of cloudy chicken fat. It was to let the words ferment, she'd say. To let their power seep into her thoughts, a compost for dreams.

I was much younger when Baba first showed me how. We'd just tended the narrow garden behind her maisonette, and my thumb snagged a splinter, its sharpness stinging bitterly. The special teapot had been dusted off, the pearly one used for baptisms, birthdays and always, always the whisperings. Her wizened hands set it down softly on the kitchen table like a round-bellied relic, before sneaking a carrot biscuit into my palm. Babcia's magic was like that, sly and sweet-toothed. "Don't worry, *myszka*," was all she said, and blinked twice. All smiles. The exact words that followed were a blur, whispers expelled in a jumble. Eyes half-lidded, knotted fingers tracing patterns along her knees, Baba seemed so frail, so distant. But the pain of the splinter soon faded entirely. It went on like that for hours. Until the odd strands of her plaited hair burnt like white-hot filaments, catching in the dying gold of a setting sun.

By winter, Baba's kitchen had changed so much. No more penny rolls crusted in trays, cooling in the oven. No more nets bursting with eggs or cloth bags slouching with poppy seeds. Now there were only books: piled high over countertops, in griddle pans, on dough bins. Their pages lay shucked, their words culled for one almighty spell to aid the Allies and still the oncoming storm. Yet no matter how many cuttings she made, it was never enough. Her anxieties were like shed skin that she couldn't see, a dust of worry that powdered all but her obsession.

It made days hard helping Baba, her mind being half-captivated. She'd lay in bed past noon, clicking her fingers at forgotten things. The notebook beside her bed was blackened with mangled words. Summers crawled by with the only way I knew to help: housework, gardening, picking hedgerows near Hainault forest, our bags stained with sloes and blackberries, and rose hips. Most evenings, we'd wait for the hedge-jam to cool on the stove, watching tufts of thistledown swirl past windows flung wide open. She'd smoke her Woodie cigarettes, and I'd perch on her lap, crisp and drowsy, socks haired with cockleburs. And when the moment was just so, she'd start to sing the old songs of her homeland, her tones earthy and prowling.

"You must collect words as well, Isabel," she said. "Collect words like berries, and commit them to your heart, for that is their water. Do this and I will show you the most sacred treasure I have. Handed down from old to young, generation to generation."

We enrolled in the public library and for months she'd read to me; fairy tales, Arthurian tales, eyes wetted if a word pleased her, her tongue examining the sound like a boiled sweet. When I was fluent enough, she taught me embroidery as well. How to sew flower centers with spiderweb stitches, satin stitches to render changing light on meadows, gobelin stitches for skies. French knots for dense scrub. Her work was beautiful and mine nothing but childish forgery.

It wasn't until the coming of autumn that I had a true inkling of her gift. One hot September morning, after finishing my music lessons, I ran back home to Baba only to be greeted by her gaping front door. The neighbours sat in the living room, huddled around the wireless, its stern, crackling voice ringing out. Their faces were ashen, forlorn. The boy from across the road was amongst them. Trevor. We caught eyes, an exchange of fresh, deep meaning that something big was brewing. Baba was in her kitchen, and stubbed out her cigarette on a saucer, saying, "My *kochanie*. Today is the day *you* shall whisper."

Countless times I'd rehearsed begging to be taught and now, here it was. The thrill coursed through me like Christmas morning as we hurried to the allotment, Baba following close behind with a bag slung over her shoulder, clutching the teapot, and in her other hand: a cheese hoop filled with freshly cooked *golabki*. We devoured the cabbage rolls in the shed. Baba took down a rusting pie tin, emptying its contents: a dead bird, which unravelled from its bandages leaving clumps of moss and tiny feathers. A starling. Its eyes had milked over, each one crawling with black ants.

"I should have shown you sooner," she said, threading a needle. Her mouth chewed over the next sentence, determined not to falter. "You must figure things out for yourself now. But know this, our knowledge will grow again, even when cut and buried. It is restless. It calls to be reborn."

Baba took out a heavily embroidered quilt, unfurling it over her galoshes. It displayed a hodgepodge of styles: some fine stitching, others of crude needlepoint, reworked and reworked, until certain patches were tangled with words. Baba pointed out her section, which had a rough depiction of a bird, and burgundy drops of blood by its feet. Underneath read: *to hold, to bind, to live,* and finally, she sewed: *starling* above its head. Placing the quilt over the brittle creature, she repeated the saying, her spittle-flecked words clogging my ears. And with a movement of her hand, she implored me, too. The words were moths in my throat—dry, unsure. When she drew the quilt back, my scalp tingled. A talon twitched. Wings shivered. Scraping back my seat, I was ready to scream. Babcia merely opened her eyes a slither, and raised a pale hand, a liver-spotted totem. The bird scrambled upright. Feathers ruffling into place, its speckled head darted about, taking in the cramped little space. Its beak worked open then closed,

154 ⚜ DAMIEN B. RAPHAEL

testing its luck. Baba got to her feet, unbolting the wireframe door, and shooed the bird back into its house of sky.

"It's yours now, Isabel," she said, folding the quilt. "Your heart is strong, my girl. And the words will work for you, as long as you've that. Men in their war machines will soon be flying. The world is at war."

I started crying. Not for all the innocent blood to be spilled. But, more selfishly, the loss of our little realm together. Of it being cracked open for others to glimpse and the burn of such a gaze fading its delicacy. In a tight hug, my face mashed against Baba's cardigan. And I drank her in: camphor, *golabki*, lavender.

The last time I saw her was on a Paddington Station platform, peering through dusty glass. She was dressed in a black coat of rayon wool, square tan shoes, her silver hair haloed into a braided crown. Amongst the throng of waving parents, she brought her hand to her mouth repeatedly, kissing goodbye. Then she linked her thumbs and fingers into a bird, a little and furious thing. It was a secret gesture. I was unsure what it meant. Perhaps to be strong in my journey hereafter. Or that her words had woven us together. Binding us. Inseparable. Yet even an hour out of London, when I tried to picture her face, her soft chin and solemn eyes, it was a watercolour that bled and ran, no matter how hard I tried to recall it. To fix it in place by sheer stubbornness seemed to have the opposite effect.

Trevor was the only child from my street on the train. The only one who'd lasted after trams and buses and billeting officers, then the final walk from a community hall to our new life under star-studded lanes. A stranger named Mrs. Phipps came to collect us with not a word of comfort. The pace she set was greyhound-like on the walk back to her cottage, her frame of bones and sinew used to the farmyard and little else.

Our new Cornish life should have been idyllic under cottony, rolling skies. It wasn't. Farm life was physical to the point of tears. And we were made to work for every nub of butter we tasted, every spoonful of lamb stew. I would have foregone all of those dinners, though, just to have one sip of Baba's cold cucumber soup.

Trevor fainted on the very first day we were put to use, hefting bags of crop. And when the harvest mites burrowed into our skin, he muttered and whinged until I threatened to summon Mary, to which he wept and pined for the parakeets of Hampstead Heath. Yet for all his whimpery there was something cheerful in his cockney tones, a reassurance of home when he chatted endlessly about his die-cast battleships. It was a familiarity to dip into, exchanging fields and brooks and wheatsheaves for London's asphalt and chimney pots.

The children of the Phipps were devils, though. Trevor was right to cry. Mary, more than Michael. She had a clean foot of height over her brother and was the oldest of the pair by two years. Her skin was perpetually clammy, her eyes greyer than dishwater. A queasiness in them. A furtiveness.

It was a look I'd catch almost daily, through windows, out swimming, or collecting firewood. Had Mr. Phipps told me there and then of the dead farmyard animals she kept, the dissections of them, the whitening of their bones with sour milk—I would've believed him without question. It was all practise to become a doctor, she'd told me once, out spotting crayfish in the stream by the rusting chisel ploughs. The smell of rot never bothered her.

Most of my days were spent avoiding almost everyone, child or adult. And there were plenty of places to shelter in Cornwall. Like the abandoned lime kiln half a mile away from the farm, tucked behind some ballast heaps and meadows of prickling poppies. If there was one thing easier to do in Cornwall than London, amongst its smatterings of dilapidated barns and uncut corners, it was hiding more than seeking, and to be hidden was to survive.

Yet by the middle of our first year on the farm, Mary and Michael began to seek me out even in my secret places, to goad Trevor and me into trials of mischief: to run through the cabbage fields south of Bagburrow Farm, trespass into the Langley Estate, or scrump apples from the orchard by the tollhouse. Things we had no measure of, no means to gauge their prohibition. Mary's games would inevitably crumble into our capture. And Mr. Phipps, smelling of diesel, muck and sweat, would scold us by the fireplace in the parlour, looking at Mary as if he feared the woman she'd wriggled into, a stranger under his own gabled roof. A stranger perhaps even to herself, animated by cunning as deep as unused wells and colder than their waters.

The first spring was when their games went truly raw. It was a cool morning, soft unfailing light ruffling through trees. Mary wanted to show us the newly born calves in her father's remotest barn. The doors were unlocked and the animal sat on mounds of hay, unguarded and unchecked.

It began as a dare. A lark to see how much a calf could drink. But Michael and Mary made no attempt to stop it, even after pail after pail of milk and bran, its eyes sick with greed. Its belly swelled beyond hope, skin ripe to burst. That afternoon in the parlour of the cottage, Mr. Phipps accused us all of sickening the calf. He hurled an enamelled washbowl against the floor when Mary couldn't contain a giggle any longer. The clatter was like gunfire; the bowl rasping for an age until silent.

"Hell," said Mr. Phipps at long last, "I don't care who done it. The fault lies with you, Mary. You know them calfs'll drink far too much, given a chance, and it's damn near gone with swelling, now. Meant to be caring for them 'til Turnbill gets back, for Christ's sake. Best you keep away from his farm, you hear? Them folk spells trouble. I shall have to have words with him myself."

That night I took Baba's quilt out from under my bed. I'd hidden it in one of my suitcases, never daring to let anyone know. Unlatching its straps, Trevor watched on from his bed at the far end of the attic, a moon face peeking out of cotton sheets, ignoring my concerns about whether a vet needed to be called.

"She didn't mean to hurt it," was what he'd said, "she told me so." Why he defended her when he'd get the lion's share of Mary's punishment, from lashings to smacks to thorns dropped in lemonade, was a mystery. He seemed to soak it up like bread. Before I left our bedroom, I warned him not to tell anyone. Especially not *them*. "I'm going to help it," I whispered. "You stay put." He nodded in silence, and far away—past the orchard, the woods, the ancient barrows—thunder rumbled like iron bombs.

Outside, the night air was sweet with sneezeweed and I bathed in the darkness of Cornish skies: a cool cloudless ocean. The lean-to behind the diary building was only a short walk across a courtyard, the stubby outbuilding where they'd housed the words-affected calf. Lighting a candle inside an old bottle was enough to see it, a mound of panting muscle and blood. Veins under its fur were fattened with panic. I shushed her when it made pained gurgles and scratched cuts into dirt with its hooves. There was no plan, other than to sew through the night, and have it healed by morning. There'd be enough time. I was so certain. Yet even before a needle could be thread, the door to the lean-to burst inward. Michael and Mary stood watching me, flannel robes cinched firm around their bellies. The light of two lanterns danced across their raven-black eyes before Michael jumped inside, punching my arm, grabbing the quilt.

"What's this then?" he said, in a tug of war, "something dear to yer? Give it over you bleddy incomer." And in the struggle to keep the quilt, the stitching chirruped in distress, resisting to be torn.

To save Babcia's quilt was to let it go.

The act sliced my heart.

Over the following days, I was rendered mute around the farm. Hollow-boned, heavy-limbed. At once sinking and floating—a churning weariness, indivisible. It had the effect of turning the walls of Bagburrow Farm to glass, like the jam-

jar traps Mary had set everywhere. They'd been cobbled together from paper, string and dollops of honey-bait, seething
with piles of jailed, dying insects. Mary would always hold
them up to the sun, flicking a glance to my way, like I was a
dying thing in her hands, too.

For weeks, breakfast times in the courtyard were a bat-
tleground. Mary kept quizzing me about the purpose of the
quilt. I told her it was only sentimental.

"Why then take such a thing to a filthy dwelling?" she
asked, and immediately spoke things to Michael behind
curled hands, laughing. Rage fizzed in my gut, in those moments. I daydreamed dark things: to throw boiling tea in
Mary's face, stab a fork between Michael's ribs. But at what
cost? To lose Baba's quilt forever?

The games became worse from Mary's blackmail. She'd
threatened to piss over it once, chin held high. There was no
option but to relent. I told her through gritted teeth that she
shouldn't, that it held a power and confessed its properties:
to heal and mend. To take things that were broken and raise
them up.

"You're a bare-faced liar," she said, face pinched. She didn't
know how to take it.

I stole pretty items from the local smithy as demanded,
miniature seashells fashioned from hammered tin. Threw
eggs at Old Angie's house, cracking shells and windows. The
line was drawn at sinking a bag of kittens in the River Tamar.

Two evenings later, when we'd finished a picnic on Shar-
row Beach, Mary insisted to be shown the quilt's true craft.
The failing light was lessened by the driftwood fire we'd made,
and the shimmer of flames hid my pursed lips as she brought
out the quilt from her satchel, having carried it the whole
cycle ride there—unbeknownst to me. What happened next,
happened quickly. Mary took out a wooden cudgel, a piece
she'd stolen from the above her father's inglenook hearth.
And without a word, she brought it down swiftly against Trevor's face, a blunt claw, and twice further before I had time
to reach them. In a festering daze, Michael held me back as

I watched Mary's spindly form stagger, dizzy with bloodlust, biting the tips of her fingers.

"You've gone and killed him," I kept repeating. "He's dying."

Trevor laid in a heap on his side, feet buckled. His face tucked into darkening sand.

We dragged his marble-white body to a disused beach hut. The procession was like a dream. Yet certain details were woven into my memory, never to be unpicked. How Mary's boot fell off, her brown sock lolling like a dog's tongue caked in mud. How Michael kicked Trevor to make sure he wasn't asleep. How sick threatened my mouth when Trevor's ragdoll limbs caught on kelp. How Mary dabbed my cardigan against Trevor's wound, and said, "You did this, see? If you don't make it better, it's your fault. The guilt is yours."

She stayed with me all night in the hut, as I sewed a barebones copy of Trevor underneath Baba's starling. Placing the quilt over his body, a small hand flopped out, fingers curled and waxen, mottled blue, sapped of youth. I did not remember falling asleep and woke to wind battering the corrugated sheet roof, a flock of seagulls keening overhead.

Mary and Trevor were on the beach when I found them, Trevor staring out to sea. Mary stood behind him turning to greet me, her mouth wide as she scooped up seawater in the bowl of her hands and baptised the matted gore away from his face.

It would have been better if Trevor had died. In some ways he did. Mr. Phipps could already tell the change. A dismalness in the boy's eyes, perhaps. His newfound taciturnity. One Saturday—maybe through guilt or remorse at pushing him too hard—he took us all to town for some homemade blueberry sherbet. The local ice cream maker had dolled up his van with peonies and snapdragons, its chromed bumper and grille liquefying like mercury in the noon sun. As we joined the queue, the people of Landrake cast us scornful glances and muttered disapprovals under straw hats. By the light of full sun, our shabby clothes were at their most striking against normal folk: the darned shirts Mrs. Phipps made do with, Michael's grease-spotted shorts. Some crossed the street as if we were cursed. The Phipps' reputation was a diseased thing, a septic smell that clung to us, moating us from acceptance. Trevor didn't eat his ice cream that afternoon. Just held it until the clotted cream pooled in the crook of his thumb. Mr. Phipps slapped him for that, and the ball of ice fell into dust.

"Look what 'e gone and dun," Mr. Phipps said, and grabbed his hair shaking sense into him. He gave no cry, uttered no yelp. Trevor took the punishment like a donkey. Silent. Pitiful. It was the first time I'd ever seen Mr. Phipps afraid.

At night, he was my worry alone. I'd make sure his pillows were plump, and his blankets well tucked in.

"It will be alright," I'd say. "Baba's magic, it is like summer and rose petal jam and goose wine, you'll see."

I turned his face to look at mine, but his eyes were never still, watching invisible spiders crawling over the oaken beams above. There had been something wrong in my stitching. Or perhaps my prayer. Trevor was now a baby again, the snivelling boy of hay fever, complaining, and laziness, had dissolved into slate untouched by chalk. A malformed corner in the between London, Baba, and the quilt.

Sometimes when Trevor screamed in the thick of full moons, I'd lay with him, lavishing hugs upon his docile body, and confided in him as if he were Baba. One night after talking to him for what felt like hours, I saw his tilted face, watching with intent unjustness, each wide pupil a cupful of longing. His meaning was obvious: *you are all thieves.*

The evening that Mr. Phipps had ordered me to the kitchen was the last straw. He'd laid the quilt over the long table and quizzed me on its magic. Mary had told him it was the reason for Trevor's change.

"I don't know if ye a witch," he'd said. "But we don't abide cunning folk on this here patch of England." He tore a scrap from a frayed edge, throwing it to me as a consolation—on the promise never to use it again—and put the rest on a bed of embers in the hearth. Within moments, it was gripped in flames. I howled the whole night long. Mrs. Phipps visited me, with wild strawberries and cream, but I lashed out and set the whole lot to the ground.

The greyness that swept over and into me, behind my sternum was a second self, one that took over my limbs, a substitute for living. In those days of halfness, as Mr. Phipps celebrated a good harvest with mulled ale, and barnyard jigs that descended into rounds of candlelit prizefighting with his farmyard worker friends, it was easy to slip away.

So, one morning, when Mr. Phipps and his children were still sprawled out in the yard, I led Trevor to the farthest field, the one where we used to unlatch the coops, feeding the bantams. There was a galvanised bath used as a watering trough, filled with tepid water. Trevor sat down in it as instructed, the knitting of his tank top darkening by degrees. There was not a flicker of emotion as I cut deeply into his wrists. Only ribbon-like plumes of blood. When I turned to look at him one last time, his head was lolled to the side with a warm and painless smile.

———

London would have been too obvious. The trek north was made by hitchhiking, arriving destitute in Birmingham. The city had been laid waste by heavy shelling; walls of buildings left standing like blistered skin.

For months there was nothing but homelessness amongst the ruins, selling stolen coats from washing lines at rag markets. Eventually, there was work to be had in the factories along the canal, long after the war had ceased. My first proper job was in machinery, making whistling kettles and irons. It was enough to get a room to rent in a family home in Sparkbrook, a back-to-back terrace crowded with offspring. My room was no bigger than a closet.

Seasons flowed by in a blur of working six days a week. Joy was a scarcity: the six-penny crush at the local picture house, a cone of spuds from the potato man on the corner. What money was left over after bills and food was spent on material and thread, and oil for a lamp to sew by. Baba's precious scrap soon grew into a patchwork of equal size or more. I tested its power by sewing a failsafe against nightmares of Mary dragging me along a beach, back to the farm. I dreamed of Baba, instead. Sitting on her lap, ensconced in her aura of cigarette smoke and song.

Years passed when the last spell was finally sewn—a depiction of a boy with a moon face, whose life had been cut short. Above him, I sewed a new prayer to Trevor: *grow again, be restless. Be reborn.* It was a spell to peel back the error that Mary had made, a means to right those wrong farmyard days.

It was a winter's night when I slid myself underneath it, and as I intoned the words on the quilt, memories flooded my head. Of Christmases past. A dazzle of red foil crinkled around baubles, candles in brass fittings lighting a tree. And Baba's guessing games before Midnight Mass, melted wax in cold water for the face of my firstborn. Or inspecting the meat of the first cracked walnut for the profession of their father. And at its yield, her smiling lips: the flesh inside the husk, dark and shrunken.

DAN COXON

COME
SING
FOR THE
HARROWING

JACK stands in his Y-fronts in the basement while Big Mike holds the cold measuring tape up against his chest. He can smell an odor coming off him like pig fat and onions, with just a hint of lavender curdled into the mix. His skin pimples with gooseflesh.

"Not bad," Big Mike mutters as he works. "Not bad at all."

It's his first day in Historytown and he's already regretting it. He only agreed to the job because he still owes his mom two hundred for the window. This is a penance of sorts; he is paying for his mistake with his humiliation.

"No back pain or injuries?" Big Mike asks, stepping back to appraise him from a distance. "Allergies?"

Jack shakes his head and wonders if he can put his clothes back on. "Nope and nope. Neither, I mean."

The older man stares at him, his shoulders hunched beneath his sackcloth robe. The moment stretches and stretches. He hears a faint *drip-drip* of water in another room.

Eventually, Big Mike's body shudders with what may be a shrug, or possibly some kind of nervous spasm. "Good. All good. You'll do, I guess."

Jack bends and reaches for his clothes, but Big Mike grasps them first, tucking them under his sweaty arm.

"You won't need those. All costumes and uniforms are provided. I'll stow them in your locker."

Jack didn't even know he had a locker, but he follows as Big Mike leads him out of the basement and into the light, his naked legs shivering in the cold.

They put him on stable duty. There aren't any horses, and it isn't really a stable. The shed looks like it's built from oak planks and thick iron nails, but when you stand close, what looks like texture is actually flat, a plastic laminate stuck over plasterboard. The knots in the wood repeat every four planks. It's near enough to the real thing that the overall effect is disorienting and slightly sickening.

The hay, however, is real. Jack has to fork it into a barrow round the back of the Black Death Experience, trundle it along the rough dirt path, then unload it again in the stable. People watch him as he does this, cameras clicking, fingers pointing. It's meant to be interactive, but nobody speaks to him; he might as well be a mannequin, an animatronic Jack wound up each morning and left to do his thing, back and forth, back and forth. Once he stops to pose for a cute girl taking pictures on her phone, but she tuts and waits until he starts moving again.

Each morning, when he arrives at work, the hay is piled back behind the BDE. Each day he sweats and toils, doing the same job for a new audience.

Nobody warns him that the hay will invade his life, working its way into the weave of his clothes, his private thickets of hair. Big Mike's question about allergies suddenly makes sense. From dust particles to strands as long as his fingers, it finds its way into everything, digging drifts of it from his ears, spitting blades from his food. It's scratchy, too, and where it has worked its way beneath his coarse sacking tunic there are red welts across his skin, like he's been whipped by tiny flagellants in his sleep. He itches almost constantly, fine slivers of hay burying themselves as splinters in his flesh. The rub of the sackcloth keeps them from healing.

The paycheck is welcome at the end of the first week, he won't pretend it isn't. But once he's paid his mom the first installment for the window and taken out the cost of his travel and lunches, he's barely made enough to buy a mid-priced Xbox game. His arms and shoulders ache from lifting the hayfork over and over, his eyes are scratchy and pink from all the dust.

Still, Mom seems happy with him, for once. He supposes the money is better than nothing.

Plus, there's Julia.

He's sitting with Julia at lunch when he first sees it. Well, not *with* her—he doesn't know her well enough to be that familiar. She's sitting on a haybale with two of her friends, the huddle of them laughing over something on her phone. He's opposite, perched on the hard edge of a half-barrel, the metal band digging into his bony thighs. Watching her.

He thinks she knows he's watching, but she's pretending she doesn't, possibly because she likes him, too, and is playing hard to get, or maybe because she actually doesn't like him and would rather that he just went away. He finds it so hard to tell. Her friend, the dark-haired one, whispers something then looks over at him. They erupt into fits of giggles, which again might mean anything or nothing at all. He does his best to look cool and down with it despite the heat blushing into his cheeks. Trying not to look their way, he examines his food, pulls out a piece of hay, stares meaningfully into the trees behind them.

And that's when it happens. He's staring at nothing, trying to tune out their muffled laughter; then it isn't nothing anymore, because there's something there. Something dark and formless, but heavy, like smoke made solid. He can see its eyes smoldering under the canopy of the trees, set too far apart to be human. Most of all, though, he *feels* it, the way you can tell when someone walks into a room, even before you see them.

"Holy shit!" He jumps to his feet, spilling the contents of his burrito down his front. "Did you guys see that?"

He's pointing without even realizing. The three of them follow his finger, conversation interrupted.

"See what?" This is Julia, turning to look at him; and he can't help it, the words stutter and die in his throat.

"The...thing? Something, I mean. I don't know...in the woods? There was something there."

She looks at the trees and then back at him, as if trying to decide who to believe.

"Where? There? I see nothing."

She's right, of course. There's nothing there, just the shadows and a growth of bracken, broken in places as if someone has trodden it underfoot.

"It's not...I mean, it's gone. It was there. Honest."

The dark-haired one puts her hand to her forehead as if she's about to faint. She cries, "Oh who will save us from the foul beast?" as the three of them start cackling again, no mistaking who their laughter is aimed at now.

They gather their lunch things and push past him, avoiding the spoiled heap of rice and beans at his feet.

He hears one of them mutter to her friends as they walk away.

"Freak."

———————————

From that moment on, he only sees the watcher when he is alone. It's never in the same place but always under the trees, in the shadows. Just dark enough to sow a seed of doubt.

He's gone to fetch another barrow of hay when he spots it in the woods, closer than usual but still hidden, a blot on the undergrowth. Clearer than before. A hint of weave in the darkness, like it's shrouded in coarse black cloth. It's slightly bigger than a man, bulky, and Jack wonders if it's Big Mike playing a prank. He can't imagine what the purpose might be, but it feels like something he would do. Scare the new kid. Terrorize the weak.

"Hey!" he shouts, letting the barrow drop. "You! What are you following me for? Mike? Is that you?"

"Is what me?" says a voice behind him, and he turns to find Big Mike stood there, not in the woods at all, two full bin liners slung over his shoulder. "Can't a guy do his job around here without getting yelled at?"

When he turns back, the watcher is gone. He wonders if it was ever there at all.

That evening he mentions to his mom that he thinks he might have sunstroke, and the following morning they give him a new assignment. No more hay, no more dust. He's still in the stable, but there's a pile of sticks in there now, dry and brittle like bones. Big Mike has sketched a picture on the back of a ketchup-stained napkin. It looks like a giant star, the top point smaller than the other four, a complex scaffolding of branches holding it upright. They want him to build it.

"But what's it for?" he asks as he organizes the pile into thicker, sturdier branches and thinner sticks. "What is it I'm making?"

Big Mike shrugs and smiles, the expression sickly and unfamiliar on his face.

"A thing. Medieval thing. The crowds'll love it, you'll see. Build it nice and strong, we don't want it falling down."

The job is harder than it looks. Jack knows nothing about engineering or the use of trusses in transmitting loads. His first efforts collapse into piles of kindling, a game of Jenga that he keeps losing, over and over. Splinters work themselves under his nails, under his skin. After two days he's back where he started.

He learns, though. If he winds the twine around a joint before tying it off, it can support a greater load. If he ties the main branches together like this, they hold each other up. There are still a few stumbles along the way, but by the end of the day he has created the framework of the star: five points, the uppermost level with his head, the bottom two rooted in the dirt. He gives it a shake and it barely moves. There's a swelling of pride in him for a moment, stood in this dusty arena in his sackcloth robe, admiring his structure of sticks.

He wonders what comes next.

It's Julia who suggests the game. They're litter-picking after the park has closed for the day, the last children ushered out clutching plastic swords and castle-shaped sippy cups, leaving a wave of garbage in their wake. Jake makes sure he's on the same clean-up detail as her, just in case the opportunity arises to chat. He has no idea what he'll say if it does.

In the end he doesn't have to. She's the one who speaks.

"I like what you've done there." She points with her litter picker at the wooden star. "Looks pretty sturdy. Take you long?"

He shrugs, as nonchalant as he can manage. His stomach is churning.

"A while. It was hard…kind of hard work. Kept falling down. But the big branches there, the beams? They bear the weight of the rest of it, see."

As he says it, he knows that the finer points of stick-structure engineering are of little interest to her, but he doesn't know what else to say and so his mouth runs and runs. He thinks he might need to visit the bathroom.

"Uh-huh," she replies, looking at it properly now, testing it with her hand. "Pretty sturdy. Big, too. I have an idea—" she says this like it has only just occurred to her, but he senses this is where her mind was going all along, "—why don't I tie you to it? Might be fun?"

Oh god. It's almost certainly some kind of joke, her friends must be just around the corner, waiting to laugh at the gullible idiot…But if it isn't? There's a tiny chance she might actually want to do this, and that's all his brain fixates on, the hot girl in front of him who's paying him attention for the first time in his life.

"Umm. Okay?" he says. "Just don't tie it too tight, please? I get eczema really bad."

The star, it turns out, is exactly the right size for him. She binds his wrists and ankles far too close to the frame, the rope cutting into his skin—where she found it, he doesn't know—but he doesn't complain. If he did, she might stop, and he doesn't want that. This close he can smell the coconut shampoo on her hair.

"I'm going to take your clothes off now," she says, as he tries not to cry. "Don't wriggle. I don't want to cut you."

From somewhere inside her robe, she pulls a knife, crude but sharp. The cutting edge shines where it's been sharpened recently. It makes a loud ripping noise as she runs it through the sackcloth. When she pulls it away, he's left in his Y-fronts, half-aroused and half-petrified. There's no backing out now, though. He couldn't if he wanted to; he can barely move his fingers.

With a deft slice she removes his underwear, too.

Jack doesn't know what he'd hoped for, but it wasn't this. She looks uninterested in him, occupied with wiping the knife on the rags of his clothes and replacing it inside her robe. There's a brutal efficiency to her movements that kills any sexual thoughts.

"He's ready," she calls.

Her dark-haired friend is the first to enter the stables, and a procession follows her. Jack lowers his head in shame before they reach the end of the line. He recognizes Miles from the gift shop, and Sharon the ice cream lady, and Big Mike. They're chatting among themselves as if he isn't there, although some of the girls are laughing and pointing. A few of them have brought snacks.

He's only aware that he's started to cry when the sobs rack his body, pulling tight against the ropes on his wrists. His cheeks are wet. He tries to turn away, hide his exposure from the crowd of onlookers, but there's no give, no respite. A cold trail of sweat runs down his belly and along his inner thigh.

A hand reaches out with a napkin to dry his eyes, and he looks up into his mother's face. She's smiling at him in a way that he wants to interpret as compassion, but actually looks more like excitement.

"Here you go, sweetie. No need for that. This is all for the best, you'll see."

"Mom?" He can't think what else to say, so he says it again: "Mom?"

"Don't worry now," she says, throwing the wet napkin into the dust at his feet. "I'm sure this isn't what you expected, but it's for the good of everyone. I'm so proud of you, sweetie, really I am. Everyone is. Look at you! The changes you're going through—it's a gift. We're all here for you, to witness what you're doing for us."

She doesn't use the word "sacrifice", but he hears it hovering in the air between them, implied but unspoken.

"Mom? I don't understand…?"

Then she's walking back into the crowd, joining them as they eat their pretzels and laugh and joke, as if he isn't tied there, naked and already aching.

The party lasts for an hour. The sun is dipping as the last of them leave, and the shadows stretch across the stable floor. Out in the darkness, Jack feels the watcher's presence, waiting, observing. He squints to see it better, but his eyes are still filled with tears. Once or twice, he thinks he hears a labored breath.

It's only later, as he stands shivering in the middle of the night, that he recalls his mother using the word "changes", and wonders what she meant.

———————————

They take turns visiting him. Big Mike lifts a dirty straw to his lips, gives him a few sips of brackish, stale water. Julia and her friends avoid looking too closely when it's their turn.

His mom comes once a day with a bucket and cloth, wiping his body down, scooping up the excrement beneath him with a shovel. He'd like to think she does it out of kindness, but it seems more like a chore. She barely speaks to him. When she does, it's all greetings-card platitudes, impersonal and trite. *Hang on in there. You're stronger than you imagine. Your time will come.*

Time runs in fits and starts, darkness the only measure of the days as they pass. Jack exists on the edge of sleep, not quite conscious; unable to find rest, strung up as he is on a giant star of wood. Sometimes he screams and shouts for help, testing the capacity of his lungs, but it makes no difference. They must have closed the park. There are no tourists to hear him.

After a while, he starts to think of the watcher as a friend. The others spend as little time as possible in his company—even his mom hurries out once her duties are done. But the dark shape in the woods sits with him all night, never showing itself fully but present all the same, the black within the black. He hears it shuffle and move, his ear attuned to its ragged breathing. Once, he thinks he hears it whisper—but he can't make out the words, or whether there are words at all.

———————

The flesh shrinks as his body consumes itself. Soon he can see his own ribs standing tight against the skin, his hipbones jutting like scythes. He feels his mind shriveling, too, only a tiny flame remaining of who he was, guttering, before it is snuffed out. He is more animal than man now, but still man enough to recognize the horror of it. The splinters of wood and hay that have worked their way under his skin itch and weep, the flesh around them angry and raised. His failing body is too weak to reject them. He can't move to scratch.

He doesn't know how long it has been when he first notices. Two weeks, maybe? Three? It's a wood splinter in his shin, one of the most troubling. It itches and itches until he feels his skin will catch fire; then suddenly, unexpectedly, there's relief. Tipping his chin to his chest, he's able to see down past his hollowed-out belly, the raised ridges of his ribs.

The wood is growing in him. What was barely more than a pencil line beneath his skin has divided and spread, a tracery of black threads buried beneath the surface. From the open wound where it entered there stretches a single white fiber, tapering to a hairy point. It must be three or four inches long, almost reaching the ground.

A root.

He watches it for any change, a sign that it is growing. Nothing. Eventually his head nods and he loses consciousness; when he wakens, the first thing he does is check it again. Now it's touching the dirt. He's able to move his foot ever so slightly, and when he does, the tip of the root stays fixed. It's already worked its way into the soil.

A hay splinter in his arm is next, its root snaking down from where he's tied in place, twining around the sticks that support him; the rest come too fast to note them individually, a hundred tiny tendrils descending from his body. There's relief from the itching at least. As more of them work their way into the dirt he'd swear he feels stronger for it, like they're feeding him, drawing nutrients from the earth and dripping it into his veins. After all he's been through, it's almost a balm, this new source of sustenance. It floods his head with green light.

More than once, in his lucid moments, he wonders what they put in the water they fed him.

The watcher's behavior changes, too. It draws closer at night, snuffling around him like a pig after truffles. It's near enough for him to see now, but in the darkness his eyes struggle to make out more than its hulking shape, seven feet high and strangely formless. He can smell it, though. Its musk is rich and earthy like leaf mold, the black gold of fertile soil. It smells like it lives in the ground—or more than that, is part of the earth itself, a creature of peat and loam. Tentatively it touches his roots and a shudder ripples through his body.

His mom and the others tend to the roots like any other part of him. Occasionally Big Mike will appear with a spray bottle and mist them with fine droplets of water, like he's a rare orchid or fern. They appear unfazed, as if this was what they expected all along. If anything, he senses a growing excitement.

He no longer needs the sips of water. His new growths take care of him.

There's a change in the season, the night air turning colder and raising pimples on his skin, when Julia comes to him with something cradled in her hands. He can tell by the way she holds it that it has meaning. She lifts it in front of his face, and he sees a tiara of holly branches, the supple stems woven together into a circlet.

"Here," she says, standing on tiptoe to place it on his head. "This is yours."

The leaves prickle his forehead but he doesn't mind. He laughs and smiles for her, whoops of joy coloring the air as she steps back and curtseys before him.

One by one they come, the crowd gathering as the day wears on. Each of them is singing the same song, though he cannot make out the words, or what language it is in. They all carry gifts and lay them where his roots kiss the ground, a semicircle of plenty at his feet: gourds and pumpkins, a bag of plums, five turnips bunched together with twine. Big Mike carries an entire sack of potatoes, laying it on its side so the tubers spill out across the dusty earth; his singing voice is surprisingly sweet. Jack's mom carries a basket of apples, each one with a thread tied delicately through its stalk, the other end tied to a fishhook. With care, she pushes the hooks into the withered flesh of his arms.

As the sun dips to the horizon, they stick torches into the ground at regular intervals around the shed, lighting them with Miles's Zippo. The leaping flames bathe the crowd in flickering orange. Jack smiles at them all the while, his head floating with a kind of euphoria he has never experienced before: a sense of oneness, of belonging. Noises escape his lips that may be laughter or might be him singing along with the chorus that swells as the daylight fades.

Once the light has disappeared, and the torches have died down to a steady glow, the song changes. Some of them are ululating now, raising shrill warbles into the night. Their arms wave in the air like reeds. They part down the middle like a field of wheat and Jack senses its presence, actually *seeing* it now in the torchlight as it shuffles down the aisle toward him.

The watcher.

The sackcloth draped over its body is blackened with mold and dirt, crusted in places with what might be scabs of dried blood. The form beneath it holds Jack entranced: heavy and shapeless, some ancient thing dug up from beneath the ground. That smell washes over him, dirt and rot, so heady it overwhelms all the other senses. Jack feels sick and dizzy and filled with an inexplicable joy.

Then a clawed hand, its nails like giant thorns, emerges from beneath the sackcloth and lifts it, the shroud falling to the floor as the watcher stands before them, unclothed and magnificent. Some of the crowd fall to their knees. Jack searches for his mom but she's nowhere to be seen.

He doesn't know what he's seeing. Not really—his mind is too far gone to process this creature made of dirt and leaves, twigs and burrs. The worms crawling from its eyes as it bears down on him with its huge, stinking bulk. He hears its teeth like river stones crunching down on their offerings: the gourds and the plums, the potatoes and pumpkins. In three bites they're gone. Swallowed inside of it, to be digested by the bugs and the microbes, broken down and shit out again as all life must be.

Then the watcher steps forward and the feasting begins.

MELISSA A. SZYDLEK

BACK
YONDER

WE are what City folk would call a "porch setting" people here in Weirman Holler, Kentucky. After a hard day working the crops or the coalmines, watching the day ease into a blaze of twilight from our porch swings and rockers is a treat. Free time is scarce, and we are content to let it tick by from our porches, watching the roads from our well-worn spots, waving to people we know, sometimes to those we don't. We watch.

Here in the hollers, we share our porches, and our sweet tea and lemonade, doing what I call "spreading the colorful commentary of the mountains." It's not just friends and neighbors, Lor' no. Should a stranger come to call, sellin' something, or asking directions, most likely we'll ask them to sit a spell with us on the porch. The women call it gossipin', but us men call it passing on vital information—as Internet and cable television is sparse up here. I'm a beacon for information because my house sits closest to what passes for the "major" highway up here—Highway 542—closer than I'd like, really, because I can feel the breeze from some of them vehicles that go whipping by sometimes. Now, I know Highway 542 is more dirt than asphalt, but it's busy. I've lost enough beloved cats and dogs, and even a goat, to that road to account for that. It's the main road from town to these mountains and all the hollers scattered in its valleys. Highway 542 is mostly unpaved, hard to travel, and has no guardrails separating it from the sharp drops off the mountainside. We have a healthy respect for it up here, and those that don't pay a heavy price—ending up not only at the bottom of the mountains, but also part of our day's porch news. By far, the biggest news I'll share with strangers and kinfolk alike is to not go messin' around back yonder. My little, beaten-down house sits close to Trace Fork, a beautiful, green, and hilly place. Most of us back here are related one way or another. Some City folks might make fun of our rural location or our mostly farming and mining professions, but we are close-knit and take care of our people up here—and not going back yonder *is* taking care. Back yonder of my place is a maze of overgrown roads that lead way up the mountain, and—some say—to places in between. Places our kinfolk told us, as children settin' at their knees on the porch, never to go.

The car was a 2013 Infiniti G37 IPL. That was a mouthful to be sure, and a fancy car I'd reckon, but Crystal—Mrs. Nicholas to most—wasn't prideful in owning it. It was an older car, but she'd had her husband rebuild it with air intakes, turbos, a high-performance engine, and all kinds of things I know nothing about. Mr. Nicholas just wanted to get her a brand-new car—said she could have anything she wanted—anything! But Crystal, she loved that old car and didn't want to give it up. So, Mr. Nicholas rebuilt it for her. He had the work done in town by my brother, Fiddler, and I was there the day she came in, riding in her husband's pickup truck, the Infiniti on a flatbed. She had all the specifications and part numbers exactly as she wanted and told Fiddler not to skimp.

"OEM parts only, Fiddler," she'd said, narrowing her eyes at him, and Fiddler nodded with an Eagle Scout's honor.

"And don't you change the color," Crystal said. "You keep that malbec color."

"Aww honey," her husband said, "They don't even make that color anymore. Infiniti is going to charge me extra to mix the color!"

"Malbec!" Crystal called as she left my brothers garage and hopped into her husband's pickup. It took Fiddler near six months to get the parts, rebuild it, and paint it, but when it was finished, it was like new, and was beautiful.

It was certainly a showy car, obvious to any who saw it, but Crystal said nary a word about it. She just drove it, which was her second favorite thing next to snuggling up to or petting an animal. Beautiful was only its second-best attribute—that car was a fast, you could tell by the way she drove it around the narrow holler curves and how it purred—loud and deep like an angry Kentucky bobcat as it zoomed by our porches. The gossip vine started the minute she drove it onto the Holler. The first time Crystal drove the car home, I was sitting on the porch with Junior Jacobs, Lee Wayne, and Lovely Phillips—we were talking about Jolanda Flemming's new baby and how ugly that poor young'un was when we saw blackish-purple blur go by on 542 and Junior exclaimed how Carter, Mr. Nicholas, was spoiling Crystal again. Then, I had to explain the whole situation at Fiddler's and how he'd been working on the car for almost six months. Lovely said it wasn't like Crystal didn't deserve it and we started recounting how Crystal volunteered most of her time to the nursing home and animal shelter in town and how Carter was all the time busy at his company in Lexington. They were a happy couple, though they didn't see each other too often, with Carter traveling.

Crystal drove all the way out to the big city when Carter had to work late, or even sleep in his office, to bring him a homemade dinner. The point was, the four of us said, Crystal was a good'un, a keeper, and a genuine and heartfelt soul who very few could say anything bad about, and that was that. We sipped our sweet tea and didn't have much to say after that.

About a week after Crystal got the car, I was sitting on my porch swing on a quiet Wednesday morning, watching the sun come up. It was hot and it was only early May. Nights were almost always cool, but summer days were scorchers, but lately it had just stayed hot. The sun was sitting mid-sky, its rays blazing right into my eyes, and I had them closed against the light. I heard tires on the gravel road and knew it was a car, even without hearing the engine. As the car drew closer,

182 ♣ MELISSA A. SZYDLEK

I knew it was Crystal because that engine of hers roared like a panther. I held my hand above my eyes to shade them from the sun and watched as she pulled into my driveway.

"That there a ninja car Crystal?" I called.

She smiled. "Sarcasm will get you everywhere with me," she said. "Wanna race?"

"Well, I reckon my old pickup would give you a good run, especially on these mountain roads. You might go fast, but I can go anywhere with a four-by-four."

She laughed and walked up my rickety wooden steps, joining me on the porch swing.

"How you been, Chester?" she asked.

"'Bout as good as I can be, I reckon. How 'bout you?"

"I'm good. 'Bout sick of this heat and summer hasn't even started."

"You got a/c in that fancy car?"

"I do. Haven't used it, yet. Trying not to. Eats up gas and slows me down. Uses up my horsepower."

She laughed again, and it was beautiful. A quiet but hearty laugh. She leaned back in the swing and lifted her feet from the porch, letting them swing free.

"This reminds me of Mamaw and Papaw's place; they loved their porch swing," she said.

"Your grandpa was working in the fields so much he hardly ever got to see the sun go down while settin' on the porch."

"He hardly ever sat anywhere," she said. "Both of them had jobs and then came home and worked the farm. I miss them."

"They touched a lot of lives up here," I said. "Hell, they fed me when I was a young man and could barely keep myself in work boots."

"Well Chester, what are you doin' home on a Wednesday mornin'?" she asked me.

"Got the day off from the mines," I said. "Switched a shift with one of them young'uns. He's tryin' to get into Big Sandy up there in Paintsville and needed the day to fill out his college forms."

"You ole' softy," Crystal said.

"Well, he'd be a might better goin' ta the college then workin' the mines for 50 years and making his lungs black."

"Amen," Crystal said.

"What brings you here so early?" I asked her.

She didn't answer right away, just looked out across the road, over the mountain. Her look was far away, and I let her have the moment. Finally, she said, "I was just out driving this morning, Chester. I was back yonder." She pointed behind my house.

"On them back roads?" I asked, sitting forward, and spilling my morning lemonade on the front of my overalls.

"Yes, sir."

"Lord, girl," I said. "You can't take that car back there. As low as it is, you'll get stuck. You can't even drive that thing out onto the fields to check on crops."

"No, I guess not," she said, smiling. "I'll have to borrow Carter's pickup truck if I need to go out to the fields. But it's okay back yonder. Some spots I can just gun it and go and go. The ground is flat and if it's not wet, it's smooth sailing, no gravel."

"Girl, you best not get that car scratched up," I said, struggling to find any excuse to keep her from going back there. "Carter's liable to blow his top." I knew that wasn't true at all, Carter let Crystal do whatever she damned well pleased because he knew she always did the right thing. If Crystal was happy, so was Carter. But deep down, I was a-scared for Crystal. Back yonder on those roads—it was a different place, a different world. No one, not one person, traveled back there. Too many people back in my papaw's day had gone back there and never came out. Never.

"You know back yonder is not a good place," I said.

"I've always come back," she said. "It's so peaceful back there, Chester. Seems like time stops and my worries just wash away. I roll the windows down, open the sunroof, and even the air seems fresher."

"Not much sun back there," I said.

"No, not much. Trees are too big and thick back there. But I like it."

"Crystal," I said, taking her young hand in my wrinkled one, "Be careful. Them back roads ain't for you, ain't for the young. Go up to Lexington or Louisville and drive one of them racetracks to your heart's content. Hell, I bet Carter would lay some asphalt down for you on your property."

She looked straight at me, and my heart leapt at how beautiful her green eyes were.

"Chester, it's all right. I like the tree cover. I don't want some wide-open racetrack."

"Well, why the hell are you goin' back yonder, anyway?" I asked.

"Don't reckon I know," she said. "Was just drivin' the new car a few days ago and had nowhere to go and nothing to do, but still wanted to keep driving. I saw the turn off, barely visible these days, right past your house, and on impulse I took it."

"Anything but trees back there?"

"Not yet," she said. "But I haven't explored it all."

"Young'un," I said, "Stay off them back roads. Ain't nothing but trouble waiting back there."

Crystal patted my knee and stood up. "I've heard the stories, Chester, and I know your family has lost kin back there, but I don't believe the folk tales. I'm a City girl, remember? We don't worry about what's back yonder."

She looked at her watch.

"I better get going," she said. "I'm volunteering at the nursing center today."

I watched her walk back to her car. When she pressed the button to start the engine, it was like a pride of lions waking up in my yard. She pulled out onto the road and zipped around the bend, headed for town. As I watched her pull away, I felt a foreboding for that woman. Something back yonder was calling to her, and I feared what would happen if she kept driving on those back roads.

"She been back yonder," I told Cledith, my closest neighbor and friend. He lived about two miles down the road, deeper in the holler. He walked to my place at least twice a week, arriving not long after I got back from the mines. We often shared a supper, and he brought squirrel noodle soup, my favorite, securely contained in Tupperware, and then we'd have a beer, or two, on the porch. Watching the sun get low in the sky, we'd wave at the few passersby, and talk.

"On them back roads?" Cledith asked, finishing his first beer and leaning down in his rocker, setting the bottle carefully on the porch. "Hain't nothin' back there. Maybe trouble."

"Maybe more," I said. "Momma wouldn't let me play back there."

"Well, I reckon our mommas were superstitious," Cledith said, getting that ponderin' face he gets when he doubts something he's said.

"Well our mommas both called back yonder a bad place," I insisted, "And when my momma was a girl, she said her ole' white Shepherd dog ran off back there one Spring and came back all funny."

"Funny? Funny how Cledith?"

"Said he walked like he was blinking in and out, like a lamp with a bulb about to blow. Said she swore she saw something little near his ear, always moving around, but by then the dog had gone mean and wouldn't let anyone near him."

"Not even your momma?"

"Not even my momma."

"Your momma who could tame the wildest dogs in the County?"

"My momma who tamed ol' Rowdy Roscoe, Ted Howard's hound, and momma was near 90 when she did it."

"Lo'!" Cledith yelled. "That City girl of ours is gonna find trouble back yonder."

"I told you. She's got me all riled, and I'm too old to be worried like this. Her drivin' around back there like 'at."

"She drivin' that new car of hers?" Cledith asked.

"Yes. Funny car, fast, and she somehow seems to make it go faster. But she's careful. I've seen her driving on these twisting mountain roads, and she's calculating. Every turn, every touch of that steering wheel, she knows what she's doing."

"I seen her driving around," Cledith said. "She is careful, but speeds. Speeds something bad." Cledith laughed, a smile lighting up his old face.

"Fast, but careful," I said. "She's like Niki Lauda, 'member him?"

"I reckon I do," Cledith said.

"She drives like that," I said. "Careful, calculating. She takes that sporty car of hers to its limit sometimes, but doesn't want to hurt the car, herself, or anyone else I reckon."

"That young'un shoulda been a racecar driver," Cledith said.

I laughed. I had said that to Crystal more than once.

"Ole' Sheriff Gavin popped her yet?"

"Nope," I said, "Not yet. He keeps saying he's gonna but he's never around when she's zipping up and down the roads."

"Hell, he's no count. He's too busy over at Virgie's Diner, ettin' up her rhubarb pie," Cledith said.

"Lord!" I said, laughing loudly, "He is, sure enough!"

We laughed till our eyes watered up and then sat a few moments in silence. The bugs were buzzing around and the frogs in the creek across the road were singing their nightly song.

Cledith broke the silence and asked me, "Do you believe in haints? Spirits? Ghosts? Whatever they is?"

"I think so," I said.

"Well, I reckon I don't believe in ghosts and such," he said, leaning back in the rocking chair and folding his large hands across his ample stomach, "But there might be something more on the back roads. Why's she doing that, running back yonder? She don't need to be poking around back there."

"I told her that," I said, "Told her back yonder wasn't right, people going missing all those years ago, and such. She said it calmed her down, gave her time to think, relax."

"Hmmm," Cledith said. "I didn't go back there when I was a boy and I surely hain't been back there in my 70 years."

"Me neither," I agreed, leaning back on the porch swing. "And it's right there against my property too, but I ain't goin' back there. Won't let the dogs run back there neither. Not after what happened to my momma's white Shepherd, and not after what all the people that have gone missing over the years. We got our mountain folk that wander up there – desperate for food when they go hunting and they never come back. And we got our City folk, who take a wrong turn, and they never come out of there."

"Mmmm hmmm," Cledith agreed. "Well, after our talk the other night, I was up to CJ's Country Store …"

"You went to CJ's and not John's?" I interrupted.

"Oh hell, CJ's got them circus peanuts I love John won't stock them."

I laughed then, slapping my knee. "Lo', Cledith, you better not let John find out. He gets his feelin's hurt real bad you know, and he'll refuse to sell to you for a month."

"Yeah, he won't find out if you don't tell him. But I was talkin' to CJ and he said he had a real estate man from Lexington come down here years back, got lost back yonder, and when he saw him drive back down – he was funny."

"Funny?" I asked.

"Pulled into CJ's parking lot and just sat there. Didn't get out of his car so CJ went out there and was about to tap on the window when he saw something…awful…in the back seat and ran back into his store. Didn't know what it was. Called the Sheriff but by the time he got there, the man had taken one of them curves too fast and was down the hill and dead."

Our conversation was cut off when an engine roared, loud, and the switching of gears filled the quiet evening. Someone was coming up the road. An old white and red Ford flew by us, the driver throwing his hand out the window and waving.

"Was that Peach? Becker's boy?" I asked.

"Naw," Cledith said, "That's the twin, Panda. I only know cuz of that dang hat he wears all the time. It's a Detroit Tigers cap."

Cledith pronounced Detroit as "Deeeee-Troy-It."

"Detroit?" I said, aghast, and then laughed.

Cledith slapped his knee and leaned forward in his chair. "I know! Can you believe it? That boy went up there once with his momma to see his Aunt Seline and acted like it was the best thing he ever saw. Got that cap up there and won't stop wearing it. Gonna make hisself bald wearing that cap all the time. His momma, Sarah if you remember, said being up there was like being in hell, but her sister had to stay up there for work and cuz she married a man from there. Sarah said all she heard at night were gunshots, and not from the police neither. It liked to have given her the vapors. Lord have mercy."

Cledith slapped his knee again and we both laughed.

"Well, what's he barreling home so fast fer?" I asked.

"Oh hell, Chester, you know he's late for supper. His momma puts it on the table at six sharp and if you're late, and not because of work, you don't eat. You gots to make your own dinner. And Panda don't work, you know; he gallivants around town with those young'uns from Gunlock. His momma won't put up with it and Panda likes to eat, so he's got five minutes to git home."

As we laughed, we heard tires moving on the gravel, must have been a car turning off the small highway and into the holler.

"That hain't no truck," Cledith said.

"I bet that's Crystal," I said.

"Vesta said that car was quiet until she slips it into gear and takes off," Cledith said, referring to his daughter. Vesta lived in town and sometimes worked with Crystal at the old folk's home.

We both turned our heads to the right, waiting. Sure enough, a dot of blackish-purple peeked through the trees lining the road and Crystal's car came into view. She slowed when she saw us, waved.

"Pretty car," Cledith yelled.

Crystal smiled and beeped her horn, driving slowly. The noise of the tires on the road was steady, slow, and then stopped.

"She didn't go home," I said.

"Hell no," Cledith said, opening another beer. "She went back yonder."

We both shook our heads, a mostly involuntary reaction.

"How many people you reckon have gone missing back there?" I asked.

"Hell, Chester, I been on this earth 70 years and my Mamaw was talking about missing people back there in the late 1800's. Shoot. Hundreds. Thousands if you go way, way back when it weren't no one here but the Native Americans."

"You lost anyone back there?" I asked.

"Not directly," he said. "My cousin Lemmings kid, Vernon, he went back there in the early 70's. You remember Vernon?"

"I don't believe so."

"Well, Vernon went back there one day, said he was gonna see if they was any fish on that small pond they say is back there. Never came back. Twelve years old and nary a word, a sign, or a clue about him, not one. Nothing in all these years."

"Cops go back there?"

"They said they did, told Lemmings they did. I reckon they may have poked around back there a bit, but they never found Vernon. Damn shame, too. We were the same age, and he was so damn smart. We all said he'd be the first to get to college from our branch of the family. He never did, though. Never got the chance."

I nodded my head, both in sympathy and understanding.

"It's not good back there," Cledith continued. "You better call Carter tell him his Missus is driving around back there. She's liable to get hurt, crash that purty car, or something worse."

"Well, I don't see Carter too much," I said, "But I might say a word or two about it to him next time I see him. Heck, I'll even wave him down if I see him drive by."

"That *is* a purty car," Cledith said as he cracked open another beer. "But I don't see how it's practical. She won't be driving out to the fields to visit anyone in that thing. She used to drive out when the fancy caught her, 'specially when her cousins Martin and Thelma was working the fields. Sometimes she'd bring them a lunch."

"She said she's still gonna do that," I said. "Said she'd borrow Carter's truck or use the old one they got settin' back of their barn."

"Carter still got that massive Dodge Ram? That is a nice truck, yes sir."

"He's got it all right. Big thing. Takes great care of it, but I hear he'll loan it out to anyone who needs it, not even worried if the paint gets chipped or nothin'."

"I know. Randall Tackery, up the next holler? His truck died and he had to haul all that corn to Lexington a few weeks back. No one would, or could, loan him a truck. Carter was in town, overheard the kid asking and handed him the keys then and there. Can you believe that?"

"I can," I said. "They are good people, Crystal and Carter."

"That they are. He walked all the way from Happy's gas station to the nursing home, in a suit no less, to take Crystal's car to work. She got a ride from my Vesta."

"Good people," I said, looking up the road. "That's why she shouldn't be back yonder."

"No, she should not," Cledith agreed, putting down his second empty beer bottle. He shook my hand and tilted his hat to me. He pulled a flashlight out of his bib overalls and walked down my porch steps, setting out on the road for his house. He looked back to me once before he got around the first bend and called out to me, "Good people get et' up back yonder."

I worked double shifts for the next two weeks after that dinner with Cledith. Didn't see my family or friends for a while. People around the Holler whispered that Crystal was spending more and more time on the back roads, some of them saying she was looking different. I hadn't seen her so I couldn't comment on it. After my fourteenth straight double shift, I came home a weary, weary man. I had the next week off, a bonus from my boss for covering so many shifts. We had a lot of the younger people quit, going off to enjoy what was left of summer or getting ready to head back to schools in different towns. Until the mine could hire more crews, they were begging us old boys to pick up the slack, offering triple time and a one-week vacation. I snatched it up. I was glad for the money, but my old bones couldn't work like that anymore. I found myself thinking more and more about retiring, about my last day at the mine. I might miss it, but I was ready to settle down with Tullie, my wife, and relax a bit before I kicked the bucket.

At dinner that night Tullie rubbed my shoulders and served me a grand dinner of grits, gravy, fried eggs, bacon, biscuits, and a steak. With Tullie being a vegetarian, I was mighty pleased with this dinner, knowing how hard it was for her to touch the meat let alone cook it up. But she was a good wife. She sat down with some lasagna made from zucchini, cheese, and roasted vegetables and looked happy. I touched her hand for a moment, and we locked eyes, smiling.

"Eat your dinner, old man," she said.

"What's this running through the rumor mill about Crystal?" I asked.

"Oh Lord, Chet, she's been spending less time at the animal shelter and old folks' home and more time on them back roads. Happy down to the gas station says she bought five large gas cans and fills them all up every single day. Everyday Chet! Where is she going back there?"

My stomach started to hurt right then and there from the awful feeling I had, the terror I felt for Crystal. I had to put my fork down.

"What's wrong? Does it taste bad?" Tullie asked me.

"Lord no," I said. "It's great. I'm just really worried about that Crystal. Carter been home much?"

"Not too much," she said. "But it's not our problem."

"No, I guess it ain't," I agreed, "But we take care of our own up here, and she's gonna go crazy or something spending so much time alone."

"Maybe," Tullie said. "I don't know."

Tullie got a dark look in her eye that I hadn't seen since our daughter, Tulip (now grown), started asking her momma questions about growing up, being a woman, and having sex.

"What?" I asked.

"Nothing. Ain't nothing," Tullie said.

"Woman, you tell me."

"Chet, she looks different. Crystal plain looks different. I was settin' on the porch yesterday round twilight, and she come out of there, headed for town to fill her gas cans I reckon. She looked wild, Chet. Not crazy, just wild. Feral. I didn't like it. I waved but she didn't even turn her head. And…"

"And what?"

"And I saw something in that car, too!" Tullie yelled. She put her fork down.

"What'd ya see? A person?"

"Weren't no person," Tullie said. "It was *something*. A creature, something wrong. Just wrong. Something that didn't belong in this world."

I didn't have even one second of doubt about what Tullie said.

"She brought something from back yonder," I whispered.

―――――――――

The next morning, my first day off, I caught up on chores around the house while Tullie went to work her shift at the Winn Dixie supermarket in town. She didn't have to work, not really, but it sure did help us out. Truth is, she likes talking to people, and being a cashier for four hours three times a week lets her gossip. If she's happy, it don't bother me none.

After chores and feeding my hounds, I took the truck down to John's Place, the only thing resembling a store in the Holler.

John ran the store from his house and kept nary a useful thing, like milk, but instead had candy and soda; things that didn't spoil. I walked in to indulge in a Mello Yello. John, sitting on a stool behind a small wooden counter, waved.

"That neighbor of yours never stops driving," he said.

"Which one? We all seem to drive a lot up here, John." I laughed.

"That Nicholas woman. Zooming up and down. Carter was in here yesterday throwing a fit, says he hasn't seen her for days."

"Days? What do you mean?"

"She ain't been home," John said.

"Lord," I whispered. I got my Mello Yello out of an old glass case and paid for it, gulping it down before I got back to my truck. My heart was heavy, and I just knew something bad was coming.

Pulling up to the house I saw Carter's Dodge Ram in my driveway. He was pacing, wearing a crumpled brown suit, his hair a mess.

"Jesus! Chester, thank God," he said, grabbing my shoulders. "Have you seen Crystal?"

"No sir," I said. "I been working doubles for two weeks, hardly seen my own wife."

"She hasn't been home, not at all," he said, panic in his voice.

"Calm down, Mr. Nicholas," I said. "Come sit down a spell. I'll get you some sweet tea and we can figure this out."

"Yeah, okay," he said, following me toward my porch. As I walked up the steps, I heard Carter yell out Crystal's name and turned to see him running across my front lawn to the road. Once he hit the gravel, Carter stood in the middle of the road, his arms outstretched in front of him. Crystal's car was coming up the road kicking up dust from going so fast.

"Stop! Crystal, stop!" Carter yelled.

As the car drew closer, I closed my eyes and held my breath, sure that Carter was about to get hit. I expected to hear a thud as Carter's fate surely was drawing close, but it never came. Opening my eyes I saw Crystal swerve around Carter, passing me on the lawn, and then slowing as she neared my driveway. Carter stared after her, looking lost and pained.

"Crystal," he whispered.

He shuffled down the road toward her car. I looked into the driver's side mirror and what I saw was not the Crystal that I knew. She looked younger, almost a teenager, her hair pulled back in a tight ponytail. Honestly, she looked happy. I noticed movement in the mirror, something in the backseat. I shifted my gaze to the rear window and saw...something. It was like I was watching an old television on a channel that wasn't quite coming in clearly. The way a picture on the TV would flicker and jump is how I saw whatever was back there. It seemed to me it was trying to steady itself into a form that would be recognizable, it struggled. Finally, the thing stuck its head out the rear driver side window and stared at me. It was clearly not human, more a mass of slithering and moving liquid. The image that came to mind was the Blob from the old 50's movie Tullie and I had seen in the theater when we were kids. It was wrong, and horrifying.

Carter appeared not to notice as he neared the car. I touched his shoulder and said, "Don't. Let her go, son. Don't you see that thing staring at us?"

"I don't care," Carter said, and approached the car.

The thing bellied back inside the window, ducking down behind the seats, secreting itself away. Crystal opened the driver's side door and stepped out, but the teenaged Crystal was gone. An older version of the thirty-something woman I knew stepped out and stood, looking at her husband with sadness in her eyes.

"Don't," she said to Carter.

"Come back home," Carter pleaded.

"I can't, not now," she said.

As Carter got closer to his wife, I heard the thing in the back seat start in with some sort of high-pitched growling. It sounded like a turkey call that had been stepped on one too many times. It hurt my ears and I backed further away from the scene in front of me. Something bad lived on them back roads, and whatever it was had got to Crystal and changed her.

"Why?" I heard Carter say.

"It's better," Crystal said. She paused, looked at the ground, put her hand on the car's roof and almost smiled. "No one is dead anymore," she said.

"What the hell are you talking about?" Carter asked. "Come home. We can make this right."

"It's not wrong," Crystal said. "Mamaw and Papaw, my momma and daddy, they're all back there."

"No," I said, not realizing I had spoken it out loud. "Whatever's back there ain't your kin," I said louder. "It's a lie."

"I don't care," Crystal said. "I don't care."

She looked at Carter. "You're a good man," she said to him. "I love you."

She got back in the car, drove up the road a piece, and we heard the tires grinding in the gravel, turning onto the back roads.

Carter collapsed on the road, crying.

I hugged that big man like he was a toddler. I never saw such sadness, such loss, not even at a funeral. I called Cledith and some of the other neighbors, and we got Carter home. He didn't stay there.

That was six years ago. Carter left that very night, signed his truck over to the Tackery boy who had borrowed it to haul corn, left a note leaving the house to his sister in Memphis, and said he was moving. He sends me notes now and again and seems happy in his new life. He moved all the way across the world, to some small town in Denmark. He told me once, in a letter, that he wanted to go somewhere so foreign, so different from anything he had ever known so not to think of Crystal. I suspect he thinks about her every day.

We still see Crystal. Near every day, someone spots her driving the roads. The car don't look a day older, nary a rust spot or a dent exists on it. Crystal changes, though. People have seen her younger, happier, and smiling. Others say they've seen an ancient crone with wild hair driving the car. Most don't see the thing in the back seat, not anymore. One look is enough for most folks to pretend the car doesn't even have a backseat. They avert their eyes, ignore that slithering, flickering mass back there.

I've seen Crystal. Sitting on my porch, more often now that I'm retired, I see her go by a few times a month. She never stops, she never waves. She usually looks the same to me, a thirty-something woman with brown hair and fair skin. But she don't look happy, not to me. She looks scared, ruined. I just hope whatever is back yonder doesn't travel past this holler, doesn't spread its evil and ruin into the world.

Because here in Weirman Holler, we see things, a lot of things. And we know things. We know to never go on them back roads, to never, ever let our children or our animals stray there. We tell kin and strangers to stay away. Whatever is there is best left ignored and unattended. Whatever is there is best left, forever, back yonder.

RAF KNOWLES

MULBERRY SILK

BECCA

curls her arm around our Intern, a waste of her delighted smiles and flashing eyes. He is one who comes to visit. We are those who came to stay. She knows he will be Indigo, as do I. Yet I watch her chatter from behind my steaming vat with palms stained plum. The wooden oar splinters as I stir, as I waft vapors into my own face. Dye so thick I can't see the bottom.

"Don't overdo it," Oliver says. He stirs vermillion beside me.

Our Intern points and gawks. Stares at our towering looms like a fascinated bird. Sparrows blush with embarrassment from their high perches in the trees. Becca giggles, though I'm too far away to hear.

I followed her to The Collective. Eighteen miles off the exit, ten down a dirt road. Past the gorge and into the woods. An orange cottage with white trim on the left, the one with daisies in the rock garden. That's where we live now. Our first day I'd pressed my palm against our new home, been surprised by the chill of waved metal. Shipping containers. We live in a village of shipping containers, converted and stylized, not one the same as another. There's purple with teal trim, charcoal with red, one modern, one craftsman, one painted like wood. On a haphazard gravel street that twists and juts off to each property, for walking only. No cars allowed. *Exhaust ruins the dye,* The Widow had said. Not said, but wrote in a letter.

I slide my oar from the vat, scrape it on the side to spill as little plum as possible. I rest it against the vat and push the tin lid on top. Becca weaves her delicate fingers through the overhead loom. The Intern puffs his chest, leans into her while he talks. She is not thinking of me.

"Have you met her?" the Intern asks. He is a city person through and through, from his slicked hair down to his shiny leather shoes.

Becca rolls blonde hair between her fingers. "Not yet." She bats her lashes.

The Intern huffs. I hate him. "Do you think I might … she's a legend in the fashion world."

"You won't." I'm upon them now, fixing my sour gaze on Becca, who straightens and glares back at me.

"You don't know that," she says.

I must stand between them. "How would you like to help prepare the leaves?"

The Intern's eyes grow wide. He's hungry. Desperate. He rattles his head in greedy agreement.

Judy and Raul carry deep baskets overflowing with cuttings. Tina gathers mulberries in an aluminum box, the corners of her mouth stained plum like my hands. The leaves must be collected. Must be washed. The Widow has been clear. I show him how to pinch the stem, clip it clean between my nails, but he's clumsy. Yanks and tears. He does not belong here.

A few more days, I remind myself.

━━━━━━━━━━━━━━

Two rubber bands wait for me on the wooden railing. I stretch the yellow one between my pointer finger and thumb. Dawn's light pushes its way through a blanket of fog that has settled around the lowermost branches of the Eastern Hemlocks. I spy Hendricks. He watches me with a crooked neck, his black feathers shining an oily blue. *Indigo.* Four peanuts wobble on the woodgrain.

"Good morning, Henricks."

He doesn't respond. Though we've struck this bargain— peanuts for rubber bands, or screws, or pieces of wire—he does not trust me. That is okay. He is a crow. I know this is his nature. It is not personal.

Becca didn't come home last night. I woke and I woke and I woke. 12 a.m. 2 a.m. 4. Her bedside cold. I imagine his grubby fingers pushing her golden hair behind her ear. His filthy claws pawing at her milky skin. This is her nature. But she is not a crow. It *is* personal.

Steam rises thick from the vats, blends with the falling fog. Oliver heats water in a kettle over a gas stove.

"Coffee?" he asks. He asks this every morning.

And every morning I say, "Yes."

It's instant. Quite terrible really. But I stir and I thank him. I've become accustomed to that. Stirring and lying.

"Have you seen Becca?"

He slurps, all ten fingers wrapped around the warm mug. "You two still fighting?"

I swallow the lump in my throat. "We're not fighting." Another lie. Becca is cross with me. She says because I cut my hair off. But I know the truth. It's because I love her too much.

"Well, better shake off all this weirdness soon. Only two more days. We need to bring our best selves." Oliver smooths his black hair over his ivory skin. Perfect for vermillion.

I nod.

One by one, naked, hanging bulbs illuminate the shipping container homes. The sun reaches further into the sky, burns up the fog. It's clear air all around us now. I can see high up into the thinning boughs. The owl nest is thicker than yesterday. Good on her. She works hard.

There's something wrong with Becca.

She wears a tunic dress, thin fabric over her hard nipples. It wafts around her, glad to be in her company. The Intern's hand is on the small of her back. I hate him. Goosebumps creep over my arms and thighs. Judy lays a wooden bowl in front of me. A fire ant snaps at my calf. Poison burns, but I'll live. It is good to hurt on the outside.

Mulberry leaves have ragged edges. They're shaped like palm-sized hearts. I chew and chew and chew, like a donkey gnawing cud. I feel the filmy green stain of chlorophyll on my teeth, viridian. That's not a color we're using this time. Indigo, vermillion, plum, burlywood, and mountbatten pink. I didn't know the last two. Had to sneak out in the middle of the night, dip white cotton into the vats to learn. My cheeks flushed with shame. If The Widow knew, she'd boot me out. Unacceptable not to know. Burlywood reminds me of khaki, a warm, sandy color. Mountbatten pink is more like purple, I'd say. But never out loud. Becca feeds The Intern who sneers while he chews. His sloshing saliva beats at my temples, a sharp pain worse than the fire ant bite. At the bottom of my bowl is a split leaf. This is her fault. A sign from the gods.

Two more days.

I wake sweating. I dreamt I caught Hendricks in a glue trap. His wings beat wild, and his eyes screamed, *Traitor!* I snapped his fragile neck. He finally spoke to me, and I popped his thin vertebrae in my twisting fist. Cold morning air chills my damp spine when I reach the porch. I run my hand along the bare wooden railing. No rubber bands. He knows. I whisper an apology. *I'm sorry, Hendricks. I didn't mean it.*

I must move on because today is the Ceremony. I wipe my tears on my forearm and join the coffee drinkers at the picnic tables. It hasn't rained in a week and the slits between my toes fill with grit, my sandals black with filth. Oliver can't stop smiling. I think his coffee might leak through his curled lips. His joy haunts me like an unyielding ghost. I have to turn away to hide my displeasure. Judy shows her teeth, making small talk with Raul, but there's no honor behind it. Not like Oliver. Her smile is all nerves. She'll be mountbatten pink, which is perfect for her. Though, I still think it's more like purple. Burlywood is still up for grabs.

Breakfast is day five of leaves. My stomach growls objections. The Collective's morning greetings are white noise against chirping crickets in the forest. Their music is something I love, but not as much as Becca. The mattress is thin in the guest cube. I hope her back aches with betrayal. When she emerges from the seafoam door, The Intern is with her, followed by Tammy, plum. His fingers strangle Tammy's hand. Three sets of eyes glitter with shared secrets. My rage is white hot flame. A fistful of leaves keeps my scream inside, cheeks so full the air barely reaches my lungs. Not enough oxygen to jump over the table. Definitely not enough to poke out their leering eyes. She can't do this much longer. It's the last day. She will have to face me.

It's her nature. I try to self-soothe.

Somewhere she loves me. I breathe again.

I know it.

Tammy catches my eyes before I can lift my mug to block her. She smiles and I smile back, awkward. She is coming my way, pulling The Intern behind her by his clammy fingers. It's too late to move.

"Morning, Gem."

How dare she smile and greet me like nothing's wrong? I smell Becca's desire on her breath. "Morning."

Becca sits beside The Intern, half an ass cheek wobbling off the wooden bench. She faces him and Tammy, like I'm a bit of fog, a memory, something forgotten.

"Do you all always eat leaves?" The Intern grabs a handful of them from his bowl, lets them cascade back inside one by one. "Not that they're not … great." He rolls his eyes.

Becca pretends she doesn't notice the disrespect. "It's only for the ceremony. Actually, Tammy here is quite a good cook." They make eye contact. For far too long. Perhaps I hate Tammy, too.

"Oh stop." Tammy bats her bony shoulder.

I suck at my lukewarm coffee.

"So, what's next?" The Intern asks. "For the ceremony?"

"The dyeing starts tonight," I blurt, more to remind Becca than to inform him. *It's your last day.* I wonder if she can read my mind. She glances at me, but only for a moment.

Tammy's maroon hair is tangled in the back. Dyed. A shame. Before the dyeing, they will have to cut it off. Extra steps.

"Where do you keep the worms?" he asks. I've been waiting for this question.

"Worms?" I raise a brow.

Becca's cheeks flush.

Tammy's eyes wander away.

"The silkworms." His overly plucked brows furrow.

"Of course." The air is lighter. Becca and Tammy both remember to breathe it. I wouldn't mess it up for us. They should know that. Becca should know me better than that. "I'll show you tonight. If you'd like."

The Intern's greedy eyes eat up half the world. He wobbles his head like a wooden toy. I hate him.

Crisis averted, Tammy excuses herself to shower. "Scrub hard," I say. It's a tiny dig. One she well deserves.

The Intern slaps a hand onto Becca's thigh like he owns her. I see the spark in her amber irises. She is immune to ownership. Allergic. "Shall we ..." he trails off. Like she should know. As if they're some long married couple. She pulls away from him. I don't hide my smile. *I know you.* I try to think it hard enough so she might hear.

"Actually, I'd better head home for a bit," she says.

His shoulders fall. Smile fades. My insides dance with delight.

Crestfallen, he retreats to the guest cube. It's only she and I now. Her golden hair is greasy at her crown. She needs me to wash it.

"Burlywood is still up for grabs," I say. I want to scare her. Can't help it. Want her to fight for me.

She shrugs instead. "Maybe you should volunteer." Her clear words are a hiss.

"Maybe I will."

She shrugs again. "Maybe you should."

Becca saunters to our porch. Her hips sway in the passing breeze.

I am made of fire and hate.

There is something wrong with Becca.

Evening closes in around us and the gods paint the sky mountbatten pink. This is a sign. They have seen my lack of faith and I am naked before them, shivering.

It is not purple. I whisper my apology.

Hendricks returned to eat the peanuts. He left a bobby pin in their place. He loves me at least, and he forgives me. The gods shoot the sky through with vermillion as I fix the pins into my hair. Clouds bleed through the tree cover. Becca's outfit has laid on the bed for hours—an A-line dress, white silk and a sheer shawl to match, like a bride.

She taunts me.

I linger on the porch like I'm not allowed to see her. I know it's not real. It's not *our* Ceremony. I am not stupid. I know Becca can't love me. Not all the time.

The mice are hiding. They don't like what comes next, but know it must come, as do we all. The Intern paces with excitement, stammers about wishing he had his camera. He still doesn't understand. Cameras aren't allowed. No cars. No cameras. No phone. The Widow has been clear. The vats rest in a semicircle behind our picnic tables. Looms net us in from above, keep the birds away from the dye, though this is not their purpose. The Intern is talking about fashion now. About runway shows. About silk and satin and polyester blends. This is not the purpose. He still doesn't understand. "Can we go see the worms?"

I stare at him, wriggling. Imagine him coated in dirt.

He holds a small notebook in one hand, a pen in the other, and he jots down details.

"Yes, we're going now." From the porch I can look down at him, which seems right.

"It's for my paper," he says. "My professor will never believe it. I still can't believe—" He blushes. Men are stupid. "This is a once in a lifetime opportunity."

"It's every five years," I correct. I tower over him. Look down my nose. He ought to know.

The peach color about his stubbly cheeks turns scarlet. "Right, yeah. I know." His pen scrapes against the pad.

The Collective is gathering now, like ants trailing from their colorful shipping containers. They gather around the vats, all wondering the same thing. *Will we see The Widow?* I eye the rock face of Her natural stone home from the path. The Intern babbles behind me about threads and runway shows and I don't know what. I listen for trilling crickets, whose music I love, but they have gone quiet out of respect. The Widow is a homebody. I've not met Her yet in all these months. She sometimes leaves notes, elegant script formed on scrolls of treebark. Those days are so wonderful. She is like a mother to me. The vats await us. Plum, vermillion, mountbatten pink, burlywood, indigo. My very first ceremony.

Angela cleared fallen sticks and spider's webs from the overhead looms. They are ready and waiting to spin the threads. The Intern's voice is nails on porcelain, something about the worms again. Why doesn't he understand?

Becca will be late. I know this. She must always be a spectacle. I love her for it. Angela wears a cloak of many colors. It drags behind her in the dirt, despite its couture making and beauty. Nothing is too beautiful for the dirt. Her blonde hair has been dipped into the dyes. It gleams with every color of the Ceremony: indigo, vermillion, mountbatten pink, burlywood, plum. She bridges between the worlds.

"The Ceremony begins. We have waited many years for this moment. Prepared. I thank you all for your service and faith and sacrifice."

Oliver beams.

The color has gone from Judy's eyes.

The Intern waits to see the worms.

I glance over my shoulder for Becca. The light shows through our bedroom window. She is dressing.

"Our ancient ways bring the silk. The Widow feeds and spins the thread. The Collective weaves thread into cloth. The outsiders send us their money so the cycle may continue. We please the gods."

"Where is The Widow?" The Intern whispers.

I fold my arms. The gall of him. To expect after such little time to meet a god. "Don't worry. You will meet her."

"Where are the worms?"

I smirk.

Angela's voice is a roar. "I call upon our Intern, who has traveled far to witness this Ceremony. So few outsiders have the honor."

Tammy grasps his hand. I hadn't seen her in the crowd. She wears a navy cloak, hood pulled up, but I can still see her shaved head beneath its folds, nicked at her temple. She leads him to the vats. The lid is lifted off and The Intern stands beside it. Indigo dye so thick you can't see the bottom.

"It's tradition," Angela says.

Tammy grabs onto his shirt hem, lifts it up. Instinctively, he raises his arms, and she punishes us all with the sight of his naked, hairy chest and too-large nipples. She whispers into his ear, and he pulls down his pants and underwear. His pointed canines fall over his bottom lip.

The audacity of men.

"You honor us," Angela says as he swings one leg over the rim of the vat.

Tammy helps him inside and he slumps down so the dye is up to his chest. It's already joining with him, a pale cerulean tinge on his skin. He grins, still thinking of fashion and runways and worms.

When Raul and Oliver creep up from behind, The Intern doesn't notice—too impressed with his own sloshing and foolish grins. They lift the lid, and together bring it crashing down with such a force, that The Intern clunks against it and disappears like whack-a-mole. He struggles, legs beating against the metal sides.

Clunk, clunk, clunk, clunk.

I feel Becca behind me. I turn and see my bride. Her eyes are big as scrolls, her smile wider.

Clunk, clunk, clunk.

There is something wrong with Becca.

Clunk.

The rest of us, The Collective, we know this must be done. *Clunk, clunk.*

For The Widow, for the gods. It is our honor.

Clunk, clunk, clunk, clunk.

But Becca ignites with joy at the sight of it, her shriveled heart made full.

Clunk, clunk, clunk. A bubbling groan.

I love her anyway. Not anyway. This is *why* I love her. She is more like The Widow than human, or maybe some other nasty god. She is beyond. I see her.

I see you, I mouth. Her smile changes. This one is only for me.

Clunk.

Oliver and Raul release their grip on the lid. I hear Judy breathing, a tiny whistle from her thin nose.

"It is finished," Angela says. "He is transformed." She gazes up at the sky, her cloak sliding down her shoulders. "Gods, with great honor, we present Indigo."

"For The Widow." It comes from all our mouths in unison.

There are no more clunks now, and the other vats are opened: vermilion, mountbatten pink, burlywood, and plum. It's a symphony of screeching metal and rustling cloaks as Judy, Tammy, and Oliver align in front. They stand beside their colors, soon to be one. Tammy and plum. Oliver and vermillion. Judy and mountbatten pink. I wave Becca over, but she resists me. Burlywood remains vacant.

"As always, we have saved one spot for a volunteer. This Ceremony's volunteer will have the great honor of becoming Burlywood. A fine, warm color." Angela scans the audience.

I look to Becca. She urges my hand into the air with her thick, shaped brows.

Betrayal. It's icy as it sinks in, from a jagged stone in my throat, to an anvil in my chest, to an emptiness in my gut. My raised palm casts long shadows across my face, hides me from the sinking sun.

"Gem! Wonderful."

There is clapping all around. It lifts me from my seat, carries me to the front with the others. When it rests, I'm beside Burlywood. Becca golf-claps behind the others, soundless.

"Now that you're all here," Angela lifts her hood over her rainbow hair, "we can begin. Our colors are as follows: Indigo is one taken. Mountbatten pink, plum, and vermillion are three assigned. Burlywood is one who volunteers. The quota is met."

The gods smile at me from above, so why does my heart not rejoice? I look to Becca instead, wait for her to intervene. She is still as death.

Angela drones on and her words make me pull off my shirt, slide my pants down around my hips. I feel them around my ankles, and I step out of them. There's a stickiness about my thighs. Sweat, I think, and I'm ashamed. If the others knew I'd forsaken my honor....

Becca points.

Angela pulls in a sharp breath. "We will need another volunteer."

My stomach turns over. They know I am afraid. They reject my sacrifice. I am made of revulsion and shame.

Raul crosses the dirt ground, picks up my pile of crumpled clothes. Clumsy, I pull on my shirt, bend down to stick my leg through the pants and—

Red smears stain my thighs. Congealed blood. I pull my pants on quickly. My heartbeat steadies. It was not shame they saw. They could not let me ruin the dye.

Becca has moved closer, circled her way to the picnic tables like a snake. She takes a seat in the center as Angela calls on the others for their willingness. I am proud to have offered. I take my seat beside her. Her hand is heavy and warm on my thigh.

"You knew?" I whisper as Petah volunteers to take my place.

She turns her hand to show me her palm, two fingers caked with blood. I lace mine into hers. This is the work of the gods. We are wedded now, in their eyes. They wish us to live, partnered.

210 ♣ RAE KNOWLES

I don't have to say it. Becca doesn't breathe a word. She squeezes my palm and Judy climbs inside mountbatten pink. She dunks her head beneath the surface and Angela sits atop the lid. She bangs and clangs inside. Fights her purpose. There are at least twenty *clunks*. It is a great shame.

Tammy holds her breath before going under plum. I'm embarrassed for her. She's quiet for a while, but *clunks* at least ten times before becoming Plum.

Oliver does much better. I knew he would. Only three small *clunks* at the end. I'm sure he couldn't help it. It's human nature. I swell with pride.

When Petah climbs inside I am looking into Becca's eyes. She is looking into mine. *You love me?* I ask with my blinks.

I've always loved you, she replies with the cadence of her breath.

The colors must sit overnight to fulfill their purpose, so the remaining Collective members scatter to their homes. Becca holds my hand the whole way. Passing lizards bob their heads in approval, wave their glorious throats at us like flags. Extra daisies have bloomed because they're happy for us.

The rising sun shakes me from my bed. I am a child again on Christmas morning. I shake Becca, and her eyes flutter as she remembers me.

"Do you think She will come?"

Becca leans toward me, plants gentle kisses on my eyelids. We are one. The gods have made it so. From our window I can squint to see through oak branches. The vats stand open, lidless.

"Becca!"

My bride rushes to join me. "She's come."

She drags me from the house, in no more than my long t-shirt. I barely think of Hendricks as our bare feet kick up loamy soil in our wake. We reach the picnic tables while the rest of The Collective still sleeps. Each vat holds remnants of spent dye. Becca tugs at my arm. My eyes follow her tilted chin to the looms overhead. Blankets of silk fiber drape over suspended netting around the looms. Brilliant swaths of Indigo, Plum, Burlywood, Mountbatten Pink, and Vermillion rest between branches. Squirrels, birds, and beetles stay away. They know better than to interfere.

"It's incredible."

The kaleidoscope of colors entrances me until I'm dizzy.

"We have spinning to do," I tell her.

"Wait, She's got to be around here somewhere."

Becca is curious. Too curious. She yanks my arm so hard it aches in the socket, and I follow her toward The Widow's stone home. Errant sticks dig into my soles. This path is not well worn. At the cave's entrance, we find the bones. They are stacked, tall intricate patterns so beautiful it makes my eyes hurt. Becca reaches out to touch them.

"Don't."

She touches them anyway, and the fragile structure quakes. I am made of fascination and fear. Becca takes quick steps back. There's a scratching from inside The Widow's home, like sticks or cartilage against rock. I strain my eyes against the darkness inside. A wing beat. Becca is a statue beside me. There's a flutter in the dark, a flash of white. A feathered antenna, taller than Becca or I. The rustling makes me reach my hand into the black. My fingertips tremble. I wait for death, but instead find pillowy smoothness against my flesh.

"Is She—"

I reach my other hand back to shush Becca.

Of course. The Widow is our mother. We are the worms.

Today we will spin the silk into threads, and Becca will love me. Tomorrow she may not, but still, I'll spin the silk. That is her nature, and this is mine.

There is something wrong with Becca.

But we are bound together now. Bound by gods and the moon and a mile of silken thread.

COY HALL

HERALD OF THE RED HEN

VINEGAR

Tom lifted his eyes towards the hilltop, and the hackles raised along his spine. Although exhausted, the greyhound stood poised for the chase. Dorin Toth moved to Tom's side and patted his neck. The dog's hide was taut. He emitted a low growl.

"It's only a deer, Tom," said Toth.

The sun had set, and long shadows covered the forest floor. A red sky framed the hilltop, making silhouettes of the trees, and making a silhouette of the stag that stood guard at the edge of the clearing. The buck cut an impressive figure. The antlers were long and gnarled. The deer watched the travelers with great interest.

Or a sentinel, Toth thought.

The air changed, growing pungent with musk.

The standoff between dog and deer lasted only moments. When the buck huffed, Tom lurched forward, springing over a ditch and into the bramble. He cut through the undergrowth, digging his claws into loam.

Cursing, Toth placed his satchel and lantern on the road.

"I warned you, Tom!"

The buck stomped and let forth with a shrill bawl.

Undaunted, Tom made haste, pressing upwards.

Failing to leave the greyhound cowed, the deer turned from his perch and beat his hoofs in retreat. Chasing deer was a grave offense in certain regions of the empire. If caught scattering a herd, woodsmen murdered canines on sight.

When the dog successfully scaled the hill, however, he stopped. Either he'd lost sight of the stag or something more threatening locked him in place. The behavior was unusual. Vinegar Tom was not cowardly.

Toth followed across the ditch. The hill was steep, so he used trees to pull himself forward through a bed of dead leaves. When he reached the top, he was huffing for air.

Tom paced on his dainty paws, his hackles erect, his fangs bared. He growled, but no bark escaped him.

"Damn you, Tom," Toth said.

As he recovered his breath, Toth scanned the hilltop. The shell of a manor house with walls of charred stone stood at the far end. The roof was burned and caved, save for blackened rafters that stretched like bone and sinew over the dark interior. Piles of stone, earth, and bowed lumber fronted the building, as if an attempt at reconstruction had been started and then abandoned. Stables and a barn, untouched by flames, stood to the side of the manor. The remains of a garden stretched over the fronts stairs, into the doorway and windows, and spilled into a courtyard of weeds.

Mysteriously, a herd of deer moved about the grounds, wandering through the ruins. The sentinel blended unseen with others of his kind.

A wave of nausea stirred Toth. A threatening pulse spread from the structure, reaching inside him. He didn't attempt to explain the sensation, but it was the same feeling that disturbed Tom. Musk thickened, making a broth of the air.

Toth had no desire to investigate the manor or its sentinel. Fear diminished his curiosity. Even from a distance, dark holes where windows once overlooked the grounds had the appearance of watchful eyes. There was depth to the wickedness here, ghosts in the earth.

The herd did not scramble from man and dog. The deer milled about, chewing grass, passing in a procession up the stairs and into the ruins, secure that neither Toth nor Tom possessed the courage to disturb them.

When Toth grabbed Vinegar Tom's collar, the dog jumped, startled. The vigor of the herd had overwhelmed and absorbed him. He looked at his master as if he hadn't realized his proximity. In Toth's shadow, he trembled despite the heat.

A chorus of insects, punctuated by the call of a tawny owl, emerged from the forest. The redness of the sky thinned to a strand.

"Come now," Toth said, patting Tom's prominent ribs. "It's getting too dark to travel."

He led the dog down the hillside, passing tree to tree, towards a lantern that glowed against the dirt. Tom offered no resistance except for peering over his back now and then.

It was fully dark when Toth reached Erlendorf. Treacherously, the road edged a cliff, skirting high above the village. A path forked to the right and winded down the hill into a valley where three lanterns made islands of light in the main thoroughfare. Houses, trees, shops, and a spired church crowded into a wedge between the cliff and a dark stream.

A tower of white stone stood to the side of the road. Hanging from poles, twin lanterns lighted a cathedral doorway. A young man with a matchlock harquebus leaned against the wall. A banner near his side waved in the breeze. Against the white background of the flag was a Red Hen, a symbol of fire to some, a herald of the Hell prince Asmodeus to others. Toth assumed the former held true in Erlendorf, although it was bizarre, nevertheless.

Holding his lantern high, he strolled towards the tower. Tom hugged his side.

"Ho there," the guard called.

The soldier put up his hand, then he hefted his weapon, aiming the muzzle. He met Toth on the road. The lantern threw shadows on his face and made shadows out of his eyes. His manner was that of a gruff peasant, despite the honorific title he assumed for guarding the gate. He wore the insignia of a militia captain on his lapel. He smelled of beer.

"What business brings you to Erlendorf? Hold that light closer. I want to see your face when you speak."

Toth adjusted the lantern.

"We're traveling through to Vienna," he said. "I only wish to stop and rest for the night."

The soldier steadied the harquebus. Over the barrel, he examined Toth and the dog.

"You're a gypsy foreigner," he said. "Is that right?"

Toth nodded assent.

"The road is too dangerous to travel at night, even for your kind. You can try the inn, but I doubt they'll allow a gypsy indoors. There's a widower miller who takes in travelers, as well. He's more forgiving of your faults."

"You'll allow us to pass then?" Toth asked.

The man lowered his firearm.

Before proceeding down, Toth asked, "What is the meaning of the Red Hen on your banner, friend? Is that the mark of your prince?"

"It's for a festival, but that's none of your concern, gypsy. I expect you to leave Erlendorf in the morning."

———————————

The mill stood in a cattle pasture, edging the tributary, away from the other homes of the village. Mills were often loud with machinery, but this mill was quiet and dark. The wheel did not move. Water sloshed against its base, while frogs croaked in its shadow. Huddled cows watched the intruders with limited interest. Toth had the idea that the innkeeper directed him to an abandoned building for amusement.

Tom, delirious with fatigue, walked in circles, sniffing and tasting manure. The dog remained behind as Toth climbed the mill's front steps.

The wood was soft and weathered, brittle as a rotten log. Toth knocked. He lifted the lantern to keep his face out of shadow. He didn't wish to appear a threat, although any presence was ominous at this hour. He steeled himself and expected the worst.

Footsteps from within broke the silence. A voice came from the other side.

"Who goes there?" a man asked. No one who'd lived through the war appreciated visitors. Too many soldiers had spoiled hospitality.

"A traveler with money to pay for shelter," said Toth. "Despite having rooms to let, the innkeeper pointed me in your direction, friend."

Tom, curious, joined Toth at the head of the steps. He sniffed the door. He pawed at a stray acorn on the porch, and then he clawed the crumbling wood, dislodging splinters.

As Toth nudged the dog to stop, the door creaked, opening inward.

The miller observed Toth and then Tom. He was an old man, gaunt, diseased. He held no lantern or candle. He faced the stranger's light with darkness over his shoulder.

"Your hound smells what's below," he commented. "The heads are fresh. The skin's still on them."

Toth grabbed the dog's collar out of frustration. The greyhound wanted to be home with his things, and Toth couldn't begrudge him for that, but his tolerance was gone.

"What would that be, friend?" Toth asked, struggling to keep his grip on Tom.

The old man furrowed his brow. "Don't tell me you never heard of burying cat heads beneath your door."

Toth knew the superstition, distasteful as it was. Cat skulls guarded the entryways of peasants in this corner of the world, thwarting curses. It was ancient folk magic, benign to all except the feline sort. However, it was wise for Romani to be unknowing and subservient, so Toth pretended ignorance and introduced himself.

"I'm Dorin Toth. I was told a miller named Endris resided here. I was told that you offered shelter to my kind."

The miller nodded. He showed his palm.

"Will you accept a *sou*? I've recently been in France."

When the miller had the coin in hand, he opened the door fully.

"Come in," he said. "Both of you. Bring the lantern. It's dark."

Toth and Tom stepped inside.

Endris took the lantern and placed it on a table. Two wooden chairs stood nearby. The home, what Toth saw of it in the dark, was austere. The miller lived without wife or children. There was no sign of pets.

"I apologize if I woke you, friend," Toth said. "We didn't intend to travel so late." He removed the satchel from his aching shoulder. His back, legs, and feet throbbed.

Endris offered a chair to Toth. Vinegar Tom made a circle, and then he flopped down on the floor. The dog sighed his frustration.

Endris brought out a loaf of bread. He tore off a piece and threw the morsel to Tom. He slid the rest towards Toth.

"You look like you could use that," he said. His voice was low and rough.

Grateful, Toth smiled. He ripped off a chunk. He was famished, having walked twenty miles since daybreak.

"Thank you for the hospitality," he said between bites. "The inn wouldn't allow Romani to sleep under the roof."

"You wear the red scarf of the gypsy," Endris observed. "That shows a great deal of pluck, sir."

Toth nodded.

"They're witches and swine at the inn," the miller continued. "What do they know?"

"A guard at the watchtower aimed a harquebus at my head." Toth laughed. "At least the woman refrained from such histrionics."

"No one is trustful these days."

"Aye. That's true enough."

"Ever since the godforsaken Swedes came to plunder. They turned everybody inside out," Endris said. "To this day, the Count pays to keep soldiers at the tower."

"The Swedes are long gone," Toth said. "Why does he keep the soldiers?"

"Oh, highwaymen, arsonists, cutthroats. They call the road you traveled 'The Vagabond Road'. There are always travelers moving to and from the Danube, easy prey. The night's no friend there, especially between villages. I hope you were armed."

"Only a blade," Toth admitted.

Endris shook his head. "Not enough. That bag should be full of ammunition and ready wicks, more like." He eyed Toth's satchel. "If I might be so bold, what is it that you're carrying?"

"Books," Toth said.

Endris laughed. "A scholar. I should've known. It's in your manner, sir."

He stood, walked to a cabinet in the wall, and returned with a decanter of wine. He filled an inelegant stein that smelled of rust.

"Here. You'll need it after I tell you why the ammunition is warranted."

Lantern light cast shadows over the miller's bearded face. He had sunken cheeks and deep-set eyes. His hair had gone white. Around his neck, he wore a bundle of elder blossoms to combat his ailments. The man was quite forlorn. Like many millers, he was an outcast in his village, a suspicious pariah.

Toth ate and drank.

Endris gave Tom another chunk of bread. The dog held the morsel between his paws on the floor, peeling it like feathers. Anger remained from his embarrassment with the stag, so he treated the bread as prey.

"Did you not find anything strange on the road?" the miller asked.

Toth finished the wine. Pleasantly, the alcohol went to his head.

"As a matter of fact," he said, "we did." He dried his mustache on his sleeve.

Endris tapped the table with the delicacy of a harp string. "The stag," he said. He raised an eyebrow. "Eh? Is that what you saw?"

"Indeed, friend. A stag. How would you know that?"

Endris poured more wine. He slid the stein to Toth.

"You're a learned man? What is your line?"

"A doctor of theology," Toth said.

"I'm certain you've encountered sorcery then."

Toth nodded.

"Then you knew about the cat heads better than you let on. Why deny it?"

"Romani are servants to the Germans. It's best to play the inferior until you know the man with whom you speak."

Endris leaned on the table. He poured himself a dram.

"We're both servants here, so no more of that. Let me tell you about a piece of magic you might have missed, Master Toth. Everyone in Erlendorf knows about the stag. If you thought he was watching you, it's because he was. He's a guardian, sir."

Tom rolled onto his back, reaching his legs into the air. He stretched his toes.

A warm breeze moved through the open windows, carrying the stench of cattle from the land and tripe from the slow current.

"A guardian of Erlendorf?" Toth asked.

"Far from it. A guardian of one particular soul—the same man who placed the mark of the Red Hen on the manor."

"I saw that fire devastated the house."

"You traveled so close? You do have pluck."

After another drink of wine, Toth asked, "Miller, what's the Red Hen? I noticed it on banners in your village. You fly it with pride."

"Is this the servile gypsy or the truth?"

"The question is sincere."

"It's flown with more wariness than pride, sir. Don't tell me you haven't heard tale of Jaroslav the Arsonist. He caused quite a stir after the war."

Toth shook his head. "The man escaped my notice."

"Here is his method: Jaroslav paints the Red Hen on your home, demanding ransom. If the ransom goes unpaid, he puts a torch to work. Once, he traveled with a gang of heathens. They burned homes and barns over several years."

"What happened to them?" Toth asked.

"All his men were captured and hanged, save for Jaroslav. He disappeared." Endris' face neared the lantern. He was jaundiced. His eyes were full of blood. "An arsonist, sir, and a man of sorcery."

Toth asked, "How so?"

"Smart men ask questions while dumb men talk."

Toth smiled.

Endris drank wine.

"Jaroslav is gone," he said, "and yet the Red Hen appears, and the fires continue. The stag guards him, warns him, hides him, so he is untouchable. Everyone knows he's up there. Even the Count, God save him, knows it. The Count's Jurist owns the property, but he's too frightened to reclaim it. These aren't thick-skulled fools. They're men of the world, sir."

"When did Jaroslav disappear?" Toth asked.

"It's been five or six years now."

"Six years of fires, but no one has seen the arsonist?"

"Aye, but he's there."

"Would you know him if you saw him?"

"I'll tell you how I'd know him. He was a boastful lad. On his forearm, sir, there's a tattoo of the Red Hen. Clear as day. The very same he paints."

"That's all clear enough, but why celebrate the arsonist with a festival? That's a bizarre rejoinder for a man who causes you grief."

"To placate him, more like."

Toth pushed the handle of the stein, thinking. He said, "I find it curious that he needs a festival and guardian. That speaks of weakness, does it not?"

"How do you mean, sir?"

"Why would Tom and I vex the stag?" He gestured at the dog. "We had no intention of visiting the manor. Does he attempt to frighten everyone who passes?"

"It's a story I hear often," the miller admitted. "Most travelers see it if they're on foot. Aye, I imagine the stag threatens everyone that nears."

"Go on. Why the festival? What's the purpose?"

Endris stood, upsetting Tom's sleep. He lifted the lantern.

"Come, Master Toth," he ordered. "I want to show you something."

Toth stood, as did Tom.

Endris led his guests through the mill to a back door. He opened it and stepped into a bed of mud near the water. The air was cool over the current. Toth and Tom followed, squelching through the morass.

Moonlight silvered the motionless wheel.

"Look here," Endris said.

He extended the lantern until a crude hen, painted red, appeared on the wood. When the miller looked at Toth, he was frail, helpless, and alone.

"The festival decides who will be burned. One is selected to spare the others. I was chosen, sir. Of course, a ransom would save the mill."

"The people of Erlendorf chose you? Or was it the Count?" Toth inquired.

"Jaroslav the Arsonist did the choosing. It's his festival, sir. We court him to do so. He obliges. Then he abides."

"This Red Hen—did it appear in the night?"

"It was there to greet me one morning three days past. It just appeared in the night."

"I suspect your enemy is larger than a simple arsonist. What, may I ask, is the ransom?"

"Well, sir, a *sou* won't cover it. People believe millers hoard gold. Look at how I live, and this Jaroslav believes such a thing." Endris gestured at the dark, clustered shapes of Erlendorf and its lighted tower above. "Of all the people he could choose, he put his mark on this wheel."

———

The white houses and burgundy roofs of Erlendorf reflected morning sunlight, painting an Arcadian scene. Hanging from poles, the Red Hen banners flowed in the street. Peasants led livestock through crooked alleys. A pair of merchants on horseback departed from the inn, split through Dorin

Toth and Vinegar Tom without apology, and rode past the watchtower. The soldier, a different guardian than the night prior, waved them on.

Tom walked ahead of Toth, moving towards the russet-haired lad. The soldier wore a mismatched buff coat, helmet, and bandolier. He gripped a harquebus. Several feet of wick wrapped his neck.

In a guttural accent, he said, "Ho there, gypsy!"

Tom trotted forward. The man knelt, glad for the dog's attention, but the acerbic greyhound slinked away from his touch.

Toth smirked.

"On to Vienna, I hear?" the soldier asked, rising, pretending the dog hadn't slighted him.

Toth brushed past with an affirmative nod.

"Ho there, gypsy," the soldier called from behind.

Toth stopped. He closed his eyes and clenched his fist.

"Vienna lies in the opposite direction. Your hound knows it."

Toth looked to his right. Tom was on the road to home, trailing the scent of the riders.

"Where then?" the soldier pried.

"An errand for the miller to repay his kindness, and then onward to Vienna," Toth said. He kept his back to the man. "Tom! Here!"

"You aren't welcome in Erlendorf tonight, gypsy. Move on or get the stick. Is that clear?"

Toth adjusted his satchel. "Quite clear," he said.

Grudgingly, Tom followed his master.

———

While Endris related the tale of Jaroslav the Arsonist, the idea had come into Toth's mind. The miller was loath to believe in things beyond Satan and artless witchcraft, so Toth didn't trouble the old man with details. Endris' fear was immediate and practical: arson and inability to pay. He was a simple soul, simply taught. Regardless, Toth recognized the shape and pattern of the tale.

Toth dealt with a similar recalcitrant spirit near Luxor. In Egypt, it wasn't a matter of a criminal secreted away, hiding from authorities, although it was believed thus, just as it was believed with Jaroslav. Rather, the matter was one of shapeshifting—glamour magic accomplished through Sobek, the crocodile-headed deity of the Nile. A nomad speared the perpetrator through the skull in animal form, however, a grisly dissolution that provided no closure to Toth's investigation.

With a month remaining on his sabbatical from the university, he could afford an additional day near Erlendorf. If this were a case of shapeshifting, the time could prove enlightening. There was a passage in the *Hieroglyphs of Ba'al*, a recent grimoire acquisition, that Toth hoped to better understand. Shapeshifting, even for occultists, remained obscure, delicate magic, notoriously difficult to achieve, let alone discern. He doubted a lowly arsonist could accomplish transformation into a stag, but it was worth the pursuit.

Curiosity drove Toth, certainly, but he also pitied the miller. Endris was in no position to be extorted. Further conversation revealed that his wife had died a decade prior, and the mill was in a state of disrepair. The Count ignored the man's entreaties for relief. While apathy consumed the mill, another cancer consumed the old man's body. At best, Endris had only months to live, but the months needn't be homeless. He deserved a modicum of comfort in his dying days.

Unlike the soldiers in the watchtower, Toth possessed the tools to solve the problem of the Red Hen. Neither cat skulls nor firearms would suffice, and an event along the lines of a festival only made things worse. One doesn't feed the pride of criminals or deities without consequence.

As Vinegar Tom left the road to pursue a feline scent through the bramble, Toth rummaged in his satchel. The sun was high and the sky clear. Birdsong filled the trees. He retrieved the *Hieroglyphs of Ba'al*, opened to the troublesome shapeshifting passage, and studied as he walked.

Toth was less than a mile from the Jurist's manor when the woodsman appeared. He crossed from shadow into the light of day, emerging from a grove of conifers. Standing at the edge of the road, the man gripped Vinegar Tom's collar with one hand and held a cudgel in the other.

"Is this your hound?" he asked.

Toth stopped, peering up from the text. Under normal circumstances, the matter of a quarrelsome woodsman was commonplace, but several factors combined to stoke Toth's unease and put him on his guard.

First, and most strikingly, the woodsman spoke Toth's native Hungarian rather than German, as if the man forgot his country. Hungarian was not a lingua franca. Second, the man dressed in old-fashioned garb that looked out of time and place, as if he forgot his century. He wore breeches of thick hide and a woolen tunic clasped at the waist. Pinioned behind the band was a long sword, unsheathed, catching the sun. A felt cap wrapped his hair and ears and tied beneath his chin. He dressed like the peasant described in the shape-shifting passage of *Ba'al*. Third, although young and strong, his face ticked with palsy. His mouth quivered, pinching to one side. Alone, an unfortunate disorder. Combined with the other incongruities, it was another flag of mimicry. Maintaining an illusion through glamour magic required tremendous strength. Toth suspected the tic was a fragile keystone.

Although wary, Toth indulged the woodsman.

"Indeed, he is," he answered in German.

The woodsman denied the invitation to speak the local tongue. Proceeding in Hungarian, he said, "The forester doesn't approve of hounds chasing his deer."

With a flash of rage, he studied the greyhound. He pulled on the collar, straining Tom's neck. As the dog squirmed, the woodsman lifted the cudgel to bludgeon him.

"Hold," Toth ordered. "He wasn't chasing deer. Let him free."

The man's mouth ticked. "Smash his skull or open his belly to the red? You'll be the one to decide with the next stag he troubles."

"Free him," Toth said, the tang of fear creeping from his stomach into his throat.

The woodsman released Tom. The dog rushed across the divide to his master, panting and trembling.

Thank God, he thought. Toth stroked the greyhound's back and grasped his collar.

Curious, he switched the exchange to French. "I'll do more to keep him in sight."

"I'd hate to see a good hound laid waste due to the negligence of his master," the woodsman replied, undaunted. He gestured with the cudgel. "I'd hate to see a good hound opened to his red because of his master's ignorance."

"What language is it that you speak?" Toth asked.

"It'd be a shame to—"

"—What language do I speak?"

"—see a good hound laid waste—"

"—No doubt it's German in the land of the Germans. Perhaps, you've forgotten how German sounds," Toth said. "Perchance, you're cribbing the words from here." He touched his forehead. "You're a thing of mimicry, aren't you? You caught me thinking in this tongue back along the road."

"—a shame to see him opened to his red."

"Come, Tom."

Toth put away the *Hieroglyphs of Ba'al* and started up the path. His tension and fear swelled. He wanted to project strength, but his heart failed him. It took substantial willpower to keep from breaking into a run.

The woodsman, with a few yards between, followed.

Vinegar Tom tucked his tail. With every other step, the dog peered back.

He held the dog's collar, Toth thought. *A thing of mimicry or not, he's corporeal. He can harm us. He can strike.*

"The forester doesn't care for hounds chasing his deer," the woodsman said, planting his cudgel. "Or for prying men scattering his herd." His mouth pinched, allowing a trickle of smoke to escape. He had no pipe. No tobacco burned in his hands.

For half a mile, the woodsman followed, maintaining distance. When Toth stopped, the woodsman stopped. When Toth spoke, the woodsman spoke. When Toth walked, the woodsman walked.

Finally, the burned manor came into view. On this side of the hill, a road curved through beeches up to the courtyard. Blackbirds moved between the trees. Rain had carved deep ruts into the path, so that wagon travel was impossible.

Everything here is a deliberate barrier, Toth thought. The idea gave him courage. *Scarecrows,* he reasoned, *like the ever-present Red Hen. Only the weak have need for scarecrows. Why would the woodsman follow without striking? Why would he release the dog after managing to grab hold?*

Impotence. He holds a weapon with an inability to thrust.

A murky idea began to uncloud, and Toth's mind moved from the shapeshifting postulation.

Like the stag, the woodsman is the grasping hand of something more powerful.

Erlendorf, he decided, had worse troubles than an occult-dabbling arsonist. A larger shadow loomed. The fix wouldn't be as simple as the nomad with a spear in Luxor.

Toth watched the woodsman.

"Show me your arms," he demanded in Hungarian. "Are you painted with the Red Hen?"

The woodsman had no reaction. He persisted in his refrain. "The forester doesn't care for hounds chasing his deer—"

Toth looked at the manor. As with the night prior, a herd of deer moved about the grounds, both in the clearing and through the surrounding woods. Their number had grown. There were more than fifty, standing, milling, chomping grass, or lounging in shade. Watchful stags moved among the herd. The air was heavy with musk.

"—or prying men scattering his herd."

The woodsman stepped closer, closing a gap he'd maintained since his emergence. His eyes were dark like pitch. In them, Toth saw the reflection of fire.

Tom shook in Toth's grip, fighting, growing angry over his shame.

"Is the Red Hen on your arm?" Toth asked, girding himself. The man's aura seeped through the casing he projected. Toth's constitution waned. He had a deep desire to run.

The woodsman placed the cudgel on the ground. Rising, he touched the hilt of his blade.

Vinegar Tom lurched, and Toth freed him, releasing the collar. The dog leapt, his paws raised, his mouth agape. The animal's teeth were high enough to clasp the woodsman's throat, and Tom had jaws like a vise when angry.

The woodsman drew his blade.

Tom, rather than smashing into the man, passed through the body, landing prostrate on the other side. The dog scrambled to his feet, puzzled, prepared to leap again.

The woodsman was gone, passing like a snuffed flame into the crook of a nearby tree. A patch of darkness moved over the bark, and then shadow made the shape indistinguishable.

Tom shook off the blow. He turned a circle, looking for the man.

Toth gathered himself. *Indeed, apparitions,* he concluded. *Not shapeshifting. Hence the stag's inability to stand and fight Tom. Extraordinary. If we remain long enough, we'll be bombarded by apparitions. Bombarded until we break and flee. Phantasms guided by what? Perchance Jaroslav, but doubtful. Perchance a spirit, one associated with fire.*

"Come, Tom. What a brave lad you are. Braver than me. I suspect the arsonist and his Red Hen are useful tools for something more terrible," he warned the greyhound.

The dog, bewildered, followed Toth up the road.

Fire left the manor exposed to the elements, with the roof and windows reduced to gaping holes. The upper floor had

fallen into the first, and the first floor crumbled into a foundation of dirt and stone. The high walls remained standing,
including the interior walls that divided rooms. The manor
had been a fine home, fitting for a member of the Count's inner circle. There were hints of tapestries, gilded frames, and
a mechanical clock in the charred walls. Stumps of melted
sculpture and globular pedestals rested in corners. Portions of
furniture stood in open spaces, sometimes colored by smoke
and bird droppings with no other damage, other times burned
to a nub.

Deer wended through the ruins. Toth observed a routine
among the animals. A deer would ascend the steps, move into
the ash, wander through rooms, mark a trail along the floor,
sniff char, room to room, and then the animal returned to
the courtyard to clean its hoofs and taste grass. As one deer
exited, another deer entered.

Toth and Tom, despite the proximity of two perturbed
stags, watched five deer move through the manor in this
pattern. Each routine was precisely the same, as if choreo-
graphed.

The motion of ritual, Toth thought.

He patted the dog. In the shadow of the stags, Tom managed to remain calm.

Even if the stags and woodsman were phantasmagoria, the
roaming deer were real creatures driven by force. Although
indecipherable from the ground, the deer were locked in step,
outlining a hieroglyph or rune of some sort.

A bird above, Toth thought, watching blackbirds exchange
trees, *could discern the shape.*

Toth started from the courtyard towards a deer that entered the manor. He trailed the animal up a flight of stone
stairs canopied by weeds. He entered a dark passage that twin
doors once barred. A weathered Red Hen remained on stone
at the base of the threshold. Tom followed Toth, and the huffing stags followed Tom. Ash, deer pellets, leaves, and shards
of wood laced the floor inside.

232 & COY HALL

The feeble-minded deer did not mind Toth's intrusion. The animal made no attempt to gauge his intentions. Rather, it moved by rote, going about its business. The ritual began in the hollowed-out antechamber, moved through a study of blackened books, and then entered a final bedroom. A headboard had melted into the wall here, maintaining its shape. A window cavity, penetrated by vine, opened to a stand of beech trees. The ground, a stone slab rather than dirt, was swept clean of ash. A door with an iron handle, unsullied, waited in the floor at the far corner.

The stags stepped into the bedroom, filling the quarters, as the smaller deer passed back into the hall, tracing its rune.

If they were going to gore us, they would've done so already, Toth reasoned. *They're apparitions, real as they seem,* he reminded himself. *They're incapable of harming you.* Believing was not an easy task under the circumstances, but he persevered.

Toth knelt and gripped the cool handle.

Tom shuffled, oscillating his gaze between his master and the stags.

"They're phantasms," Toth said to the greyhound. "Remember the woodsman."

The door possessed nothing to bar it, so Toth pulled it open. Sunlight over his shoulder illumined the cavern below.

Jesus Christ in Heaven, he thought, jarred by the sight.

On a rock lay the coiled form a man, shrunken to a size that was little more than that of a child. The form was without clothing, the skin bloodless and grotesque. Of its limbs, one leg remained, long and malformed, while the other leg was gnawed to the hip. Ragged sinew spilled from the socket. The arms were misshapen, the fingers reduced to bone.

On the right forearm was a tattoo, and the tattoo was that of the Red Hen.

So, this is what became of Jaroslav the Arsonist, Toth thought.

The man was in an advanced state of suffering, rotten except for a firing brain and nerves. His body was drained. There was no blood in the open cavity at his hip, no blood wetting the sinew, no blood in the chewed holes covering his stomach and groin. His facial features had decayed into a puddle in which maggots swam rather than crawled. The eyes were emotionless black knots that darted in the liquid flesh.

Rat and roach scavengers had entered his chamber. Their debris filled the stone corners.

The stench that rose from the vault was that of putrefaction, trapped to an almost poisonous state in the sarcophagus. Vinegar Tom's tail trilled at the odor. Toth touched the dog to calm him.

A deer passed through the stags to enter, observed the scene with indifference, and passed through the stags to exit.

Toth studied the repulsive figure and deduced his conclusion.

The case of the Red Hen was not one of shapeshifting, nor was it a simple matter of a criminal in hiding.

A deity, or a spirit that desired to gain the rank, reduced Jaroslav the Arsonist to this state of existence. Perchance, the arsonist dabbled, invoked, was subsequently overcome, and then paid the price. The old forests possessed many forgotten spirits, some created by God, some by man, some by lower animals, some worshipped, some feared, some ignored. Whatever it was that Jaroslav conjured, it kept him entombed in the ruins, using him. No blood meant no vessel for the man's soul, so he was as much a shell as the manor he burned.

If the villagers of Erlendorf are willing to pay, I could unearth the culprit.

No, Toth thought then. *I say to Hell with the lot of them. Endris won't live to experience the wrath of the thing responsible for this. My interest might not end there, but my concern does.*

Toth looked into the darting eyes.

I imagine, Jaroslav, that your preservation is necessary for the fires. Why else would the thing keep you alive? It uses the fear of your Red Hen. In pagan times, this would've preceded worship. The festival, the fear, the symbol—all would beget a cult. The ambitious thing you conjured usurped your symbol.

The genesis of a cult, an extraordinary thing.

"*Et in Arcadia ego,*" Toth said. Even in Arcadia, there am I.

He watched Vinegar Tom.

"Unfortunately, for the sake of Endris the Miller, we must kill it," he said.

Tom, emboldened, leapt into the rancid vault. Toth hung his legs over the edge and followed. His boots crunched insect husks. The chamber was four feet deep. The floor upon which the stags stood was level with Toth's chest. He removed the knife from the scabbard at his waist.

Another deer, oblivious, entered and exited the room.

The stags huffed, stomped, and bawled, making a show of their anger.

The woodsman's voice, the final act of desperation, sounded from the corridor. He shuffled through the ash.

"It'd be shame to see a good hound laid waste," he echoed. "It'd be a shame—"

Tom sniffed the withered man, made a circle around his slab, and, when the shape offered no resistance, he took the neck between his teeth. The thing's mouth, or the indentation that constituted a mouth, quivered. A maggot squirmed through his liquid cheek, spilling down to his ear.

Tom gnawed, but death in such a manner would take minutes.

It was evident that Jaroslav experienced pain. His eyes quickened.

God forgive me, Toth thought.

He brought down the blade, opening a chest as delicate as a rotten gourd.

The stags were vanquished, and the woodsman silenced, as three apparitions blinked from the ruins. More apparitions, unseen by Toth and Tom, blinked from existence on the surrounding hills.

With the fork to Erlendorf approaching, the watchtower loomed. Toth kept his eyes to the dirt, hoping to avoid more interaction with the soldiers.

As he came into sight, however, a guard stood at the mouth of the road, waving his arm.

"Ho there, gypsy," the man called. "Endris the Miller sent word."

Toth approached. The dog sauntered past.

"Hold up, Tom," he called. He adjusted his satchel and stepped into the grass that surrounded the tower.

"Does he wish for me to see him?" Toth asked.

"I said what I said this morning. We don't want you here, gypsy. He sent word is all. He would've remained to speak, but he is too ill."

"Very kind of you to relay the message. What is it?"

"The Red Hen is gone from the wheel, the miller says."

Toth smiled with relief. "Very well," he said. "Very good."

The soldier shook his head.

"That troubles you, friend?"

"Certainly, it does. It could be my home next."

"For now, I believe you're safe from such a thing."

Vinegar Tom circled back, his tail erect.

"Ho there, what's that in your hound's jaws?"

"Looks to be a skein of hair. I told him he couldn't take it home," Toth said, "but he rarely listens."

The soldier grimaced. "On with you, gypsy," he said, "and don't return."

"I won't," Toth promised. "Even when you send for me."

ZACHARY ROSENBERG

THE GODS
THAT DRIFT
WITH US

THE land between Mirador and Venice was vast for the great stretch of space it encompassed, but it was only empty because it was godless.

Alejandra Kahan had crossed that vast and empty land to return to the lakeside village of Mirador six decades after her family's exile from the newly united Spain. Standing upon the prow of the boat, steered onward by her silent bodyguard Beatriz, she dared to hope for answers that had eluded her people since the Diaspora. She could feel the power from the waters beneath them, her gaze drawn to the banks. Where a great shrine had once resided at the banks of the lake, now there were only burnt remnants by this majestic stretch of water.

They had come to the right place.

Alejandra was a tall woman, though Beatriz still towered above her. While Alejandra was slender and lean, Beatriz's body was thick with muscle. While Alejandra's black hair fell to her shoulders loosely, Beatriz's was short, her brown bangs covering her broad forehead.

Alejandra wore a simple traveling pack, and no symbol of faith adorned her neck. It was dangerous for even *conversos* in Spain these days, where the Inquisition hounded them relentlessly. In remote villages like Mirador, it might be a death sentence. Villagers were rarely less zealous than those who wore the Inquisitors' robes, their frenzies often fatal.

"We are here, Beatriz." It pleased Alejandra to speak Hebrew, a reminder of what Spain had not been able to rob from her people. "We have returned at last." Sixty years since her people had been driven from this territory. She was the first of them to set foot back in this land in the fourteen hundredth and sixty third year of the so-called Lord. Through all the lands of Italy and Spain, Alejandra and Beatriz had walked in places notable for the absence of Gods. They had encountered the licentious and the avaricious, those who knelt beneath crosses expecting to be showered in golden ducats.

Beatriz did not speak, calm and reserved as ever. She helped Alejandra to shore, turning her face in the direction of the village, betraying no emotion.

"We will be in time for the festivals shortly," Alejandra reminded her, speaking to reassure herself more than her bodyguard. Her God drifted alongside her, she reminded herself. Even here, there was no danger.

But Alejandra knew her God was her ally, beside her at all times. Scarcely had they begun their walk when Alejandra saw a group of men hacking away at a downed tree. Alejandra called a greeting and the men's eyes turned to see a stranger in their midst, their whispers falling silent so Alejandra might hear her own footsteps while she trod upon their roads. She hid her apprehension behind the veil of a friendly smile, knowing that the first impressions might decide everything.

"My name is Alejandra! My companion and I are travelers seeking sanctuary for this night!"

The men of Mirador dipped their heads, huddled as though in secret conspiracy with furtive smiles lighting sun-darkened faces. Alejandra followed their gazes, their eyes fixing upon Beatriz with wonder, for she rose head and shoulders above any of them. The men then focused back upon Alejandra with wolfish stares, lupine smiles frozen upon their faces.

"Welcome," one called out. He was a tall man, powerfully built, the axe in his hand more the toy of a child than a weapon or tool. "Have you traveled long?"

Alejandra had only ever needed to learn Italian in addition to Hebrew, but she had honed and perfected her Spanish before she had set out upon her journey.

"Days upon the road. Aragon is our destination. We are meeting family there." She adopted the most vacant of smiles with her thin lips. "My cousin is mute, but a good laborer.

Our kin are merchants in the city. We have the coin to pay for lodgings."

"We have an inn," the axeman said with a gesture down the road. "You are not far from the town!" His smile could not have been more inviting if he had escorted them to pull the door open for Alejandra himself. "Your coin is no good in Mirador, Madame. We always receive visitors around this time of year. Please stay and enjoy our hospitality. We would not want you to miss our festival."

"Festival?" Alejandra asked, feigning surprise as she blinked her dark eyes with questioning sincerity. "I was not aware of such a thing this time of year?"

"It is the festival of the wood, Madame," another man called out. "To the saints, so they may bless us with good harvest!" He gestured to the woods around them, shadows shifting in time to the tender sway of the trees.

Alejandra pretended to consider it, turning to consult with Beatriz. "Would it take too long out of our journey, Beatriz?" Beatriz shook her head slowly. "Wonderful! It has been so long since we have known a celebration!"

She waved to the men, who waved back, directing her where to go. She and Beatriz walked on, down the path through the woods for the village ahead.

Mirador meant "lookout," the town having been built upon the north of Spain to overlook the water, not far from the pools and lakes that meant it was only accessible by boat, a peninsula unto itself. Alejandra could smell the smoke from the village over the thick copse of trees. They were getting close.

She walked upon the brown and fertile soil. Trees stretched up in all directions, the pools of water clear and blue all about her. She paid no attention, walking forth to Mirador, a town without walls. The buildings were made of wood and stone, coming into view while Alejandra walked forth, flanked by trees.

She felt eyes upon her, from the woods. Through the thick canopies, between gnarled and grasping bars of wood, she could sense the furtive movements in the wilderness. She walked forth, fist clenching at her side. Alejandra forced her fear downward, frigid nails in her stomach as she realized she had reached her long-cherished goal.

Beatriz walked beside her, a mighty, silent shadow. Alejandra smiled, the presence of her guard buoying her confidence.

"Thank you," she murmured to Beatriz. Beatriz did not respond, though Alejandra believed she could see the barest smile upon her guard's placid features. Without Beatriz, Alejandra knew she could never have come this far.

They were in time for the time of giving, the festival of Mirador. Alejandra had come prepared. She told herself again she did not need to fear, not with Beatriz and her God beside her. Both comforted her in equal measure, even if the fear of the deep and dark woods could not be fully chased away.

Alejandra's feet rested upon old soil and though pains had been taken to disguise it, she could feel the burnt remnants of old foundations that had been scorched to the marrows of the earth. She could feel the memories all around her, whispers for vindication that refused to silence their rasps in her ear.

Alejandra bowed politely and set her course to the inn. It was placed next to a modest church with a cross in front bedecked with leaves and flowers. Near one of the walls was a wood carving of the Christian savior, a floral crown shaped around his brow, his smile beatific and wide.

She passed it to enter the inn, murmuring to God for strength. She clasped a hand over her heart, desperation bleeding from her words as she pushed herself onward. For many years, Alejandra's people had worshiped here as they would, glared at with suspicion and envy all the while. Her people were allowed to exist, but never quite accepted. Alejandra had lived it in Venice, glared at with suspicion by the Christian citizenry. She had seen her people spat on and cursed for engaging in banking, even as it was one of the few professions the authorities would allow her people to partake in. She had lived comfortably in the Jewish Quarter but was never accepted. Always isolated, sneered at.

The fervor with which their good, devout Spanish neighbors had taken to the persecutory fury had been relayed to Alejandra by her grandfather. Their homes had been burned, their property seized. The symbols and houses of their worship had been razed to the ground and the ashes scattered throughout the woods.

Her people had been forced into boats, upon threat of death. Nobody in Mirador, nor anywhere else, had bestirred themselves to care what might become of them in their exile. They were sent to drift and drift alone, like so much flotsam. To drift and drown if that was the will of the heavens, taking their God with them.

Never had her own parents been able to reassure her that she was safe in the land where she had been born. Nor any other. Not even her mother's studies of the Kabbalah could secure that. Alejandra had known from an early age that eternal vigilance was the price of her security.

There were likely none yet living who would recognize Alejandra for what she was in Mirador. Six decades were so far removed from the event as to be eternity. Nobody could have imagined such a return. They were only delighted that someone had arrived in time for their harvest festival.

The wind tickled the trees, the leaves rattling with soft laughter. The woods darkened behind Alejandra while she and Beatriz crossed the threshold into the inn. Behind a desk of aged wood was an elderly woman, creases on her cheeks deepening as she witnessed Alejandra arrive. "I am here for the festival," Alejandra said mildly. Her voice was meek supplication, the tender request of the wayward lamb. "I am looking for a room."

"A room you shall have," the woman said firmly. She bade Alejandra follow her, down a small hallway. "Shall your companion have a second room?"

"Beatriz stays with me," Alejandra said. Beatriz nodded in response, her thick arms threaded through their packs. "I will require food. We have dined upon nothing but berries and tubers for the past few days."

"Yes, of course. Food and wine, fine wine. We have stew tonight, made of hare and deer alike." The woman's smile was boastful. "From the woods. The woods provide."

"I am honored by your hospitality," Alejandra said as the door swung open with a whining creak to expose a room with a small bed and no windows.

"Are you so certain that we cannot interest your companion in another room? I would not wish her to be uncomfortable if she sleeps upon the floor. Such a hale and hearty lass she is."

"Beatriz will be fine," Alejandra assured the innkeeper with nothing more than a smile and a wave of her hand. "But she appreciates your concern. Forgive her silence, she was rendered mute as a child."

"But of course," the woman said, turning her eyes over Alejandra's face. "Have we seen you here before, my dear?" She studied Beatriz closely, her brow furrowing. "I would remember such a woman as she, and yet I feel such familiarity from her."

"I am afraid Beatriz was born from the soil of *Italia*." Alejandra's smile was as harmless as an empty scabbard. She slid a hand to her companion's arm, thick as a mighty branch. The innkeeper excused herself as Alejandra allowed her tired feet to rest, her body cradled by the softness of the sheets while Beatriz remained standing over her, an ever-watchful sentinel.

The stew was thick with chunks of hare and deer, flavored with rich spices. A small plate of fresh fruit rested beside the bowl. After confirming the stew contained neither pork nor cream, Alejandra passed the bowl to Beatriz. Her guard took a spoonful in a huge hand, sipping slowly. She placed the spoon back in the bowl and pushed it back to Alejandra, who devoured it in short order, pleased it was not tainted.

She murmured a prayer over the wine. Sweet and tart all at once, the liquid was a deep purple color. The innkeeper had told her the berries came from the woods, harvested regularly by the men of Mirador.

"You will be staying with us long? The festival is not to be missed."

"Beatriz and I are expected soon in Aragon." Alejandra feigned contemplation for a moment, her brow furrowing at the plea in the woman's face. "But I suppose a day or two shall make no difference."

Though there was no window in her room, Alejandra felt her gaze pulled again to the woods. She stood in a village that had sought to purge its past, to erase her people and strike them from their records with blood as a cheaper substitute to ink. They had settled with their kin in Italy, confined to the quarters of Venice, joining exiles from England and France.

They had endlessly drifted away from their homes with faith as their most stalwart companion. With a long-cherished dream at last fulfilled, Mirador witnessed at long last, Alejandra sank into the bed and slept, cradled in silk.

She awoke to Beatriz pushing her shoulder delicately. Her eyes fluttered open in the dark and Beatriz tugged her to her feet, though Alejandra murmured protestations. The shadows in the inn were the shade of dull pitch, but Alejandra's ears detected the noises outside. The firm crackle of flames and the clicking of steel set upon steel. Beatriz gestured, but Alejandra shook her head, donning her shift and slowly opening the door.

She crept down the hallway, down the small inn with no other breathing soul in sight. Beatriz was a silent shadow at her back, Alejandra finding the entrance, a portal back into Mirador.

She gazed upon the villagers, swaying as one in a single line before the trees. The woods shivered as though receiving their worship, Alejandra concealed from sight as to witness what she had expected.

No Christian crosses adorned the people before her; strange symbols hung around their throats, their faces masked by wood and clay carved to resemble the features of bestial things from the times before man. Before the woods, they bent and writhed. They danced, holding blades in their hands and sang in hymns from a tongue older than Iberia itself.

Mirador was a remote village. The superficial trappings of Christianity by day would be enough to fool the Church and allow them to practice their true vocation far from the eyes of the Inquisition.

And doubtlessly the murder of the Jews had convinced the Inquisition the good villagers of Mirador were nothing but devout. The Inquisition had withdrawn its eye in ignorance, but now Alejandra watched.

The people of Mirador waltzed before the woods. In their midst was a lamb, bleating out in frightened fervor as it struggled against the fetters that bound it. It shrieked when its throat was opened, the blood spilling before the earth. Alejandra felt pity for the creature, keeping her position as the villagers knelt as one before the woods.

The shadows grew dim, and Alejandra could hear something moving through the trees. Slow, stealthy, though measured as though it wanted to be heard. Her eyes pierced the umbral gloom and beheld a shape that was not borne of mankind. Its head was crowned as a stag's, its eyes orange moons. The blood from the lamb ran to the ground, a steady little river that flowed into the woods, past the trees. Alejandra crept from her hiding place by the church. The villagers had removed the church by night and replaced the image of Christ. In the torchlight, Alejandra beheld this Yeshua's smile was full of sharp teeth, the flowers he wore decorated with bone.

Alejandra doubted there was a single true Christian left in Mirador now. The Pagans had decades to convert or slay all such believers, with the trappings of Christian faith serving only as the lure into a trap. Alejandra could not have cared less for the fate of papists. Her chief concern now was what lurked in those woods.

The people intoned again, behind their masks as they knelt and prayed. Alejandra knew what she beheld: she saw a god.

It was a god that had drifted here long ago, for she knew the old stories. A god that had brought its followers in an unholy melding of old ways and new. Alejandra knew the blood being shed was to nourish the thing in the trees, the ancient god that blessed the village with harvest and crops.

But gods were possessed of hungers older than the earth. Gods required acts of devotion, tokens of worship before they might cast favors unto their followers.

It was a festival without a name, yet it was one she had expected. The God of the Wood beckoned, uncurling a thin and tenebrous digit. It pointed in Alejandra's direction and one by one, masked faces turned to her. Hungry eyes glittered through the darkness, the moon reflecting upon gleaming blades.

They advanced upon her as one, men and women alike. They came silently, more extensions of what lurked in those woods than as individuals. A faceless mass of fanatics bearing the weight of devotion upon their shoulders.

Alejandra did not fear. Beatriz was with her. Her own God was with her. She turned and did as they expected; she ran, the act of a frightened lamb. Alejandra called Beatriz's name and her companion raced alongside her with shocking swiftness for a woman of her height and bulk.

Alejandra heard them at her back, hurtling herself headlong from Mirador, a victim in flight. She ran from the village, along the paths that flanked the woods. She ran across a land that was vast for stretches of miles. She ran across a land that belonged to a dark and hungry god.

"Beatriz! Beatriz, with me!" Alejandra shouted her companion's name. They were at her heels, ravening wolves that sought to hamstring her and take her so the ruler of their pack might sup on her blood and marrow, granting them plentiful harvest in turn.

In the woods, she sensed their great ruler in its ravenous majesty. Her lungs burnt as the lake came into view, black crystal waters behind a wreckage where a shrine had once stood.

She stumbled forth, falling into the waters. The cold embrace drew her in, and she came up sputtering. The villagers had paused, their god behind the trees, even its burning eyes not enough to erase the darkness of the woods about it.

Beatriz flung herself in front of Alejandra, arms outstretched. Alejandra watched the blades bite into Beatriz's flesh, her guard making not a sound. Beatriz stumbled back, the waters darkening as her wounds wept into the lake. The villagers paused there, a sudden trepidation overtaking them.

They halted at the edge of the waters. Alejandra discerned a primal fear in their eyes and the trembling hesitation in their limbs. A smile spread over Alejandra's face as she came to her feet. She stepped back, feeling the water come up to her hips. She did her best to look concerned for Beatriz.

"Take them," one man urged. "The big one is wounded."

Indeed, the waters around Beatriz were stained darker still, a black ink that blotted away the reflection of the round moon.

"Into the water?" Another man asked, his voice halting and weak.

The God of the Wood rumbled its displeasure, the clopping of cloven hooves upon the earth drawing nearer.

"There's nothing there anymore," the first man protested. "Take her, before He grows displeased." They followed her into the waters, sinking to their ankles, hesitating

"You would not want that, would you?" Alejandra ran her hands through the cold waters, awaiting them. Her smile was triumphant.

Vengeful.

"Years ago, the Inquisition drove my people from these lands. The hidden Pagans of Mirador used us as a shield to hide your ways and joined the slaughter before converting this village. For years, you have remained hidden with your worship, your prosperity purchased with the lives of Jews. You used our blood to feed your drifting god," she called. "But in our flight, we saw another you had wounded. Another you had devastated. One whose shrines you burnt. One in whom we recognized a kindred soul. One who did not take our worship, but our companionship."

THE GODS THAT DRIFT WITH US ❧ 249

Alejandra's scriptures said that Hashem, God of the He-brews would not allow any other gods before Him. Hashem was rather mute on gods allowed to walk beside her.

Beatriz rose and swept her hair from her forehead. It was not blood that poured from her wounds, but thick, dark clay. Her forehead was exposed and upon it were golden words "EMETH," the word for "Truth" in Alejandra's mother tongue.

With curved fingers, Beatriz reached to her own stomach and began to pull. She pried open her own body, unfurling it. There was no blood, just an outpouring of clay that ran into the waters. Alejandra's mother studied the Kabbalah for years; the result was embodied in the mighty golem who had been by Alejandra's side since childhood.

From the hollow earth within Beatriz, something spilled into the waters. Something thick, dark, and scaled, with eyes that burnt with a fire of revenge that it shared with Alejandra. The God of the Wood faltered and took a halting step back, for it knew what the waters now held.

One man screamed and was pulled downward, his cry swallowed first by the water and then by something else. The once-still lake became a chaotic tempest. The men and women of Mirador were pulled into the depths, flailing and shrieking as they learned of older hungers than they might have dreamed.

Alejandra watched, floating beside Beatriz, who offered her a confident smile. Alejandra put a hand to her cheek, feel-ing the warmth of a life that pulsed so brightly, whether it was clay or flesh. She kissed the words of Hebrew on Beatriz's head as the screams continued.

Gods were creatures of sacrifice and rapacity, ancient and with long memories. They were beings possessed of mighty grudges and mightier hungers. Alejandra remained without fear, even as the darker shadows in the water grew and grew, something coiled and sinuous sliding there as the flesh and blood of its sacrifices renewed it. Strengthened it.

The God of the Wood had once faced a weakened being, starved and robbed of worship. It now faced something more ancient, pulling it to the waters from its sanctuary of the trees.

And though the woods were full of depth and darkness, deeper and darker still were the waters.

Alejandra watched. She waited. She heard the thrashing and the inhuman howls that might have been fury or pleas for mercy. Beatriz held her, shielding her. The golem's smile was confident and gentle, the eternal reassurance. Alejandra put a hand to Beatriz's warm, dark cheek, gazing tenderly at the friend who was far more than construct or guard to her. She waited until the fight was over.

The god that had drifted here with Alejandra, contained within the golem, stilled its motions at last, victorious. Of its rival, there was no sign. Something brushed against Alejandra in the water, and she gazed down at the great body that now returned to the depths it had longed for.

"How I envy you," Alejandra murmured. "For you have come home. Something we cannot do."

Beatriz as ever was silent, but the God of the Lake and the waters shuddered in sympathy. Alejandra took herself from the water and Beatriz took up mud from the banks. The golem placed the mud upon herself, sealing the hole she had crafted. Alejandra heard a splash behind her, facing the unbroken, stilled surface of a lake with no reflection of a moon anymore.

The blood had drowned it away.

She looked at woods and a town that were now truly godless, the smile on her face lingering. She would burn down the church before the night was through. Any survivors would fear her too much to retaliate.

Just as it had happened before. There were yet other gods Beatriz contained who had drifted in the Diaspora with their friends and protectors.

There would be more Miradors. Alejandra's vengeance was far from over.

A smile lingering on her lips, she set back on her way to town with Beatriz silent at her side. Alejandra prepared to walk again through a land that was vast for the great stretch of space it encompassed. And empty because it was godless.

Save perhaps for the gods drifting with her.

J. M. FAULKNER

RADEGAST

A DOLLOP of sweat kited from the bridge of Honza's nose and splashed the toe of his hiking boot. Wind blew the map in his hands ragged. Ahead of him, Miroslava scaled the flysch outcrop with the finesse of a mountain goat. At sixty-nine, she weighed little more than a feather, and was by far the sprier of them.

"*Pospěšte si, městští chlapci,*" she called into the bluster. *Hurry along, city boys.* She grabbed a protruding tree root and bounded onto the grassy rise overhead, where the ground gave way to a cliff.

Panting, Honza leaned his head on the bedrock that had come up beside him. When he rested his eyes, it only wrung more sweat from his forehead. Could be his pores were intent on sweating out the night's plum brandy, Miroslava's *slivovice.* His heart pounded in the dark of his eyelids.

Dear Lord, how was she doing it? He was twenty-two, for heaven's sake, and slivovice or no, he should have—

Vilém lurched beside him, skidding on stones grinding underfoot. Mister Perfect at least had the decency to look flustered.

"You look a little green," he said, scanning Honza from shoelaces to dripping fringe. He chuckled and grabbed the strap of Honza's rucksack. "Let me hel—"

Honza snatched it away. "Don't!"

Vilém threw up his hands, retreating. Brow bunched in a look of derision, not outrage, he said, "Suit yourself."

Miroslava's Alsatian, Dubček, had come to a stop not far from where the brothers had flared up. Ears bent, the dog pocketed his lathered tongue and leered reproachfully.

Guilty in the Canine Court. Just what Honza needed.

They trudged after their grandmother without word and joined her on the crest overlooking the valley below. Her arms were crossed behind her back, cupping her twig-thin elbows. She stood bolt upright, as if in anticipation of an audience, and didn't stir when Honza and Vilém dumped their rucksacks in the gravel behind.

The brothers looked at one another. Vilém cocked an eyebrow: *What the hell?* Honza shrugged: *Beats me.*

Miroslava said, *"Nemyslíš, že lesy jsou jako kostely?"*

Don't you think that forests are like churches?

All around them the thick and ancient canopy of the beech forest carpeted the Beskid Mountain range. The density was such that the sun scarcely touched the forest floor, though humidity fairly permeated within the steel-grey trunks. Titanic trunks, Honza thought, that reduced the hikers stumbling through them to insignificant, ground-dwelling things.

"Škoda, že nepřišla tvoje matka." Miroslava sighed, hunching a little. *"Možná má Anglii radši než rodinu."* *It's a shame your mother didn't come. Perhaps she likes England better than family.*

When Vilém made no defense of their mother, Honza took a step in the gravel and said she would never forget the sight of Soviet tanks crossing the Vltava, fleeing home with twins in her belly, nor the student that—

His Czech dried up in his mouth. He looked to the nearest beech, where Vilém rested his cheek on a bough. His brother had always taken Czech language seriously, reading and re-reading books by Kundera and Kafka, and sneered at Honza for not doing the same. But he doubted even Vilém knew the word for self-immolation.

Miroslava turned and drew in her chin, as though repulsed by an eye-watering stink. She said everyone knows about Jan

Palach. Your mother left Czechoslovakia behind—see how those who couldn't flee suffered?

What could he say to that? Less than a year ago, there were two kinds of people: those who lived west of the Berlin Wall, and those who didn't.

Honza exhaled through his nostrils. "Mum didn't—"

Miroslava asked if their mother had at least told them the family legend.

The brothers peered at one another, wondering if one of them had heard it but kept it from the other. A family legend? That was an interesting prospect—like finding out a long-lost uncle had died rich.

Miroslava went red in the face, pumped her fists and squawked. Perhaps that beat weeping in front of the grandchildren she had met for the first time only forty-eight hours earlier.

To the squawk, Dubček let out a bark that echoed around the valley.

Miroslava scratched him between the ears, her petite hand disappearing into the fur. She recounted the family legend.

Afterward, Vilém turned on Honza with a face of contempt. "She's right, you know. Mother should be here."

———

Don't you think that forests are like churches?

Honza closed his eyes and listened: behind peals of birdsong, the knock of a woodpecker, the soft caressing of leaves—the aroma of nuts, berries, and wet earth—there existed a sacred quiet. A stillness.

Trekking through a thicket of steepled pines became all the more tranquil for the storm that had battered Miroslava's cottage through the night, the groaning timbers that had followed Honza into sleep, and saw him dreaming of an old brig cresting Atlantic waves. Dubček whining from the cupboard. Vicious winds that even now Honza felt as a dying zephyr upon his neck.

But the forest tempered his rage, smoothed it out like pastry dough on a long, flat kitchen surface. He brushed a trunk with his fingertips, satisfied with the metaphor. The forest was a rolling pin thinning the bile in his blood.

Is that what Miroslava had meant? That however the world wronged you, in the forest you could turn the other cheek? Forgive?

Church was anything but reconciling when they were children. Honza could weave a tapestry of the scene behind his eyelids: naves, echoes, flickering wicks and candle wax—the pinches he and his bored brother inflicted on the soft, easy-to-bruise flesh of their underarms. The pew creaking, their flustered mother hissing "Don't fidget", the tutting congregation sitting so piously firm through the sermons that Honza imagined motes of dust settling on their Sunday best.

And yet he was eager to visit the small Orthodox Chapel atop Mount Radhošť.

A church within a 'church'.

Vilém was more interested in seeing—

"Well, fuck."

The outburst jolted Honza out of his thoughts. Neither of them had said more than a few words since leaving their grandmother an hour earlier, each cautious of the sharp retort the other might make to an innocuous comment. Better to keep *stum*.

The trail ahead was smothered in deadfall. A great cleft had been torn from the escarpment above, and a monstrous tangle of brush and fallen trees now hung precariously over the mountain shoulder. A couple of dead, leafless snags fidgeted in loose soil nearby, threatening to make another landslide of the debris.

Hackles raised, Dubček slinked to the nearest trunk blocking their path and sniffed the shredded bark.

Honza unzipped his rucksack and took out a thermos flask. Across the deadfall, a red flag was painted on the bark of a steadfast oak, pointing them up the mountain. "There goes the hike, I guess."

Vilém tipped his head back and rinsed his mouth with water from his own flask. He gestured to their right, where the slope opened into a narrow gully piled with dead leaves. "We should go around."

Honza gritted his teeth. Was just like Mr. Perfect to snap his fingers and, hey presto, conjure a detour. As if the deadfall wasn't omen enough to turn back. Come to think of it, when had he ever seen something so...*impressive?*

"The summit is that way." Honza stabbed a forefinger at the red flag. "Miroslava warned against straying."

"Hm." Vilém clicked his tongue. "You mean *Grandma?*"

Honza shut his own tongue behind his incisors. Spending two days with an old, selfish bat in twenty-two years didn't make her *his* grandma, not by a long shot.

"Well, we can't crawl through it," Vilém said, already packing his flask away and trudging into the gully, leaves rustling against his trousers. Dubček dove in after him, swimming up to his neck in the foliage. Vilém called out, "Not unless you want to be skewered like a fricking shish kebab? Hey, don't look at me like that. At least it'll be an adventure, won't it?"

Fifteen minutes later, according to the arms on Honza's wristwatch, and thoroughly lost, the brother's scaled the slippery gully bank into the forest proper. The bed of leaves had preserved moisture from the night's storm, and they had been forced to squat under deadfall spanning the gully, ensuring a good dunk in the sopping greenery.

Honza clapped the sludge from his palms and removed the map from his rucksack. The names of landmarks were hard to make out, the bluster having given the paper a solid thrashing earlier. A raindrop walloped the map, suffusing in all directions and discoloring the print. The wind was picking up, yet again. He sighed his most aggravating sigh.

Vilém didn't take the bait. "We know which way is up." He made a cap of his fingers and arched his neck. "We can find another trail down from the summit. Get home before dinner, if we're lucky."

Honza scowled at the gully behind. He could kill his brother now, beat him senseless with the weight of his stainless-steel thermos flask, coat him in a grave of leaves if he liked hiking so damn much, and he'd be long gone before anyone suspected anything.

Don't you think that forests are like churches?
Forests are hushed. Like funerals.

Climbing Radhošť where the trees were thinnest, Vilém asked, "Who do you think the man was, the one in Grandma's story?"

Honza chewed his underlip. He reminded himself of the promise he had made to their mother: get along with Vilém. He pushed a branch out of his path. "Not sure what to think, really. Maybe she made it up."

"It's an allegory," Vilém said, leading them upward, ignoring Honza's last remark. "There's a deeper meaning. Something."

"Yeah?"

"Think about it: all those people traveling mile after mile across the Carpathians, outsiders everywhere. Might've been shameful if somebody caught you rolling in the hay with, say…a Jew or Gypsy."

"Lots of *Vlachs* journeyed from Transylvania through the mountains," Honza grumbled, tired of speculation, tired of walking, and all out of patience for his brother. "Hell, could be a Jew or Dracula himself."

Vilém fell quiet. And not a happy quiet.

"All right, smartarse," he said, "who do you think it was?"

"I don't think," Honza hissed through his teeth. "But—but! It could have been a bad man, a bad man who spotted a peasant girl alone in the fields and took what he wanted. And in that case, maybe Great-Grandma Zita concocted a wee story. What else do you tell your deeply religious parents when your belly starts swelling? What's safer? Feed them a superstition. And I don't want to rain on your parade, but if you were Grandma, what version of the tale would you believe? You'd parrot the family legend."

What Vilém said next, he muttered under his breath, but there was no hiding it in the pitter-patter of rain: "You're such a prick."

"Sorry, what?" His brother was storming ahead. Honza called after him, "Hate to break it to you, Vilém, but the Tooth Fairy ain't real."

Vilém spun on his heels and punched Honza clean across the jaw.

In darkness, Honza felt the hard, unforgiving earth catch him. A tree root drove into his lumbar spine. Dubček barked in alarm, and ever so distantly, Vilém stammered something placatory in a warbling voice.

A great shadow beat in front of Honza's face: his eyelids exerting themselves against closing consciousness. He watched Vilém's gangly, jittering silhouette inch toward him in snapshots.

"Honza? Jesus…Honza?"

Just then, a monolithic snag towered over Vilém's shoulder—a spying villain from on high, a demon conjured for episodes of paralytic sleep.

But Honza smiled.

Radegast? Look, Vilém, there's the statue of your pagan god. The hike wasn't a waste of time, after all.

"Honza, are you…laughing?"

The Slavic deity leaned to, closer and closer, as though to whisper in Vilém's ear.

Before Honza's eyelids lost their battle, the earth shook beneath his outstretched body, Vilém screamed, and Dubček whined like a tire going flat.

———

A willow-thin girl walked through the field, picking cabbages for the wicker basket that rocked to and fro on her hip. She wore a white, button-down dress and an apron covered in soil: Zita Vaculíková, born to a family of Vlach shepherds in 1899. When she wasn't gathering vegetables at the foot of Mount Radhošť, she enjoyed the stories her grandfather told her about how their family had crossed the Carpathians from Transylvania. Nearing adulthood, she spotted the inconsistencies in his retellings but didn't mind.

Honza scarcely had time to question how he knew all this or ponder how he came to be spying on his long-dead ancestor, when the rat-a-tat-tat of rain punctuated by Vilém's wailing untethered him from the vision.

Pain. Pain unlike anything Honza had ever experienced. He felt as though his legs were being steadily submerged in lava, stripping the flesh from his bones. He bolted upright from sleep, howling.

The snag lay across his shins, crushing them against the packed earth beneath. He heaved against the smooth, bare trunk with all his might. It didn't budge. He swung at it, bruising the meat of his palms, and went at it again and again with all his strength, forehead beading sweat.

Nothing.

His head spun. He slumped to one elbow and threw up the morning's scrambled eggs. A bubble burst from his nostril and trickled down his chin.

Vilém lay face-down in the dirt a few feet away, a patch of blood and mud smeared across his stubble. The snag lay across the back of his thighs. "Water," he croaked. Honza wasn't the only one to have screamed himself hoarse.

He groped for the straps of his rucksack but couldn't find them. Twisting, he spotted it lying just out of reach, where the ground dipped. Fuck.

Teeth gritted, he dropped his left hip and bent toward Vilém. Pain shot through his legs, whistled in his ears. He unzipped the rucksack on Vilém's back and fumbled the flask into his brother's hands. Vilém accepted greedily, propped himself up on his elbows so that he appeared to emerge, sphinxlike, from the snag and poured the water down his throat.

"How long was I out?" Honza asked. He tasted vomit.

Vilém swallowed. "Dunno. T-ten minutes?" His eyes appeared to be wandering in their sockets, but vaguely he looked at Honza's legs. "Bad?"

Honza wiggled his toes. No, he tried to wiggle his toes but felt nothing. He shook his head. "And you?"

"I heard a s-snap, Jesus Christ, but I can't m-move the trunk. And I've tried and tried." He gnawed his sleeve, warding off the pain.

Dubček lay nearby, watching with his snout propped between his forepaws, emitting a soft whine. But he didn't appear hurt.

"Get help," Honza yelled, and the Alsatian raised his head. "Babička, Mirsola—home! Jdi domů!"

Dubček merely stared.

"We need to tell someone we're here," Honza wheezed. Vilém blurred in front of him. He looked like an overly diluted water painting. "Miroslava warned against straying from the trail, said park rangers would clear it for hikers, so that's where we ought to go. Vilém, what if it's days before anyone finds us? Dubček! Move!"

"I've tried that already," said Vilém, sullenly. "He looks miserable enough, but that dog ain't got two brain cells to rub together. No help there."

Honza looked at the snag stretched out across their mangled limbs. "So what now?"

Craning his neck, Vilém nursed hungrily on the flask, his glugging a boisterous echo in the minute clearing in which they were trapped. Water trickled down his chin.

"You should take it easy," Honza said.

The rim came to rest on Vilém's lips. His eyelids flicked open. He screwed the cap back on with a sigh.

"This is bad, isn't it?"

Judging by Vilém's pallor, things were past bad; things were *bad* bad. He had the complexion of a man reaching the transpolar railroad's last stop. A man stepping onto the platform and setting eyes on the gulag where he was to serve his indenture. That wasn't going to improve in the forest, not without immediate medical care.

But there was a chance they could be discovered by park rangers. Before separating, Miroslava had advised them to stick to the main trail, as the rangers would salvage the deadfall and clear it for hikers. If Honza and Vilém waited until they heard chainsaws growling, they could kick and scream until somebody came running.

Then again, Vilém had led them far from the main path. And curiously, when Honza recalled the gully through which they had ascended, he saw a dreary tunnel leading down rather than up, covered by cloying branches that parted at his approach but promptly shut in his wake. Had Vilém hit him so hard?

"I'm sorry I hit you," said Vilém, suddenly, as though reading his mind.

Honza peered up. His brother's gaze was lowered to a patch of dandelions. The apology felt…genuine.

Honza exhaled through his nostrils. It was almost a chuckle. "Suppose I don't really give a shit what you did or said anymore."

Vilém's laugh was cut short by a hiss of pain. "Fuckin' leg."

Dubček trotted over to inspect him. Not knowing what to do next, he set about sniffing Honza's regurgitated breakfast.

"His stomach must be grumbling," Honza said, thinking of pangs in his own stomach.

"Hey, there's some biscuits in my bag, if you want them. Can't reach them myself, though."

Honza bent to one side and removed the biscuits. He tossed one to Dubček and shoveled another in his mouth. He held out the packet and mumbled, "Want one?"

Vilém waved them away.

"Does it…you know?" He nodded where his brother's legs disappeared under the trunk.

"Hurt? Comes in waves. It's k-kind of going numb."

"That's not a good thing, dude. If your legs don't get blood—"

"Hey, I wasn't born yesterday. Let me enjoy whatever relief I can get."

Honza had to respect that. "When the pain subsides, I'm sure your appetite will pick up. We'll need energy."

Vilém said nothing.

"You couldn't have fallen on your backside, could you?" Honza shook his head and tried to inject some levity into his voice. "I almost had the tree off us when pushing. If only we could push together, at the same time…." He trailed off. Dubček was dribbling beside him, chewing the stem of a dandelion. "I'm sure Miroslava will know something's wrong when Muttley doesn't turn up. Can't see us being here more than a night."

As the horizon dimmed, Dubček snuggled between the brothers, his thick coat warm to the touch. For what he lacked in brains, he made up in heart.

Night came but sleep did not. Honza and Vilém made small talk, skirted around uncomfortable topics, and dozed in the brief moments when their pain was outmatched by exhaustion. But the pain kicked in when they quit talking for too long, and the hopelessness of it all. The surrounding canopy flapped, branches creaked, and an unseen owl hooted.

Honza hadn't been afraid of the wind or dark since before he could remember—those were primal fears, but he felt them now, stirring. Only when the sun reared up behind the snag did he feel any relief.

"Good morning," he said, drily.

Vilém looked at him. "Are you making breakfast?"

"I've got biscuits…."

Vilém's lips sashayed on his mouth. "One won't hurt."

The morning wore on and around afternoon they started hollering. Honza pried a stick from the earth and drummed

266 > J. M. FAULKNER

the trunk with it. They yelled until they were hoarse, and the stick had snapped.

Not a sound stirred in the forest.

They lay down exhausted, how they were pinned, neither willing to exert themselves for conversation, until Vilém said, "I had a dream." He shook his head. "Try not to look so shocked, even the worst of brothers have them. I saw Zita, our great-grandmother—" he stayed Honza from speaking with a raised hand "—in the field, and I felt danger."

Honza wanted to tell him he had experienced the same thing but kept stum.

"Don't look at me like that," Vilém said. "You think I'm waffling on about Czechoslovakia again, and I know you hate talking about that side of us, where our parents were born, but really I—"

Dubček growled. A low, unsettling thunder from the dandelion patch that made Honza's innards clinch.

The Alsatian prowled toward the brothers, his fur on end, glaring past the deadfall across their legs. His lips stretched to reveal his canines.

"Honza…?" Vilém's voice was caustic with urgency. He was pushing onto his palms and twisting around, desperate to glean something of the world past the deadfall.

Keeping a low profile, Honza eased himself upright so that his chin met the snag. Aside from Dubček's rib-jangling growl, nothing appeared out of the ordinary in the forest: birds trilled in the canopy, a bumblebee buzzed here and there, and sunlight filtered through the branches in strands as thin as cobwebs.

That was why the lidless amber-yellow orbs spying down from a rock evaded Honza's first supervision of the silhouetted trunks within.

Dubček snarled and drool sprayed Honza's cheek. In the forest, the levitating eyes blinked and reappeared several paces forward, seeming to have grown in the interval.

"Honza…" Vilém's pitch grew high and timid. Perhaps he had seen the expression on Honza's face, for although Honza's chin motioned up and down, no words left his shocked, rounded mouth.

A wolf lowered its broad, shovel-like head out of the gloom—and a fantastic specimen it was, its bushy fur an incredible white. Deep-set eyes under its sharp brow twinkled, and even as Honza reminded himself that wolves were skittish creatures, as the wolf smacked its lips and quivered all over, his stomach sank.

They were trapped, and the wolf looked too observant and curious for Honza's liking. Their only means of defense was to shoo the damned thing. And if that didn't work? There was no time for speculation.

The wolf sprinted at the deadfall, launched—

And collided with Dubček in midair. Snaps and snarls and crashes and claws exploded between the brothers, who could do little more than ball up and shield their faces from the strikes bearing down on them.

But as quickly as it happened, it finished. The wolf took flight, and Dubček charged after the wolf into the gloom.

"I'm bit," Vilém yelled, his throat choked in disbelief. "I'm bit, I'm bit, I'm bit."

Honza uncoiled himself. How had Dubček managed to fend off the gigantic wolf? Vilém groaned beside him, and Honza bent and seized him by the sleeve. An indistinct, uneven stump pumped blood from where Vilém's ear used to be.

"...Christ."

"What? What is it?"

Honza shook his head. "J-just lie still, okay? We need to wash your face, otherwise it'll get infected."

Grunting, breathing heavily, Vilém obliged and braced his uninjured cheek against the grass. Honza was unscrewing the flask when a high, strangled yelp went up in the forest.

The brothers looked at one another, wide-eyed: *Dubček.*

"Maybe he got the wolf?" Aside from pain, the doubt in Vilém's expression was plain as day. The wolf had looked a third bigger than Dubček. "It's got my blood on its fucking

268 ♣ J. M. FAULKNER

tongue, Honza." He shoved onto his hands. "Help! Somebody, help!"

Honza slapped a palm over his mouth.

Over Vilém's shoulder, twenty paces away and in the sable depths of the shrubbery, the amber-yellow eyes burned.

"It's back," Honza whispered between them, and Vilém's eyes swelled round and fearful above his firmly-clamped palm. "Maybe if we stay still…."

Vilém mumbled against his skin. Honza eased the grip on his brother's lips. "There's a p-p-pocketknife in my rucksack"—The wolf's head began to coalesce as it descended from the forest into a pane of sunlight—"Maybe you can get it"—The wolf lowered its snout, stalking forward—"slowly, then cut the fucker's throat—"

The wolf leaped.

Honza swiveled to his brother's rucksack and yanked the zip. The wolf's awful weight landed on his shoulder and took a large, blind bite of his arm in the scramble.

He reeled away, fortunately tearing little more than his sleeve. He tried to flee but was tugged downward:

The deadfall.

It forced him to watch as the wolf snapped at Vilém's rucksack and heaved, stripping the fabric in place of his innards. When this didn't draw blood, the wolf circled and snatched onto Vilém's elbow, yanking vainly in an attempt to pull him out from under the fallen snag and into the forest.

Honza twisted toward his screeching brother and fished into the rucksack. His hand came away with the pocketknife!

But the wolf was attacking Vilém from the far side, biting and shaking him with dizzying ferociousness.

"I can't get him," Honza shouted.

Vilém struggled with the wolf, clawing at it with his free hand. The wolf pulled and had him at full stretch. Only when the wolf let up for a victorious moment did Vilém have any success. He crunched toward Honza and covered his head, folding into a turtle position.

The wolf pounced, and Honza swung his tightened fist with all his might, and he felt his closed hand thump against the beast's muscular shoulder.

It whimpered and darted away, ears drawn in confusion.

Honza held out the sodden knife, ready to strike. A string of carmine flicked from the blade's tip. "Now fuck off. Get the hell out!"

And the wolf did just that. It retreated into the trees, head twisted over its shoulder so that it never let Honza out of sight.

Come evening, the sun had slipped behind the Beskid mountain range. The softest light lay on Vilém's slumbering form, in his bed of blood. Honza had cleaned his brother's wounds—the punctures in his back, the hole where his ear should have been, and the gouges that exposed his collarbone—with what remained of the water, save for a few drops that scarcely qualified as a mouthful.

To that realization Honza did something astonishing. He bowed his head and started praying in earnest. He hadn't spoken to God since he and Vilém's unruly behavior, and the congregation's xenophobia, had driven their mother from the church. That had to be fifteen years ago, and he felt awkward and vulnerable to be seen in prayer. To spare himself distress, he waited until Vilém had fallen asleep before he began.

At first, he had been adamant that Vilém should fight off sleep, but seeing him wrestle to keep his chin lifted, the grass and dandelions crushed all around, Honza had decided against torturing him further. Didn't sleep heal, after all?

But when Vilém awoke, his voice had taken on a hoarse, pained quality that made Honza think he had been mistaken. He spoke in short, sharp sentences with tension written on his jaw, and he talked about anything but his wounds or the situation at hand. He said how delighted he was to visit Czechoslovakia, and other things Honza couldn't reciprocate. He could but listen and look earnest.

270 🝐 J. M. FAULKNER

"You know," Vilém continued, a mischievous twinkle in his eye, "I s-saw you praying. If only you could wait, there's a chapel atop Radhošť. Your god will hear you better there, although, you'd do just as well to kneel before Radegast's statue. Mount Radhošť *is* Radegast. Unless you've already joined the Slavic pagans in ancient dance, their worship of nature and the sun? Or do you sit a pious Christian still?"

"Neither," Honza answered tersely.

He was tired of being drawn into debate, as Vilém relished at home. Usually, it was capitalism versus communism. Even as communist governments dissolved across Europe, closer and closer to the USSR, Vilém opined that it was because the governments had lost their morals and didn't follow *The Communist Manifesto* closely enough—in short, their communism wasn't *his* communism, the right communism.

"But it doesn't matter," Honza said, now sounding matter-of-fact. "Whoever I pray for, it won't magic us water."

"Are you thirsty?" Vilém held out the flask.

Honza accepted it and shook. There was a gulp at the bottom. "Not much left. Should pace ourselves."

"Do you know," Vilém smiled mockingly, "how many people die of thirst with water on them? How many lone figures tramping through dunes think to themselves 'I'm hella thirsty, but I'll hold onto this precious jug until I'm desperate'?"

Honza held out the flask. He wasn't in the mood for know-it-all, ill-fated humor. "If anyone needs this, it's you."

Vilém stared past him. "Read about a man once, trapped at sea, surrounded by *all* that water and not a drop to drink." He laughed. It had a weak, gravel-like quality. "Survived by drinking rainwater, turtle blood and catching fish with his bare hands. To stay hydrated, he ate their eyeballs, said he craved it like nothing else he'd ever felt before. Imagine... 'magine craving eyeballs, huh? Pity there's none around here."

"You shouldn't talk like that."

"Think I'm being plenty realistic, Honza."

"What about the knife? I could cut—"

"What, through the whole tree?" He tracked Honza's gaze. "...Wait, really? Cut off your damned leg, how are you going to make it down the mountain? We don't even know where we are. And there's a wolf about."

"We need to do something."

"I *need* to apologize," Vilém said. "I've not exactly been... the best brother. I've given you a hard time, I know it. Sorry I dragged you into my pilgrimage of self-discovery. This was all about me, who I was, and making you see the importance of our heritage."

"Doesn't matter now, does it?"

"The truth is we never really liked one another, did we?" Vilém frowned. He pinched his lips together and shook his head. "No, we don't like each other much. The thing we have in common is our parents—and with one dead and one to go, well, what's the odds of us calling the other when Mum's gone? Who'd pick up the phone?"

I would, Honza thought.

But would he? He wanted to say yes, because that was the compassionate thing to say, but that didn't make it true, did it?

Vilém continued, "You'd have fucked off with that Welsh girl—what's her name, Braith?—got married and put that degree of yours to good use. I'd be somewhere behind the Iron Curtain, hitchhiking and playing the accordion for pennies. Do you think we would have been happy, in our own way?"

On the morning of the fourth day, two days after the attack, a deafening squawk ripped Honza out of a cold, deep sleep. He clapped his hands around his head and ears, feathers blurring his vision, a chorus of beating wings scarpering in every direction. When his assailants fell silent, he peered out from behind his forearm.

A crow's silhouette leered down at him from the deadfall, the sunset over its shoulder. Honza swung at it, and the bird flapped away.

Another crow, however, remained unperturbed nearby. It was perched the length of Vilém's neck, beak-deep in the orifice of his missing ear.

Honza lurched and threw a clumsy chop. "Fuck off!"

That evening, the sun retreated behind the watchful beech trees more gradually, to the point of voyeuristic leisure, leaving Honza to witness the fastening shadows zip up his brother's corpse in a body bag of darkness.

———

A wicker basket filled with freshly plucked cabbages swung from a petite hand. Even as Honza questioned the shortness of these fingers, that he felt himself squatting on loose soil, and faintly registered he was a passenger inside Zita Vaculíková's body, the free hand reached down to reap another cabbage.

A shadow blotted the sun. A broad, bare foot crushed the cabbage lying between Zita's knees. The leaves crunched savagely.

He daren't peer up from that naked foot to look upon its owner. His heart—Zita's heart—pounded his ribcage, he couldn't breathe, it was as though the foot bore down upon *his* chest.

A sonorous, drum-like voice said, "I will take the eldest son, and he will know my name."

———

Honza rolled the biscuit on the grass. He had tied it carefully with a piece of string from his brother's bag, hoping to lure a bird or other animal. He was all out of water, and the thought of juicy animal eyeballs, like the ones Vilém had mentioned, was beginning to make his stomach rumble like an explosion deep underwater.

But he needed to remain still. Anything more than a twitch could mean a lost opportunity. Too many of those could spell disaster now that the August weather had returned in force. He squeezed his eyes shut and played dead, and sure enough the tap of avian feet crept closer.

How many hours passed before he perceived a tug on the string, he could not say. His insides clenched, he leaped, the bird squawked, and he caught a handful of earth.

The bird flapped away while he hammered the ground. "Hell with you!"

Hell? If Hell's not to your taste, say the name.

Honza didn't know precisely when Vilém started whispering in his ear, only that each time he heard the voice, and saw his brother's limp body under the deadfall, mouth packed with the dandelions he had been masticating when his body surrendered, he reminded himself that he needed to drink if he didn't want to slip into desperation-fueled insanity.

It's your destiny, Honza, inherited from me, your elder brother by seven destiny-deciding minutes.

"You're in Hell, and I don't need you. You did nothing but make my life miserable. Dragged me into this godforsaken place. You got me killed. *You* killed me. You're going to Hell—"

And so Honza shrieked, on and on, as the sun slid down the mountainside.

Scooping out Vilém's eyeball was sticky business. A sticky, slippery business. But the knife was sharp, and Honza's desperation to live was sharper still.

He pried the optic nerve from his brother's head like a worm and knotted it in his fingers so that it didn't wriggle away. It wouldn't cut easily, he realized. It felt elastic under his blade, like a copper wire protected by insulation. He severed it with a full-body yank.

The eyeball popped on his molars as he choked it down.

"I'm s-sorry," he blubbered, unable to scrub the tears from his cheeks for the gore webbed around his fingers. "I had no other ch-choice. Had to do—"

The wolf leered at him from the tree line, where a pane of sunlight fell on its thick, blood-stained coat.

Honza grabbed for the knife with sodden fingers. "Now fuck off. I already got you once. I got you once!"

The wolf lowered its head and stepped forward. Honza swung, and although the wolf was more than a dozen paces away it stopped. Its tongue flicked in excited observation.

"Back off."

But the wolf came on, cautious to keep Vilém's corpse between it and Honza's knife. It ducked his wild, desperate swings that were far out of reach until, with a last flick of the tongue, the wolf buried its snout in Vilém's ribcage.

"Noooo." Honza screeched and sliced thin air—the deadfall restrained him. Blood dyed the wolf's bushy cheeks. "Get the fuc—" He dropped the knife, seized Vilém by the sleeve with both hands and pulled.

But Vilém didn't budge under the deadfall's grip, and what little distance Honza closed between them, the wolf undone with a quick tug of war.

Honza beat the packed earth, howling. This was the final act of humiliation, the final assault on his threadbare sanity.

"Viléééééms—"

A low rattle sent shockwaves through Honza's sternum. Dubček stood at his shoulder, flashing his canines. The Alsatian appeared thinner than he remembered, fur knotted with blood and filth. A forepaw was bent awkwardly.

But the wolf backpedaled into the forest, and Dubček settled into Honza's embrace, letting out the occasional whimper. Honza tangled the dog's fur in his fingers, weeping into its shoulder. "Good boy," he repeated. "Good boy."

He was wondering whether he and Braith had ever held each other this passionately when he saw the flicker of amber-yellow eyes from the trees, several fanning from a central figure.

Dubček detached himself from Honza and staggered to his feet. He couldn't outrun the pack with a broken leg, but he could stand his ground, and he did so loyally, between Honza and the sleek figures exiting the forest.

Honza swung the blade wide over his head, endeavoring to make himself as large and threatening as possible. Dubček barked and snapped thin air, his teeth a menacing clatter.

But the wolves came on without a huff or a howl. They stalked forward with unhurried, unflinching purpose. Glaring at Honza and Dubček, sniffing, they nuzzled up to Vilém's corpse and began devouring him.

Dubček stumbled away in the commotion, tail tucked between his hind legs, as the pack filed around the feast.

"Don't leave me." Honza flailed against the deadfall, bawling like a child abandoned to the dark of his bedroom. "Please." Whether from exhaustion or remorse, the Alsatian hesitated. "I'm not ready to die. Somebody, somebody…"

The wolves stripped Vilém's corpse, and neither Dubček nor Honza found strength enough to protest. After what felt like an eternity, they ripped him out from under the deadfall.

Without warning, the white wolf leaped at Honza—

Dubček intercepted. The canines clashed and tore one another, and in his desperation the Alsatian fought an even battle.

But the other wolves were quick to react.

They seized Dubček by the forelimbs and dragged him several paces away. There they pinned him to the ground, whereupon the white wolf clamped onto his throat and shook him until he stopped fighting. When Honza cried out, the faithful dog twitched, and the wolves went at him again and again, until Dubček remained still.

The grey wolf came for Honza first, slow enough he cut its snout open with the knife. It bolted backward with a whimper.

"I'll gut you," Honza cried.

But he couldn't fight them all. Thanks to Vilém's shortcut and the snag, he was condemned to the worst death imaginable: to be eaten alive.

He thought of the family legend. He knew what he had to do, had known since Vilém's corpse had started whispering to him, if not before.

When the white wolf slipped under the flash of Honza's knife, sank its jaws into his arm and began thrashing, Honza screamed for the old god by name:

"Radegast!"

An incandesce whited the beech forest. His vision cleared and he saw the white wolf crushed beneath a muscular foot, spine broken.

Honza had no choice but to look upon the owner of that dreaded foot:

Above an emerald skirt buckled with a sun emblem, the old god had a muscular torso, a cornucopia in one hand and an axe in the other, a lion-like face and a golden, horned helmet. Expression stern and unreadable.

The nearest wolf pounced. Radegast chopped it mid-flight with a meaty, sickening club of his axe.

Blood showered the clearing, but Honza couldn't help but smile as the wolves fled. Miroslava had been right about the family legend: it was their destiny to visit Czechoslovakia, the Beskid Mountain Range, Moravian Wallachia's Mount Radhošť, and Vilém had been Zita Vaculíková's eldest living male descendent until passing the baton, and now Radegast was here to play sage to his forgotten son.

Honza crawled hand over hand in the grass to paw the old god's knee. It felt like iron. "Forgive me, I didn't believe, but now I understand: I am the first-born son. I—"

He had crawled...

Squinting back over his shoulder, he saw the deadfall, the old snag that had pinned he and Vilém for days, had vanished.

"But..."

Don't you think that forests are like churches? Radegast *was* this mountain, this forest, and Radhošť was but another variation of the name Radegast. The old god had been here all along, waiting....

Radegast plucked him off the ground like a broken puppet and held him aloft, so close their noses touched.

Dazzling, earthly eyes of eons. A low, hideous grumble:

You are the first-born son.

"No." His head shook frantically. "No—"

Radegast opened his hands. Honza crashed into a crater stomped by the gigantic foot. A snap echoed from his femur and pain pockmarked the forest with flickering lights. The sound that escaped him was guttural.

Frantic, he scrambled through the grass, past the destroyed wolves and toward Vilém's remains.

The earth crunched at his heels, and Honza reeled around to see a monstrous axe blotting the sun.

The blade fell and severed the wounded legs from his torso with a single stroke.

"Please," he gasped, head swimming. "Plea—"

The old god jammed two beans from its cornucopia into Honza's mouth. Tears streamed down his cheeks as his tongue erupted with sour, blood-tasting blisters.

"I'm not ready to die," he choked. "I'm beggin—"

Radegast scooped him from the ground and barreled him in the crux of his armpit. Belly over the god's bulging forearm, Honza watched as the forest turned upside down and blood chuted from his legs, as hooved, faun-like limbs sprouted in their place.

The old god made off with his purchase into the forest until the howls of life over death had all but ebbed away.

DIE BOOTH

PAPER COINS

THE road was a scar. Either side to the horizon rolled moors of scrub, still holding pockets of winter snow under a colourless sky tumbled with a steely underbelly of cloud. No traffic. No people. No noise, except the minute tick of melting ice.

"This is where you're from?" asked Andy. His words steamed briefly around his face, no breeze to disperse them. They sounded hollow in the stillness and that hollow threatened to creep inside him: he wrapped his arms around his chest to ward it off.

Gwyn didn't answer. When Andy turned to look, he was staring away across the low hills with a hint of a smile haunting his red mouth and in that moment, Andy truly could believe him sprung from this place, a part of the landscape as much as the rock piles and craters and wind-bitten heather. Andy glanced back, a couple of hundred yards down the uneven tarmac track, to where he'd parked the car. It looked like fiction amidst the terrible desolation of the hills; a refuge time-travelled from a future century and Andy wanted nothing more than to run back to it and bang his cold-burned fists against the rusting orange paintwork to prove that it was solid and real. But Gwyn said, "It's beautiful, isn't it?"

"It's something else all right. I can't believe we're only a few miles from the main road. It's like another world."

"It *is* another world. It's World's End."

"I never believed you when you told me that name." Andy scuffed his toe into the roadside grass; his boot glittered with frozen crystals. "It sounds like something from a fairy tale."

Gwyn's secretive smile widened. "Come on. I'll show you where I found the coins."

The walk took them out of sight of the car, until the only sign of civilisation was the battered strip of road. It seemed from another time. When Gwyn stepped off the track with casual sureness Andy's heart plummeted like a dropped stone, iced over with the fear of falling. "You really know your way around this place, hey?"

"Yep." Gwyn didn't look at him.

Andy kept his gaze fixed on Gwyn's back. Followed his steps, placing his feet in the green melt-patches of Gwyn's tread, too irrationally afraid to even glance back to check that the road was still in sight. "Even as long as it's been?"

"Yep."

Andy shivered. He pulled his jacket closer around him and gazed out across the blankness, certain suddenly that if he did turn around, the road would have disappeared like a mirage. "Are you sure there's no quicksand?"

Gwyn's laugh took wing and cawed like birds. Snatched up by the stinging air. His cheeks were pink, and his eyes sparkled, and it seemed like he certainly must come from this place—a strange and beautiful and intimidating place where people did not go—because no matter how often you explored it and how well you knew it, it must still be a mystery. He said, "There's no quicksand."

Andy almost believed him. "But it *is* marshes, right?"

"It's moorland, not marshes."

"Then what's that?" Andy pointed off the path to a mire-y dip some hundred metres long, the floor of it black-water-logged and bristling with dead sticks of sedge that cradled a small, shining figure. "Hang on, what *is* that?"

His boots squelched as he scrambled down, sunk inches into the sump while he ascertained: a child's foil balloon, shaped like a cartoon character, deflated and drowning. Obviously, people did come up there after all. Looking around, he began to notice more debris: beer cans and tobacco packets, biscuit wrappers and pop bottles and a rain-soaked magazine, scattered as though those who'd left them had departed in a hurry, or just disappeared. But wasn't that always the way with places of natural beauty?

"Litter," Gwyn said, wrinkling his nose. He waved a hand, his fingers crooked in a way that was certainly coincidence, but made Andy think of curses. Picking through the withered woody grass, he wound up the side of one of the low hills that undulated not-so-low up close, with Andy gingerly following.

At the top of the hill, the wind found them, like knives. All there was were more hills, with sporadic hummocks of piled rocks of no immediate purpose or origin, stretching out into a misted blue distance. They looked like cairns. Like the dead lived there.

"How come the stones?"

Andy nodded in the direction of the nearest mound and Gwyn said, "Building rubble. All fallen down, now."

"What, there were houses up here?"

A nod. "Aye, and walls and industrial buildings."

"Don't tell me you lived up here on the moors?" He could picture it, little Gwyn waving goodbye to a red-cheeked mother in a checked apron, before embarking cheerfully out into rain-swept bleakness, unaware of the rest of the world with its BMXs and Playstations and cinemas.

"No. Farther along." Gwyn shot him another hard glance and Andy felt suddenly foolish. "All these places have been gone hundreds of years."

Andy squinted into the grey distance, picking out the scattered white map-pins of the few farmhouses still standing. "And your house is still there?"

"No."

Andy didn't press it. "So, what was the industry here?"

"Lime quarrying. And mining, lead and silver."

That made sense: they'd driven here past derelict shacks and the foundations of mines, with yawning shaft entrances shrouded in wire mesh now curled and orange with rust. The landscape that looked so unearthly had been carved by centuries of hard labour; now it mistrusted men.

"There." Andy followed Gwyn's pointing finger to a spot not far away. At first, he took it for a formation of rock, but on arrival closer inspection revealed it to not appear quite natural—a capstone, perhaps, with a single, perfectly round hole bored through the middle.

"What is it?" Andy said, as the wind took that moment to mute, and his voice sounded far too loud. He dropped down onto one knee, peering into the hole in the centre of the stone. "What's under there?"

"Tunnels."

"Tunnels," Andy repeated. The cold from the ground seeped into his bones, making his knee ache in only moments. He ran a finger around the mossy edge of the hole in the middle, then, feeling odd, stuffed both hands into his jacket pockets.

"They run right under all around here," Gwyn said, "There were always tunnels under these hills, but the tunnels weren't always mines." He crouched down next to him, and Andy felt his heat, like light; like a solid light. "Listen." Reaching out, Gwyn picked a chip of stone out of the grass and held it for a moment over the hole, before it dropped, like a craven heart. "One."

The wind held its tongue. The silence pummelled their ears.

"Two." Gwyn took a long breath between each number so that Andy could see the word *Mississippi* almost form on his lips, "three, four, five—wait—six, seven, eight, nine," his eyes widened expectantly, "ten, eleven."

From way down below, a faint echoing plop sounded, like something landing in water. It was a dark noise that flew out of the hole in the rock to find them.

Andy shivered. "Eleven seconds. How far down does that make it?"

"A long way," said Gwyn and even though he was looking into the distance, Andy could tell his attention was down far below the earth.

"And this is where they found you?"

"Yes."

Andy folded his arms. "I don't believe you." He was lying. He did believe it, maybe more than anything he'd believed before. He just didn't want to.

And Gwyn said, "I don't care."

"Andy!"

"Lola!" Andy called back, "How goes it, babe?"

Then they air-kissed, because that was a thing right then, which Andy would later look back on and feel fleetingly self-conscious and silly about. He had to angle his head to avoid the giant acrylic squares of her earrings, slipping in next to her in one of Bar Delta's booths. "So, when do I get to meet the new boy, then?"

"Tonight." Lola stirred a paper straw in her drink, and took it out, and sucked the liquor off it with anodised-red lips that left a bloody smear. "I can't wait to show him off to you. He's *exotic*."

"Wales is exotic now?" It kind of was, after years of inner city jading.

Lola raised the bleached arches of her eyebrows. "You'll see what I mean. He's different."

"You mean weird, don't you?"

She frowned and half nodded. "Yeah, but—you'll see. *Good* weird. He's good. The things he turned up to the studio with, they're mind-blowing."

Andy sipped his G and T and nodded at her to go on, but she looked adrift in thought and he had to prompt her. "So, what were they?"

"Oh. Paper. Paper sculpture, I suppose."

"Like Valérie Buess?"

Lola shook her head. "No, no; not like that. Nothing like that. He turned up with nothing, just the clothes on his back and a handful of cash; you would have taken him for home-less. And he had a rucksack with this suit in it. A full suit made of paper, beautiful flawless white paper with no stitches and no seams, and when he unfolded it, it wasn't creased at all..."

"Origami?" Andy asked, but he knew as the words left his mouth that she hadn't heard him, and he felt a sudden jab of jealousy—jealousy of this artist he had not yet even met.

"Coins, too. Paper coins, beautiful flawless white paper stamped with letters."

"Doesn't sound too original to me," Andy said, hiding his expression with a sip of his drink. He hoped he sounded pragmatic and not just bitter, but Lola didn't appear to care.

"No, it doesn't. But you have to see them; then you'll see. He said he found them up on the moors. He has this whole crazy story constructed around it, how he lived in the hills and loved walking on his own in the wild deserted places. Then one day he went missing. His family called the police and they searched for him for weeks, thinking he'd got lost in all this wilderness, like ramblers get lost on the Yorkshire moors, you know? He knew the place like the back of his hand; it just wasn't like him to go missing. But they never found him. Filed him dead. Then five years later, apparently, he just turned up again, all wild and unkempt like he'd been living outdoors, with no memory of where he'd been and all this exquisite paper sculpture. A local guy found him, he said, just found him again, there on the hillside. You have to hear him tell it though, he does it way better than me, I swear you'll actually believe him, I hope I—" She fell silent and Andy swivelled in his seat and followed her gaze to a young man who was headed for their table, and the second he saw him, he knew. An unremarkable man, average height and average build, dressed in blue jeans and a black knit jumper, with short, mousy hair and the most piercing eyes Andy had ever seen. When he reached their table, Lola said, "Andrew Degare: Gwynfor Aberthol Bach. Gwyn, this is Andy."

"Pleased to meet you, mate." Andy stuck out his hand, and the man, Gwyn, took it warmly and shook it and smiled the shy smile of the London initiate.

He said, "You, too," with no trace of weirdness and more than a trace of an accent. The splinter of resentment in Andy's heart immediately began to work free. He knew, too well, what it was like to be the outsider looking in. To go away and come back changed.

"So, how are you liking the big city so far?"

"It's…big." Gwyn's eyes were large and blue and new, like a child's eyes in an adult face, seeing a place for the first time. "There's a lot of history but not enough grass." He grinned a fresh-air grin and Andy downed any lingering misgivings with the dregs of his gin.

"True enough. You get used to it though. We'll make a local of you no problem." Given half a chance. Lola was right: Gwyn had an aura, a glow around him that belied his mundane appearance. Realising he was staring, Andy said, "Anyhow, I've heard great things about your work with paper. I'd love to see some of it one day."

"Here." Gwyn shuffled on his seat, fidgeting a wallet out from his back pocket, and opening it. From one of the credit-card compartments he drew a wisp of tissue paper, unfolding from it a white disc that looked to Andy's first glance like a Communion wafer, something sacred and terrible. He held it up. It was simple, a circle of thick paper about the size of a two-pound coin, with what looked to be a stamped or embossed design of beading around the edge and a medieval-looking letter S in the middle. Andy held his hand out and Gwyn passed it over, but his eyes never left it.

Lola was right again. There *was* something about that coin that defied explanation and awoke desire. It was heavy, for one thing, heavier than paper ought to be and it was the same on both sides, but, holding it up to the light, Andy couldn't detect any form of adhesive line between two identically stamped halves. That would suggest that it was moulded, but the paper seemed too fine for that; too white and of such petal smoothness that it couldn't conceivably have been fashioned by any but the most skilled of artists. Of course, there must

have been some simple method by which he'd made it, but …
feeling Gwyn's eyes still on him, Andy handed it back.

"Lola wasn't kidding, that really is something else. Very
unusual. I'm impressed."

Some kind of deep emotion flitted across Gwyn's face—
sadness, or bereavement. Maybe homesickness. He turned
the coin over in his hand, flipping it smoothly between two
fingers so that the spotlights in the bar caught its spin and lit
it up red, blue, sunshine yellow. He said, "They were supposed
to turn to gold."

━━━━━━━━━━━━━━━━━━━━━━━

"You knew him best," said Lola. "Know him. You *know*
him best." Her voice on the other end of the telephone line
deteriorated momentarily into feedback and then clarified
again. "Sorry, I'm on the train. I just keep thinking, what if
that stuff—the stuff he said about him disappearing—what if
it was true? All this time everyone thinking it was an artist
thing but it was really like, a cry for help or something. Andy,
was it true?"

"I don't know." He didn't. What she said about him knowing Gwyn best, he couldn't contest it. He'd spent time with
him, talked for hours with him, taken his bronchial old Astra
on a whimsical road trip back to his home county with him
so that they could play at *Withnail and I*. One hundred and
eighty miles to see Gwyn's place of birth: that haunted, des-
olate expanse of moorlands and abandoned farmhouses. One
week out of a lifetime for city kids wandering with a burning
uncertain hole opening further in their hearts. But he still
couldn't claim to know Gwyn Bach at all. Couldn't claim that
Gwyn Bach had truly known him. "He was kind of private."
The words felt a little inadequate.

"And this is kind of important! It's been nearly a week.
We'll need to tell the police, what if he's flipped out or something and run off somewhere? What if it *has* happened before? He could be freezing to death on a mountain somewhere

or something! Great friends we'll look like. Does his family still live in Wales?"

"I don't know."

"Has he *got* any family?"

"Lola, *I don't know*. You know he never talked about stuff like that."

An audible shudder shook the phone connection; Andy couldn't be certain if it was an irritated sigh or more signal interference. Lola said, "I know." She sounded resigned. "I just presumed he talked to you. Didn't he know anyone properly in London? He must have been lonely."

"I think he was used to being lonely," said Andy.

It was one thing to tug the tail of winter in a place familiar to its own kind; but going back to that place on your own is an entirely different matter than going with someone who knows it.

Andy put the car in neutral and opened the door onto a glaring day that would look hot in photographs. Around him, steam rose from the bracken as the night's dew evaporated in the warming rays of sunlight. For as far as he could see, waves of grass like water made solid were rendered flat as poster paint by the brightness. Opaque blue sky met infinite green in a horizon that looked drawn on. It was that horizon that Andy made his way toward, the nape of his neck prickling. Around him, the hills seemed to breathe. To watch, quiet and wily, this foreigner setting foot into their world. This interloper, there by their tolerance only.

Aside from being a vast expanse of virtually featureless nothing to start with, the moors looked different in spring, the duns and greys giving way to gold and jade, brighter but no less foreboding than the bleakness of winter. It was luck rather than judgement that brought Andy once more to the pierced capstone in the hills. Or perhaps it was something else entirely.

He kept his distance and looked.

You can drop a stone in and wait a full eleven seconds before you hear it hit.

What's under the hills?

The temperature rose with the sun, climbing to midday as Andy climbed the hill, but it was still somehow chilly. If he let his mind run, he could imagine that Gwyn was there with him like on his first visit, climbing just behind him. He seemed near, he seemed all around, but that surely went to show how much Andy associated him with the landscape. Like Gwyn, the moors were keeping secrets. He could have been murdered or anything. He could have been lost forever. He could be just over the next ridge, sitting on the spring grass in his suit of pristine white.

At Andy's feet the capstone was an island in a sea of green, the hole there in the middle comma'd now by a sheep's jawbone. Ascending the hill Andy felt his feet drag, his legs heavier than a walk across the moors should have made them. On his hands and knees, he gazed for a second time into the black mouth of the hole, that bone-cold feeling reaching up again from the ground despite the warmer weather. Around him the grass seemed to swirl in whirlpool eddies and, feeling dizzy, he pulled back and cast around for a stone.

One Mississippi, two Mississippi. Make sure you take your time and breathe and count properly. Seven Mississippi, eight Mississippi, nine Mississippi. We're getting close now. Eleven Mississippi, twelve Mississippi, thirteen Mississippi. This is definitely breaking all records. Sixteen Mississippi, and Andy was down on his hands and knees with his ear held closer to the hole in the capstone than he liked, but all he could hear was the low, narcotic drone of insects in the heather.

Ten minutes and four stones later, Andy had heard none of them land. Of course, it was possible that something was stopping them, catching them, that the hole had been blocked up inside, choked with some overgrowth of foliage. That something down there in the dark was preventing the stones from making any noise. There could be any number of explanations. In the brilliance of early spring, surrounded by awakening life, Andy stared at the hole in the stone and swore it stared back at him. He bent towards it one last time.

"Hello?"

Nothing. Not even an echo; his voice swallowed up by the blackness as surely as the stones he'd dropped. How was that possible? Had it echoed before, that time Gwyn had dropped the stone in?

"Hello?"

There *was* something.

It sounded like rushing air, but it was certainly something. His skin crawled to do it, his mind conjuring things that sprang from that flat blackness onto his face, but his need to know outweighed the fear and so he crouched closer to the opening in the ground and listened. It sounded like whispering. Turning his head slowly, Andy's lips grazed the pelt of moss that dressed the edge of the hole like a kiss. He shouted, "Gwyn?" and then he listened to the sound returned to him.

It could have been an echo at last, but what it sounded like was voices—and one most familiar to him. A chorus of other voices in the deep, calling out *his* name.

CATHERINE McCARTHY

THE
SICKLE
AND
THE TITHE

I MUST have been around the age of five when Mamgu Begw disappeared. She was the first, though not really. She was *my* first, is all. Mam told me later that the same thing happened after every Reaping. Like all significant events, you remember your first, don't you? It sticks in your head, like honeydew to an apple tree.

I remember waking to the screams. Remember running to the window and wiping away the cloud of condensation that revealed an image of Mamgu's daughter, Carys, standing barefoot in the village square, dressed in a white cotton nightie and clutching something to her chest. If I close my palm, I can still feel the cold damp of the glass.

She caught my eye and screamed again. "They've taken her! For god's sake, help me!"

In one hand she waved an object—a doll of some kind—and with the other she tore at her hair, until my mother went out and ferried her by the elbow into our kitchen. I ran downstairs to see what all the fuss was about, but was shooed back to my room. Ear pressed to floorboards, I listened.

Carys had woken to an empty bed with wrinkled sheets and a harvest token in the shape of a doll where Mamgu should have lain. Not a speck of doubt in the women's minds other than the band of Reapers had taken Mamgu and replaced her with a doll, hewn from the very last sheaf of wheat at the furthest end of the field.

By the time I was allowed downstairs Carys had gone, taking the doll with her as paltry compensation for her missing mother.

Was there blood? I remember asking, to which my mother replied, *Of course not, silly. Mamgu Begw's gone, that's all, like a puff of dandelion seeds on the wind, she's disappeared into thin air.* She'd blown on the palm of her hand, as if to demonstrate.

My mother seemed to be taking it in her stride, but I refused to believe our elderly neighbour had blown away on a puff of wind—there had to be a more sinister reason for her disappearance. Questions galloped round my head like a jittery horse. Questions such as: Who took her? Was she dead? Why did they leave a straw doll in her place? But the question that burned brightest was: Will I be next?

Mam offered little in the way of explanation, thinking it best to deprive me of the facts. Grown-ups fail to understand that children's questions should be answered rather than ignored, because if ignored, children will make up their own answers, and the horrors that lurk therein are often more fanciful than the reality. The only reassurance she gave me was that no, I would not be next, nor would she, because you had to be old to be taken, and neither of us were old enough—yet.

So that was the end of Mamgu Begw, beloved member of the close-knit community to which both she and I belonged here in the heart of Wales. No one baked better *bara brith* than Mamgu Begw, and no one sang *A'r Hyd Y Nos* more sweetly. I would miss the lilt of her voice and the taste of her candied tea-bread, filled with raisins. But what I would miss most was the blissful ignorance, the lack of understanding that when something is given, something else is usually taken in exchange. Every subsequent year that followed Mamgu Begw's disappearance, the same thing happened, and one of our elderly would go missing. Sometimes an old man; sometimes an old woman. From then on, the joy of Harvest Supper would be tainted by the woe of loss.

Funny the things children take for granted. It took some time before I realized the farms surrounding our village produced the most abundant crops in the whole county, and that they sold for a higher price. Our ears of corn were the sweetest, our heads of wheat the most golden, our potatoes free of blight, and all because of the pact our ancestors had made with the Reapers.

Unlike others hereabouts, we never went hungry, nor did we suffer the hardship of drought or flood. Each year, the band of Reapers arrived on the first day of September and left with the rising harvest moon. And it was what they took with them that enabled us to thrive.

They came with the dawn, a silhouette of six men ambling down the hillside with their sickles and scythes until they reached the first farm, Dolau Fawr, where they would commence Reaping without so much as a word to anyone.

They partook of no food or drink other than what they brought with them, nor did they request a place to stay. Instead, they set up camp among the oak and wych elm in the little copse at the foot of the hill and returned to their makeshift beds each and every night. From dawn till dusk, no matter the weather, they worked in the fields alongside the men and women of the village to harvest the crops and grains. Always at a little distance, and never a word exchanged.

To look at them you'd suspect nothing, for they did not stand out from the rest of the Reaping party. Same linen shirts and braced breeches; same straw hats and weathered complexions. Indeed, you'd struggle to pick them out. You had to get up close to see the difference, and that was easier said than done since they kept their distance. It was in the eyes, see. A sorrowful expression that spoke of hardship and toil, and something else, something far more mystical and beyond my childish understanding.

With each passing year, as summer's curtain fell and the final Reaping drew near, I grew more and more fearful, because with it came greater understanding of what would come to pass.

"Why do we let them come, Mam? We should tell them they're not welcome, then no one else will disappear."

My mother had sighed, sick of being asked the same question year after year. "I've told you before, Alys, it's not as simple as that."

"But why?"

"It's been tried in the past. Many times." She handed me the carpet beater and pointed towards the back door. "You'll understand when you're older."

But I didn't understand, not until much later.

It was during the celebration known as Harvest Supper that they chose their victim, or rather their reward, for that was the night when every villager and all the farmers from further afield gathered together in the square to make merry. Labourers and landlords were one and the same on that night, no more than a blade of straw to differentiate rich from poor. Even the vicar attended the feast. Over the weeks, each of us had done our bit to reap and bind. Shed sweat, blood, and tears over the land together, and now we came to celebrate the hard work and rejoice in its rewards.

As soon as the sun dipped below the horizon, the merrymaking began. A hearty supper of *whipod* and *whigin* was served to all—the first to fill the belly, the second to free the mind of inhibitions.

Then came games like the blanket-tossing *rhibo* and *dai shon goch*, a curious dance with walking sticks. Air blue with banter and pungent with hops, even the braziers joined in the fun, spitting and cackling with joy to see folk make fools of themselves. And try though I might to join in the celebration I never lost sight of the band of six who sat on the church steps—watching.

Earlier that day, the very last sheath of wheat, from the furthest corner of the field, would have been cut by one of the six. No one else was entitled to reap the final straw; it was their unspoken right. Now it lay at their feet, a symbol of death, struck down by the Reaper who had cut its neck. Yet even in death its fertility lay dormant, not snuffed, for we believed the spirit of the Earth Mother lay within its grains, waiting to be reawakened the following spring. All She needed was a little help. A transference of power—old for new. A life lived to maturity, sacrificed for the sake of the young and able to pass on its worldly knowledge to seed not yet sown.

Festivities underway and an eye to the crowd, the Reapers would pass the last sheath back and fore, fashioning a doll. Deft hands, swift fingers, plaits and knots transformed into an androgynous thing, with a straw head, tufted tunic, and blackberry eyes that provided it the gift of sight, though god knows it might reel in horror if it knew what it would witness, for that night, one of our elderly would go missing, never to be seen again, just like Mamgu Begw.

My teenage years did not arrive alone. Instead, they brought with them enhanced curiosity, and since my mother refused to answer my questions, I turned to my *tadcu* for help. At the age of sixty-five, I wondered if my grandfather grew fearful of becoming the Reapers' next victim and asked him one day while he toiled in the allotment.

"Why don't we turn them away?" I said, my heart full of angst and my mouth full of questions.

He raised a white eyebrow and faced me square-on. "Do you really want to know, Alys?"

I nodded.

"Then I'll tell you a story. A true story, mind—none of your make-believe nonsense."

Perched on the pig-bench that stood beneath the apple tree, I smiled and gave him my full attention.

He set down his spade and came to join me, so I shuffled across to make room. We faced towards the stone circle known as Waun Mawn, the place of legend where giants dance on the grass as the summer solstice rises within its entrance.

No flights of fancy now, Alys, I reminded myself. *He's about to tell you the truth.* I took a deep breath and folded my hands in my lap, eager to hear what he had to say.

A whiff of pipe tobacco as he spoke, spicy vanilla and the scent of the earth. "Right then, Alys." He swiped his hands together, brushing away the dirt. "This story has been passed down from generation to generation, but it's as true today as it were back then." He glanced my way with fire in his eyes, as though daring me to contradict him. "Turn of the last century, and a cold winter was followed by a cool, wet spring. To make matters worse, a drought occurred in early summer, which meant the wheat harvest was halved. Like the thermometer, prices soared and so did tempers. Bread was scarce; folk took to rioting, and all hell broke loose."

I wondered when he'd get to the bit about the Reapers but dared not interrupt. He cleared his throat, propelling a gobbet of brown sputum in the direction of the apple tree, then continued where he'd left off.

"With folk on the brink of starvation things got desperate, till one day, from out of nowhere, six strange men arrived with the dawn. When they got to Dolau Fawr, they paused and looked around at the barren fields, shaking their heads and pointing. Disturbed the sheepdog, they did, by all accounts, which snapped at the intruders' heels.... Now then, where was I?"

He paused, squinting in the direction of the sun to gather his thoughts.

Fingers clasped round the wooden bench, I willed him to continue, knowing how easily he could wander off-course. He mumbled to himself while counting on his fingers.

"Would have been Dewi Jones's great grandfather who owned the farm back then, I believe. Well, he came out to see what all the fuss was about, and what did he see but six strange men stood in front of the gate. The same men that return every year to help with the Reaping."

I stopped him in his tracks. "But that's impossible, Tadcu. Dewi Jones is close on eighty, so if this happened in his great-grandfather's day they'd not be alive now." My heart sank. Not a true tale after all, then, I thought. Just another fairy tale to fob me off.

Tadcu shook his head and frowned. "Ah, but there you're wrong, my girl. The same six men have been coming for over a hundred years. Same now as when I was a lad. They never get any older, see."

I stood from the bench so abruptly it wobbled, causing Tadcu to dig in his heels to save himself from falling. "None of this make-believe nonsense, you said. So much for your true story." I spoke through gritted teeth. "Why will no one tell the truth?"

He pointed at the bench. "Sit down, girl, and hear me out, then you can have your say."

The look in his eyes told me I should do as I was bidden, so I plonked down next to him once again and bit my tongue.

"They'd made a pact there and then," he said. A pact written in the soil with the farmer's finger and sealed with spit and sawdust. The Reapers would bless the land with power invested from the Earth Mother and harvest its rewards each and every year in return for the sacrifice of an elderly member of the community. As a symbolic token, a doll, hewn from the last sheath and therefore possessing the most vigorous spirit of the earth, would be left in his or her place where it would be kept until the following year. Then it might be buried according to the will and custom of the family.

"But what right did Dewi's great-grandfather have to agree to such a thing? How dare he make the decision on behalf of others?" I said.

Tadcu pocketed his pipe and turned towards me, a look of earnest resignation written on his face. "He did it because he knew they'd agree, Alys."

"But what if they hadn't? I mean, surely many would have considered it madness. And what about the future generations, how dare he speak for us?"

He folded his arms across his ample middle and nodded, his eyes never leaving my face. "So that's what you think, is it? I'd lay down my life to save you from suffering, and so would your mother and father."

"Of course, I know you would, but—"

He raised a hand. "But nothing, Alys. There is no *but* about it. It's simple. Us old folk have lived our lives, and now it's time for you to live yours. It really is a small sacrifice, you know."

"But it isn't! And in any case, I wouldn't let you. Just because you're old it doesn't mean you should want to die."

My words tickled him, and his chest rattled as he laughed.

"Oh, I don't want to die, Alys, believe me. Nobody wants to die, no matter how old they are, but if it means you living without ever having to beg for food, then I'd give up my life in a heartbeat." He paused, allowing me to consider his words. "So, there you have it. The old made the decision to sacrifice themselves for the sake of the young, and that's the way it's been ever since."

He stroked the back of my hand with calloused fingers, though gentle as a lamb. "Remember how you made room for me when I sat on this bench?" he said.

I nodded, but my eyes remained downcast.

"Well, it's the same thing, except other way round. In honouring the pledge, we make room for you. It really isn't much of a sacrifice."

I balled my fists and my throat constricted. "But how do you bear not knowing if it might be your turn next? I don't want to wake up after every Harvest Supper wondering if they've taken you."

He gave another chuckle. "Oh, they won't take me, Alys. Not with these old lungs." He slapped his hands against his ribcage and coughed. "They take the old, but not the sick, see. They want someone ripe in age but not riddled with disease. Affect the crops, it would. No, what they want is someone who is able to teach the young seeds how to grow, someone whose decaying corpse will feed the soil with knowledge as well as nutrients. Think about it—you ever known anyone sick to be taken?"

I thought back to Mamgu Begw and her crop of white hair that smelled of sunshine and lavender. Apart from a slight limp, she was fit as a fiddle. Then there was Siôn Griffith, still capable of walking all the way to the top of Mynydd Carningli without pausing for breath, despite the fact he was approaching his eighth decade.

I failed to remember all who had disappeared, and some I hadn't known very well, though it seemed Tadcu was right in what he said, because I could not picture one of them infirm.

We sat in silence for a few moments, each digesting our thoughts.

"Tadcu, you know you said the decaying corpse would feed the soil, does that mean the Reapers bury the person they choose in the fields? And if so, how do they die?"

He looked at me then, tongue poking against his cheek, uncertain as to how much he should reveal. "Mm-hmm. Furthest corner, the place where the last sheath will be cut the following year."

I shuddered at the image. "But there's no saying goodbye; no funeral. It's awful." I held my head in my hands and pictured his body in the ground, all alone, even though he'd assured me he would not be chosen.

"No different to being buried in the churchyard, girl. Not really."

I remained unconvinced. Of course, there was a difference. "But surely, we have no need to continue the practice these days. I mean, our crops are the best for miles, and there's always plenty to eat."

"And why do you think that is, Alys?"

I shrugged. "Good weather? Skilled farmers?"

He said nothing, just gave me one of those looks, the kind that could turn you to stone, so I tried another tack. "When it comes time for Reaping, we don't need six more men. There are enough of us to do the work. Can't we undo the pact, you know, tell them we no longer wish to be held to ransom?"

"What you're suggesting is out of the question, Alys. Trust me, it's already been tried, back when I was a lad." He shook his head. "Worst year ever. Nothing grew, not as much as a stem of corn or a single potato. I guess they were punishing us."

I thought back to the previous Reaping, recalling how the six strange Reapers had sat on the church step, fashioning the doll as they studied the crowd. I felt certain they selected their victim as they watched.

"I know," I said, brightening. "How about we hide all the old people? Stop them attending the party. That way they won't be able to choose someone, will they?"

He shook his head. "Oh dear, oh dear. If only it were that simple. Over the years we've not only hidden the elderly but shackled them to their beds. We've had relatives sleep in the same room as them, too, but it was no use. Trust me, Alys, no stone has been left unturned." He stretched his arms wide and yawned. "No, we made our bed and now we have to lie in it. It's as simple as that."

He glanced at my crestfallen face, then turned away.

"Wait until you're older, then you'll understand." He faced toward the mountain as he spoke, watching the sun set on the horizon. "As you grow old, you learn to live with the fear of death. It doesn't come easy, but it creeps up on you with every ache suffered and every tear shed, until one day you realize you're no longer afraid. That's how you beat it, see, by switching off your fear."

He never did answer my second question, the one that asked how they died. Perhaps it was best I didn't know.

———

It is the evening of the Harvest Supper, and I am an old woman. I sit in the garden, facing towards Carningli and remember Tadcu's words. The setting sun bruises the sky with peaches and plums and turns the summit of the mountain into a liquorice peak.

My son is six-foot-tall and strong as an ox; my daughter is vivacious and wise. Between them they have raised five children, all of whom are kind and curious. They take after their grandmother in that respect.

How right Tadcu was; I would give my life for any one of them. To see them grow up strong and healthy, without ever needing to wonder where the next meal was coming from has been worth the sacrifice.

Down the decades I've witnessed many come and go. Some to places far from here, preferring to take their chance with whatever the earth provided. Others went to an early grave, a natural death, like my dear husband who died of pneumonia just days before his sixtieth birthday. And then, of course, there were those who were taken after the Reaping.

As for me, I've always known how I will end my days. I've known it since the day Mamgu Begw disappeared. And yes, for a long time I feared it. I'd be lying if I said otherwise.

The Reapers have never missed a harvest, and just like Tadcu told me, they have not aged a day. They've had their eye on me for many a year, my harvest doll already in the planning stages. When they come to collect, I will ask them to remove its blackberry eyes so my spirit will not bear testament to my children's grief. It is but a small favour to ask.

"You ready, Mam?" My daughter, Catryn, appears as if by magic, wearing her best dress and a smile as wide as the ocean. The setting sun adorns her with a golden halo, and I think to myself how clever the sun is to have chosen her. She is my golden girl; always will be.

She takes my hand in hers and helps me to my feet, then arm in arm we step through the gate and on towards the village square where the sound of the harp soothes my soul.

Catryn settles me on a stool and brings me a plate of vittles which I feed to the larks while she dances. I am not afraid, but in truth cannot say I am hungry.

The six sit on the steps of the church as they have always done, the last sheath lies at their feet, awaiting its fate. I glance at them out the corner of my eye and realize this is the first time I am able to enjoy the Harvest Supper without feeling afraid. Tadcu was right—once you accept the inevitable, it loses its power over you.

Eventually, the flames from the braziers wither and die, tainting the air with smoky breath and insisting we away to our beds.

They arrive just after midnight, catching me with eyelids aflutter as I dream of whispering wheat that spreads gossip on the breeze. Something hides among the stems, and I search for it, desperate to be reunited with the thing that eludes me.

The smell of tobacco wakes me, and I open my eyes, expecting to see Tadcu. Instead, I see six men, two either side of the bed and two at the foot.

"Wyt ti'n barod?" the tallest asks. *Are you ready? So, they speak in the mother tongue, then.* But I do not answer, because I cannot help but wonder if we are ever ready.

The tallest Reaper places the doll on my pillow as the others help me out of bed.

"Wait," I say, turning to face the tall one. "Please—take out its eyes."

He pauses for a moment, then does as I ask, popping the blackberries into his mouth and grinning, though the smile soon fades as he tastes their bitter tang.

Then the world turns cold and silent, and we breeze through the house like ghosts.

TIMOTHY GRANVILLE

SARSEN WOOD

WE were down by the pond when Barnaby Creed found us. The village pond, I mean, where each year the little ones catch tadpoles to keep in jars on the windowsills of the school. We were all there—Peggy and Olive and Roger and Tommy, everyone. We had been larking about in the meadow, and now we were hot and had come down to the pond for the coolness. Some of us had taken off our shoes and socks and had our feet in the water. No one was swimming though because we never swim there, only in the millpond. It has always been like that, although the village pond is quite safe.

It was a still day, the harvest already in, and when we were quiet, there wasn't even the hum of a faraway tractor. That sort of stillness always gave us the feeling that something was about to happen, though, of course, nothing ever did. And then Barnaby Creed appeared from nowhere. He didn't say anything, just came and sat down with us, his fat pink tongue poking from the corner of his mouth. And we let him, though we wished he'd go away. I suppose he'd been looking for us that morning, sneaking around the village from place to place where he thought we might be. Don't ask me why. None of us had ever known what thoughts went through his head, and we weren't sure we should like to, either.

Our parents always said that Barnaby was harmless. They looked at his flattened face and his tongue which kept slipping out no matter how many times he swallowed it and they felt guilty, as if they were God and had made him wrong. From guilt they gave him work picking fruit or mending fences so that he didn't starve. They called him touched, simple. Or, like Father, they used more proper terms. "Barnaby Creed is

one of the afflicted, Mary, to be remembered in our prayers…
Barnaby is subnormal…he is childlike." But though he sometimes seemed to want to join in our games, we knew that he
was not like us.

There were things we didn't tell our parents. We hardly
told each other, though we all knew, all the same. How we'd
sometimes come across Barnaby in lonely places, whispering
to himself, or kneeling with his ear pressed against the turf, a
horrid smile on his face. How he had tried to get some of us
to go off alone with him—Olive and Mabel and even Tommy
once. Into the woods, or the old Whittaker barn. Offering
a pocketknife, a precious rationed toffee, a blown lark's egg.
Or there was something to see, something exciting, though
his thick tongue never quite managed to spell out what. And
maybe there was. But none of us ever went.

That day though was oddly warm and still, and we had the
feeling that something would happen. And when Barnaby
tried to get us to go with him, we decided we would. We just
did. There was something about the stillness egging us on.
And we didn't really think that anything would happen. And
they say there is safety in numbers.

We followed Barnaby away from the village and across the
stubble fields and up onto Ferne Green. He was excited, telling his own sort of muddled joke and tumbling on the grass.
It only made Derek Hodgson laugh, and he is the small-
est. The rest of us were quiet, watching Barnaby, wondering
where we were going. When we reached the pasture at the top
of Ferne Green, he stopped his clowning, all of a sudden. His
slack face got a sort of sly look. We heard him talking about
having a lie down and a bite to eat, a titbit. He started peering
at the grass, his tongue lolling out of his mouth like a thirsty
dog's. We were puzzled. None of us thought Barnaby such a
simpleton that he grazed with the sheep.

But it didn't take him long to find what he was searching
for. He plucked it out of the grass and held it up by its thin
stalk so we could see. A crooked little mushroom, looking

tiny in his big grubby hand. We all noticed that. He was the size of a man, and we had never thought of him as harmless.

After the first mushroom, we quickly discovered more and more. A carpet of them all across that part of Ferne Green. And we picked them, like Barnaby told us.

You see, it wasn't our fault. We ate the mushrooms, but Barnaby said they were good to eat, and we believed him. He had two or three first himself, so they couldn't have been poison toadstools. And we were tired and hungry, and the day was warm and close and so, so still. Thinking about it now, I imagine he knew that's where the mushrooms grew and led us up there on purpose. I suppose it was a trick. And it worked, because we ate them, all of us, even Derek Hodgson, who tried to spit his out, and we had to hold him and push a piece between his teeth and make him swallow. Yes, we admit we ate the mushrooms.

At first, nothing was different. We lay in the grass looking at the sky, and the clouds were only clouds. The fields down below were normal fields. The trees took no interest in us. A few of the little ones played at this and that, but the rest of us were quiet and still. Barnaby whistled bits of songs out of tune. Perhaps some of us dozed. But in any case, time passed, and we heard the grass begin to whisper, and Ferne Green groaned in its sleep. Panic and joy came creeping up on us. Soon we were running in laughing circles or clinging to each other for dear life. The trees turned their faces towards us and opened their knotted eyes. It was very queer and frightening. And all the while, Barnaby Creed sat there rocking back and forth and grinning.

Then Barnaby said we should go to Sarsen Wood. It was his idea, we all remember. And some of us were afraid because though we went where we liked in and around the village, that was the one place we were not allowed to play. But others were full of the joy of the mushrooms—so much joy hiding in that little cap and crooked stalk!—and said, "Yes, yes, Sarsen Wood!" And they started running and skipping, and those of us who were full of panic ran as well, and so we all went as one across Ferne Green, panic and joy together.

That was the peculiar thing about the mushrooms, the feeling of *oneness* that they gave us. Both among ourselves and with the land beneath our feet. We had always been tied to this place and to each other, we knew almost nothing of life outside the village, we thought we could be no closer. We were crying as we ran. It was like all joining in the hymn together. Except it wasn't like that in the slightest. It is impossible to say to anyone not from here.

So, we came down into the fields again and went on till we had crossed the Bowditch farm. The way grew more tangled. Brambles slithered like nests of snakes. Branches reached for our hair. We saw strange birds flit from bush to bush. We talked to each other about them and understood, though we sensed the words we used were wrong. The mushrooms told us where to turn, which path to take. Soon, very soon, we were at the edge of Sarsen Wood. And we thought of the faces up on Ferne Green, and all the faces that must be waiting in there, and we nearly couldn't go in.

But something happened, didn't it? Oh yes, old Davey Gaunt the wheelwright. He saw us at the edge of the wood when Barnaby was leading us inside, and if he says any different then he's a liar. Yes, old Davey called out to us, telling us to stop. But he'd always had a gammy leg, mangled long ago in Gallipoli, and we just laughed at him and ran into the trees, knowing he'd never catch us.

Though why would Davey be anywhere near Sarsen Wood? It might not have been him. Perhaps there was no one there.

But whoever it was, we soon forgot about them. On we went into the trees, deeper and deeper. Sarsen Wood is very old, all those great gnarled oaks and hornbeams with their ancient eyes. Tall things like men wearing robes of yellow leaves stood far off among the huge trunks. And we were frightened and walked in a hush as though we were in church. Though the joy never left us, it made itself small, crouching at the back of our minds and peeping out. We knew we were being watched, you see. And we knew we had something to do, and we weren't sure even then that we would be able to do it. We were like a slow child going to the front of the classroom to write on the blackboard. All those eyes on us and not knowing if we could.

But Barnaby didn't see the tall things or the wizened tree faces. He walked with one of us holding each of his hands, making lowing noises and still grinning stupidly. Now and then he would talk about the pretty colours, or nod and say, "Oh ah," as though agreeing with someone who wasn't there. I don't believe he even realized he was in Sarsen Wood. But that changed when we reached the Nine Teeth.

Not even a village fool could mistake them. The circle of tall standing stones hidden in a clearing in the trees. The scanty grass between always reminding me of the crown of Father's head. We had all been here before, at the old festivals and those times when God seemed to have turned his back on the village. Despite the pretty colours, Barnaby knew straight away. He showed us the whites of his eyes like a frightened horse and tried to run, but we dragged him on towards the circle, telling him not to fret, it was only a game. He was our friend, we couldn't play without him. Giggling so much we could hardly get the words out.

So, yes, we led Barnaby to the Nine Teeth. But it was the mushrooms which led us. And it was the Ones Under the Ground who told us about the mushrooms. No one could say that was our fault. We had to listen to them. You would have listened, too.

And so now we left our hush behind us because we were not in church, but somewhere God does not care to set foot. Now it was time for the panic and the joy and the joy-panic and the I-don't-know-what. And we found that we could, that we really, really could, do what we were here to do.

We had all picked up stones and branches on our way through the wood. Though Barnaby was the size of a man, he was dazed with the mushrooms and everything that was happening to him, and we were many. Some of us tried to hold

314 ❧ TIMOTHY GRANVILLE

him, and others struck him 'round the head and on the legs
and pelted him with stones till his hair was wet with blood.
Even so, he nearly escaped us, staggering and pleading and
almost twisting free. But he slipped, and as he was getting up,
Wilf Barker caught him sweetly across the back of the head
with a good, heavy branch. Then his eyes glazed and down
he went.

We beat him and beat him. The girls bit his face, the boys
emptied their bladders on him. Roger waved a bloody clump
of his hair. That wasn't like us; it was the mushrooms making us do those nasty things. But it was also only then that
we understood how we hated Barnaby. Always getting in our
way, spoiling our games. Wanting to be a part of us. We hated
him so much that it was hard to make ourselves stop in time.

But eventually we pulled each other off him and helped
each other up. We left Barnaby slumped in the middle of the
Nine Teeth, his flat, round face a shambles, but breathing,
just about. We collected ourselves, we smiled left and right.
And we began to dance.

We had seen our parents talk to the Black Earth. And
we had practised the steps out in lonely places where no one
would catch us. We knew what to do. In and out of the Nine
Teeth, first widdershins, then deasil. Stopping to kiss the
stones and speak the words, then on again, deasil, then widdershins. And sure enough, we felt Sarsen Wood begin to
turn, too. And all the trees looked towards us, and the tall
shapes dressed in dead leaves gathered around to watch. And
the ground stirred beneath our feet.

The dance went on till we were faint, till Barnaby had begun to moan and twitch. But at last it was over, and we stood
footsore and swaying among the stones. The trees span sick-
eningly. The ground trembled, knowing it was time. Then we
made the signs which we had not been allowed to practise.
And the Black Earth answered.

While we have seen the Black Earth roused before, it was
quite different with Barnaby. Usually our parents bring a
goat, or perhaps a lame gelding. Thinking to toss the Black

Earth scraps of pain and fear and then go sneaking back to God with clean hands, hedging their bets. But from feeding on scraps so long, the Black Earth grew hungry, ravenous. The Ones Under the Ground could not rest. That is why they started speaking to us—in our dreams, in the lonely places, in the stillness of our empty homes when only the clock ticks. We were to bring the Black Earth a man. And now we had.

So, though we all knew what would happen, it was still very exciting. First the terrible rumblings under the ground, and then the surface of it beginning to buckle and lift, breaking open as though being turned by some great invisible plough. Parts of it thrust upwards, spraying dirt and revealing long-buried bones, while other parts drained down into pits like sand running from an old hourglass. Soon the whole circle between the Nine Teeth had come to a kind of boil. Barnaby was flung back and forth as the Black Earth toyed with him. He moaned louder and groped at the living ground and tried to raise his head. We joined hands, and the trees span faster and faster. The sky darkened. The God of heaven drawing a curtain, looking away. We held our breath.

Then the Black Earth fastened on Barnaby, sucking his legs beneath the ground. His limp body flailed and twisted in a funny way so that we heard something snap. Barnaby's eyes sprang open, and he screamed like a vixen in season, only worse. And some of us didn't want to watch, but the others made them.

And in its own time, the Black Earth stopped worrying Barnaby and held him there, with the good soil churning all around him. And we stared and stared, and the whole spinning wood pressed closer to see. And then very slowly, lingeringly, so that he could know what was happening, the Black Earth drew Barnaby down screaming into its own depths. And the ground slowly grew still.

Afterwards, we walked back to the village. The little ones asked for their mothers or cried in a confused way, overtired. The mushrooms wore off somewhere on the Bowditch farm. We found ourselves alone again, with bloodstains on our faces. We couldn't stop shaking. None of us felt very proud. But even so, we hushed the little ones and cleaned ourselves up and promised not to tell our parents. Then we went home.

So that is everything that happened that day. Now you see we can't be blamed, we had to do it. We didn't even want to at first. But it was the best thing for the village. We couldn't have gone on with horses and goats. The Ones Under the Ground would have given us no peace. Besides, it was only Barnaby Creed. An idiot, not so different from an animal, really. And a foreigner, too, born halfway across the county.

Of course, there is no going back now the Black Earth has feasted. The mushrooms will be there to help us, though, and with Barnaby we have proved to ourselves what we can do. There are plenty of old folk in the village, half-dead already from farm labour and wars, and plenty of others that come rambling this way and won't be missed: hitchhikers, tinkers, tramps. We will feed the Black Earth and thrive, working the soil and gathering in the harvest and having children with each other. Tommy and I are nearly ready for our first. When the children are big enough to toddle, we will blood them at the Nine Teeth. We will show them where the mushrooms grow and tell them never to play in Sarsen Wood. We will teach them to swim in the millpond. We will take them to church on Sundays. We will live all together in the village and never leave, and nothing, nothing, will ever change here.

ALEX WOLFGANG

MALLEABILITY

WHEN Manos's clocktower struck midnight, Sophia lay awake and listened to the Creators as they scuttled through town. They dragged crates through the dirt to replenish the grocery shop across the street. They fed and watered the animals in the stables. A hailstorm had erupted that evening, so they scraped and hammered as they patched up damaged rooftops nearby. Sophia was glad her family had a broad tree hanging over their house. Her skin crawled at the thought of them coming closer.

She used to find the sounds soothing. When she was younger, she'd imagine a Creator sticking out a finger to lift the window and creep into her room. She'd dream of it wrapping its fingers around her body and shifting, cracking, molding her into an artist greater than she could have ever imagined.

The thought of making art was now sickening.

When the Creators were gone and the night's silence resumed, she crept to her window, opened it, and stole out into the night. She tiptoed past the hundreds of sculptures her mother and father had left around the yard, their sharp pieces of shattered glass laid to waste by hail. As usual, the Creators had taken none of their offerings.

Out on Main Street, her heart sank at what she saw beyond their yard. Once again, her parents would not be the only disappointed artists in Manos. Across the road, every easel in the Nelsons' yard was still occupied. Another house down, there lay untouched pots and bowls. She traveled further in hopes there might be something missing anywhere, but every yard in town still had its offerings.

She could already see the accusing gazes of her fellow townspeople. They'd whisper more about what a freak she was, about how they were losing the Creators' favor thanks to her failure. Tomorrow would be another miserable day.

She returned home to the sounds of her parents shouting and glass shattering. Nothing new, but it still churned her gut to hear it. They shared an artistic medium—that seemed like a sacred thing. A natural union. Why would the Creators make them both glassblowers if not to guide them to each other? They must have fallen victim to that conclusion in the days before Sophia was born, when the Creators were more accepting. They probably loved each other then.

Even when the fighting stopped, sleep didn't come. Instead, she laid awake for hours and dreaded the day to come.

It was time to leave this place.

Sophia had tried to be Created many times before—the earliest five years ago, when she was fourteen. There were only ten children her age growing up in Manos. The sun came up early in the summertime, and they often gathered for games in the schoolyard before their classes began. Just down river from the school were the Badlands, and somewhere in that rocky desolation lay the Creators. It was an easy walk, almost as though the adults had built the schoolhouse there just to tempt them.

Sophia was the first one to suggest they visit.

"We're too young," said Constance, an older girl who lived two streets from Sophia. "My mother says we can't be Created until we're older."

"If that's true," Sophia said, "they'll just ignore us. We should try."

"How?" Lisa asked, her voice measured and self-assured, as if she'd been waiting for someone to bring it up.

"I don't know," Sophia said. "Have you ever even been to the Badlands before?"

They all shook their heads.

"Come on, what's the worst that could happen?"

Sophia led the group along the river—then just a trickle in the dry season—until the grass gave way to forests, then plain dirt which dipped sharply into the canyons that made up the Badlands. In less than half an hour, the scenery had morphed into a different world of sepia dirt and rugged cliffs. She stepped to the edge of a rock jutting above a shadowed abyss. Her stomach fluttered as she gazed into its infinite darkness.

"Hello?"

There was no answer, as the Creators spoke no language. Instead, there came a scuttling from deep in the shadows as arachnoid shapes scaled the walls with spindly limbs.

Gulping, Sophia stepped back, the rest of the children with her.

"Maybe we should go."

The children cried out and looked to one another for a cue to run, but the Creators arrived too quickly. From where Sophia had stood before at the cliff's face, a hint of flesh peeked from the shadows.

With the grip of its fingertip, one of the Creators pulled itself into full view. The children screamed and cowered at the sight of a human hand, complete with nails and muscles and joints and wrinkles, though it was so large it could have carried any one of them in its palm. It reared back on its rounded stump of a wrist like a trapdoor spider ready to pounce.

They screamed and ran as fast as they could back toward the schoolhouse. Behind them, a thud sounded as a body was tackled to the ground. Lisa cried out for help, but no one looked back or responded, not when her cries suddenly stopped, nor when the cracking and crunching of her bones echoed through the trees.

When class started that day, they all agreed no one had seen Lisa that morning.

That night Sophia couldn't stomach her parents' stew and feigned an illness to be alone. She tossed and turned in anguish while the Creators tended to their business. She was responsible for a girl's death. Nobody could survive the effects of those horrid sounds.

Yet the next day, Lisa returned to school. The other kids stared at her like she was a ghost passing through the building's wooden doors. She radiated a peaceful aura—blonde hair brighter, toothy smile wider than ever before. Silence hung over the class, and Lisa looked intoxicated by it.

"Lisa, would you mind coming up front?" asked Mrs. Appleton.

Lisa made her way past the other students, the sharp echoes of her footsteps piercing the quiet.

"What happened?" Constance finally blurted out.

Lisa looked to their teacher, who nodded. "I was Created."

Whispers emerged among the children.

"They shaped me," Lisa said. "I guess I won't be in class anymore. Got more important things to do now."

"Did you know you're the youngest in over fifty years?" Mrs. Appleton asked.

Lisa nodded. "I won't let you all down."

"Do you know your medium yet?" the teacher asked.

"Ceramics. I'm sure of it. I already felt the rush when I touched clay this morning. It's incredible. We were right, there's nothing like it."

───────────

Nobody knew it then, but Manos was living through a golden age. No art lay untouched for long—the Creators always hungered for more. Her parents' glass offerings rarely remained in the grass long enough to leave an imprint. Yards were often left with only empty easels. The town buzzed with artistic fervor. As far as anyone could remember, this was how it always had been.

Some days Sophia would take evening walks down Main Street to watch her neighbors set up their offerings. She liked to admire their art before it disappeared forever, bound for whatever purpose the Creators intended, a purpose that sparked constant debate among the young ones and cryptic answers among their elders.

The old woman down the road, Joanna Nelson, always gave Sophia a fresh apple when she came to look at her paintings. Joanna depicted fantastical things from faraway lands—fairies, gnomes, mermaids. They'd delighted Sophia since she was a child.

Other artists were kind to her, too. Peter Wood sometimes gave her an extra wicker basket, and the Merrimans delighted her with tellings of the fables they'd depicted in stone.

Sophia returned to the Badlands often, each time trembling as she stood atop the cliff face, but nothing ever happened. Not when she screamed or begged or threatened to jump if they refused her. They must have known she wouldn't follow through—that or they didn't care.

Lisa's talents developed quickly. The girl was dedicated—her fascination with ceramics bordered on obsession—but each time Sophia passed her at work, her eyes looked sunken, empty. Still, she always forced a smile at Sophia from behind her studio-front pottery wheel, an inviting, desperate look that always unnerved her. Even when surrounded by admirers, Lisa always seemed to be looking.

By the time four years had passed, all her classmates were Created. Some went to the edge of the Badlands every day until their time came. They became painters and glassblowers, sculptors, and weavers. The classroom emptied of her peers and filled with younger ones as the days ticked on. Embarrassment became a daily plague. Stares from the other townspeople became more frequent as time ticked on. Adults hushed children who asked what was wrong with her.

No golden age could last forever. On a cold November night, the Creators began to lose their appetites. Sophia hadn't slept well, but she woke early the next morning and set off for a walk through town. Her parents' sculptures remained untouched in the yard. Dew on the glass reflected the early

324 ✠ ALEX WOLFGANG

sun, so the entire display twinkled. A closer look revealed
that only two pieces had been taken.

A knot formed in her stomach, one that got heavier the
more she explored the town. Untouched, dew-soaked artwork
remained in every yard on Main Street. When she passed Peter Wood's house, she found him drinking a cup of coffee and
staring at the hundreds of baskets that still lined his property.

She started to speak to him, but when he turned and shot
her a look of unfiltered malevolence, she cut herself off and
turned around. On the way home, more glares peeked out
from behind windows and around corners. She was on the
verge of tears by the time she was back in her room.

That was only the beginning. As months came and went,
as the people of Manos saw no respite from their disinterested
audience, those poisonous looks became more frequent, more
unbearable.

One night she lay in bed, watching the clock's minute
hand tick by on her wall. Thoughts of returning to school the
next day chewed away at her. The clock struck 11:30. In half
an hour, the nightly rearrangement would begin, and it would
be too late to leave. But if she ran, she could reach the edge
of the Badlands in ten minutes flat. Her muscles ached with
desire to flee.

She rose and dressed as quickly as she could, then lifted
her window from the sill. With a deep breath, she pulled herself through and into the night.

Manos's darkness was aided by a new moon and the cover
of trees, so Sophia relied on muscle memory to take her toward the Badlands. Twice she tripped and fell, cursing at a
skinned knee and a sore elbow. Desperation and gravity pro-
pelled her. Sweat dripped from her forehead and evaporated
into the humid air.

Soon she reached the same cliff she'd always visited. She
listened to the darkness and heard nothing. Nerves tingled
her skin; dread manifested in her stomach.

"Hello?" she cried out.

At first, only echoes. Then a distantly familiar clicking echoed against the canyon walls. She forced herself not to flee. The scuttling sounds grew louder, and soon the entire canyon was awash in the static roar of chitinous movement. Sophia trembled and waited.

Silhouettes of fingertips blotted out sections of starlit sky over the Badlands as they leaped above her. A hand curled over the cliff's edge, followed by a dozen others.

The Creators surrounded her, barely visible but unbearably present. This was her time, surely.

Two of the hands reached forth their fingers and covered her limbs, pushed her down on the hard rocks and knocked the wind from her. Pain erupted through her back, and she squirmed against her entrapment.

One hand crawled over her, and she could just make out the divots in its pink flesh. A hungry void opened on its palm and revealed a soft, wet tongue, which caressed her cheek, leaving viscous blobs of saliva that dripped down her neck to her shoulder. Its breath was a hot cloud that stank of paint and clay. It came closer, and hard, jagged teeth scratched her cheeks. Nobody had ever talked about this happening. Was this Creation? She began to cry.

"Wait," cried a voice from behind her. "Let her go!"

The Creator reared back. Sophia craned her neck and saw Lisa standing near the spot where grass became hard rock.

"Please," she said. "Take these instead."

She slowly removed three pieces of pottery from a sack in her shaking hand—two vases and a bowl— and set them on the ground.

The Creators hesitated. Something like giggles or the chit-terings of deranged squirrels erupted from their mouths. They released Sophia, moving slowly toward Lisa's offering. There were wet smacks as their lips parted. They lunged on the pottery, but the girls didn't stay to watch what happened next.

They ran together. Lisa offered her no explanations, but Sophia didn't ask. Her thoughts were only on returning to her room before those things could make their way into Manos

326 ♣ ALEX WOLFGANG

once again. When they reached Sophia's house, Lisa turned to leave.

"Wait," Sophia said.

Lisa looked back.

"What do you think they do with the art they take?"

"Constance says they have an enormous gallery somewhere, and there's lots more who admire it. My parents say—"

"I want to know what *you* think."

Lisa thought for a moment. "I think...I think they're learning from us. They study it and try to make their own."

"What makes you say that?"

"I don't know. It's a beautiful thought, that maybe we're the ones helping them instead of the other way around. Plus, it's not like we'll ever know. Might as well believe what feels good, right?"

Crickets chirped in the night's silence.

"So why do you think they stopped?"

Lisa cleared her throat. "I...I have to go."

The next day, Sophia ditched school. She paced along the main road, gazing at the busy studios that lined the main street. The townspeople averted their gaze at the sight of her. They focused on their tasks, arms mindlessly maneuvering paintbrushes or gathering molten glass from a furnace. Joanna Nelson peeked at her over the top of her canvas, eyes watering beneath tufts of grey hair. Most of her yard's easels were occupied.

"Morning, Joanna," Sophia said.

The old woman sunk behind her painting and said nothing, just scowled. Her canvases were just visible. Gone were the fairies and gnomes, now replaced by black goat-men and decrepit witches.

Peter Wood lay passed out on his front lawn in a wicker basket, one so large he must have weaved it for this explicit purpose. Beside him, a mostly empty bottle of whiskey lay tipped over in the grass.

A little further down, the Merrimans' sculptures had also evolved to a grotesque state. Angels and animals were now headless bodies slumped in death or frightened children screaming to an unseen void. Their newest work showed an old man stabbing himself in the neck with a screwdriver. He grinned in ecstasy.

Near Lisa's studio, soft weeping emerged from behind a wall. The Creators had built her a studio that was half-inside, half-outside—a large red barn with an absent wall that allowed passersby to watch her work. Hundreds, if not thousands, of ceramic sculptures surrounded her.

Sophia followed the sounds into the workshop, past hundreds of bowls and vases strewn haphazardly across the ground. The crying grew louder.

Lisa lay in a heap beside her kiln, face buried in her hands. She jolted when Sophia approached, trying to wipe the tears from her eyes.

"Hey," Sophia said.

"Hey."

"I like your pottery."

"Thank you."

A long moment passed. Sophia wanted to speak of the previous night, but the words wouldn't come.

"Why were you crying?"

Lisa bit her lip. She gestured around the studio, at all the unclaimed pieces. She'd likely made some of these years ago.

"Why don't they like them?" Lisa asked.

"I think they're beautiful."

"They liked Constance's portraits," Lisa said. "They took them all last night. Every single one. You know how many pieces they've taken from me? Five, Sophia. Five. I've been doing this for four years now. Why did they make me this way if they didn't like what I could do?"

"They liked what you gave them last night."

Lisa looked away. "I didn't make those. My father did."

"Oh. What were you doing there?"

328 ♣ ALEX WOLFGANG

"I wanted ... I wanted to see if they'd believe they were mine."

Sophia's heart sank, but the feeling was coupled with guilt-ridden relief. For the first time, she wondered if maybe she was the fortunate one.

That feeling lingered. Her departure felt inevitable long before it happened.

———————————————————

The morning after she'd decided it was time to leave, Sophia awoke early and strode through Manos's morning chill, examining the Creators' handiwork in fixing the hail-damaged rooftops. Her resolve hadn't dissipated. Just after dawn she passed Lisa, whose blonde hair was matted with sweat and clay, her eyes bloodshot. She held a vase but struggled to find a place to put it. Before her lay a sea of ceramic, dirt peeking through the spaces between.

"Still no luck, huh?" Sophia asked. "How long since the last time?"

"Year and a half." Lisa said, her voice weak, eyes averted from Sophia's. "Anyone else?"

She shook her head. "Nothing."

Lisa looked at her feet. "Damn."

"It's because of me," Sophia said. "It won't get any better while I'm still here."

Lisa's cheeks reddened. "You've got no reason to think that."

"Doesn't really matter. Everyone thinks so."

Lisa shrugged. "I don't."

"Well, I'm finally leaving," Sophia said. "I hope it helps."

Lisa laughed, then cut herself off. "Where are you going to go?"

Above them, a gust of wind pulled brown leaves from an oak tree and sent them spilling down the path that led toward the edge of town. Sophia looked longingly toward the expanse of blue sky on the horizon. She pointed toward it, and Lisa scoffed.

"You think they'll let you through the Badlands?"

"Why not? They don't care about me."

Lisa's eyes swept over her compulsive creations. "I'm sure they care. Why else would you be here?"

Sophia ignored her question. "I think you should come, too."

"Sophia…"

"I'm serious. We can leave together. You don't want this either, I know you don't. You're just as miserable as everyone else."

"I can't." She stared at a bowl near her feet.

"Tonight," she said. "After they're done. Meet me by the schoolhouse. If you aren't there by 1:30, I'll go without you."

"I—"

"Think about it, okay? Don't say anything else, just think about it."

———

That night, as the Creators moved through Manos, Sophia laid in bed and wondered if Lisa would come. Once an hour had passed, and the Creators made no more sounds, she climbed from her bed and headed into the night. She brought a sack containing clothes, water, meager food rations, and a lantern. Hopefully it would be enough to get her through the Badlands, but who knew how far that aimless desolation stretched? Who knew if they would let her pass? If she died out there, maybe that would be alright.

Still, calm blanketed her as she strode through the moonlit town. The hundreds, maybe thousands of art pieces still sat unmolested where they'd been left. Her parents' glass reflected stars; dim faces gazed at her longingly from portraits. Relics of artistic anguish and unfulfilled desires. Maybe someday the Creators would be hungry again, but in the meantime, she wouldn't be here to watch everyone suffer.

She waited for half an hour by the schoolhouse. The clocktower counted the minutes away from a few blocks over. With each passing moment, she became more desperate.

She was a fool. Lisa was Created. Lisa was an artist. Why would her companion throw that all away for her? When these thoughts overtook her, she forced herself to remember the empty, hollow eyes that plagued Lisa, that plagued every single artist in Manos.

Finally, footsteps. Lisa emerged through the trees. She stepped into the moonlight, her face expressing pain and shame. She carried nothing.

Sophia's heart sank. "You're not coming."

Lisa's lip trembled. "No."

"Why not?"

"I want to, Sophia. I really do. But there's nothing else for us out there."

"You don't know that."

Lisa sniffled. "I'm sorry. I don't think you should go, either. You're going to die if you leave."

Anger flashed through Sophia. "Good. I'd rather die than stay here."

They stared at one another for a long moment. Lisa's face was beautiful in its melancholy, its hopeless resignation.

If I had become a painter, Sophia thought, *I would have painted you, and I would have looked at that painting every day.* The thought was absurd—nobody made art for themselves.

"Bye, Lisa."

"Goodbye. I hope you find something out there."

Sophia turned away, forcing herself not to look back. Her slow pace became a sprint, and she didn't stop until she reached the Badlands.

She bypassed the cliff where everyone else had been Created, instead carefully descending the canyon walls in the spots least steep. She tied the lantern to her pack, straining her eyes in its soft glow. There were no stirrings from the Creators.

As she descended the canyon's walls, her sense of calm returned. Her heartbeat slowed; her mind stopped racing. She could die here and that would be perfectly fine. They could choose this moment for her creation, but even that didn't frighten her. Were they to lay their fingers on her, break her bones and reform her, she'd allow herself to tumble deep into the Badlands and die, never giving them the satisfaction of watching her develop her pointless artistry. Never causing her the true misery they seemed to desire.

Within half an hour, she'd fully descended the canyon, only slipping twice on loose rocks that cracked and tumbled to the bottom. She looked up at the steep cliffs. The darkness around her swallowed up all but her lantern and the faint light of the moon above.

She weaved through the Badlands for an hour or more, following the carved-out sections and letting the natural pathways determine her fate. She didn't stop until her feet knocked against something soft and fleshy.

Blood buzzed in her ears. When she looked down, she nearly screamed. A Creator was balled into a fist, slumbering away silently. She squinted and looked further, only to see dozens more, all dozing like penned cattle.

The one she'd bumped stirred. Its fingers unfurled, lazily feeling the stones around it. She staggered backward as quietly as she could. Her courage waned, and terror flooded her veins.

The Creator lifted itself onto its middle and ring fingers, stepping toward her as though they were legs. It opened its mouth and yawned. The others began to stir, too.

Sophia stood frozen, awaiting whatever was coming to her. The other Creators rose on their fingertips, and they surrounded her silently, moving without apparent threat. There was no leaping or tackling like there had been before.

As they stood, they revealed what looked like chunks of garbage surrounding where they slept. When Sophia dared look away from their towering figures, her lamplight revealed what was truly there—shredded canvases, shattered glass, pots, and vases lying in ruins. A Creator moved and revealed a passage that led further into the canyon. In it lay endless mounds of art which stretched further than her light could illuminate. It did not look consumed, nor did it look examined. It looked as though the Creators had simply taken the pieces and tossed them on the ground.

A few feet behind a Creator was a painting she barely recognized—one of Constance's. It depicted a family sitting beneath a tree, sunlight streaming through the branches. Constance had showed it to her just a few weeks ago, beaming with pride. Now it was little more than a mangled hunk of shredded fabric and wooden framing. She'd been so proud when it was taken, so validated.

The answer to Manos' greatest question lay before Sophia, and for a moment, she wished she could have died without ever knowing. She wept for her town, for its empty existence, for its fruitless misery.

The Creators encircled her, blocking her view of the discarded art. One by one, single eyes opened at the base of their palms. They glowed a pale, lunar blue. She felt their pupils sweep her body, question her form and presence.

"Please," she said. "Please let me go. Just let me go through. I won't bother you again. I won't tell anyone, if that's what you want."

The Creators looked at one another, puzzlement in their eyes.

"I don't want to be an artist. I just want you to leave us alone."

Two Creators stood on either side of her as if standing guard while the others gathered in a circle to confer. They pressed their flesh and fingernails into the stone ground, rubbing patterns like words. Some got heated, their movements frantic, others remained stoic and peaceful. After several agonizing minutes, they broke from their huddle.

One approached Sophia, who closed her eyes and awaited her fate.

There was a light pressure against her forehead. She opened her eyes, and the world was awash in a haze of blue—she could see perfectly through the darkness. Distant trees became visible, striations in the canyon walls now clear and vibrant. Water vapor seemed to sparkle.

She was calm again. Like a drug entering her system, her nerves settled into a peaceful bliss.

The two Creators that were guarding her backed away. She no longer wanted to flee, nor did she feel the urge to create, at least not in the usual sense. Instead, another compulsion drove her back the way she came. She walked slowly, but the Creators didn't follow. She climbed the rocks back toward Manos.

Once at the top she felt she could see her town for the first time. The shapes of the trees and houses were immaculate and fascinating; the starry night sky a flurry of sublime light.

She walked until she reached Lisa's studio, the sea of ignored creations. Her good mood faded.

An aura of pointless misery oozed from the pieces. Such effort and torment, all of it amounting to nothing but frustration. But her sadness was short-lived—she could fix this problem.

Sophia giggled, then laughed hysterically as the rush overtook her. She brought her foot down on one of Lisa's vases, smashing the fragile porcelain into a hundred tiny shards. The feeling was incredible. She did it again. And again. Soon she was dancing in the moonlight, crushing everything underfoot until she was too tired to go on.

A third of Lisa's pieces now lay in shattered shambles. Panting, Sophia searched inside the shop until she found a large burlap sack. Bit by bit, she picked up the shards of porcelain and filled the sack until it was full to bursting.

She dragged the bag down the pathway, through the forest and out to the edge of the Badlands. There she emptied it, sending the shards raining to the canyon floor where Sophia knew Lisa would never venture.

Her euphoria renewed. She glowed the entire way home.

Sleep came easily, her last thoughts lingering on how happy Lisa would be in the morning. Tomorrow maybe she would save someone else—if she decided anyone else was worthy of being saved.

They could judge her, ridicule her, mock her. It wouldn't matter. Should she ever tire of her role, she was capable of ruining everything they thought they knew, of exposing the cavernous void of their lives and sinking Manos into a deeper despair, one they could never escape from. She'd been Created, or something close enough to it, and she felt her art might be the greatest medium of all—the art of the gods, the Creators, the Destroyers.

TRACY FAHEY

WITCH
WALKING

THEY call me the Witch On The Wall. The Hag Of The Castle. The Evil Eye Stone. The Idol. Síle-na-Gig. I stand here, on one foot, in the magician stance. One arm is raised above my head. My open mouth is a channel of stories as old as the land. Between my legs, another opening, fearlessly displayed; an uaimh, a cave, a secret grotto. It is the origin of the world, the passage between places.

I stand in silence. The Great Mother, stone echo of the goddesses. Áine. Boann. Banbha. Cessair. Brigid. Gobhait.

They come to me here, the women. They do not fear me; my frozen shout, my open womb. They perform rituals in my honour. They pray to me for strength, they touch me for fertility. They keep me safe. They move me at night, from standing stone to church, to castle, and back again, to hidden stones in the forest. The centuries slip by as the trees around me thrust from the ground, grow from saplings to huge oaks. I stand in the ticking clock of the land, and life rolls round me.

But wait. Here is another. Her footsteps crackle on dry twigs. I stare into the summer sun. Come.

On the thirteenth day I find her. Another night of broken dreams, of half-heard noises. I wake in a twist of damp sheets. Birds tweet insistently outside. The curtains are fringed with early sun. My body is sore and stiff, a rush of vinegar reflux in my throat. I lie and visualise stretching out, my legs moving easily under me, muscles flexing and aligning. *A walk.* The perfect place glows green in my head, the tangle of old woods at the back of this unfamiliar house.

338 ❧ TRACY FAHEY

The sun climbs as I do; crushed grass under my feet scents the air with green warmth. The white cat from next door follows me for a while, purring and winding around my legs. From the darkness of the forest, a low bird-call, ominous: *Oooo. Ooo. Ooo.* The softness of the gravelled path is a revelation, tiny stones crunching under me. I'm a city girl. My feet are used to concrete footpaths, the only trees I'm accustomed to are dusty, diesel-fumed, leaves half-crackled with brown.

But here. *Here.* I stop and breathe in the air, rising from the earth, damp and delicious. Here is a peaceful, green, early-morning paradise. The lemon-sour bile rises again; I swallow it back. To my right, there's a barely-perceptible lane of trampled grass. It spools out into the woods, a viridian ribbon of invitation.

Under the trees on this path, it's darker. Greener. Sunlight glows far above, filtered through leaves. I hesitate, and then deliberately turn to walk this new path as silently as I can. There's the faint rustle of my steps, the occasional crack of a tiny branch underfoot, the soft *thud* of a dislodged stone. It's magical. I look around, half-expecting a witch cottage, a trail of breadcrumbs.

The path comes to an abrupt end in a clearing. Light spills down, steady and golden. There's a small circle of stones, no higher than my knee. And in the centre—

Her. She blazes forth, her outlines burn clear under the sun. The stone is cared for; I can see the darker patches where the moss and lichen have been scraped away. She faces me, oversized face blooming hard with strength—staring eyes, bald head, piano-key ribs, open mouth. Her body is smaller, twisted. Even though her limbs contort, arm over her head, body pivoted on a small foot, she is perfectly balanced. Unafraid, she exposes herself, the crevasse of her interior. She peels back her folds and I'm hypnotised, a newborn in front of her, standing before the birth channel. I blink. She's the oddest thing I've ever seen. But strangely powerful.

I touch her with a hesitant fingertip.

"Ow!" A shock, a sting. I snap my finger back, stick it in my mouth. A tiny bloom of tinny blood on my tongue. There's a bright speck of red snagged on a rough crevice. I eye the carved figure with a new respect.

In front of her, a collection of objects; tarnished coins, a broken rosary, pieces of glass pocked with dirt. A rusty miraculous medal, a photograph bleached pale. Some old bones, frail and yellowed. Unbidden, a thought—*This is a witch place.*

I swallow, shake my head. No. I've seen these places before as a child. They're shrines for praying, grottoes of saints. Places of petition, special spaces. I pause. My head blurs, fills with a tangle of voices, running down a dark road, the cold, jolting bus. I pat my pockets. I've brought nothing here.

Instead, I pull out three strands of hair. Three momentary pricks of pain. I tie them carefully to a piece of speckled bone and murmur a simple prayer. "Keep me safe."

In the trees, the women nod to each other.

I came to life here, in this rough stone. The woman who carved me did so as an act of simple veneration. She knew who I was before I did. She called me Áine. Anu. Bright stones encircled me, anchored me, the still point of the wheel of the year. This was a wide plain then, only a few small trees marking the boundary. The came to me then. Not just the women, but men, children, to mark the turning points of the year. Imbolc, the birthing season, Bealtaine, the start of summer. Lughnasa, the harvest. Samhain, the death of the year. And as they celebrated Imbolc and Bealtaine, druid men and druid women joined together, the sacred sensuality of coupling. Divine feminine met divine masculine, and the children who ensued were special, blessed. The wheel of stones counted their nine months, and they were birthed here, attended by midwives. As their flowers piled around me, offerings, I stood proud and powerful among them.

And slowly I learned who I was. The Great Mother Goddess.

Years slid between my parted legs, and all was good with the land.

In bed, there's a low, slow prick of pain from my finger. The woman in the woods has stung me. I sleep a little more, but she follows me there. In my dreams, she raises her imperious arm. From her mouth, a torrent of sound; susurration of leaves, the bright, pulsing flow of a river.

I wake, and the dark folds round me, my duvet a mortuary sheet. I claw it down, stare into the corners, the soft blackness there.

I don't put on a light.

When I came to this house, I came in darkness, fumbling my way in past the stiff lock, the inky hall. For the first few days, I didn't even switch on the lights at night; I went to bed when the sun did. Lying in the dark, my stomach roiled, every slight noise waking me, alert and sharp. Night after night I imagined sudden, heavy steps, always waking with a start.

I lie there till sun leaks in, gilding the ceiling. Over morning coffee, I try looking her up on my laptop. Nothing. No statue listed on any of the sites I've found. Not even the stone circle is mentioned. Strange.

A knock at the door. I freeze, heart thudding noisily against my ribs. An impulse to hide. Then it comes again. Another knock. I move noiselessly down the hall, press an eye to the porthole of magnifying glass. In the porch, a bulky, older woman, face wide in a comfortable smile, letters in her hand. I breathe deeply, open the door.

"God save all here." Her face is cushioned, a web of wrinkles dance around her grin. "You're new here." It's a statement, so I don't reply. Instead, I take a letter from her outstretched hand. *It must be it. It must be.*

"Settled in now? Lovely place, here."

I pause. I want to ask her, you know. 'do you know the place well?"

"I do, sure, wasn't I born here." She points behind me, to the woods. "I live the other side of the forest. Always have. Kathleen O'Neill." She nods, head to one side, inquisitive.

"Sheela." I say. It's not my name, but it's the name on the letter. "Tell me, do you know the path in the woods? To the stone circle?"—I hesitate—"To the carving of the woman?"

Her eyes lock on mine, a steady stare. "Aye."

"Who is she?"

For an instant her eyes crease again in a smile. "Same name as you, girl. Sheela. *Síle-na-Gig.*"

━━━━━━━━━━

Over the tops of the trees, I saw them, the bright stones rising. There is a new worship in the land; a man hangs on a cross, his tortured body a site of veneration. But they don't forget me. Instead, a woman comes, Inghean Bhaoithe, a daughter of Boathe, Boann. She recognises me, this woman, this abbess. She feels my power. And in her soul, she knows that a new man needs to be balanced with an old, wise woman. She tells some strong men to take me from my circle, to their buildings, to place me there.

From my new position, high over the door of this Christ-church, I watch them come in, the old druids turned priests and priestesses now. They come in from the village, the men and women whose ancestors conceived and birthed in my circle. They eat the body and drink the blood of the new god.

The men leave. But the women stay. They build a little cairn of stones by the main door, stand on it, stretching, tip-toed, to touch my divine mother-womb. They believe it brings them fertility. I point to the sky, imperious.

They pass between my thighs from the old world into the new church.

━━━━━━━━━━

I find myself wandering instinctively back into the woods. I tell myself it's the shade that draws me, but it's not. The letter brings some relief, the order is passed. My steps are lighter on the path. I follow the thread of beaten grasses back to the

342 ☙ TRACY FAHEY

clearing. The tiny spot of red on finger throbs like a beacon, steady and low.

I catch my breath in quick surprise. There's another woman there in the stone circle, her ripe belly swelling out a floral summer dress. As I watch from the trees, she draws a length of yellow ribbon from the pocket, and holds it to that other, strange Sheela. Her lips move in a silent prayer as she does so. She takes out a pair of scissors, snips the ribbon neatly in two. It's so quiet here, I hear the *snick* of the blades. She loops one end around the stone and ties it, the other she ties around her own waist, or where it should be. I hesitate, a voyeur, lurking in the fringe of trees. I move, and as I do, a twig snaps, brittle, under my feet.

"Oh Jesus!" The woman presses a hand to her throat. "You frightened the life out of me! Come on, come out of the trees." She beckons me, laughing now.

I join her at the stone. "What were you doing with the ribbon?"

"It's an old thing we do, here in the village." She smiles at me. "Síle protects expectant mothers. We all do it. Our mothers did it too, and way back, I imagine our ancestors did too."

"Who *is* she?" The question bursts out of me.

"We call her 'St. Síle' here. She's a saint for women. You'll see"—She stops short, then looks me over, carefully. "Well, you'll see that women come here. All of us."

I like this. A saint for women. Even if she looks alarming, crude, weird. There's something elemental about her. Here, I feel—I draw in a breath—I feel almost safe.

"I'm Sarah," says the woman, extending a hand.

"Sheela." I take her hand solemnly and shake it. It's like an agreement.

Her face lights up, just like Kathleen the post-lady's did. "You were meant to come here with that name."

"Maybe." I like her, but I'm giving nothing away. She places a hand on her bump and burps slightly. "Sorry," she says, but in a resigned way. "Heartburn, all the time. Lucky I've only got a month to go. It's wicked."

I stand and look at her. My throat bubbles up, battery acid. *I can't be.*

But that evening, after I've caught the bus to the next village to get the kit, I pee in the café loos. Two blue lines well up. *I can't be.*

I am.

Fuck.

―――――

For a time, all is well in the monastery. The new priests and priestesses do not cast off the old ways. They are part druid, after all. Instead, they welcome the beautiful parts of this new faith, the sacrifice, the love. And they knit it together with the old cycles. The Great Mother is celebrated again in the body of the new Madonna. Above the door, I watch as the holy women and men of this monastery join together in prayer and ritual. The scriptoriums flower new manuscripts, ornate with Celtic strapwork, folding strips of leather translated onto the page. Birds and beasts play in the margins.

But this old Coptic system, which travelled to Ireland from Egypt, via Gaul, poses a threat. There is a bigger Church now, a symbol of a new Empire, stretching from Rome. It speaks the language of power and authority. The kingdoms and their sovereignty must bow down. This Roman Church wants to purge women from these mixed monasteries, to render them subservient instead of equal. Their men speak of woman as sinful and point at me, an illustrated stone sermon, the subject of which is lust. My womb is a site of sin, a dark cave that frightens them.

There is no space here for the old sites of veneration.

There is no space here for a wise, old woman.

―――――

How could I be such a fool? What was I *thinking?*

The truth, I wasn't. I wasn't thinking about anything but escape. My rucksack lay underneath a carpet of clothes in the wardrobe, a guilty passport jammed with money, clothes, and mementoes of my life before. At nights, when you lay beside me, snoring, I fancied I heard it beat thickly in the darkness, a tell-tale heart, disclosing my intention. By day, when you were gone, I planned my route, I made phone calls to women who were ready to help me, carefully erasing the call list before evening. With all of those things in motion, I forgot the most important thing: the foil packet of pills in the bathroom.

And now here it is. A souvenir of the worst timeline. I press a hand to my stomach, still flat, and do the unthinkable, wish it away, a bad dream.

But there's no awakening from this one. My body refuses to repel the invader. The waves of heartburn are stronger now. In the mornings I'm sore, nauseated. My breasts are fuller, painful. I am slowly reforming, resentful, around this small seed: an envelope full of bad news.

The old anxiety floods back. When the shadows fall, I pull the duvet over my head. My hot, quick breath slicks my limbs in sweat. Whenever I close my eyes, the unfamiliar walls resettle themselves; reformed in the shape of those old rooms. I hear your footsteps now, constantly. On the gravel outside. Coming upstairs, one heavy tread at a time. Circling my bed, where we lie, it and me. In the darkness these rooms resolve themselves into a memory palace, theatre sets for old nightmares. I suck my finger, the soreness subsided, just a little hard lump now under the skin.

Once, I wake up and see a dark figure standing over me. *I'm here*, breathes the dream-voice, harsh and unpleasant. When I wake fully, you've dissolved, melted in the rays of weak morning sunshine.

I don't stir outside for a few days. Instead, I look out my window, at the children playing, at the white cat stretched out, sunbathing in the untidy patch of grass. The only contact I have is with Kathleen. Some days she knocks even when she's not delivering post. She tells me the news of the village, comforting anecdotes populated with names I don't recognise. I let her talk. She never asks questions, I'm glad. But sometimes I see her eyes scan me, concern in her kindly eyes.

When I finally go to the shop, sick of drinking my tea black, I see Sarah with her shopping basket, bump resplendent and proud in front of her, knotted with yellow ribbon.

"Sheela!" Her face is warm and welcoming. I'm absurdly touched. We chat about her pregnancy. Part of me wants to tell her—why? I've barely admitted it, even to myself. But I don't. I carry it inside me, pushed to the edge of my consciousness.

"Come home with me, have tea," she urges. And I do. But I'm not expecting company. When we get back there's two other women waiting at the gate. Another of them has a gentle bump, and a string around her middle too.

Sarah sees me looking at it. "Told you it wasn't just me! Anne believes, too."

"It's a good luck charm," offers one, a little older than the others. Ellen, I think. "I did it for all three of mine. And all were fine." She beams and sips her tea. "You have a lucky name, Sheela." I don't tell her I made my own luck.

"You must come there for her feast day. St. Síle's," says Anne. "It's the eleventh of next month." The women nod. I feel a warm glow of acceptance, even though I'm still wary.

"Definitely." Sarah refills my cup, smiles.

Maybe. Maybe not. I put on an interested expression. "What happens then?"

"We walk the rounds."

"Witchwalking," says Ellen. They laugh. I join in, though I'm not sure exactly what I'm laughing at.

When I get home, I turn on my phone. *You have missed twenty-seven calls.* They're from an unknown number. I switch it off, throw it in a drawer.

That night I curl around myself. Around it. It's the size of a large kidney bean, I've worked out.

"Hello, little human bean." And there, in the darkness, the pact is sealed. I'm committed.

The morning rain falls soft and relentless. I walk over the sodden grass to the stone woman. I unroll a red spool of thread, tie it around her. There are six other rags tied there, including Sarah's ribbon. I knot it on, and then tie a secret girdle around my waist, under my clothes.

"Keep us safe." No more than a breath in the moist air, but Síle-na-gig's mouth seems to soften in a smile.

I still stand over the church door. But things are changing here. A new bishop travels around the land, face set in resolution. His holy book in one hand, he drives out the old ways. As he does, he casts out serpents; symbol of the neart, the energy of the divine masculine and divine feminine combined, the snakes that weave around Greek healing staffs. They slide before him, hissing in the dust.

The bishop continues to travel around the country. As he comes closer, he banishes the old Hag of Carrigogunnell, the Cailleach of the rock. He blows out her candle, she disappears in a blink. Afterwards, rumours blaze that she was a wicked old woman, a sorceress who could turn men to stone with a glance. Witch. The older ones know the truth; she was the Watcher On The Hill who guarded them. But they say nothing. The new power glitters bright and sharp as a sword in the land.

The women still come to me, but quietly now, and always by night. I have become the Witch In The Wall.

A new myth rises, of the Bishop's wife. Her name is Sheelagh, Sheela, Síle. It's no coincidence that they speak of her as a Hag. Disgruntled, she sweeps the earth with angry brush-strokes after his feast day, a vain attempt to clear his new rituals and restore the old ways. People speak in hushed voices of Sheelagh's Broom, bringing foul weather to the land; blasts of snow and wind.

No. I am the land. I bring no misfortune. I bring fertility, Sovereignty.

The abbess looks in my direction from time to time, a worried expression on her face. One evening she comes to me. She stands before me at the magical time of twilight, intersection of day and night. Beside her is a royal woman, I can tell by her dress. She points at me, they talk. The abbess nods, steps back. From behind them, a troupe of men emerge. They climb up to me, chip around the rough stone.

This place is no longer safe for me.

It's the powerlessness that hurts the most. I'm hidden here in this small village. Occulted. But I never feel entirely safe.

By day it's not so bad. I keep myself busy, cleaning these new rooms. The old, flagged floors gleam, mopped till they shine. Grey spiderwebs cling and coil around my fingers. I'm building my magpie nest here, piece by piece: an old woollen blanket from the charity shop, washed soft; an embroidered cushion, glowing with flowers; a cheap glass vase brimming with Michelmas daisies.

Some days I venture out. I go to the shop. I go to the library, breathe in the scent of old wood in the converted church. Sometimes I see Kathleen, bag slung over one shoulder. We wave to each other. Once I meet Sarah for a coffee in the village café by the river. She's with her husband Paul, a quiet man. Her bump swells hard against her dress. It fascinates me. She talks about her plans, a natural birth, she says. Better for the mother, better for the baby.

"It's a girl," she tells me. Paul smiles at her with such loving, intense pride that I have to look away, embarrassed. I go home and wash my windows till they gleam.

Yes. By day it's not so bad. Nights are a different story. As soon as the summer light fades into grey shadows, the unease grows. The cheerful noise of children playing, only half-heard by daylight, disappears. Silence falls, only broken by the intermittent drone of a passing car. I draw the curtains tight and switch on the low glow of a lamp, the only light I now permit myself. And here—in the twilight—*here* is where my anxiety blooms.

In these rooms, shadows tangle in corners. The contours become liminal now, shifting whenever I turn my back. I sit, one hand on my belly, a tiny clock ticking below the surface, counting down till…till what? I don't want to think about it. It's flowering now in the darkness, no longer a bean, but a peach. Soft-skinned, fragile.

One night, there's a soft *thump* on my window. I jump up, heart thudding. Another bump. For a second I see it, clear as day. Your big hand splayed on the pane, testing the surface for a crack, a chink. I switch off the lamp, grope my way to the kitchen, slide the phone out of a drawer. It glows green as I power it on. Forty-three missed calls. I key in 9-9-9, pause, breathe deeply and move the curtain a fraction. A white shape, two sharp green eyes. *The cat.* I sit down in the darkness, knees weak with relief.

I still dream of you. You snake through my nightmares, that tumbled jangle of trees and streets I walk through in the dream world.

The night I discover the cat on the windowsill, I dream of Síle. I dream I press my face to her cold stone one; it becomes soft, yielding. Her stone grin fades, reshapes to become yours, mouth open now in rage. *I'm coming*, you whisper, wet lips moving against my check. *I'm coming for you.*

I wake then, and cry, long and hard, arms wrapped around myself and the peach. The frail bloom of its skin, a treasure to be protected. I get up and huddle on the sofa.

Kathleen finds me there. She passes by the window, frowns, knocks.

"Are you okay?"

I open the door reluctantly. "Fine." But my red eyes tell the truth.

She comes in, uninvited. Sets down her bag on the worktop, fills the kettle, clicks the switch. "Go on," she says gently. "Tell me."

And I do. Not all of it. I don't tell her the worst bit. The bruises. The broken jaw. The sleeping pills I crushed up and poured in your beer can. "It was a bad situation," I say, and leave it like that. She sips her tea, unsurprised.

"And now I'm pregnant." It's the first time I've said it. The words fall like stones. "I'm pregnant and I don't know what to do."

Her face changes, brightens. "Sure, that's wonderful news! And you're in the best place for the baby. This village is a sacred place for births. Lots of happy mothers here." She looks at me searchingly. "You need to come to walk the rounds on Síle's feast day. The witchwalking."

This is the second time I've heard of it. "What exactly *is* witchwalking?"

Kathleen pours herself another cup, tops mine up. "Drink. It's good for you." Stirring her tea, she smiles at me. "Witchwalking is the old name for it. We walk the rounds, walk around the stones, and pray to St. Síle. Pregnant women go first, then the rest of us, all praying for good pregnancies, safe deliveries, and healthy children. It's lovely."

"It sounds it." Almost imperceptibly, I've relaxed. Under the table I press a secret hand to my stomach. *We're safe here, little one.*

Kathleen's gaze is shrewd. "You're safe here, Sheela. You were meant to come here. She'll protect you."

Now I am the Hag of the Castle. I stand at another entrance, but this time I have a new role. The woman who brought me here knows my power. She uses me to keep her and her family safe within these walls.

But here, I do not welcome, I repel. My body has transformed over the centuries, once a cypher of power and sovereignty, then a syncretic symbol, then a site of sin. And now it transforms again, its function apotropaic. I am the Evil Eye Stone. On this wall, I repel invaders. My body, once celebrated in fertility rites in the shivering, long-grassed fields, is construed differently here. My twisted body, my stark ribs, my shouting mouth, the threat of death-in-life between my legs. My womb reveals a dark passage into the next life, warning for trespassers.

The years spool by. I stand on the castle wall, a warning written in stone. But from time to time, the women still come to me, secretly, under the cover of darkness. They touch my stone body, they pray softly in the night. And in the mornings, small heaps of wilted flowers lie below me.

And still the dreams continue. Even though the women surround me here in the village, I'm still haunted by you. You've soaked into my skin for so long, you're in my bones. The seed you planted, our little peach, *my* little peach nestled dark inside. The house colludes with you. Curtains rustle in the night breeze, whisper in your voice. *I'm coming.* Walls melt and flow, like time does. I'm here, but not. Part of me is still there, still waiting for your footstep, for the alarm to sound noiselessly within me.

I know I need to sleep. The peach needs it, and so do I. But instead, I fall into the habit of napping during the day, reassured by the soft glow of sunshine that falls over me, a blanket. *If you come, you'll come at night.* That's when I stay awake.

And so, the days drift by. It's getting hotter every day. The peach is now an apple. I watch the flowers in the garden dry and curl and remember to drink water for it. For her. Somehow, I feel it's a girl. Outside, the white cat yawns and stretches itself out, stiff-legged and splayed in the midday sun.

In the shop, in the library, I meet the women, sometimes singly, sometimes in a group. Their company makes me brave. I tell them my news, slowly, one by one. Sarah is delighted. "Another baby for the village. It'll be a bumper crop this year. Me. You. Anne." Her bump, enormous now, moves as she speaks. It writhes, the lump of a foot kicks, retreats. It's queasily magical. I smile.

"Not long now." Her eyes radiate contentment. "Not long at all."

They know, the women. They know that the land is out of kilter now. Waves of new invaders come from across the water. Apotro-

paic symbols no longer hold the charge of fear for these foreigners. They take the land as a gift from English kings and queens. The marriage to the land, the sacred union of ruler and landscape, disappears.

All around the land withers. Sovereignty has been dispersed to a city, with no connection to the rituals. Leaders no longer kiss the Hag, no longer look to women to be appointed. The old goddesses lie dormant, buried in new clothes in stone tombs, under holy wells, in hiding places on mountains, in secret places.

The women gather around me and talk. They decide to occult me, to remove me again, to keep me safe.

They hide me where no one will think of looking. They hide me in plain sight. They hide me where I came to life, in the forest.

I fall asleep on the sofa, woollen blanket pulled up, tickling my nose. I'm too warm. *I'll push it down in a moment,* I think, but I'm already asleep, swimming, descending. The world outside blurs and fades.

I'm in the dreamhouse now, walking through the old, dark rooms with uncertain steps. Every sound is amplified here, echoes bleed into the still air. There's something here. *Somebody* here. I feel my way around the bedroom, wall by cautious wall. No. Not here. I move out to the landing, slow, careful. There's an abyss there, a dark staircase of nothing in front of me.

From downstairs, a rustle.

I step into the abyss. One foot meets the wood. I swallow, hard. Next foot down. Another rustle. Somewhere below me, a large animal, shifting, restless.

"Who is it?" My voice is an airless croak. The sound disappears into the air.

A thump now. Big. Menacing. *This isn't the cat.* I move, faster now. The fear of the unknown is worse than the reality.

I push open the kitchen door. There you are, silhouetted against the window. I've forgotten to draw the blinds. The cold light of a full moon pours in. You are silver-edged, huge.

I'm here.

Fear rises thick in my throat. I can't speak. I can't move.

You take a step.

"No!" And I'm awake, cold, blinking. You're gone. Moonlight on my face. I rub my face. I've been sleepwalking. The terror clings to me still, obstinate cobwebs. I shiver.

I have to get out. I don't think, don't delay. Instead, I pull on a coat over my pyjamas, stick my bare, chilled feet into boots and run, stumbling, out the back door and into the woods.

———————————

I am safe here. Safe and worshipped. Even though the rituals are lost in time, the women know my function. I stand back in the circle again, a clock of fertility and birth. In this forest, I rest, a green secret. Grandmothers whisper of my legend to their children, mothers to daughters, all down the long line that stretches back to when these woods were young nubs of branches.

Outside the stones, another circle of trodden grass as the women walk the rounds. Treading the path. Witchwalking.

Remember this: all it takes are women to help us rise.

———————————

The woods are strange at night, darker. Leaves brush my face—a soft, blind caress. There's a torch in my coat pocket. I click it on, move more confidently through the press of trees. The wavering line shows me where the paths diverge. I hesitate, but only for a moment. Somewhere, deep within, I *knew* where I was going.

All around me, a hundred tiny noises.

I'm not scared. It was the house that trapped me. The walls sliding, silent, inward, compressing me with my thoughts. The roof a lid that kept my nightmares in.

On this old way, my feet sink noiselessly into the mossy floor. A cold scent rises, pure and green. The pencil line of the torch draws my path.

A cry. I freeze.

It's a woman. I click the torch off, grab a tree trunk for support. Another cry, a longer one. I've heard that noise before, coming out of my own bruised mouth. *She's in pain.*

I'm braver than I think. Torch on. I stumble faster and faster down the path, following the red thread of cries, as they grow louder and louder. Lights glow ahead. I push the trees outside. And there they are.

The women.

Torches surround them in a neat ring. Shadowy figures stand at the stones. In front of the Síle-na-Gig, illuminated in the light, Sarah lies, her dress rucked up. She moans as I watch; her breath jags in a sharp cry.

"Hush, now," says Ellen, stooping between her knees. "I know what I'm doing."

"She does, you know." Kathleen, nodding, beside her. "She's delivered many babies here. And her mother before her. Eat this now, it'll help." She holds what looks like raw meat to Sarah's mouth.

Sarah takes a bite. Her mouth is smeared crimson. She moans again, a raw, guttural sound. "It hurts." Her face gleams with sweat, her hair plastered to her skull.

"Of course it does, lovey. Your body is birthing." Ellen's hands are busy. "I can see her head now. It won't be long."

The women move around the stones, slowly, clockwise. Ellen raises Sarah's dress. I catch a glimpse of the red, slick wound between her legs, a flash of pale skin inside.

"Push, there's a good girl." Kathleen wipes Sarah's face. She's making wet, animal sounds now, it hurts to listen. "Push."

Sarah arches her back, screams. Ellen reaches, pulls. "She's coming." There's a rush, a blur of movement, she sits back on her heels, arms full of a tiny, red bundle. "Here she is!"

Anne comes out of the shadows, a white cloth in her hands. Her face is pale, terrified. "Here." The women cluster round, blocking my view.

I'm an intruder here. I back away into the soft darkness of the trees.

I stand in the centre of the circle.

They call me St. Síle now, but in their hearts, they know. They know me for what I am, bigger, older, more powerful than this new name. And so they walk the rounds, praying to me for fertility, safe births, healthy children. Here I am both protector and giver. Within my circle, a place of safety and strength.

And in return, their prayers and offerings.

They come for me in the morning. I see them, the small group at the gate. Kathleen, Ellen, Anne. Kathleen knocks gently at the door.

"Ah, you're up," she says, pleased. "Wonderful day, isn't it?"

I look at the sun gilding he hills. "It is."

"A fine morning for St. Síle's Day. Are you coming with us?"

I hesitate. The strange scene from the night before dances in front of my eyes. "Where's Sarah?"

Kathleen's eyes slide to one side. "She's at home, resting."

That makes sense. I don't ask more, and she doesn't volunteer any information. Instead, she points at the assembled women. "Do you have anything you want to bring?" I look closer. Ellen and Anne are both carrying bags.

"Flowers?" I'm already picking them, warmed with early sun. Daisies. Marigolds. Bright and celebratory.

"Lovely," says Kathleen, squinting at the sky. "It's nearly time. Let's go."

We wind our way through the trees. The air is cooler here, restful. Ellen hums as she goes. Anne chatters away to Kathleen, bright and inconsequential village gossip. I watch them all, wondering if I should bring up Sarah, confess that I watched the birth. But I'm shamed by my voyeurism, so I don't. Instead I ask, abruptly—"St. Síle, I'd never heard of her before I came here. Is she venerated anywhere else?"

Ellen stops humming. "Not that I know of, precisely." She turns to me, her voice low. "But I'm sure there are plenty of hidden places, like this, where ancient, sacred women are still quietly celebrated. Even in this modern world, we women are still rooted deeply in the old ways. She is one of those vital connectors."

I nod. Being here, in this village, with these women, feels *right*. Here in the forest, the contemporary world slides away. With this little apple seeded and sprouting inside, I recognise I've always felt this hunger to tap in to an older, more vital life-force.

"And we're here." Kathleen, her face alight. "What a glorious day for it."

We step into the clearing. The sun beats down steadily on Síle, her stone mouth open in celebration. Although it's early, she's already strewn with garlands, part-wilted in the sun. In front of her, a larger pile of offerings; a jumble of objects. On top is Sarah's yellow ribbon, spotted with blood.

━━━━━━━━━━━━━

Ellen takes charge. "Anne, stand at the stone nearest her on the left. Then you, Sheela." She smiles at us. The women take up their places. A hush falls, the only sound the whisper of the breeze through the leaves. *Shhh, shhh, shhh.*

Ellen sings. It's the song she's been humming as we walked through the forest. It's an Irish song, unfamiliar, her voice sweet, rising and lilting. The tune is hauntingly familiar. Anne walks to the Síle stone, pauses, touches the crevice of her open womb. Her lips move silently, she passes on, taking her position at the next stone.

My turn now. I stop in front of the Síle-na-gig, drop my flowers in front of her. My foot brushes against a small bone, crusted with dried blood.

"Touch her." Kathleen's voice, behind me. I don't move for a moment. *Sarah isn't here. The blood. The bone.*

"Touch her." Ellen.

I reach out blindly. Síle's vulva is worn smooth as marble. For hundreds and hundreds of years, women like me, bellies budding with fruit, have performed this ritual. The thought soothes me. She fixes me in a wide stone grin. I touch her. The stone is strangely warm.

And like a thrown switch, the sun disappears. From the forest, a sharp sound; a branch cracks. I turn around, and there, among the trees, the one person I've run here from.

You.

———————————————

Kathleen is beside me. "Who is it?"

"It's him." My voice is a frightened whisper. Silently, they surround me; her, Anne, Ellen.

"Leave her alone." Ellen, her face grim. "You have no place here." She takes my hand. Kathleen takes the other. Anne touches my shoulder. I feel their strength, their purpose flowing through me.

You step out from under the trees. Tall, terrifying. That face that I once thought so handsome is transfigured in a snarl. "Thought I wouldn't find you?"

I find my voice. "Go away. I've got a restraining order. You're breaking the law."

You laugh, unpleasantly. "Think I care about that?" You step closer, insolent. "Think those old biddies can protect you? You're coming home with me."

"No."

I pull my hands free, place them on Síle's head. *Keep me safe.* And everything falls silent. The stone hums under my palms. A quiet power flows outwards, filling the clearing, encasing us within it.

"What the hell?" Your face, unfamiliar. *You're scared.* I straighten my back. When I speak, my voice is not my own; harsh, loud.

"This is a sacred space for women. I protect them here. Men with evil in their hearts cannot come closer."

I watch you try to move forward, but it's as if you're stuck in glue. You push against an invisible shield.

"Go. Forget what you saw. This is not your place."

Slowly, the anger and confusion leaches from your face. Blank and calm, you step back, disappear under the trees.

I lift my hands from Síle, trembling.

"You did, good, girl." Kathleen puts a hand on my shoulder.

"He won't trouble you again." Ellen's face is grim. "He made a bad mistake coming here today. You channelled her power, and he witnessed it. She has wiped it from him now, but some part of him will remember. And fear you."

We embrace then, all of us.

"Have I missed it?" Sarah stands there on the fringes of the forest, a tiny baby swaddled in her arms. She is pale but smiling.

"Oh Sarah!" I pull her and the baby into the group hug. "Congratulations."

"And well done, you," whispers Sarah. "I saw it, Sheela." She puts her cheek to mine.

I am here. I am filled with power and strength. My hand slides down to my belly. From deep within, a movement; a contented wriggle. You are safe now.

I am safe.

I am Sheela.

One hand above my head. One leg in the air. I dance. I dance and the power radiates from me.

I am the Witch On The Wall. The Hag Of The Castle. The Evil Eye Stone. The Idol.

I am Síle-na-Gig.

FINIS

BIOGRAPHIES

DIE BOOTH is a queer indie author who likes painting pictures and exploring dark places. When not writing wild lies, he DJs at Last Rites—the best (and only) goth club in Chester, UK. You can read his prize-winning stories in anthologies from Egaeus Press, Flame Tree Press, Neon Hemlock, the Cheshire Prize for Literature and many others. His cursed new novella *Cool S* is available online, along with short story collections *My Glass Is Runn, Making Friends (and other fictions)* and *365 Lies* (one flash fiction a day for a whole year, with sales proceeds going to the MNDA) and his horradventure novel *Spirit Houses*. He's currently working on a queer coming-of-age Folk Horror novella. You can find out more about his writing at diebooth.wordpress.com or say hi on Twitter @diebooth.

RYAN CASSAVAUGH is a playwright and author originally from the cold frozen wastelands of New Hampshire. He's written a whole bunch of plays. *Jimmy's First Christmas on Parole* is good; *Three Glorious Weeks* is even better. He wrote and directed over 30 hours of original scripted audio for the live radio series and podcast *Don't Close Your Eyes: Live Radio*

Theatre, which he co-founded with writer/director/Jeopardy winner Keith Suta. Ryan is best known for writing the book & lyrics for the psychedelic rock-and-roll horror musical/comedy/giant puppet show "Freak Out!" (With music composed and arranged by well-known guitarist, the late great Joe Knapp.) He used to write horror stories when he was young, but then he got busy and stopped; then all the theaters had to shut down nationwide for some reason, and he started writing them again. He now resides in the cold frozen wasteland of Montana with his amazing wife Sadie, brilliant daughter Rosemary, and two sneaky dogs who like to steal trash and, therefore, will not get mentioned by name.

DAN COXON is an award-winning editor and writer based in London. His non-fiction anthology *Writing the Uncanny* (co-edited with Richard V. Hirst) won the British Fantasy Award for Best Non-Fiction 2022, while his short story collection *Only the Broken Remain* (Black Shuck Books) was shortlisted for two British Fantasy Awards in 2021 (Best Collection, Best Newcomer). In 2018 his anthology of British folk-horror, *This Dreaming Isle* (Unsung Stories), was shortlisted for a British Fantasy Award and a Shirley Jackson Award. His short stories have appeared in various anthologies, including *Shakespeare Unleashed, Unspeakable Horror 3: Dark Rainbow Rising, Beyond the Veil, Mother: Tales of Love and Terror* and *Great British Horror 7: Major Arcana.* His latest fiction anthology—*Isolation*—was published by Titan Books, while the sequel to *Writing the Uncanny*—*Writing the Future*—will be published by Dead Ink Books in September 2023.

MATT ELPHICK is a writer of dark fantasy and Folk Horror who draws inspiration from the countryside he grew up in, local folklore, and mythology. He is a Lecturer in Creative Writing and lives in the South East of England. When not parenting or reading, Matt can be found watching obscure horror films and preening his excessively styled beard.

Despite wanting to be a writer since he was four, Matt has so far successfully procrastinated his way out of writing his first novel. This may (or may not) change in 2023.

TRACY FAHEY is an Irish writer. She has been twice shortlisted for Best Collection at the British Fantasy Awards —in 2017 for *The Unheimlich Manoeuvre* and in 2022 for *I Spit Myself Out*. Fahey's short fiction is published in over thirty American, British, Australian and Irish anthologies including Stephen Jones' *Best New Horror, Nightscript V,* and *Uncertainties III,* and her work has been reviewed in the *TLS* and *Black Static.* Fourteen of her stories have appeared on Ellen Datlow's "Recommended Reading Lists" from 2016-2022.

Fahey holds a PhD on the Gothic in visual arts, and her non-fiction writing on the Gothic and folklore has appeared in Irish, English, Italian, Dutch and Australian edited collections. She has been awarded residencies in Ireland and Greece, and Irish funding from Limerick Grants Under The Arts, and in 20232, an Individual Arts Bursary. In 2022 she was awarded Saari Fellow status for 2023 by the Kone Foundation, Finland to research her new collection which examines the relationship between women, folklore and power.

J.M. FAULKNER teaches English in the Czech Republic, the perfect place to steep himself in a tumultuous history that fuels his curiosity. Outside of work, you can find him hiking in North Bohemian forests with his Czech-British family, Kat and Jasper.

As of yet, they haven't met any old gods in the forests or mountains of Bohemia. They will keep trying until they do. He has work published or upcoming with *Solarpunk Magazine, Cosmic Horror Monthly, Allegory,* Nosetouch Press, and Eerie River. Find out more at jmfaulkner.com.

TIMOTHY GRANVILLE lives with his wife and daughter in rural Wiltshire, U.K., with convenient access to a range of eerie barrows and standing stones. His horror stories have appeared in anthologies from Flame Tree Press, Egaeus

Press, and Chthonic Matter, as well as publications such as *Nightscript, Supernatural Tales, ergot., Ghosts & Scholars,* and *The Ghastling.*

COY HALL lives in West Virginia, where he splits time as an author and professor of history. As a historian, he studies Medieval and Early Modern Europe. History influences his fiction, with many of his stories set in the distant past--sometimes the real past, sometimes an imagined one, but most often a mix of the two. His books include *Grimoire of the Four Impostors* (Nosetouch Press, 2021), *The Hangman Feeds the Jackal: A Gothic Western* (Nosetouch Press, 2022), and *The Promise of Plague Wolves* (Nosetouch Press, 2023).

FOX CLARET HILL is a transgender fiction writer who has been writing horror stories since he was old enough to spell. However, writing was nothing more than a shadow-shrouded hobby until submitting his first short story in November 2021. That same story saw the light of day, and he has been confined to his office ever since. Born in Mothman's home state and raised in the hills of Malvern, Fox now resides by the water in Australia with his husband and two dogs. You can find information about his works by going to foxclarethill.com or following him @foxclarethill on Twitter.

CHARLIE HUGHES writes dark suspense and horror stories. He lives in South London his wife and two children.

In 2016, Charlie took the 1st prize in Ruth Rendell short story competition. Since then, his work has been published by *Ellery Queen Mystery Magazine, the Magazine of Fantasy & Science Fiction, NoSleep Podcast* and *Mystery Weekly.*

Flame Tree Press recently included Charlie's story "Remains" in the *Close to Midnight* Anthology, alongside work from Steve Rasnic Tem, Alison Littlewood and Adam Nevill. Author Stephen Bacon described "Remains" as, "...one of the best ghost stories I've read in years."

In 2023, "Fell Mill" appears as Charlie's second contribution to the *Horror Library* anthology series, following "Riverman" in Volume 7. His story "The Collection" will be reprinted in the *Best Horror of the Year, Vol.15* anthology, edited by Ellen Datlow.

Many of Charlie's stories, including "The Motley", are inspired by and set in his hometown of Shipston-on-Stour, Warwickshire. He hopes the locals forgive him.

Find Charlie on Twitter at @charliesuspense, and a full list of published and forthcoming stories is available on his website charliehugheswriting.blogspot.com.

RAE KNOWLES (she/her) is a queer woman with multiple works from Brigids Gate Press. Her debut novel, *The Stradivarius*, was released May '23, her sapphic horror novella, *Merciless Waters*, is due out winter '23, and her collaboration with April Yates, *Lies That Bind*, in early '24. A number of her short stories have been published or are forthcoming from publications like Dark Matter Ink's *Monstrous Futures, Nightmare, Seize the Press, Ghoulish Tales*, and *Taco Bell Quarterly*. Recent updates on her work can be found at RaeKnowles.com and you can follow her on twitter @_Rae_Knowles.

THERSA MATSUURA is a graduate of Clarion West (2015), a recipient of the HWA's Mary Wollstonecraft Shelley Scholarship (2015), and the author of two short story collections, *A Robe of Feathers and Other Stories* (Counterpoint Press LLC) and *The Carp-Faced Boy and Other Tales* (Independent Legions Press), the latter of which was nominated for a Bram Stoker Award (2017). She's also had stories published in various magazines, anthologies, and serialized in newspapers. Her short story "Zipper Back" is coming out this year in *Horror Library Vol.8* (Dark Moon Books).

Thersa has lived in Japan for over thirty years and uses her fluency in the language to do research into parts of the culture—legends, folktales, and superstitions—that aren't well known to a western audience. A lot of what she digs up informs her stories or is fodder for her podcast *Uncanny Japan*. She also has a Patreon page where monthly she reads an obscure Japanese folktale that she's translated and (sometimes) reimagined. There's also recipes, videos of temples and shrines and travels, etc. at patreon.com/thersamatsuura.

CATHERINE McCARTHY weaves dark tales on an ancient loom from her 19th century Welsh farmhouse. Her love of supernatural fiction is an ever-present ghost, and she enjoys haunting others through her words.

She is the author of the collection *Mists and Megaliths* and the novella *Immortelle,* both of which are set in Wales.

Her short fiction has been published in various anthologies and magazines, including those by Black Spot Books, Alienhead Press, and Dark Matter Ink.

In July 2023 her Gothic novel, *A Moonlit Path of Madness,* was published by Nosetouch Press, and in August her novella, *Mosaic,* publishes with Dark Hart Books.

Forthcoming works include a YA novel, *The Wolf and the Favour,* from Brigids Gate Press (October 2023) and a weird psychological novella, *The House at the End of Lacelean Street,* with Dark Matter Ink (April 2024).

Time away from the loom is spent hiking the Welsh coast path or huddled in an ancient graveyard reading Poe.

Find her at catherine-mccarthy-author.com or at Twitter @serialsemantic.

DAMIEN B. RAPHAEL is a writer who lives and works in Oxfordshire, England. His work has appeared in *The Ghastling* and *AHH! That's What I Call Horror: An Anthology of '90s Horror.* You can find him on Instagram as @damienbraphael.

ZACHARY ROSENBERG is a horror writer in Florida who practices law by day and writes scary and fantastical tales by night. His works have been published in various anthologies and will be forthcoming in *Unspeakable Horrors 3* and *Shakespeare Unleashed,* as well as publications such as *Seize the Press, the Deadlands,* and *Dark Matter Magazine.* You may find his books published by Brigids Gate Press, Darklit Press and Off Limits Press.

MELISSA A. SZYDLEK is a writer of horror fiction and horror science fiction. Her short stories have appeared in the anthologies *Twisted 50 Volume 2: A Second Serving of 50 Contemporary Shockers* and *The Singularity: 50 Sci-Fi stories about the transcendence of technology and the obsolescence of humanity.*

STEVE RASNIC TEM's writing career spans over 40 years, including poetry, plays, short stories, and novels in the genres of fantasy, science fiction, horror, crime, and regional fiction set in the Appalachian South. His collaborative novella with his late wife Melanie Tem, *The Man On The Ceiling,* won the World Fantasy, Bram Stoker, and International Horror Guild awards in 2001. He has also won the Bram Stoker, International Horror Guild, and British Fantasy Awards for his solo work. His novel *UBO* (Solaris, January 2017) is a dark science fictional tale about violence and its origins. Steve's southern gothic novel *Blood Kin* (Solaris, March 2014) won the 2014 Bram Stoker Award. His other novels include his YA *The Mask Shop of Doctor Blaack* (Hex, 2018), *Deadfall Hotel* (Solaris, 2012), *The Man On The Ceiling* (Wizards of the Coast Discoveries, 2008, written with Melanie Tem), *The Book of Days* (Subterranean, 2002), *Daughters* (Grand Central, 2001, also written with Melanie Tem), and *Excavation* (Avon, 1987). A handbook on writing, *Yours to Tell: Dialogues on the Art & Practice of Fiction,* also written with Melanie, appeared in 2017.

Steve has published over 500 short stories. His first collection of stories, *Ombres sur la Route,* was published by the French publisher Denoël in 1994. His first English language collection, *City Fishing* (Silver Salamander, 2000) won the International Horror Guild Award. His other story collections include *The Far Side of the Lake, In Concert* (collaborations with Melanie Tem), *Ugly Behavior, Onion Songs, Celestial Inventories, Twember, Here With The Shadows, Out of the Dark: A Storybook of Horrors, Everything Is Fine Now, The Night Doctor and Other Tales,* and *Thanatrauma.* Coming soon: *Rough Justice: The Complete Noir,* from Centipede.

Visit his website at www.stevetem.com.

RICHARD THOMAS is the award-winning author of eight books: three novels—*Disintegration and Breaker* (Penguin Random House Alibi), as well as *Transubstantiate* (Otherworld Publications); four short story collections—*Staring Into the Abyss* (Kraken Press), *Herniated Roots* (Snubnose Press), *Tribulations* (Cemetery Dance), and *Spontaneous Human Combustion* (Turner Publishing); and one novella in *The Soul Standard* (Dzanc Books). With over 170 stories published, his credits include *The Best Horror of the Year* (Volume Eleven), *Cemetery Dance* (twice), *Behold!: Oddities, Curiosities and Undefinable Wonders* (Bram Stoker winner), *PANK, storySouth, Gargoyle, Weird Fiction Review, Midwestern Gothic, Shallow Creek, The Seven Deadliest, Gutted: Beautiful Horror Stories, Qualia Nous, Chiral Mad* (numbers 2-4), *PRISMS, Pantheon,* and *Shivers VI* (with Stephen King and Peter Straub). He has won contests at ChiZine and One Buck Horror, has received five Pushcart Prize nominations, and has been long-listed for *Best Horror of the Year* seven times. He was also the editor of four anthologies: *The New Black* and *Exigencies* (Dark House Press), *The Lineup: 20 Provocative Women Writers* (Black Lawrence Press) and *Burnt Tongues* (Medallion Press) with Chuck Palahniuk. He has been nominated for the Bram Stoker, Shirley Jackson, Thriller, and Audie awards. In his spare time he is a columnist at Lit Reactor. He was the Editor-in-Chief at Dark House Press and *Gamut Magazine*. His agent is Paula Munier at Talcott Notch. For more information visit www.whatdoesnotkillme.com.

ALEX WOLFGANG is a horror writer from Oklahoma. His debut short story collection, *Splinter and Other Stories*, is available now. You can also find his work in *Cosmic Horror Monthly, Nocturnal Transmissions Podcast*, and the anthology *Howls From Hell*. When not reading and writing horror, you can find him hiking and camping, playing tennis, and watching movies. You can follow him on twitter @alexwolfgang92 or visit his website: www.alexwolfgang.com.

THE EDITORS

DAVID TYLER NEAL was born in Missouri, grew up in Ohio, and settled in Chicago, and has always written fiction, but only got really serious about it in the late '90s. He brings a strong Rust Belt perspective to his writing, a kind of "Northern Gothic" aesthetic reflective of his background.

Writing his first novel at 29, he then devoted time to his craft and worked on short stories, occupying a space between genre and literary fiction, with an emphasis on horror, science fiction, and fantasy. He has seen some of his short stories published in *Albedo 1*, Ireland's premier magazine of speculative fiction, and he won second place in their Aeon Award in 2008 for his short story, "Aegis." He has received Honorable Mentions for "Aegis" and "Rotgut" for *The Best Horror of the Year* series edited by Ellen Datlow.

He has published six novels with Nosetouch Press, *Saamaanthaa* (2011), *The Happening* (2015), and *Norm* (2022)—collectively known as The Wolfshadow Trilogy—*Chosen* (2012), *Suckage* (2013), and the cosmic Folk Horror-comedy thriller, *The Cursed Earth* (2023). He has also published three novellas with Nosetouch Press—*Relict* (2013), *Summerville* (2013), and *The Day of the Nightfish* (2022), and two collections—*The Thing in Yellow* (2023), stories based on The King in Yellow mythos, and *Singularities* (2023), a collection of science fiction stories.

He is the Co-Publisher and Editor-in-Chief of Nosetouch Press and its nonfiction imprint, Aster Books. He co-edited *The Fiends in the Furrows: An Anthology of Folk Horror* (2018), *The Fiends in the Furrows II: More Tales of Folk Horror* (2020), *The Fiends in the Furrows III: Final Harvest* (2023), *Wax and Wane: A Gathering of Witch Tales* (2015), *Blood, Sweat, and Fears: Horror Inspired by the 1970s* (2016), *The Asterisk Anthologies: Volumes 1 & 2* (2017–2018).

He has lived in Chicago since 1993, and is a passionate fan of music, a student of pop culture, an avid photographer and bicycler, and enjoys cooking.

CHRISTINE MARIE SCOTT has been a professional graphic designer/website developer & brand consultant for thirty years. She is an ardent book designer, intent on creating works that support the vision of the author and provide a pleasing yet unobtrusive experience for the reader that both refer to and expand upon the methods of the art of bookmaking.

Born and raised in Youngstown, Ohio and currently residing north of Pittsburgh, Pennsylvania, Christine is a freelance graphic and web designer, brand developer and consultant operating under the name Clever Crow Consulting and Design.

She is the Co-Publisher and Creative Director of Nosetouch Press and its nonfiction imprint, Aster Books. She co-edited *The Fiends in the Furrows: An Anthology of Folk Horror* (2018), *The Fiends in the Furrows II: More Tales of Folk Horror* (2020), *The Fiends in the Furrows III: Final Harvest* (2023), *Wax and Wane: A Gathering of Witch Tales* (2015), *Blood, Sweat, and Fears: Horror Inspired by the 1970s* (2016), *The Asterisk Anthologies: Volumes 1 & 2* (2017–2018).

Additionally, Christine creates visual art as Vrana. She uses mixed media to craft a world-within-a-world that communicates a playfully unnerving take on the contradictions, absurdity, and strangeness of postmodern American life, with a focus on reuse of the discarded and philosophical interpretations of the unseen through a lens of Modern Mysticism.

She sells her handcrafted items under the brand names (if she's breathing, she's branding) of Jane Dee Peculiarities, Cerys Crowe, Lady of May, and Magpie's Mischief. All can be found at her shop, Monmouth & Clark.

Several of Christine's handcrafted creations were selected for inclusion in *Game of Thrones: The Compendium,* a promotional book published by HBO in 2016.

Her interests also include art and art history, the decorative arts, history, architecture, music, costume design, bookbinding, printmaking, assemblage, photography, found-object jewelry creation, paranormal and occult studies, paganism, cemeteries, old buildings, historical preservation, and living history documentaries. She loves a really good ghost story, mysteries, corvids, clever turns of phrases, haunted and mystical places, woodlands, libraries, and liminal spaces. She takes her coffee blonde.

For a complete list of links on where to find her, please visit christinemariescott.com.

COPYRIGHTS

EDITORS' NOTE

In an effort to maintain the spirit of the authors' intent and their use of the English language as an expression of Folk Horror, Nosetouch Press has retained English spellings from the writers who used them.

A NOTE ON THE TYPE

The text of this book is set in Adobe Caslon Pro, and is based upon the typeface first created by English typefounder, William Caslon I (c. 1692–1766).

The distinction and legibility of his type secured him the patronage of the leading printers of the day in England and on the continent. His typefaces transformed English type design and first established an English national typographic style.

Caslon worked as an engraver of punches, the masters used to stamp the moulds or matrices used to cast metal type. He worked in the tradition of what is now called old-style serif letter design, that produced letters with a relatively organic structure resembling handwriting with a pen. Caslon established a tradition of engraving type in London—which previously had not been common—and was influenced by the imported Dutch Baroque typefaces that were popular in England at the time. His typefaces established a strong reputation for their quality and their attractive appearance, suitable for extended passages of text.

Caslon's typefaces were popular in his lifetime and beyond, and after a brief period of eclipse in the early nineteenth century, they returned to popularity, particularly for setting printed body text and books.

Adobe Caslon is a popular revival designed by American designer, Carol Twombly. It is based on Caslon's own specimen pages printed between 1734 and 1770 and is a member of the Adobe Originals program. It added many features now standard in high-quality digital fonts, such as small caps, old style figures, swash letters, ligatures, alternate letters, fractions, subscripts and superscripts, and matching ornaments.

Composed by Clever Crow Consulting and Design,
Pittsburgh, Pennsylvania

YOU MAY ALSO ENJOY

THE FIENDS IN THE FURROWS I
An Anthology of Folk Horror

THE FIENDS IN THE FURROWS II
More Tales of Folk Horror

THE CURSED EARTH
D.T. Neal

THE THING IN YELLOW
D.T. Neal

SONG OF THE RED SQUIRE
C.W. Blackwell

THE PROMISE OF PLAGUE WOLVES
Coy Hall

GRIMOIRE OF THE FOUR IMPOSTORS
Coy Hall

NOSETOUCH PRESS

Nosetouch Press is an independent book publisher
tandemly-based in Chicago and Pittsburgh.
We are dedicated to bringing some of today's most
energizing fiction to readers around the world.

Our commitment to classic book design in a digital
environment brings an innovative and authentic approach
to the traditions of literary excellence.

NOSETOUCHPRESS.COM
We're Out There

Science Fiction | Fantasy | Horror | Gothic | Supernatural | Weird

Printed in Great Britain
by Amazon